My Life at Sea

by

William Caius Crutchley

My Life at Sea

by William Caius Crutchley

Copyright © 2024

All Rights reserved.

ISBN: 978-93-63058-94-1

Published by

DOUBLE 9 BOOKS

2/13-B, Ansari Road
Daryaganj, New Delhi – 110002
info@double9books.com
www.double9books.com
Tel. 011-40042856

This book is under public domain

ABOUT THE AUTHOR

William Caius Crutchley, a seasoned mariner and captivating storyteller, shares his extraordinary adventures in his masterpiece, "My Life at Sea." Through vivid narration and firsthand accounts, Crutchley takes readers on a captivating journey across the vast expanse of the ocean, offering glimpses into the trials, triumphs, and profound moments that define a life lived at sea. From harrowing storms to breathtaking sunsets, he intricately weaves together tales of courage, camaraderie, and the timeless allure of the maritime world. With a keen eye for detail and a deep appreciation for the sea's beauty and unpredictability, Crutchley invites readers to immerse themselves in the rich tapestry of his experiences, from the bustling ports to the endless horizons of the open ocean. "My Life at Sea" stands as a testament to Crutchley's resilience, passion, and unwavering dedication to his craft, offering readers an unforgettable glimpse into the heart and soul of a true seafarer. This captivating memoir is sure to leave a lasting impression on all who embark on this remarkable voyage alongside him.

CONTENTS

FOREWORD

My good sailor friend Captain Crutchley has asked me to write a foreword to his autobiography. It is a pleasure to comply.

The author began his life at sea in sailing-ships, in the age of the Black Ball liners, the Baltimore clipper-ships, and those perfect specimens of naval architecture built in Aberdeen for the China tea trade.

Captain Crutchley tells of the hardships of the sea. He gives stirring descriptions of the performances of the ships in which he sailed. His narrative may perhaps be briefly supplemented. Sir George Holmes, in his book on ancient and modern ships, quotes many examples of record passages. In 1851, the *Nightingale*, in a race from Shanghai to Deal, ran on one occasion 336 knots in twenty-four hours. In the same year the *Flying Cloud*, in a voyage from New York to San Francisco, ran 427 knots in one day. The *Thermopylæ*, 886 tons register, built by Messrs. Steel, of Greenock, sailed 354 knots in twenty-four hours. The Aberdeen clippers of the 'sixties did marvellous work. Under sail, the *Ariel*, *Taeping* and *Serica* started together from Foochow on May 30, 1866. They met off the Lizard on September 6; and on the same day the *Taeping* arrived in the East India Dock at 9.45 p.m., and the *Ariel* at 10.15 p.m. — a difference of half-an-hour after racing for over three months on end.

The present writer recalls a like personal experience of more recent date. In 1905 a race was sailed from Sandy Hook to the Lizard for a cup offered by the German Emperor. On that occasion the *Valhalla*, a full-rigged ship, *Hildegarde* and *Endymion*, two-masted fore-and-aft schooners, and the *Sunbeam*, a three-masted topsail-yard schooner, anchored off Cowes on the same tide, the distance of more than 3300 miles from Sandy Hook having been covered in fourteen days.

After years of service at sea, Captain Crutchley passed from sail to steam. He filled important commands with distinguished success. He began with the comparatively easy voyage to the Cape. In the later years of his career at sea he was engaged in Australasian voyages, when his experience in sailing-ships enabled him, by the combined power of sail and steam, to make successful voyages.

In Captain Crutchley's time ships coming direct from the homeland were the bonds of empire. They received a warm welcome on their arrival in the distant ports of New Zealand and Australia. Captain Crutchley earned a deserved popularity as a representative seaman. He began his work as an empire builder while serving at sea. It was continued ashore for a period of many years in the capacity of Secretary of the Navy League.

The book abounds in valuable hints on discipline at sea. The vessels commanded by Captain Crutchley were happy ships.

It only remains to commend this volume as interesting reading to all who love the sea and admire the hardy breed of men who do business in great waters.

Brassey.

March 7, 1912.

CHAPTER I

"Ride with an idle whip, ride with an unused heel,
But, once in a way, there will come a day
When the colt must be taught to feel
The lash that falls, and the curb that galls,
And the sting of the rowelled heel." —Kipling.

Early in the year 1863 there was brought into the little harbour of Margate a vessel called the *Figaro* of Narbonne, a small craft with a cargo of wine. She had got into trouble on one of the many outlying sandbanks which make the entrance to the Thames a problem of considerable difficulty for any vessel not thoroughly qualified to meet any emergency that may arise through wind or weather. What the precise cause of this accident was escapes my memory, but whatever its origin, it was instrumental in sending me to sea, for it brought me into close contact with a London merchant, Mr. Trapp, who was interested in her cargo and who had come down to supervise her repairs. This merchant was also a shipowner, and had been at sea during the French wars in the early part of the century. He was good enough to tell me many stories relating to privateering and the customs of the sea, to all of which I listened greedily, for I was born with the sound of the sea in my ears and from my earliest recollections had made up my mind that the sailor's life was the only one worth living. Unfortunately this view was not shared either by my father or my mother, both of whom had set their minds upon making me a civil engineer. My head master was of the same opinion as myself as regards my future, but we reached the same conclusion by somewhat different roads, as will be seen.

I scarcely think I was tractable as a school-boy. I can distinctly remember that from the age of ten until I was fourteen I was always the "awful example," and my impression is that the cane was administered thrice daily with great regularity. At the age of fourteen there was a serious difference of opinion between the head master and myself; he suggested that my conduct in class was beyond his endurance, and I, considering his was also objectionable, expressed my view by launching a book at his head. When I turned to make my escape, there was no escape for me; I was headed off and cornered by masters lower down the room. And face downwards on a desk I both heard and felt the best arguments that can be used in such circumstances. When I got home, these arguments were only too palpable, and my indulgent parents brought my career at that school to a summary conclusion. Nevertheless, I bore the old boy no malice, for he was a good judge of a human boy's nature. When he asked me one day what I was going to be, I replied, "Civil engineer," to which he retorted, "A soldier or a sailor is all they will ever make of you," and it must be confessed that it was a fairly accurate forecast, though the prophecy was evidently not intended as a compliment to either army or navy.

After that episode it seemed to dawn upon my mind that it was time to learn something, and I was put as a private pupil with a man whose memory I shall always respect (afterwards Leetham of Thanet House), for he had the great gift of raising his pupil's enthusiasm for the subject he was teaching. We used to start quite early in the morning, before breakfast, take our time in the middle of the day for recreation, and again tackle the work in the evening. It was in one of the mid-day recreations that, happening to walk down the lower pier, I met my old friend the shipowner. I soon made up my mind that I must go to sea, and realised that here was the instrument by which my desire could be accomplished. A steady siege was at once commenced.

My dear old father would not listen to the scheme for a moment; salt water had no charms for him. Yet he himself had taught me the use of mathematical instruments and given me a fair grounding in plan drawing and similar matters. The shrine at which he worshipped, however, was that of Brunel and the great engineers who were then discovering the wonders of applied science. My mother, on the other hand, seeing that my mind was made up, offered no further opposition, and when the time arrived managed to give me the necessary assistance.

The scheme finally formulated was this. My friend Mr. Trapp had at that time a vessel in port of which he was part owner, and as she carried apprentices I was to take my place among them on her next voyage, but it was also stipulated that a premium was to be paid. How often, I wonder, have boys been jeered at by the old salts as being "blank gentlemen's sons that pay to go to sea," and when one considers in after life the hardships of a sailing-ship, such a custom certainly seems humorous.

Well, the appointed day arrived and my mother and I set out for London to carry out the necessary preliminaries. My father had provided funds in a surreptitious sort of manner, for when the die was cast he accepted the situation, though he never really acquiesced in it. Boys are heartless brutes as a rule where their inclinations are concerned, and set little store by the desires of those who have had the trouble of rearing them. But, after all, we none of us are asked whether we would like to come into the world. We are shoved upon the stage willy-nilly without any consideration as to the part we are to play, and expected to give unquestioning obedience to the prompter. This seemed to me unreasonable, and that is how I at length found myself in the London Docks boarding the *Alwynton*, a sailing barque of 491 tons register. To the best of my knowledge she was one of a series of outside vessels chartered by the Orient line, and a stout, staunch craft she was, good looking also in her own way.

On the other side of the wharf was the sailing-ship *Orient*, the first of her name and a clipper of renown. The officers and men of that craft considered themselves very superior beings to those who had not the good fortune to sail under the blue St. Andrew's Cross; but they in their turn were looked down upon by the men sailing in the ships of Green, Dunbar, Wigram & Smith. In those days it would have required a very careful M.C. to give the varying grades of the merchant services their due order of precedence.

We were met by a very dark, handsome man who we were told was one of the owners of the vessel, and one of the first remarks he made to me after the ceremony of introduction had been gone through was on the iniquity of my wearing kid gloves. Needless to say, I immediately disclaimed any intention of doing so in the future, being fearful that so pernicious a habit should already have prejudiced my chances of forming one unit of the ship's company of so particularly correct a craft. Let me here say that the last time I met that gentleman he was bowed in stature and quite white on the figurehead; it was at the Trinity House, and this time we foregathered on equal terms. I reminded him of the particular incident and he was much amused. I regret that he has now joined the majority, leaving behind him a name that will be long remembered for good and philanthropic work wherever seamen are concerned. I refer to Captain David Mainland.

My first doubts were raised when I met the second mate, who seemed to be what I should now describe as a particularly "hefty" personage. He was not wearing any elaborate uniform, in fact he wore neither coat nor waistcoat, and was very busily engaged in assisting to take in stores and stow them away down a hatchway in the after part of the cabin, a receptacle known as the lazarette. For many months afterwards that place to me was one of discomfort, for it was also the sailroom, and to one not accustomed to the smell of "below decks" the work of stowing and re-arranging canvas was not agreeable. It was, however, particularly the sort of operation to which a raw and unskilled hand could be usefully turned, and accordingly there fell to my lot a good deal of it.

Immediately behind this hatchway were two staterooms, so called, fine airy cabins, one of which was the abode of Captain Hole, whose acquaintance it was now my lot to make. Let me try and describe him. He was a man of more than average height and enormous chest measurement; his face was not so weather-beaten as might have been expected, but it was one mass of freckles, and was surmounted by sandy hair and fringed with whiskers of the same colour. His hands were mighty and possessed enormous power, as I was to discover later. There was withal a bluff *bonhomie* about the man that was attractive in its way, and to do him justice I think he tried to behave as well as he could, but he was the natural product of a hard school.

On this particular occasion he wished to be very agreeable, and the interview went off well, ending with the transfer of my premium from my mother's pocket to his. In this he stole a march upon my first friend, the owner, who had intended me to be *his* apprentice, in place of which I was forthwith indentured to Captain Hole.

The remainder of the day was all pure joy. I was a sailor and was measured for my sailor clothes! Some days afterwards I went back home to display to my lay acquaintances and the world of Margate in general, the full glory of blue cloth and brass buttons. Upon mature consideration I am not certain that the first wearing of a brass-bound cap is not the most satisfactory experience in a long sea life; the first command is not in any way to be compared with it.

At length the long-looked-for day arrived when I was to join my ship, and I set out without a doubt in my mind, and with a callous indifference to the tearful farewells of my family, or rather the feminine portion of it. I have since noticed that this indifference is not unusual with the human boy, and perhaps it is well that it should be so, for he is like the young bear and has no idea of the troubles that lie before him. Still, were my time to be gone through again, even starting with the accumulated wisdom of half-a-century's experience, I doubt greatly whether I should act very differently.

I was not, however, fated to join my ship that day. I was taken by my old friend, Mr. Trapp, to his house in the Minories and handed over to the care of one of his sons. He took me to my first theatre, and next morning at breakfast was solemnly reproved by his father for causing me to break that clause in my indenture which forbade the apprentices to frequent taverns or playhouses.

But the time had now come when the realities were to commence. We were five apprentices in all, and, with the carpenter and boatswain, lived in the starboard side of the topgallant forecastle. As the ship's windlass formed part of the furniture it may be imagined that the quarters were rough in the extreme, but they were in keeping with the life in general, which began to develop as soon as we reached the dockhead, prior to being towed down the river. Here we began to make acquaintance with that very authoritative person, the chief mate, who in all well-ordered ships is the ruling spirit. Mr. Coleman was a good specimen of the mate of his time. Not bad-looking by any means, very neat in personal appearance, and painfully precise in his remarks to all and sundry. There was also conveyed in some particularly subtle manner the fact that he was an accomplished pugilist, and in point of fact, there were not many that could emphasise their orders with greater neatness and dispatch. I can recall many instances where the trouble was over almost as soon as it began, and that was no small qualification for an officer in the rough sailing-ship days. This quality of command was quickly manifested on the way to Gravesend, when the work of rigging out the jib-boom and getting things shipshape commenced in earnest. Before the first day was finished we had discovered that the lot of an apprentice was likely to prove an extremely lively one.

The next few days were a blank to me—sea-sickness claimed me for its very own, and there is only a confused recollection left in my mind of wishing to die and being expressly prevented from doing anything of the sort. That state of affairs lasted perhaps two days, until one morning with a fair wind and fine weather the episode passed away like an ugly dream. There was one other difficulty, however, to be surmounted, and that was "going aloft." But with a determined boatswain behind you it is astonishing how quickly difficulties disappear; the terrors of the unknown yielded swiftly to good solid pliable arguments capable of immediate application.

It becomes evident to me that I must curtail my reminiscences of this period or my work will grow to gigantic proportions completely unwarranted by the importance of the subject, but I wish, if I may, to record one phase in the change from sail to steam.

We were bound to Adelaide with a general cargo, and made a fairly good passage. The captain firmly believed in giving the crew lots of work to keep the devil out of their minds. Consequently the ship was what was known as an "all hands ship," in other words neither officer, nor man, nor boy ever had an afternoon watch below. "Watch and watch" was a thing unknown, but as the power of the master was absolute there could be no appeal, and for reasons I have hinted at there were none who would have been willing to incur the wrath of the ruling powers. It will be shown presently how those powers were sometimes used, but that was the ship's routine, and every afternoon, no matter what the weather, all hands were on deck from half-past twelve to five o'clock. We apprentices were taught to observe the meridian altitude, and sometimes in the afternoons and evenings the captain gave us some instruction in navigation, but the mate rather resented what he termed loafing in the cabin in the afternoon. Our captain was also fond of signalling to other vessels, and that, of course, was our special work. In those days it was almost a certainty that every vessel sighted was British; a foreign flag was a matter of interest. But the great mass of the world's sailing-ships to-day are no longer of our nationality, and the training of our future seamen can no longer be carried on in those best of all possible schools for teaching men self-reliance, and the faculty of doing the right thing at the right time. The trip out was uneventful. By the time we had arrived at our port of destination we boys had learned to steer, and to use a broom, also to furl the light canvas, and generally do as we were told.

Port Adelaide in those days was still a rising town, and the facilities it offered to shipping were considerable. We were consequently soon discharged and loaded up for Auckland with a cargo of flour, wheat, and sheep on deck. At that time the Maori War was in progress, and we had hopes that some adventure might possibly befall, for up to this time our visions of sea life had become very commonplace, and were far from realising our youthful fancies. I may say that the experiences of the passage out had satisfied several of the men and one of the apprentices, who consequently deserted. Some difficulty was experienced in filling their places, as colonial wages ran high.

We ran through Bass Straits with a fine fair wind. There are few more picturesque parts of the sea than these grand straits, dotted with steep rocky islands like impregnable fortresses. On this passage, as I have said, we had a cargo of sheep on deck, and as these foolish animals will not drink of their own accord, it was necessary to administer to each member of the flock one quart bottle of water daily, an operation which at first took a considerable time. After a few days, however, they became accustomed to the treatment and gave no trouble.

When the coast of New Zealand was sighted and we were running through the Bay of Islands, the captain thought it prudent to overhaul the ship's armoury, and muskets, pistols and cutlasses were all got on deck for cleaning and putting in order. Here it was discovered that I was of some use, for firearms had been one of my hobbies, in which I had been encouraged by the officer in charge of the coastguard at Margate—dear old Bob Aldrich. After a long lapse of years I can recall his cheery face and the infinite patience with which he initiated me into the mysteries of powder and shot. He succeeded after a time in making me a fair marksman.

With a view to testing the hitting power of the crew a bottle was hung at the fore yard-arm, and we all fired in turn. The bottle survived until it came to my turn, and then, probably because I had loaded the musket properly, I hit it, but suffered reproof afterwards because I could not do so with a ship's pistol. I mention this matter of loading because, even with an old smooth-bore gun, if the bullet was properly centred by means of the spare cartridge paper, it was quite possible at short ranges to get decent shooting from it, but if, as commonly happened, the bullet and cartridge were rammed down anyhow, the bullet went anywhere.

There are few harbours in the world more beautiful than Auckland; it is worthy of Kipling's description "last, loveliest, loneliest, exquisite, apart—on us, on us the unswerving season smiles." I have known the apple of beauty claimed often for Sydney. Of that harbour I cannot speak personally, but I have heard a great Sydney authority confess that the apple should, in fact, be given to the harbour of Rio, and with that judgment I am inclined to agree.

The most striking object in entering Auckland is the mountain Rangitoto. It is doubtful whether it can best be described as a cone or a pyramid; from whichever side it is viewed it presents the same shape, and it possesses considerable interest by the speculation it creates as to whether it is an extinct volcano. In point of fact the whole region is volcanic, and once, many years afterwards, in a little altercation with an Auckland man concerning some point in connection with the harbour, I heard it observed that he need not put on too much side, "for he was only living on the outside of a bally cinder, anyway." Curiously enough, within ten days of that altercation, there occurred the eruption of Tarawera, and the celebrated terraces were destroyed.

Anchored off Rangitoto was a splendid-looking ship, the *Tyburnia*, as spick and span as any first-class London sailing-ship could be. My recollection of her is vivid even now. I think that she had taken troops there. As we got further up the harbour we came across H.M.S. *Miranda*, an object of admiration and respect, for the tales concerning warships that were then told in merchantmen were many and wonderful, creating an atmosphere of awe. There was also the vague idea still existing that a man-of-war could send on board and take any men she pleased for the state service. Old traditions die hard, and at the time I write of the great mass of the songs and ditties sung by seamen were reminiscences in verse of the Great Napoleon, and the men of the navy and the merchant service were more interchangeable than they are to-day.

The Queen Street wharf was not then the imposing feature it now is; but it was a very fair size and we got to a comfortable berth at the end of it, quickly getting clear of our live cargo. I have reason to think that the entire shipload was extremely welcome, for the town was at that time more than a little anxious concerning the future of the Maori War. We, however, saw no signs of fighting.

As showing the vast changes a few years make, twenty-one years later I lay at that same wharf, in command of a splendid mail steamer fitted to carry frozen mutton and produce to the home country.

One great characteristic of Auckland in the early days was the peculiar abruptness of some of its streets. It was not lit at night-time with any degree of brilliance, and the sudden inequalities of road surface required some practice to deal with; still we were generally pleased with the place and the scene of bustle there was about the shipping. We, being the end ship of the wharf, often got visits from the members of other ships' companies, and in particular there was one midshipman from the *Tyburnia* of whom we heard great things. He was a good-looking lad and a gentleman, but it seemed that he was rather made much of by his captain for his smartness as a seaman; he was credited with being able to start from the deck, stow the mizzen royal, and be down again in four minutes. Our ship was not exactly popular as a rendezvous, however, for the custom of the grog tub, prevalent in most ships in harbour, was entirely unknown to us.

In due course the cargo was discharged. The mate, having kept careful tally, clapped on the hatches when he had landed the exact quantity he was responsible for. There was a considerable surplus, but how the matter was finally arranged I know not—probably by compromise I should think, for the mate, being a canny Scot, was not likely to have given much away. Our captain was anxious to secure a cargo for London, so the ship was what is called "laid on" for that port, and we commenced loading with casks of Kauri gum. These were stowed, with ballast to fill in such spaces as would hold it, for it was necessary to give her some stiffening; but one afternoon I was taken up to the agents by the captain and sent back with a message to the mate to commence and break out and land all we had taken in, as enough could not be procured to fill the ship. We all thought that bad luck, for we now had to ballast the ship and return to Adelaide in the hope of filling with wool and copper. We made rather a long passage back, for there was a good deal of strong head wind, the ship being hove-to under a close-reefed main topsail for some days. That made no difference to the work of the crew, for day after day we were kept at it scraping and oiling the woodwork of the hold, in other words the inner skin of the ship. I personally was very glad to recognise some of the landmarks I remembered in Bass Straits, and to know that we were that much nearer home. We duly arrived at Adelaide without adventure, and commenced preparations for the homeward run.

Before going further with the narration let me describe a scene, not an unusual one in those days, which took place on the passage from Auckland. There were certain epithets which were considered fair and lawful to use, and which men did not resent, on the other hand there was one term only used if he who was delivering the oration was prepared to back his opinion by muscular arguments. Our ship was fitted with patent reefing topsails, but as most good things have drawbacks to them this particular main topsail had developed a habit of carrying its halliards away, and their replacement usually caused some little trouble. For one thing, it was an "all hands job," and with the scanty rest the crew were permitted, this did not tend to increase the smoothness of current matters either for officers or men. Upon this particular evening the halliards had parted and the yard came down with a run. As the chain passed round the yard it was necessary it should be kept clear of turns to ensure smooth working of the patent, and this was a job of some little difficulty. The second mate and a fair number of men were aloft reeving the chains when one man in the top incurred the wrath of the mate, who was superintending operations from the quarter-deck. He yelled out to his subordinate aloft: "Mr. King, kick that son of a — — out of the top." King on his part addressed some drastic remarks to the delinquent, but did not appear to consider it necessary to do more, so the work proceeded until the man who had been "mentioned" came down the rigging saying loudly: "I've never been called son of a — — before and won't stand it." That was enough for the mate. As the man stepped on deck he was met by a straight one, two, in the face, and then began a rough-and-tumble about the end of which there could be no doubt. The captain came along to see what was going on, and the mate sang out: "Put this man in irons, sir." The captain did so, and poor Canadian Bill, as he was called, was duly ironed and dropped for security down the lazarette hatch, where for some days he endured the scanty bread and bitter waters of affliction. Needless to say he lost no time in deserting on arrival in port, which no doubt fitted in with the higher policy of the master, who did not wish to retain the services of men at high colonial wages during a long stay in port when the absolutely necessary routine work could be carried on by apprentices, the cargo of course being stowed by stevedores.

It may not be out of place here to say a few words concerning the power of the master in those days. It may be summed up as absolute despotism. There was seldom any attempt made to obtain redress for ill-treatment at sea, and, strange though it may appear, a ship might bear a terrible reputation through her master or officers, and yet little if any trouble was experienced in shipping a crew. It must be remembered that shortly before this had been the great days of the Australian clippers that made most astonishingly quick passages, and to do this it was necessary to keep the men in a very tight hand. This had its drawbacks, for where seamen, accustomed to the rule of mates who in many cases could have qualified as prize-fighters, happened to sail in a ship where force was not so dominant, they were apt to be very troublesome, as I shall show in the course of these pages. I give in this place one instance of the despotic power of the master. One morning shortly after we reached Adelaide for the second time we were greatly surprised at breakfast-time to see the second mate, Mr. King, walk into our quarters, sit down and commence to eat breakfast. He saw our looks of astonishment, and remarked: "Did none of you fellows ever see a man drinking a pannikin of tea before?" Then it came out that for some offence, I never heard what, the master had turned him out of the cabin to come and live with the apprentices and the warrant officers. As we took home a few passengers that trip, I believe that the captain picked a quarrel to get more room and an additional cabin aft, but King was quite an acquisition to our party, for he was a splendid sailor, and always bright and jolly, except when he thought it necessary to use a rope's end. That was pretty often, but the rope's end had little terror for me. I had been so well acclimatised to punishment at school that it took more than a rope's ending to upset my equanimity.

I must confess, however, that a system obtained in that ship which was bound in the long run to end in disaster. The apprentices were held responsible for far too many things, and if an article could not be found in its right place, or let us say the ship heeled over and a bucket came down to leeward and hit the mate on the legs, his first instruction would be: "Mr King, lick those dam boys!" and we got it. At that time the idea of possible rebellion had not taken root—that was to come later. I still think that the rope's end in moderation is a good thing for a boy, and regret exceedingly that a sickly sentimentality seems to be undermining the healthy view that corporal chastisement is good for young people. I believe it is still one of those luxuries dealt out at Eton and similar schools to the sons of the wealthier classes, and this undoubtedly constitutes a real advantage that the son of the rich man has over the board school boy.

Our life in Adelaide loading for home was enjoyable. There were many vessels in port also bound home, and there was a certain amount of *camaraderie* among the various ships' apprentices, but it seemed to me there was always a certain number of them who walked about thanking their Creator that they were not as other men were. In other words they aspired to take rank as from the ship in which they served, and when it came to a near thing between two ships of nearly equal merit, a skysail, on a fitted flying jib-boom, or a patent pump, or some such item was quite sufficient to establish a superiority which would be insisted upon with all necessary vigour. What it may be to-day I know not, but ship worship was a very strong feeling among young seamen at the time of which I am writing, and it ran high in the crews of such ships as the *Orient, Murray, Connatto, Goolwa,* and others, even including that very respectable old vessel known as *Irene*.

As may be imagined in a small port such as Adelaide then was, the younger portions of the ships' crews were something of a terror to the inhabitants, for if one could not invent some new piece of mischief, another could; and when a party of us went on shore for the evening the proceedings were seldom characterised by dulness. One great pastime of our ship in particular was swimming. We lay in what was then the river basin, and that was close to a creek where there was a fine bathing-place. In the course of time we all became good swimmers, and took an especial pride in diving. This was encouraged by the skipper, who urged us to go higher and higher from the ship's rigging, until at last some of us could dive from the mainyard. As the time of the year was the Australian summer it was a very pleasant way of spending the evening.

The independent spirit manifested by the stevedores and other working-men that had to do with the ship came to one rather as a revelation. There was a quiet assurance about these men that was remarkable; they knew what their importance was in a place where labour was scarce, and being satisfied with the wages they got did their work with a manly independence which needed no driving. I should mention that the stevedores stowing the wool were paid by piecework, and that perhaps may have had something to do with their satisfactory performances. They had all been seamen at some period of their lives, and when hauling on their tackles in the hold, screwing wool, could raise a chanty that would merit unfeigned approval from a nautical critic. Wool-screwing was there an art. There was not the hurry-scurry of the present day, and I suppose it took two months to load that little vessel with wool and copper. When this was done we shipped the able seamen we were short of through desertions, and set out for our homeward trip.

I wish I dare set down in black and white the various incidents of that trip, but I must refrain. We had three passengers, an old Cornishman and his wife, considered second class, who lived in a boarded space in the poop, and a fairly young lady who messed with the captain and mate. The front of the poop was fitted up as an immense birdcage for a great number of small green parrots that at one period of the voyage died by scores daily. I believe, however, that enough survived to make the venture a paying one to the skipper. We had shipped as steward a colonial man, the blackest I ever saw, with an immense idea of his own importance. As the steward on a sailing-ship is looked upon exclusively as the master's servant there is frequently antagonism shown him by the mate, and the present case was no exception to the rule.

Now let me say that so far as my knowledge serves me, all boys at sea are thieves so far as food is concerned. It is not considered dishonourable to steal any food that can be got at, but the great crime is to be found out. My particular chum, Fred Wilkes, however, not content with annexing potatoes, had the audacity to light the galley fire in the middle watch for the purpose of baking them. This was asking for trouble, which promptly arrived, for, being taken red-handed in the act, he was sentenced to be deprived of his forenoon watch below for an indefinite time, and this sentence of brutality was actually carried out. For the uninitiated it may be explained that, having been on deck for eight hours previous to 8 a.m., he was allowed time for his breakfast and then called on deck to begin a full day's work.

The passage home was to be made round the Cape of Good Hope (few of the Adelaide ships favoured the Cape Horn route), and we were particularly fortunate in getting round Cape Leeuwin and up into the south-east trades with a fine fair wind. There are few more pleasant passages than that across the Indian Ocean at the southern limit of the south-east trade, which on this occasion was blowing very strongly. Indeed, at times it was more than we could carry all studding sails to. I remember that in our middle watch the lower stunsail had been taken in for wind, and the captain, coming on deck during a period of lull, soundly abused the second mate, in whose watch I was, for keeping the ship "hove-to," and that with everything set except one lower stunsail which was even then being got ready to hoist again. King was not in favour with the powers that were, although to do him justice he was a very fine seaman. On one occasion on the passage from Auckland to Adelaide it became necessary to call all hands to shorten sail, and it happened that King was in charge, neither the mate nor captain being on deck. It was necessary to take in the mainsail, and he did it successfully by taking up the lee side first, in opposition to the dictum laid down in Falconer's *Shipwreck* that—

> "He who seeks the tempest to disarm
> Will never first embrail the lee yardarm."

At that time, however, there was a difference of opinion on the subject, and I think a good deal is to be said for both contentions. The truth probably is that with a strong crew and proper management a heavy course, if taken in lee sheet first, was easier to furl, as the canvas was not so much blown over to leeward, but on the other hand, if great care was not taken the canvas very often blew to pieces.

To do justice to the officers of that ship they were all fine seamen, and insisted on a high standard of a sailor man's attainments from all hands. A "job of work" badly done, or done in a slovenly manner, called down immediate reproof and punishment—which usually meant doing it again in a watch below. In modern times it may sound strange to talk about reefed stunsails, but we carried them, and night or day not a moment was lost in making or trimming sail as it was required.

It was when we were nearing the Cape of Good Hope that the mate going aloft one afternoon discovered that the mainmast was sprung, and reported it to the captain in the words, "The mainmast is a sprung mast, sir, just below the futtocks." In fact, as was afterwards discovered, the mast was pretty rotten. All hands were immediately turned to splice a big spar up the after side of the mast, and so well was this done by lashings of rope and chain, tightened up by wooden wedges, that it lasted the remainder of the trip without giving any trouble. When the mast was taken out in London every one marvelled that it had lasted as it had.

When we sighted the land about the Cape, the first view of Table Mountain was most impressive, and it is one of those great natural features that never loses its grandeur or becomes stale by constant acquaintance. I little thought that at that time there was a little maiden two years old toddling about an old garden there that in after years was to be my wife. So it was, however, and indeed I ultimately grew to regard the Cape quite in the light of a home country.

The remainder of the passage home was uneventful. The next thing I remember was being at the wheel on a bitterly cold June morning, when we made the English land, and the feeling of exhilaration that it gave all hands was a thing to be remembered. Then the run up-Channel in company with many other vessels was a pure joy. The old man walked the poop snapping his fingers; as soon as we got the pilot off Dungeness, and a tug, we commenced to furl the canvas and put the finishing touches on the ship's harbour toilet. Once in the London Docks the ship was soon deserted by the crew and left to the care of the apprentices, who were not supposed to have any desire to get away. It happened, however, on this occasion that Captain Hole was subjected to a raid by my sisters, chaperoned by that kind, gracious and beautiful lady, the late Mrs. G. E. Dering, whose wealthy and eccentric husband recently achieved posthumous fame as "The Hermit of Welwyn." As they desired to take me away at once for at least six weeks the old man surrendered at discretion, and in all the glory of gilt buttons I was borne away.

That brings to a close my maiden voyage, but one thing that struck me when I got home was the pleasure with which one remembered familiar details—even such insignificant things as old cracks in paving-stones. It seemed almost wonderful that one had been so far away and yet come back to find everything just the same, even to the same old boatmen lounging on the pier apparently in the same position they had occupied from one's earliest recollections.

CHAPTER II

"'Twas all along of Poll, as I may say,
That fouled my cable when I ought to slip." — Hood.

It is doubtful whether, if left to his own devices, any boy would go a second voyage without a very considerable amount of hesitation. Indeed, a trip as far as the Downs quite satisfied the nautical aspirations of a certain friend of mine, who put to sea in the *Roxburgh Castle* and left at the earliest possible moment. This was poor Will Terriss, whose tragic ending is still fresh in the memory of his many friends and countless admirers. My own brother also had nautical aspirations. He went from London to Newcastle to join a vessel as an apprentice. Unfortunately he went by sea, and the trip was amply sufficient to cure him, for he took train and came back home at once, without even having seen his ship. I must say this was nothing remarkable, for sea-sickness is such a sheer horror that people become indifferent to all surroundings, and are frequently so demoralised that they would hardly resist being thrown overboard. I have known a case where, touching at a port some days out, it has been necessary to land a lad to save his life, the sea affected him so terribly.

Terriss and my brother, therefore, had my sympathy in deciding not to stick to the sea, but in my own case there was no alternative. I had insisted upon going to sea, so had to stick to it, and after six weeks' holiday rejoined my ship in the London Docks. They had replaced the sprung mainmast, and the ship was again loading for Adelaide.

Without any doubt it is wrong to make boys live on board a ship in dock without any effective control. There were always three of us and sometimes four on board, and night watchmen looking after lights were easily hoodwinked. We had gorgeous and surreptitious feasts, and the seals of custom house officers on excisable goods were tampered with quite easily. I can recall on more than one occasion the mystified looks of officers who found seals intact and contents considerably shortened of what they should have been; and, generally speaking, there is scarcely any problem of food supply that boys on board ship will not find a way of solving. Very wrong indeed, many people will say; what became of your moral principle? I reply in the words of the Eton dame who, asked as to the moral qualities of the boys: said, "There was never a moral amongst them," and, after all, it wasn't much worse than orchard robbing! This is a digression, but it is a little difficult to sit down late in life to recount one's juvenile villainies without at least a half-hearted attempt to palliate them—knowing also at the time that even then you do not mean your confession to be a complete one.

In due course the ship was loaded and the crew signed on. We had a new second mate, who we quickly discovered was of a different make to the last one. In fact, I think it was hinted to him that the rope's-end régime was not to our liking, and that we had begun to discover that unity was strength, but this was only possibly because he messed with us. For the "old man," having started by turning King out of the cabin, thought fit to continue the innovation, and kind-hearted Geordie Roshwell was not the type of man to assert himself. A good seaman he was, but more sailmaker than second mate. Both mate and captain bullied him unmercifully, and destroyed the little authority he was capable of wielding.

We were detained in the Downs for many days, one ship of a large fleet, for the wind was blowing too hard from the westward for us to attempt to beat down-Channel. When at last we did make the attempt we got as far as Dungeness and spent one night under short canvas, almost constantly wearing ship on short boards and eventually anchoring again; but we finally did get a slant of wind and fairly started on the voyage. I will only recall one incident as showing the sort of treatment that was then meted out to seafarers as the ordinary custom. It was one of the desires of Captain Hole that his apprentices should be first-class helmsmen, and for some unexplained reason that they should steer better than the able seamen. One day the ship was going her course with a very strong wind just free enough to carry a topmast stunsail in addition to all plain sail. She was steering badly when I relieved an A.B. at noon; in point of fact she was a bit of a handful and the old man had been taking a good deal of interest in what had been going on. This interest he now transferred to me, and because I could not do better than my predecessor I was sentenced to stay at the wheel until eight o'clock that night. Fortunately for my arms the wind grew lighter as the afternoon wore on, and about six o'clock my chum smuggled me a biscuit along. In this, however, with his usual bad luck, he was detected, and when eight bells came he was ordered to relieve me, and spent the four hours of his watch below at the wheel. It was a rough school, but injustice never seemed to be questioned, or thought much about; the master was absolute and despotic, and there was no more to be said.

There is little of interest to record of this passage. Adelaide was reached in due course; the cargo was discharged, the crew deserted, the ship was chartered for London and taken out into the stream to load, as it was likely to be a long operation. The wool was only coming down slowly, and the apprentices had their fair share of work cut out for them. The routine was something after this fashion—called at 5.30 a.m. and got to work by 6.0, washing decks, or doing boat work; half-an-hour for breakfast at 8 a.m.; then on again to 1.0, when there was an hour for dinner; 5.30 p.m. clear up decks. Even after supper the work was not over, for two of us had to pull the skipper on shore and remain in the boat waiting for him, usually till midnight. As we were taking in the ship's water, the rest of us frequently spent the evenings in towing off a small lighter that carried water-tanks. Well, that was all right enough; it was hard work, but we were used to it and did not grumble; but I think the cause of the subsequent trouble was the interference with our shore leave, and I am also afraid that the eternal feminine had a little to do with it.

It was in this way. On the preceding voyage the skipper invited some young ladies on board to lunch, with one of whom he seemed to be somewhat smitten. Now, as it happened, I also was acquainted with the family, and as boys and girls we were on good terms together. Of this the skipper knew nothing until some kind friend gave the show away. That was quite enough for him, and I was duly informed when I asked leave to go on shore, that it was no longer permitted.

That evening we boys held a great pow-wow, at which I stated my intentions to do no more work, and two others also resolved to follow my lead. The sense of injustice rankled very strongly; we were worked most unsparingly and then denied the most ordinary privileges to which we had a right; and the proverbial worm at length turned.

Next morning came the usual summons to turn out, and as I woke up I remembered that I was pledged to defiance by the resolution I had come to the preceding evening. So when my fellow conspirators looked to me for guidance they got all they wanted.

Now that I am nearing the end of my career I can look back and see that there is, and has been, one very curious trait in my character. It is the greatest of my desires to live at peace with my fellows, and to pay the greatest respect and obedience to properly constituted authority, but once that idea has been overcome there is nothing that would stay me in carrying out my own will at any cost, or in the face of any obstacle. This characteristic has led me into much hot water, and I am not at all sure that it has left me even now.

"Now, you boys, turn out," said the voice of "old Geordie," as we nicknamed the second mate. To this we replied that we were not going to do any more work. I can see the smile of pitying incredulity that spread over his features as he listened to our resolve and pointed out the inevitable consequences. These, however, we had made up our minds to face, so, leaving us, he went and informed the mate, who, to our surprise, also tried to reason with us and pointed out, with considerable sarcastic energy, what was likely to happen if we persisted in our attitude and forced him to tell the captain. We said we had counted the cost and were solid in our refusal, but we came as far aft as the mainmast at his bidding and waited for developments.

They soon came. I can see the scene now as clearly as when it happened—a beautiful sunshiny morning. We three boys in shirts and trousers, bare-footed, and the old man just roused from his sleep looking like an angry bear, and not by any means dressed, rushing from the cabin, his eyes blazing with wrath at an act of rebellion such as he had not conceived to be possible. He began with me. Picking up the end of the forebrace, which was close to where we were standing, he gave me the order "Go to work," to which I replied, "I won't, sir." Then, swinging his shoulders, he gave me three strokes with the end of the forebrace. It hurt, but it had not the least effect in disturbing my resolve, and the mate interposed with the advice not to strike us but to put us in irons in the after cabin. This was done, our hands were ironed behind our backs, and we were left to our own devices. To the best of my belief the other fellows escaped the rope's end that had so beautifully scored my back.

The after cabin in which we were put was fitted with lockers for holding tinned provisions, wines, etc., and it had stern ports that opened outwards. Access to the deck could also be obtained through an open skylight. Our sentence involved no food or water, and it seems to me after this lapse of time that more care might have been taken as to our place of confinement, for we were fairly familiar with those lockers and knew exactly what they contained, also, being slim and active as young eels, it was a perfectly easy matter to get our hands in front of us, and ordinary irons do not prevent people from doing useful things on an emergency. During the day we were not absolutely hungry, for we were able to make provision against that, but the thirst was another matter, and that we could not remedy. At seven the next morning we had had enough, and surrendered in exchange for water that we could no longer do without. Our irons were taken off and we went forward.

I should here interpose that at the time of which I write the custom of "hazing" a man was still prevalent. In other words, if a man were obnoxious to either mate or master he would be kept at the most difficult, obnoxious, and perhaps even dangerous work until he deserted, for as a rule there was no purging an offence, and desertion was the only remedy. At the time I speak of there was a man on board a ship in the harbour who had been sitting on the end of a royal yard for some days. What he was doing no one knew, except the mate who was hazing him, and when once that treatment commenced, it was a dog's life indeed for the individual on whom it was being tried. I mention this to show that we knew perfectly well what our future lot was likely to be, but up to then we had possibly not sinned beyond forgiveness, although that seemed a little unlikely.

But now I was confronted with another difficulty, for my chest had disappeared, and I went aft to inquire about it from the captain.

"As I neither intend to allow you money or liberty," he replied, "I have taken charge of your wardrobe." I remember the words as well as if spoken yesterday, and I told him that he could put me in irons again, for work I would not. Probably this was pot-valiant on my part, but I had had a good drink of water. Moreover, I knew the letters that box contained, and also guessed that their destination would be—the father of the girl who wrote them, so I went back *solus* to my irons in the after cabin. The others had had enough of the treatment to satisfy their longings for martyrdom, ardent though these had been.

With me, however, it was entirely different. I had been hurt in more ways than one, and much as I hated the idea of deserting I resolved that no power should make me risk the passage home in that ship if I could do otherwise. As I meditated I saw through the stern port the steward sculling the dingy on shore, and that gave me an idea.

The ship was in the stream, possibly a hundred yards from the shore. I got the irons in front of me, slipped on deck through the skylight unseen by any one on board, threw the vang fall over the side, slid down it, and struck out for the shore. Although, manacled as I was, I could not swim in the ordinary way, I could paddle, and at times turn over on my back for a rest. Not a soul lent me a hand or interfered until I got to the landing-stage, where I was promptly arrested by a constable and marched up to the police station.

The police superintendent, as it happened, was imbued with an idea of fair play. He released me from the irons and told me what I should have to do. By this time my clothes had got fairly dry, I was sitting quietly wondering what would happen next when in came Captain Hole.

"Take that fellow into custody," he said, directly he caught sight of me, "for being absent from his ship without leave."

I subsequently learnt that he had called at his lawyers' on the way up and they had suggested this course as a "try on." It did not work, however. The superintendent declined, saying that I had come to him for protection and he would see that I got it, and on this the old man retired very crestfallen. The outcome was that I was granted a summons for assault, and the captain had to appear before the magistrates next day. I cannot at the moment of writing find the record of the police court proceedings, but anyhow the skipper was fined for the assault, as it was called, on the three of us, and was ordered to give up my property. We, on our side, had to return to our duties. The name of the lawyer who represented us was Edmunds, and I recollect well how he painted the terror we must be in (at which we grinned comprehensively) when one could risk life by venturing into the water with irons on.

After that episode life went on for some little time much on the former lines, except that there was shown to us a suspicious consideration which did not augur well for our comfort on the passage home. Indeed, I received a broad hint from the mate. "Bill," he said, one day, "if I were in your place I should skedaddle and get a moke," his idea for my future being some sort of a costermonger's business, then very popular amongst the runaway Jacks. That scheme, however, had no fascination for me; I had gone to sea to become a skipper, and nothing was going to spoil the idea though there might be many obstacles. However, we finally resolved that we would bolt and get up-country, our objective being a place on the Murray River called Port Mannum. We laid our plans with care, for if we went too soon there would be the more time to catch us, and also it was necessary that we should have as many hours' start as possible in order to escape immediate recapture. What we did with the clothes in our chests I have no very clear recollection. I should think we sold them, for we had to go very light for travelling; but certainly from that time I was not overburdened with clothes until my return to England.

On the fateful night Fred Wilkes and Bob Walters were the two to pull the skipper on shore, and having done so returned on board with instructions to fetch him off at 11 p.m. It was clear they would have to wait until that time or the hue and cry would be raised too soon, so it was settled I should go first and make arrangements for them to pick up their bundles. These were placed in a round washing-tub with my own apparel, and lowered over the side, followed by me. I swam on shore to the peninsula side of the river, pushing the tub before me, and gave a cooee. Then I dressed and, taking the bundles, left the tub for the enlightenment of those on board in the morning, and set off to the house of a town boy friend, who, with his mother, were aiding and abetting us. That was an evening of many incidents, some pleasant, all to be remembered, and I wonder if these words will meet the eye of any of the actors. If they do they will know that the waters of Lethe have not obliterated for me the memory of their kindness and help.

About midnight Fred and Bob duly arrived. They told me that when they had taken the skipper off they intentionally left the oars in the boat. This he noticed and had them taken on board as usual. When he had turned in they quietly replaced them and pulled on shore. As there was no other ship's boat in the water, the presumption was that we were safe from pursuit until the morning, but had the skipper had the imaginative faculty at all developed, the first omission to remove the oars might have provided him with the opportunity for a dramatic surprise. I always feel regret that I never met any one afterwards who saw what went on the next morning when it was discovered that the birds had flown. The skipper's face must have been a study when he was told that the ship's boat was to be seen made fast to the steps and the three apprentices missing. There was a fourth one, who stayed behind, but as he was delicate, and more or less used as a cabin-boy, our actions had not been any guide to him. These words are in no way intended to convey a reproach to you, Jim Powell, of Pimlico, for you were a sportsman, although you could not go quite the pace of your more athletic comrades.

Well, away we went, tramping through the hours of darkness, and when the sun rose we took shelter under a haystack and slept until awakened by the pangs of hunger. We had arrived at a place called Golden Grove, and, knowing the hospitality that was extended to travellers, had no hesitation in going to the house and asking for food, which was freely given. I cannot remember the name of the owner of the house, but he saw his opportunity of securing a useful hand on the estate and persuaded Bob to stay with him. Bob accordingly drops out of this story. Fred and I, after our appetites were satisfied, continued our journey, and I quite think we made a good time of it. The next night we spent in a place called Gumeracha, and experienced the hospitality of a landowner named Randall. I expect it was pretty clearly seen what we were, but there was always a great deal of sympathy ready for runaway seamen, and we certainly met it in this instance. The next day we started on what we meant to be the final stage of the journey. It was, but well do I remember the interminable white hills of that road. From the top of each one in succession we hoped to see the water of the River Murray, and this kept us going. Other characteristics of the road were trees and fields of water-melons. I also remember being struck with the appearance of great worn boulders perched on hilltops, and the soil turned up showing fields of white shells something of the nature of oysters. At length, however, we climbed the last hill and came in sight of our destination, a small cluster of huts by the side of a wide white river, fringed by great trees, and conveying to the mind an idea of vastness and grandeur.

Here we had reached a place where one could exist by one's own exertion, and where, if you did not like the job you had, you could leave it and find another more to your liking.

As it happened Mannum was the head-quarters of a Captain Randall, who commanded one of the steamers that plied on the Murray. They took up all sorts of merchandise for the towns on the river banks, and towed down barges laden with wool. I did not make one of these trips, but I was told they were at times fairly exciting, for what with shallow water at one time and overhanging branches of trees at another, there was usually plenty of incident. There were five carpenters there building a new barge for Captain Randall. These men were accommodated in a large tent, and in a very short time it was explained to me that I could have a pound a week and my tucker if I could do their cooking for them. The offer was gratefully accepted, especially as it transpired that there was a shot-gun at my disposal, and that I was expected to replenish the stores from the sources of wildfowl that were to be found in the lagoons on the other side of the river. I do not well remember what occupation Fred found at first, but eventually he went as a deck hand in a river steamer, and thus he also drops out of my story. I heard afterwards that he took up his quarters at a town higher up the river. Good luck to him, wherever he may be, for he was a good fellow, although we had many a scrap together at odd times.

Left by myself I waited for the time I might safely return to Adelaide, but my life in the meantime was by no means a bad one. The Murray is an exceedingly beautiful river, running as it does, almost a milky white colour, between banks thickly wooded with splendid gum trees. Of course its volume depended upon whether there was a wet or dry season, but I saw no sign of drought while I was there. On one occasion two men and myself were towed some hundred miles up in a barge, and then cast adrift to drop down the stream, with instructions to stop at intervals and cut branches of trees that would be suitable for using as knees for the new barge. I regret to say that our success in this matter was not commensurate with our expectations. The life, however, was an ideal one, the weather all that could be desired, warm and beautiful, with a bright moon at nights. Life by the camp fire, with plenty of tea, damper and beef, was an excellent stimulant to high spirits, and a night passed in Swan Reach was especially noticeable in this matter.

If we were not as successful in our wood-cutting as we might have been, we certainly had a most enjoyable time, and when at last we got back to head-quarters I found a newspaper which gave me the information that the *Alwynton* had duly sailed for home.

Well, with the least possible lapse of time I gave up my job, got a cheque for my wages, duly cashed it, and took my passage back in a sort of coach. I have no very clear recollections of any incidents in that trip, but I got to Adelaide all right and learned that a warrant was out for me as a deserter. That was no more than I expected, for it was the ordinary thing. The police, however, were not over zealous in worrying runaway seamen, for they themselves had mostly once been in the same category. The thing was to find a ship, and for that purpose I was advised to consult a certain boarding-house master, Jack Hanly I think his name was, and not a bad sort by any means, but it was rather an eye-opener to be fitted out with a discharge that had belonged to some other seaman of about my own age, and it further involved a change of name which I saw might lead to complication when it came to producing papers for the Board of Trade. The first trial showed me that it would not do. There was in the harbour a big American ship called the *Borodino*, and when Jack and I went to the captain the following conversation took place. Said Jack: "Captain, I've brought you a hand, wants to learn to be a captain."

"No, thank you," said the skipper, "looks too white about the gills for me, no deal."

That was the end of that episode, and I cast round myself to see what could be done. There was also in port another ship called the *Troas*, which I remembered we had spoken at sea on the previous voyage. On the strength of this acquaintance, I went to see her skipper, who, being badly in want of hands, agreed to see me through the police court and ship me as an ordinary seaman. When I was fined £5 or a month for desertion my new skipper paid the fine, and I forthwith took up my berth in my new ship. She was a full-rigged vessel of about 800 tons, and was bound for Foo Chow to load tea for home. So far as the officers were concerned the tone of the ship was on a fairly high plane. The mate was no great personality, but the second, George Davies, was a very fine seaman and a splendid officer. He was also a splendid athlete. I have seen him go out on a bare topmast stunsail boom to reeve a tack that had become unrove, in order to save the time it would have taken to rig the boom in. I believe he was afterwards in command of a sailing vessel that was lost in a typhoon in the China Sea—at all events his ship was reported as missing. There was also a third mate, whom I afterward met when he was serving in the P. & O. service.

The crew were a curious lot. There was especially one typical old sailor full of ancient lore and tradition. Commenting on the fact of the captain having his wife on board he predicted evil from the commencement. "You mark my words," he said, "they are bad cattle to sail with." That was not, however, the general opinion, for the lady in question was pleasant to look upon, and every one she spoke to was pleased with her charming manner.

The cause of our misfortune was something quite different, and might have been foreseen. After taking in about one hundred tons of stone ballast for the trip to Foo Chow, we took in for the remainder a great quantity of semi-liquid mud that had been dredged up from the bottom of the river. Whether any consideration had been given to the matter by those in charge I am unable to say, but the fact remains that as soon as we got to sea the ship showed a great want of stability or stiffness, and as she heeled over the moist mud picked up its lowest possible level. It was evident that this state of things would not do, so as the ship had sister keelsons we tried to build a dam amidships by driving down piles inside them and then filling up the internal space with stone ballast. The general effect of this procedure was, I think, to make matters worse, and as we could not get back to Adelaide, the wind being strong and adverse, we tried to get to Port Lincoln. Here, again, our luck was poor, for the wind came strong from the westward and cut us off.

The next idea was to run for Melbourne. We in the forecastle were dependent for our news of what was being done upon such scanty information as might be dropped by one of the officers, but we mostly recognised that we were in rather a tight fix and that we should be lucky to get out of it. Owing to the ship's inability to stand up to her canvas we were driven south of Kangaroo Island and were hardly put to it to weather

Cape Jaffa. From that point, however, the land trended a little to the north-eastward, but it was soon recognised that nothing short of a shift of wind would save us, and that there was no sign of. We had weathered Cape Jaffa about midnight, having carried close-reefed topsails and foresail with the greatest difficulty. The ship, of course, lay over tremendously, but she still carried some way. As soon as we were past the Cape the maintopsail blew away and, the foretopsail and foresail being furled, we lay hove-to under the mizzen-topsail. The next morning we were set to work to get up stay and yard tackles for the long boat, and to clear away the spars that were stowed on top of it. This was done and the stay tackles hooked on and hauled tight, but during this operation I had fallen on my left shoulder and hurt it so badly that it was difficult and painful to move my arm. Some time shortly after noon the weather cleared a little and some one shouted out "land on the lee beam." There it was sure enough, and about two miles or so of breakers I should think. There was no escape, for the ship was simply drifting to leeward. Davies, who went aloft to obtain a better view, hailed the poop: "It's all right, sir—a sandy beach;" and then scuttled down to help and advise the only thing possible, which was to run for the beach. As we discovered afterwards, it was the top of high water and fortune had directed us to the only patch of sand in the locality.

The second mate was now the man of the moment, the mate was not much use, and the master, never a noisy man, was apparently well contented to see Davies run the show. Foresail and foretopsail were loosed and set, the mizzen-topsail was clued up, the helm put hard-a-weather, and keeping her quarter to the sea we ran for the beach. Davies commanded the ship. A big German, a very fine fellow, was at the weather wheel, I was on the lee side. Needless to say, we were all a little curious as to what the next few minutes might bring about, though honestly speaking I do not think young people care very much what faces them. I perfectly well remember thinking that I might shortly be called to an account for all I had done or left undone, but decided that there was no time to dwell upon such thoughts. Just about this time the first real comber came on board, sweeping the main deck clean of everything. It left the stem and stern posts of the long boat, however, swinging in the tackles. By this time the ship was nearly on her beam ends and probably touching the ground, for the water was breaking very heavily over her, and to the best of my recollection the foreyard was touching the sand. We cut away the weather rigging so far as we could, and in long-drawn heaves and attempts to come right side up the masts and spars gradually left us to a precarious foothold on the outside of the ship's weather quarters. I can remember that episode well, for the water came over bitterly cold and seemed blown by the wind into our very bones.

In the course of an hour or so it became evident that the water was receding and it was possible to see what could be done. The ship was breaking up fast, and before three hours had passed there was a hole through the middle of her. But the ends kept together and some of the comicalities of life commenced to appear. The mate was walking as best he could in the cabin with a lifebelt round him and a musket over his shoulder, and as little semblance of order remained, it was left to the stronger spirits to do the best they could. Here John, the big German, and the second mate came to the front, and they did well. By the time it was low water a rope had been got on shore, how I know not, and some had gone on shore by it, but I know that before we left the ship we had a feed of jugged hare in Davies's cabin. That stands out vividly, but I cannot remember any drunkenness on the part of any member of the crew.

The landing of the captain's little lady was accomplished with little trouble, for she was a plucky soul, and went through a trying time with a courage that was greatly to be admired, but she could not have avoided drawing conclusions which would have been invidious could they have been particularised. The next scene in this drama was round a big fire under the lee of a sand-hill, where most of the crew were gathered. Some of the crowd had secured food, and there was a general feeling of satisfaction that we had not lost the number of our mess. Also we gained the knowledge that a bag of flour made a first-rate life-buoy for a man who wanted to get on shore with a rope. One of the big deck water-casks had been washed on shore; we knocked the head in and placed it with its sound end to windward, and its opening to the fire to make a shelter for the lady of the party, and then, hot on one side and cold on the other, we waited for day. Some bold spirits had already tried exploration, and failed to find any sign of habitation.

Shortly after daylight, we saw two men on horseback gazing at the ship, and they expressed wonderment and surprise at the good fortune which enabled us to greet them. It appeared that the general character of the coast was rocky, and the other wrecks that had taken place in the vicinity had all been attended by fatalities.

As we were the exceptions we could only be thankful that Providence had been so good to us. Then we set to work to think out the next move. As for myself, I had got on shore with little more than a packet of letters, tied up with a rope yarn, and a copy of Byron's poems. I have them both now, but they were neither of any considerable value when the world had to be faced in a shirt and trousers only.

Our friends on horseback came from a station near to Lake Albert. It was some miles away, but we went there and were hospitably entertained for days. We made occasional visits to what was left of the ship, and were lucky in finding some boots and articles of clothing. These were useful, as our hosts had begun to hint that it would be well if we made a move to see what some other station's damper and mutton were like. Davies and I had tramped to Rivoli Bay, an old boiling-down station, to see if any vessel was there, but not finding one we returned, and soon afterwards we all set out for Port Macdonnel.

There were many amusing incidents in that trip. The news had travelled that a party of sailormen were on the tramp, and at one station the cook was exceeding wrath because his master had not given him notice that we should be there for supper. He observed that the boss had done it for spite, to take him unawares. "Just," he said, "as if twenty-five bally men could knock me out at any time!" I think his confidence was not egotism, for we were well done, and the people from the big house came down to the shed to look at us all.

Words fail me to convey the surprises of the next day's tramp along the bush paths. We passed emu in droves; the wallabys hardly troubled to get out of the path; and to see the kangaroos cover the ground was a constant source of wonderment. I do not know what the record kangaroo high-jump is, but what we saw them do with apparent ease seemed absolutely marvellous.

It must not be supposed that the period between the wreck and our arrival at Port Macdonnel was only a few days. I should think it was about a month. There were certain matters regarding wages that the captain had to arrange with a great part of his crew, and he had to ride to Mount Gambier to find some one to finance him, subsequently meeting us at Port Macdonnel. My wages were no source of trouble to me, for he had paid my fine and I was consequently in debt to the ship, but with the others it was different. The skipper was the object of much wrath when it leaked out that he was not in favour of our getting a passage round to Melbourne by the coasting steamer, but preferred to play into the hands of a road constructor who was anxious to secure our services. One of the owners of the steamer was present when the altercation was taking place, and solved the question by giving a passage to those who wished to go. I shall always entertain a kindly remembrance of that action by the gentleman in question, whose name I think was Ormerod. This series of events led up to one of the pleasantest times of my life. We got to Melbourne, for the steamer went up the Yarra, and as many of us as wished were taken on to assist in loading and unloading cargo. For this we were paid one shilling an hour for eight hours' work, and we lived at the sailors' home. Strange as it may seem, we were satisfied with our lot, and the pay sufficed for all reasonable needs. When that particular ship was finished with, however, Davies, Dowling, third mate of the *Troas*, and myself thought it time to see about getting home again, and so, with our added store of knowledge of various forms of life, we got down to Sandridge Pier to look for a ship.

CLIPPER SHIP "ESSEX," 1042 TONS. J. S. ATWOOD, COMMANDER

Sandridge Pier in those days was a beautiful sight to any lover of salt water. It belonged to a period that will never again come round—the time when ships were beautiful, and no pains were spared to make them so. Steam had not then got all the passenger trade, and the ships of Green, Wigram, Smith and Dunbar were the lineal descendants of the old East Indiamen. They carried big crews, and they were mostly commanded and officered by men who were splendid seamen as well as gentlemen. The command of one of these vessels for a voyage extending over nine months might be worth a thousand pounds; that was before the world woke to the period of extreme competition. But beautiful though these ships were, they only pleased the eye because they were to our belief the embodiment of all that was the finest to be found afloat. Many of the best specimens of them can be found to-day in various ports of the world serving as coal hulks. When I made a trip to the docks some years ago to see the *Essex*, it was difficult to believe that she was the ship one had known teeming with life, brilliancy and smartness. She was, I suppose, about 240 feet long, which was then considered a very fair length for any sailing-ship.

What is known as "taking the time ball" was one of the events of the day. A midshipman belonging to each vessel would be perched in some prominent part of the poop of each ship, and in close proximity would be the boatswain and his mates, ready to pipe to dinner and grog at the instant the signal was given that the ball had dropped. The chorus of pipes was a thing to hear and remember, as it was taken up by the assembled ships; there was always a laudable ambition to be the first ship to commence.

The names of the ships there escape my memory, but there was more than one belonging to Money, Wigram & Co., and there was also a splendid old frigate-built ship called the *Holmesdale*. I am not quite sure whether the celebrated packet-ship the *White Star* was there then, or whether I came across her the next voyage, but both she and the *Champion of the Seas* were magnificent-looking vessels, and the captain of the latter ship, Outridge, I think, was his name, was in appearance quite in keeping with the name of his command.

The point I want to bring out is that these two last-mentioned ships, fast sailers and "packet-ships" though they were, did not rank among the aristocracy of the sea, such as the Blackwell ships proper were then considered. They were regarded in the same manner as, ten years later, a Union Steamship man would regard a Donald Currie ship. He would throw a condescending glance upon a Donald Currie ship as much as to say, "Very worthy, no doubt, but you are not *us*, although you try your hardest to get the set of our sail covers and to keep your yards decently square." But of that more anon.

It appeared that the *Essex* wanted two able and one ordinary seamen, and as Dowling and I both wanted to ship as ordinary, Davies, who was the wise man of the party, advised me to ship as A.B. As he put it, "You want to get home, and they can only reduce your wages in proportion to your incompetency." Accordingly, when we had concluded a satisfactory interview with the "first officer," as he was styled, I followed this advice. This first officer's name was Gibbs. He turned out to be a great favourite with all, and I can say with truth that the forecastle hands tried their best to please him always out of sheer personal liking. We used to speak of him as "Lady Jane." He had his valet with him, and on one occasion he sang "The Lost Child" in costume and was much applauded. I met him years afterwards, on more level terms, and I hope he retains as kindly a remembrance of me as I do of him.

Soon after taking up our quarters on board, we had our first lesson in "Blackwall fashion." Davies and I were on a stage on the ship's side busily painting when one of the Jacks put his head over: "Here, you chaps, you're doing too much work, that ain't Blackwall fashion," and I must confess that we immediately complied with the regulation.

That ship, of 1042 tons about, carried captain, four mates, midshipmen and apprentices, twenty-four able seamen, and a boatswain and two mates. It was a fine crew, and could work the ship handsomely. It was then considered that it took four A.B.'s to stow a topgallant sail, but I have some recollection that upon one occasion Davies managed by himself at the fore, where he was stationed as a foretop man. I was a maintop man, and, being under the immediate eye of the officer of the watch, had not that same freedom of action they enjoyed forward, and yet I seem to remember some association between the game of euchre and the maintop on fine afternoons.

The first night out on the homeward trip we had three topsails to reef at once. It was well done and quickly, and, in the curious way in which news gets forward, we learned that the old man was very pleased with the way in which it was done, and said he never had a finer crew. And let me here, as one of that crew, pay a tribute of respect to Captain J. S. Attwood, who was in command of it.

The said crew was one such as I am thankful to say I never had to deal with as a skipper. Almost without exception they were men holding Board of Trade certificates of competency, having been runaways or something of the sort. There was one man whom I had seen in command of a sailing-ship in Adelaide, the *Jessie Heyns*, he was working his passage in order to buy a ship in London. He did so, and afterwards wanted me to go as second mate with him. Fine seamen as they were, the men knew too much to be tractable. Their *bête noire* was the third mate. Now there are various ways of annoying officers. One punishment that can be served out by a crew is not to sing out when hauling upon the ropes in the night time. By the tone of the men's voices it can usually be learned in the dark what they are doing, but to shorten sail with silent men was an ordeal that was spared me as an officer, I am thankful to say. I learned a lot on that trip, however. For one thing I cultivated the art of chewing tobacco, so that I might be able to demonstrate undeniably to my people at home the fact that I was an A.B., and could, therefore, spit brown with a clear conscience.

It is a curious thing how trifling incidents come back to the memory when dealing with past events. There was one night the third mate had already given rather more trouble than we thought he ought to have done, when he put the finishing touch by giving the order to set a lower studding-sail. The night was pitch dark, and we were being as awkward and as slow as we knew how to be. The captain was on deck, and ordered the third to go forward and see what the delay was caused by. He did so promptly, and got a ball of spun yarn thrown at his head by a hand unknown, on which he retired aft and told the skipper. Now Captain Attwood was a man who feared nothing or no one, and he promptly came to inquire who had "thrown a ball of spun yarn at his third mate's head?" Such was the temper of the men that the betting was very even as to what he was likely to get himself; but after some talk of more or less lurid hue, Davies solved the difficulty by saying, "Look here, Captain Attwood, if you want the work done we can do it, but we are not going to be humbugged round by that third mate of yours; now we'll show you how to set a stunsail." And we did. But, as I said before, I am glad that I never had such a crowd to deal with. This little incident will serve to explain the temper of crews on the southern seas during the 'sixties.

We rounded Cape Horn without any striking incident. It was winter time, and beyond the clothes I stood in I had precious little. There was, however, some sort of a sale on board, for I know that I got a warm monkey jacket. We ran from the Horn to the line in under sixteen days—a good passage—and off the western islands were becalmed for some days with a number of other vessels, tea ships mostly, and vessels of repute at that. But when once the wind began to make from the westward, as it did, what a glorious spin home it was! The *Essex* was not loaded deeply, she had fine lines, and it took something to pass her. In this case I think she was the second ship to dock, the winner of the race being a ship called the *Florence Henderson*.

Blackwall dock at last, and my mother to meet me! I can see her look of horror as I jumped on shore from one of the maindeck ports, bare-footed, dressed in shirt and trousers, with a quid of tobacco in my cheek that was intended to be obvious even to the casual observer!

It is a little remarkable how one's views on the conventions change with one's surroundings.

CHAPTER III

"All the way to Calcutty have I been, and seed nothing but one—banany. Howsomever, it was werry good, so I'm going back to have another." —*Old Sailor Story*.

Back once more to the house of Trapp & Sons in the Minories, where I had to face Captain Hole, and "dree my weird."

It was essential in my sea time for obtaining my certificate that I should have four years of good conduct to show, and that could only be obtained by the cancelling of my indentures, or serving out the remainder of my time. Now Captain Hole had retired from the sea, having put the late mate, Mr. Coleman, in command of the *Alwynton*, and was, moreover, keenly bent upon getting a bit of his own back, so he utterly declined to cancel my indentures and finished the discussion by saying, "I know you like big ships; you have just come home in one in time to go out in a small one. The *Lord Nelson* is in Swansea, and you will join her at once. If you had stayed in the *Alwynton* you would have gone away second mate of her this voyage. And that's for saying 'I won't' to me."

Well, there was no help for it, but there was a touch of "I told you so" in Mr. Trapp's private remark, "If you had paid your premium to me I could have altered things." There was also human nature in this, but what Captain Hole got he kept, as he was part owner, and I proceeded to Swansea to join my new craft as second mate.

A little barque of 247 tons, built by White of Cowes for a whaler, she had made many voyages round Cape Horn and had just come home with a cargo of copper ore. She was not in good repair and was to be refitted and rigged with new wire rigging. I am not at all sure that this was not a stroke of good fortune for me, for as the operation took some months it gave me an opportunity of learning some of the tricks of the trade.

There was a captain who lived on board with his daughter; his name was Boisse, and he was very kind to me, for I lived in the mate's berth and messed in the cabin. At the same time I had the good fortune to become acquainted with the family of a Captain Outerbridge, the master of a copper ore ship, the *Glamorganshire*. They treated me as one of themselves, and

Tom Outerbridge and myself were inseparable. We both had a great liking for the theatre, to which we treated ourselves to the extreme limit of our purses. Wybert Reeve was then the manager of the Swansea theatre; I met him more than twenty years later in New Zealand and we talked over and remembered the actors and actresses of the old days, but admiration for Kate Saville lingered even then.

Captain Hole paid frequent visits to Swansea to see how the work progressed, and he was also paymaster. After some little time Boisse went on leave, and that left a great deal more responsibility for me, but I learned how caulking required to be watched when it was being done by contract, and also mysteries connected with re-coppering and rigging a ship. It was good useful work. So far as I can recollect there were three riggers and myself, and I suppose that by that time I considered that I could do a man's work, as my ability to do so had not been questioned in the last ship, and furthermore I had shown that I could do a day's work at carrying bags of wheat, which is a hardish test.

Whether there is the same zeal now concerning the details of their calling among sailor boys as there was in my time I cannot say, but we apprentices in the *Alwynton* had always striven to learn all we could about our business. Doubtless we were better in practice than in theory, but we had certain text books that we hammered at until we mastered the various difficulties that presented themselves. Consequently I thought myself equal to sending anything aloft that might be necessary, and naturally took a lead among the riggers. One morning I learned a little more.

We were sending the foreyard aloft, and age and experience said that two double blocks and a fall were the proper tackle to use—no, said Youth, hook on a top block, reeve the end of a small hawser through it, bend on to the yard, and we will take it to the windlass and heave away.

We did so, and hove the yard high enough, two men then going aloft to shackle on the slings. It was a cold morning, and Youth, having held on to the hawser while it was being hove on found his fingers cold, and not suspecting harm, as there were many turns of it round the windlass barrel, put it on the deck and stood on it while he warmed his hands. Now this shows how a fine idea may miscarry by some absurd detail being overlooked; in getting my feet on the hawser I suppose I had slacked it slightly and the next thing I knew was being on my back, a vision of flying rope, terrible swearing aloft, and the foreyard down across the rails. I laugh as I recall the scene, but it might have been far more serious. The lesson was learned, however, that a purchase was better than a single rope, even if sufficient power could be applied. In this particular case no harm was done, for as the mainstays set up right in the eyes of her—they had eased the yard as it came down. It had been a narrow thing for the men aloft, but they were good fellows and said little after the first natural outburst.

Then there came an inventor from Whitstable and fitted the barque with patent topsails of his own invention. I trust that Heaven may have forgiven him by this time, but I freely confess that nothing will ever induce me to do so. A good patent topsail, if there is such a thing (which I doubt), may be a boon and a blessing. I can say a word or two in favour of Cunningham's patent, which is not so very bad, but this particular patent in question must have been inspired by the spirit of evil, who in some moment doubting his power over the destiny of the souls of seamen, made assurance doubly sure as regards the future crews of the *Lord Nelson*. These yards were awful things to work with and had more weak points about them than even erring human nature.

By the time the ship was nearly ready for sea we received the new mate on board. He was a great raw-boned Scotchman named McKinnon, a good seaman, and not bad to get on with. His first introduction to his new ship did not seem to impress him very favourably.

We loaded a cargo of coal to take round to Plymouth, where we were to load for Australia, and with a scratch crew of ten all told we were towed to sea. The skipper, Boisse, who had re-joined to take her round the coast, observed, "Never mind about washing down to get the coal dust from the deck, she'll do that for herself when she gets outside." He showed a sound knowledge of her ways, for deep as she was it was like being on a half-tide rock.

In due course we got to Plymouth, discharged a great portion of the coal and commenced to load large iron pipes and machinery for Wallaroo. It was mining gear of some sort, but, not being content with a fair load, the skipper had some of the pipes filled in with coal to make more room, the result being that the ship was loaded inordinately deep.

About this time, for some unexplained reason, there was a change of skippers, and our new one was R. K. Jeffery. He was a most important personage, with a great deal of the Methodist about him. There were two or three apprentices and one Bob McCarthy, an ordinary seaman, who was a friend of the owners. He was supposed to be suffering from consumption and came to sea to be cured or killed. He was cured, as it happened, and we were chums for the voyage, as he lived in the deck-house with the carpenter and myself. The last I heard of him, some years ago, was that he was in command of a steamer and doing well. The apprentices disappeared from the ship before we put to sea.

This was early in the year 1866, and the winter season in the Atlantic had been bad. It was shortly after the *London* went down in the Bay, and our anticipations of the trip were not hopeful. It will be remembered that this was before Mr. Plimsoll began his celebrated crusade, and, in point of fact, here was as fine an illustration of overloading as any one could wish to see. So far as I know there was at that time no check at all upon the amount of cargo a master or owner might think fit to place on board, and I am sure that no one was ever more entitled to the gratitude of seamen than was Samuel Plimsoll. His method of procedure might have been crude, but the fact remains that his book was a fair and just account of the usages of the sea at the time it was written. Some years afterwards, when it came into my hands, I found how closely my experiences coincided with his remarks.

This matter of overloading ships was a very vexed question, and "as deep as a collier" is a proverb not altogether forgotten even to-day. The evil now to some extent corrects itself, for a deeply-laden steamer is always lightening herself by her coal consumption, but I am confident that I could go to the docks to-day and point out first-class steamers that would be overloaded if down to their Plimsoll mark, and which, if they put to sea in the teeth of a bad breeze of wind, would give considerable anxiety to those in charge of their navigation. Of this, however, I may say more anon.

We put to sea loaded as deeply as possible, and had no great luck to speak of, for after rounding Ushant the wind drew to the southward of west and began to blow hard. The barque laboured heavily, commencing to make a good deal of water. The pumps eventually got choked with small coal and we had to bale the water out by buckets. This was only possible because, owing to the nature of the cargo, the hold was not full, and we were able to clear a way pretty deep down in the coal and so keep the water under. Then the maintopsail yard (patent) carried away, and that gave us more joy, and finally the men came aft to the captain and demanded that he should put back to Plymouth or the nearest port.

To proceed with the voyage in our then condition would have been impossible, but the old man did not yield with any good grace. The crew, however, were worn out by constant work and want of sleep, and there was nothing for it but to shift the helm, and hope we might be fortunate enough to get to port. The decision to do so acted as a tonic to all hands, and eventually we got back to Plymouth Dock to unload and refit. To the best of my recollection the ship was by this time so down by the head that the hawse pipes were almost level with the water, and it was a mercy that any of us ever again set foot on shore. It is one of the dispositions of Providence, however, that a danger once escaped leaves no lasting or abiding cautions behind it, and perhaps in the interests of adventure it is well that it should be so.

When the cargo was discharged and it came to clearing the ship's hold, we found that the spaces between the ship's timbers as high as the 'tween-decks were filled in tightly and solidly with small coal, which was very troublesome to extract. In fact, a great deal of the inner planking of the ship had to be removed to get at it, but eventually it was done, the cargo reloaded, the coal being omitted, and once more we set out on the voyage.

There was nothing particularly striking on the passage out. The ship was too deep to sail well, and the captain after rounding the Cape went no further south than was necessary to get a westerly wind. He was greatly distressed, however, at the erratic course the ship made when she had a fair wind. Of course the mate declared that she was properly steered in his watch, and I do not doubt it, but I was called into the cabin, and inferentially informed that iniquities always occurred on my watch, further that it was *always* in the second mate's watch that things did go wrong. Neither of my mentors appeared to realise that they had both been in the same position themselves, and that, therefore, they must have suffered in their time from that particular original sin of which they were now complaining.

So long as my connection with sailing-ships lasted I found that this idea concerning the second mate was very firmly rooted (it would not, of course, apply to the steamers in which I afterwards served), and indeed it was not much to be wondered at. He was as a rule the least experienced of the afterguard. He was necessarily thrown much among the crew, for he had to serve out and be responsible for all stores, other than food, used by the men. And he required to be a strong character in addition to his muscular development if he hoped to obtain the same respect and attention given to his superiors.

We arrived at Wallaroo after a long passage, and were moored alongside the pier. It was not a comfortable berth, for the port was subject to sudden strong winds known as "Southerly busters." These came up against the side of the pier and consequently the stern moorings were slip ropes, which permitted the vessel to cast off and ride by the head moorings, end on to the wind. The pier is probably strengthened by this time, but in those days it was a very flimsy affair.

Our skipper was a man who used his head, and by his instruction the mate had rigged a swinging derrick that discharged our cargo with ease and safety. We then ballasted and set sail for Port Victor, where we loaded a cargo of wool for Melbourne.

Before leaving Wallaroo, however, my old shipmate Hill of the *Essex* tried very hard to get permission for me to transfer to a brigantine which he owned and was in command of in Adelaide. We had inspected her together in London, and he had then bought her, declaring I should be second mate with him. He reckoned, however, without my skipper, who was obdurate. Hill afterwards took the *Belle* trading in the China Sea, where he died suddenly, leaving a young wife on board.

Port Victor was a curious little place in those days. It had originated as a boiling-down station. It was not much more than an open roadstead, but it was sheltered by an island that afforded some protection at the mouth of the bay. We had fair luck there and, loading our wool easily, got to Melbourne, where we discharged at Williamstown, and ballasted. There were many splendid ships in port—curiously enough again the *White Star* and *Champion of the Seas*, and also a celebrated Aberdeen White Star liner *The Star of Peace*. Those ships were in a class by themselves; they made very good passages, at times records, and were kept up in first-rate style, I retain a vivid recollection of being passed by one of them when bound up-Channel—but I will refer to that in its proper order.

We beat down Melbourne harbour in charge of one of the smartest pilots I ever saw. I am sorry I have forgotten his name, but the way he worked that ship to windward was a very masterpiece of handling. He had, moreover, a fairly biting tongue, and a vocabulary that was practically inexhaustible if the least thing went wrong in tacking ship. We heard a good deal of it, but we made a fair start for Point de Galle, and nothing of moment happened on the passage.

It is not given to me to adequately describe the first smell of the East. It is years since I last experienced it, and the thought arises whether steam and modernity can have made serious inroads into the characteristics of the Garden of the World? It is no use speculating on that point, however. Here we were anchored off Point de Galle, the smell of the land wind almost giving a sense of intoxication, spice-laden as it came, the native catamarans darting about at an astonishing speed, and what was of still greater interest to us, each boat with a bunch of big yellow luscious bananas that we lost no time in making acquaintance with. There again is a new experience, the first taste of an East Indian banana is not a thing to be easily forgotten. Let no one imagine that the forced and imported things we get in London to-day can be compared to the fruit in its native state; as well compare chalk with cheese!

We lay at anchor here some days, and I remember well seeing the largest shark in my experience. He was blue with black spots and a square head, and probably between eighteen and twenty feet long; in the clear still blue water he looked an enormous brute.

Eventually the skipper came off and we got under way for Colombo, where we were to load coffee for either New York or the Continent, calling off Bahia for orders. This was indeed good news, and the work of the ship went with a snap and a swing that made child's play of it until the novelty of being homeward bound wore off a bit.

It was the fashion when a ship was leaving to send a boat's crew on board from all the other vessels in harbour to help to work her out of the anchorage. The skipper usually took charge of that job, and it was a kindly and useful assistance which tended towards good fellowship all round. At times a marvellous smartness would be developed, seeing that no proper stations had been prearranged, but to help to get a ship under way for home was always a pleasant experience.

Now it should be known that the one great day on a long voyage is that on which one gets money and leave for twenty-four hours. It was looked forward to most keenly, and afterwards served as a topic of conversation until long afterwards. This particular leave was no exception to the rule, and as I have not visited Colombo since I shall always remember it for its intense beauty. There is only one place with which I can compare it for beauty, and that is Rio. The luxuriant vegetation made it appear as a sort of paradise to men who had been cooped up in a small craft for months past. I suppose we amused ourselves pretty much the same as sailors on shore usually do. We chartered a conveyance and drove out into the country, we bathed in a fresh-water lake, and generally disported ourselves like a lot of overgrown school-boys, but on return to town, in some way or other we made the acquaintance of certain bandsmen of the 25th Regiment and found them very good fellows. They did their best to do the honours of the place, and succeeded very much to our satisfaction. A dinner in the evening in an open-air corridor attached to a big hotel completed my enchantment, and I wanted to stay there and enlist in the "Borderers." My particular friend (by this time), a bandsman named Hibbert, with a view to giving effect to this suggested that I should meet him after the officers' mess, when he would be free and would put me in the way of doing so. I sat outside the officers' mess on the other side of the street and envied them. Eventually I was taken to a Sergeant Sinclair, who invited me to his quarters and put me up for the night. I like to put this action on record as typical of the kindness shown by men of the services to youngsters when they get a little adrift. Before I turned in, in a spotlessly clean bed which was a change indeed from my usual quarters, he discovered that he had served in the 92nd under a cousin of mine for whom he had the greatest respect and regard. Next morning he said to me: "If I enlist you I shall get so much bounty (I forget how much), but for your own sake I think you had better go back to your ship. You very likely would work up to a commission, but go home and see your friends before altering the idea of your life." Whether that was good advice or not I cannot say. Anyhow I took it, and retain a grateful remembrance of the Sergeant's kindness.

So it was back to the mill once more, and an end of all the pleasant things that had been so tantalisingly held in view, back to the daily round, the wretched food, and the discomfort of poor quarters in hot weather with no chance of more shore leave.

Our cargo was being stowed by a gang of natives who lived on board at the fore end of the ship. We took the bags in, they stowed them, and a specially beautiful lot of coffee that was, in fact a rare consignment. Every possible care was taken in its stowage, and no precaution was neglected to ensure its safe carriage to its destination.

Our stock of ship's bread or biscuit had run out by this time. It was of the hard brown type that required a deal of cracking, and we were rather pleased to take in a supply of native baked biscuits that at the time we first tasted them were a great improvement upon the former supply. But before we had been a month at sea they were simply swarming with black weevils, little insects resembling ants.

Sailing day came, and with it the usual crowd of boats from the various ships to help us out of port. On these occasions it was usual to offer the visitors a glass of grog, but I cannot remember that the crew of the *Lord Nelson* ever had a taste of it, for none was put on board. The advocates of so-called temperance can say what they please, but the judicious administration of grog on board ship (sailing-ships especially) will always have my support. In a wet weary world of toil it frequently helps to put a more cheerful face upon a very drab outlook.

The commencement of the homeward-bound trip is always an occasion when high spirits (animal, not spiritous) prevail. Yards were hoisted to the tune of artistic chanties, for where a collection of sailing-ships were gathered together each ship's crew prided itself upon singing some particular ditty better than any one else. This was reserved for special occasions. The finishing pulls were given, hands were shaken with cheery good wishes, the strangers dropped over the side into their boats, and we were off under the most favourable auspices for a trip to which we all looked forward.

As I am now writing of events that occurred forty-five years ago, and as there are no notes to consult, I cannot pretend to remember more than a fair share of detail, but that fact will not form a pretext for drawing upon the imagination. We crossed the line and reached the latitude of Mauritius without any event of note happening, but we were conscious that it took longer to pump the ship out than it had formerly done. Nothing to speak of, perhaps, but as we had a valuable cargo we were naturally careful to eliminate any unnecessary chance of damage.

One evening we had a fine beam wind on the port side and the old man was rather keen upon making the most of it. As he cracked on more and more canvas the ship lay over a good deal. It was my first watch and it was spent mostly at the pump, but when the mate relieved me at midnight I was able to report that the ship had "sucked," which was equivalent to saying that she was pumped dry. Dry below she might have been certainly, but as her starboard rail was more often under water than not, on deck it was certainly more than a little damp. I had hung on to the topgallantsails for my watch, and the mate now proceeded to get these in. That, I suppose, was really the beginning of the trouble, for we all, from the skipper down, should have known that a small old ship would not stand being driven unfairly. But she had the reputation for being strong and sound, and as she had been built by White of Cowes the idea obtained was that there was on occasion a turn of speed to be driven out of her.

The starboard watch now went below. The mainsail was stowed, and we knew that the mate could handle the topsails if it became necessary to reef down. This, indeed, was very soon done, as we could gather from the various noises. We could also tell that she was wallowing into it, and that a great quantity of water was being taken on deck. Before our watch below expired "all hands" were called to take in the foresail.

It was blowing fairly hard, there was a good amount of sea running, and the ship had a very dull, heavy motion that did not seem to be quite right, but we got the foresail in, and went aloft to stow it. I had learned by that time that it was well to make sure work of such things, so as the gaskets on the lee side were rather insufficient I sent a man down to let go the lee leach line so that I could use it as an extra gasket.

While I was busy over this the day was breaking, and I saw the mate with the sounding line doing something at the pumps and making signs to me to come down. At the same time it occurred to me that the ship was rising very sluggishly to the sea. Even then the truth did not occur, but as I got on the deck, the mate yelled in my ear, "There's seven feet of water in her."

There are times when all men think alike, not frequently I will admit, but this was one of those rare cases when no one proposed to argue the point, and a rush aft was made for the mainbraces. The skipper was on deck by this time, and he also appeared to acquiesce, for he had not been specially called, and was unaware that anything out of the way was happening. There was another strange occurrence; there was a black man at the wheel—at least he was a black nigger when he went there—but as he put the helm up his face had paled to some nondescript colour that was certainly not black. I have never seen a similar case.

As we squared away the mainyard and the vessel got before the sea, the next consideration was to get the pumps going, and this we proceeded to do with a will, finding out as we did so that most of the stanchions on the starboard side were sprung and that the water was fast pouring into the hold. I am afraid that our saucy craft was not well fitted to cope with an emergency; there was a wooden pump brake to work one pump, but the double brake to work the two had for some time been used aloft as a spreader for the outriggers at the main topmast head. I soon nipped aloft, however, and got it down, and then we set to work in good earnest to see what fate had in store for us.

We ran under close-reefed topsails and the sea was not much, now that we ran before it, but our wake in the dark blue of the ocean was now a sickly olive green. I doubt if so large a brew of coffee has ever been made before or since. The water came up from the pumps green and smelling of it, and it did not require much prescience to forecast that the greater part of the cargo was hopelessly spoiled.

How long it took to clear the ship of water I do not remember; fortunately the weather became fine and enabled us to lay our course again—but the fact remained that in that eventful middle watch a great part of the starboard bulwarks had been washed away, and on the earliest opportunity as many men as could drive a nail and find a hammer to do it with, clapped on and nailed some planks to the stanchions for a makeshift, while the carpenter did his best to caulk the openings in the covering board through which the water had got below. But oh, what a mess it all was!

Naturally as soon as there was time to talk about anything, the discussion arose as to who was responsible for it all, and equally certain it was that the second mate was to be blamed if possible. I say nothing against the time-honoured custom of cursing "that second mate," who has been held responsible for everything that has gone wrong from the time of the Ark, but on this particular occasion I was not taking the blame. It commenced this way: Quoth the skipper, "William, there can be no doubt that this is all your fault, you could not possibly have pumped the ship out properly in your watch." My reply to this was that I had left the starboard bulwarks intact when I went below, that they had been washed away in the middle watch, and that if the mate could not explain how the ship got half full of water, neither could I, especially as he had had her for four hours to himself. That reasoning appeared to be conclusive, for afterwards there was no endeavour made to pile the blame upon me.

By the time we drew down to the Cape there was more pleasure in store for us, inasmuch as all the biscuits on board had developed so great a capacity for producing weevils that it began to be a matter for speculation who would eventually consume the biscuits, the weevils or ourselves? We generally tried to extrude the weevils before eating the biscuits, but in this we were not always successful, and we acquired the knowledge that they were very objectionable shipmates.

What a helping the Agulhas current is to homeward-bound ships! On this occasion we were lying-to under a close-reefed maintopsail, and all the time being set to windward thirty or forty miles a day directly on our course. I remember perfectly being passed one Sunday by one of the Natal traders called the *Alphington*, outward bound. She was carrying every stitch of canvas with a beautiful fair wind and we were lying-to under the shortest possible canvas. She reported us, however, when she got to port, as having sustained damage. In due course we rounded the Cape and drew up into the S.E. trades, heading for Bahia.

In most sea-going ships where a fair ship's company is carried, there are two cries or shouts from the poop or quarterdeck in the ordinary routine, one is "Heave the log" the other "Trim the binnacle light." In this craft, however, in my watch I had to attend to the latter business myself, and when the light required attention I would take it down the cabin companion-way, and prick the wick up as required. One night shortly after rounding the Cape I was doing this when in spite of all I could do the light went out. I thought this was funny and got some matches, but as I struck them they went out also. Then I took the lamp and matches into the deck-house, where I slept, and had no difficulty in lighting up. It puzzled me considerably why lamp nor match would burn below, when suddenly the thought arose—where a light won't burn a man can't live, so I went below and with difficulty aroused the mate and then the skipper. They both took a deal of awakening before I got them on deck, and then we came to the conclusion that the gas generated by the decaying coffee in the hold had found a vent into the cabin, which had it not been discovered in time would in all probability have been fatal to life. The skipper slept in a hammock on deck between there and New York, and the mate took very good care that the skylight was kept open and a windsail run into his berth.

The pinch of hunger was by this time telling on us all—even the rats— and I have repeatedly woke up when sleeping with bare feet in warm weather and disturbed a rat that was making a light meal by nibbling the hard skin from the soles of my feet. It was some time ere I discovered how it was that at times my feet became so tender. The failure of bread at sea is a disaster hard to overcome.

On this passage the chief point of interest to me was on the evening I went to the skipper to announce the fact that I was "out of my time." I then discovered for certain what I had long suspected to be the case, that the old man must be a Methodist with leanings towards the pulpit, for the sermon he gave me was long enough and dull enough to have run into "fourteenthly and lastly." He wound up by advising me not to forget the night I was out of my time, and I have carried out that instruction religiously.

We called off Bahia and received orders to go to New York to discharge our cargo. We arrived there without any further adventure, and as the crew were entitled to be paid off at the port of discharge the able seamen all left, only the mate and the cook remaining.

What a sight did the hold present when the hatches were removed! Not a sound bag of coffee remained. The greater part of it was dug out with shovels, and altogether it was one of the most deplorable losses that I have come across at sea.

New York in those days had a lawless atmosphere, and revolver shots could be heard on the river pretty frequently throughout the hours of darkness, for thieves were daring in the pursuit of plunder, and a night watchman if he did his duty on board a ship (ours did) had need be a very determined and plucky man to hold his own. We were not molested, however, and after our cargo was discharged we proceeded to load resin and timber of sorts, for the run home to London.

Let me mention here as a matter of interest that during this visit to New York we saw the celebrated sailing-ship *Great Republic*. She was then laid up, but I well remember that her decks were temporarily covered with loose planks, in order to preserve them from the weather. She was an enormous vessel, and carried a crew of 100 men. She must then have been near the end of her career, for she was built early in the 'fifties and a life of fifteen years was a long one for a soft-wood ship.

At this time, too, steam had not entirely driven the sailing passenger ship from the Atlantic trade. Whether I ever saw the celebrated *Dreadnought* I cannot quite remember, but she was then in her prime and had made passages across more than once in ten or twelve days. It was generally a very rough life on the Atlantic, and whether in steam or sail, canvas was carried to its extreme limit. There were in existence a class of mates who were prime seamen and fighting men in addition. The crew were a very hard-bitten lot too, but a reputation once earned in that trade was not easily forgotten, and when a man shipped in a western ocean packet, he was generally pretty well cognisant of the treatment he was likely to receive on board. That particular trade had its customs, and its laws, though unwritten, were none the less binding. It had its own rough code of honour too. I shall deal later on with a few of the methods that were put in practice in order to ascertain just exactly how far a crew would be allowed to take liberties, but I want to get home again in this chapter.

We filled up with the necessary number of "packet rats" as they were called, for the run home, and I saw these men come on board with great curiosity. They were a queer-looking lot, but fine big fellows, not extravagantly burdened with clothes, and with faces that carried plainly the marks of many a scrapping-match. But here the rough code of honour came in. These men found themselves in a little quiet peaceable ship, and they consequently did not consider it compatible with their ideas to make trouble where they could have had it all their own way. They behaved as decently as any men I have been shipmates with.

We had also on board some new stores for the trip, and it was possible to eat the biscuits, seasoned only with the remembrance of the weevils of the last lot. Still bad food will eventually tell upon the best constitution, and it took some considerable time for me to shake off all the ill-effects; in point of fact when I landed in London I had a hole in my leg that one could have put a small egg inside.

The fates were good to us and we made a fair run across. With the first smell of the Channel away went the remembrance of all troubles, and eventually the ship was docked and I stepped on shore from the *Lord Nelson* "out of my time" and a free man.

This, however, was, as I fully recognised, only the beginning of things. My kind friends nursed and fed me back to a decent state of health, and then came the ordeal of getting my second mate's certificate. In this connection I should like to pay a tribute to the memory of a good and clever man, the late John Newton, master of the Navigation School in Wells Street. He was tireless and unremitting in his endeavours to impart information, and his patience with pupils of all sorts was a thing to be gratefully remembered.

I had, of course, been preparing myself at sea to the best of my ability for the anticipated ordeal, and it may perhaps have been that knowledge that led me to pay less attention than I might have done to the advantages offered. I suppose it was a recrudescence of the spirit which earned me three thrashings a day at school, but Newton's patience was equal to the test, and his kindness was inexhaustible, although I was generally the ringleader in any attempt to adjourn the day's work.

But there was now another factor in the equation, and that was the Board of Trade. Let me say here, for the benefit of any young reader whose eyes may fall upon these lines, that the anticipation of an evil is far worse than the reality, but at the same time I do not wish to belittle the ordeal through which I now had to pass.

It is needless to say that before examining a candidate for a certificate, certain certificates of service and sobriety are required, and the Board has the necessary machinery for verifying such certificates. Hence when I went to put my papers in, it was discovered that I had deserted from my ship, and I was informed that to purge so heinous an offence it would be necessary to petition the Board. It did not by any means follow that the petition would be granted, but in this case, helped by my friend Newton, I got my petition through successfully, and I was ready to face the music.

There were certain examiners in navigation and seamanship for the Board of Trade whose names were well known—some with terror—to the aspiring youths of the Mercantile Marine; but there were two who possessed a reputation for severity that was somewhat phenomenal. Personally speaking in all my examinations I got the fairest of fair play, but it does not follow that others may not have suffered. Human nature is not infallible, and some people would try the patience of a saint. Further I have seen officers going up for their certificates dressed so untidily and badly that if they created a prejudice they had only themselves to thank for it. One case in particular recalls itself to me as an illustration.... The man in question had been a brother officer of mine, and I liked him. He was also a gentleman, but he went up looking as though he had been rolled in a hayloft, and came back failed and cursing his examiner—instead of his own folly.

The two undoubted dwellers on the threshold of certificated competency were Captains Noakes and Domett. The former had been in the East India Company's service, and I should imagine had been a leader of men. I had, therefore, many qualms when on the day of examination the usher opened the door of the waiting-room and informed me that "Captain Noakes is now waiting for you, sir." My inmost reflection was, "Shall I make a meal for him or not?" That feeling did not last long, however. He asked me a few questions about rigging gear for hoisting out weights, then about handling canvas, and it was done in so conversational a manner that one had rather the feeling of enjoying it. Finally we discussed shortening sail as per Falconer's *Shipwreck*, with a few other trifles of a like nature, and I heard him say that he did not intend to put more questions, that I had passed a good examination, and where would I like my certificate issued? To which I promptly replied Ramsgate and bowed myself out, with a feeling that the world was now a ball at my feet. As I write these lines I have the firm knowledge that the ball has been me—but nevertheless it is good to remember that the world was young once, and there were things to strive for, with the store of energy necessary to secure them.

In due course I got back home to Margate, and walked the pier and jetty with some of my old friends the boatmen, who having known me as a boy were now inclined to regard me as being rather a credit to them. I went to Ramsgate, received my certificate from the collector of Customs there, who was kind enough to assure me that I should have no difficulty in obtaining employment. In thanking him I was content to accept his assurance, which, however, I found afterwards was a somewhat optimistic one.

CHAPTER IV

"Oh, we're bound for Mother Carey where she feeds her chicks at sea." —Kipling.

It was one thing to be assured by my friend the collector of Customs that I should never be in want of employment, and quite another part of speech to find a ship. I have a very distinct recollection of the trouble I had to get suited. Without any influence in the shipping world berths were not easy to obtain, and many a long day did I pass prowling round the various docks before success attended my efforts. What the procedure of others was I know not, but mine was to pick out a good-looking ship and then get into conversation with some one on board her to ascertain if she had a second mate. Of course this action would be useless in well-established lines, for they would promote their own men, but an outsider was all I could aspire to, as I was not sufficiently pleased with my late owners to apply to them for help.

One day my eyes lighted upon a very handsome little iron ship lying in the London Docks. I thought her a beauty, and on closer inspection discovered her name to be *Lord of the Isles*; she was not the celebrated tea clipper of that name, which ten years previously had beaten the Yankee vessels in the race from Foo Chow to London. There was this similarity, however, that she was built at Greenock by Steel, while the earlier ship was built by Scott of the same place. Anyhow she was a little beauty, and, when I went to try my luck, I was fortunate enough to find the captain on board, and to get into conversation with him. I think we took rather a liking to each other, for without much trouble I secured the berth of second mate. The ship was loading for Adelaide, and it transpired that the owner was anxious the ship should make a quick passage, for I well remember Mr. Williamson of the firm of Williamson and Milligan saying to me, "Mind, Mr. Second Mate, we expect the ship to make the passage of the season." I rather liked that remark, for it seemed to give a share of responsibility to so very humble an individual as myself, and, indeed, as a matter of policy, or humbug, it might be well if people in authority realised more than many of them do, how a junior is "bucked up" by a word of encouragement. I can moralise over this now that the opportunity of putting the precept into practice has passed away, but I cannot remember that I was ever very sympathetic to my subordinates when I had them.

And while dealing with ethics, let me add the note of utility, and suggest to any young man the desirability of keeping some notes of his life's events. There is no need to go into detail, but for one engaged in such a calling as the sea a chronological note-book will in many cases save an infinity of trouble. Even now as I pen these lines I find the want acutely of some record that would fix dates and aid memory, for it entails an enormity of trouble to get together the necessary data.

My new captain was James Craigie, a Scotchman, I think, from the kingdom of Fife, and there were two apprentices on board from the same town. I remember their Christian names were "Wully" and Peter. Occasionally the old man engaged them in broad Scotch conversation, presumably lest they should forget their native dialect, for they were *broad* Scotch, and the skipper was proud of the fact. Captain Craigie was a fine seaman and a skilled and scientific navigator. He had no notion of what fear was, and although he suffered from an absurd affliction that eventually killed him he was tireless in doing everything that he conceived to be his duty to his owner. But—and it was a big but—he had little notion of what discipline was, and perhaps the education I got on that ship was useful to me afterwards. It is all very well to be on familiar terms with those you control, but you require to be very careful how you set about it. However, I think we most of us learned things on that voyage.

The mate was a little Welshman named Jones, not a bad sort, but there was a certain natural antipathy between him and that which was the fact. He was a poor hand at keeping order amongst the men, and, all things considered, it was hardly matter for surprise that we had the trouble we did.

At that time there was a good deal of difficulty with the crews of outward-bound ships. The glamour of carrying canvas was very great. There were the traditions of the *Marco Polo* with Bully Forbes in command; the Black Ball liners such as the *Red Jacket* and her kindred ships; the *Donald McKay*, and others where it was the custom to say, "What you can't carry you must drag," all of which entailed an immense mastery over the crews. In the vessels I have mentioned there was a lot of hard usage, and the masters and mates were mostly young men who could fight, and occasionally use a belaying-pin with decent effect. But, as with the western ocean men, there were certain able seamen who habitually sailed in fighting ships by choice, and if they by chance got with a peaceable crowd of officers they might or might not behave themselves, as the fancy took them. Our crew contained a fine lot of men physically, and there was no doubt that the old man intended to get the utmost out of his ship, which was a smart craft and a good sailer.

We had rather a dusting during the beat down-Channel. I got her into one mess through hanging on too long to the topgallantsails, but a mild reproof was all that I suffered, and a youngster must often pick up his experience at the expense of some one else. We made very fair progress on the way south, and the skipper stated his intention to go well south and make a passage if possible.

One clear morning we were about due south of the Cape of Good Hope, running under all the canvas we could carry and making about thirteen knots, when we sighted our first iceberg. It was about eight bells, and the whole of the forenoon we made towards it, passing it shortly after noon. In size and shape it reminded me of St. Paul's cathedral. Modern Antarctic explorers tell us that the size of these southern bergs have been greatly exaggerated, but as we saw this particular berg more than fifty miles off it cannot have been a very small one.

For some days after this we constantly saw ice. One Sunday afternoon, my watch on deck, it was misty, and we continually sighted the heads of bergs in more or less close proximity. There was a strong following wind, but the old man took in the mizzen-royal and crossjack, and, telling me that he had snugged the ship down for me, went below to sleep the sleep of perfect peace. With the gaudy confidence of youth, however, this did not give me any immediate concern.

But we did carry canvas, and I should hesitate to say how many topmast-stunsail-booms we carried away. We had got into a streak of fair wind, varying from N.W. to S.W., and made the most of it. The watch on deck was frequently occupied with draw knives helping the carpenter make new booms to replace those that went, but after a few days of this work it began to pall upon the crew, who lacked the accustomed stimulus to their exertions as supplied by a "heftier" school of mates, and for some days the men would not come out of the forecastle. The ship in the meantime was worked by the apprentices and afterguard. This was not an uncommon occurrence at the time, and should have been cured by the administration or threat of a few leaden pills, but before the old man made up his mind to apply this remedy the crew turned to again. They had secured a store of biscuits, but were unable to cook anything below, and this brought them to reason.

In the last chapter I mentioned the sort of custom that existed when there was any serious friction between the men in the forecastle and any particular officer. If action was deliberately decided upon, the development would be something on the following lines. At 4.30 a.m. it was the custom for the watch on deck to have their morning coffee. This is a sustenance that is very greatly appreciated in all ships, and I can remember that my friend Mr. Clark Russell enlarges more than once in his inimitable books upon its advantages. At 5 a.m. when the watch commenced to wash decks, one man would come aft to relieve the man at the wheel to go and get his coffee. I have not previously mentioned the custom of the sea which reserved the weather side of the poop for the captain or officer of the watch, whichever might be in possession (if the captain came on deck the officer of the watch would cross over to the lee side), but by reason of this custom if a man were out looking for trouble he would attempt to come aft on the weather side of the poop to relieve the wheel. The officer of the watch would then meet him at the head of the poop-ladder with, "Go up the lee side, you — —;" that is left blank for the reader to fill in the precise amount of profanity or warmth that had been previously generated, and consequently brought about the breach of the peace which was now certain to follow. Curious ways sailors have!

Well, in that telepathic manner in which news spreads on board ship, the hands got to know that I was not a believer in half measures where refractory men were concerned, and my watch laid themselves out to see how much trouble they could give me. They really succeeded in a most creditable manner, and the result of a little difference of opinion that became manifest, concerning the setting of a lower stunsail one middle watch, was that when the mate came on deck to relieve me he found me insensible and covered with snow. I had been rather badly manhandled, and when next I looked at my face in the glass it was not by any means a thing of beauty; in fact, I carry the scars to-day. Worst of all they were very manifest when I had to again face my refractory watch, but there was no help for it; we were making a splendid passage, and the old man was for peace at any price.

We made the run from the meridian of the Cape to Adelaide in twenty days, which was very fair work, and duly docked the ship and started to discharge cargo. There was, however, to be another unpleasant little episode before the crew were finished with, and to this day I laugh at the remembrance of the mate's coat-tails streaming behind him as he rushed forward one afternoon with a hammer in his hand, to take vengeance on some man who had aroused his ire. I forget what it was all about, but the men came aft in a body bent on mischief. The ship was alongside the wharf, the old man was on shore, and there was a crowd of onlookers from other ships, when the mate left to fetch the police. I was being roughly handled, but putting up the best fight I could, when, seeing the captain of another ship looking on, I shouted to him to ask what I was to do. "Get a cutlass and smash their skulls for them," was the answer I got, and with one in my fist I escaped further trouble. The police came down and marched the lot off to jail, and on the next day I fancy they got three months a-piece. There was a Captain Douglas, R.N., acting as one of the magistrates on the bench, and he appeared highly interested in learning the manners and customs which had obtained on board the *Lord of the Isles*.

Our stay in port after this was most agreeable; I renewed acquaintance with many old friends, and when it was time to depart did so with regret. There is a certain great artist alive to-day, who may remember an episode concerning a letter and an old boot. Do you, Mortimer Menpes? I have not forgotten.

Some pains were taken to get a decent crew together. We were towed to the outer anchorage, there to await their arrival, for we were to sail for Newcastle, N.S.W., in ballast and then take a cargo of coal for Manilla, where we were to load for home. The mate and I had by this time made up our minds that if there was to be any more hammering done we were not intending to play the passive part.

It is very curious how these things happen. The cook was the only bit of the old leaven that was left, and there was no love lost between him and the steward. The first morning we were at anchor outside, the steward, who was a very good-looking fellow, went forward to the galley to get early morning coffee for the mate and me. While it was preparing in the customary saucepan, the cook blew upon the rising steam to see if the preparation was boiling.

"Don't blow on the coffee, cook," said the steward.

"Shall if I like!" replied the cook.

The steward gave a hitch up to his trousers, and the cook brought the saucepan of hot stuff down on the steward's head, cutting it open, and sending him aft badly hurt and much scalded. The cook then proceeded to sharpen his knife on the grindstone for the edification of those whom it might concern. It did not help him much, however, for the mate told me to put him in irons, and that I promptly did, using only such arguments as were really necessary.

That day the old man came off with the crew, and we got under way, settling all little unpleasantnesses as we went. To make a long story short, there was only one more case of trouble during the voyage. I found it necessary on one occasion to stretch a man out, and the old man, who was looking on barefooted and dressed in his usual rig of shirt and trousers, kept up by one brace, quietly knocked a broom off the handle and giving me the stick observed, "Now baste him until there isn't a whole 'bane' in his body." I did not altogether obey the injunction, but that was the last of any trouble.

The experience of a coal cargo is not a pleasant one, but there were quite a lot of fine ships in Newcastle on a similar errand to ours. We got away with fair expedition and made the eastern passage up to Manilla, where every basket of coal that came out of the main hatch was tipped over the side by me. Work of that sort in a blazing sun is a fair test of endurance; however, it was done, the holds cleaned, the ship watered and loaded for home with sugar. Then we had a day's leave on shore. The place that all the skippers and mates who came to visit us expressed a wish to see was the cigar manufactory, but it appeared to be a difficult matter to obtain the necessary permission. When I got on shore (I had a brass-bound coat, as was the fashion then for young mates to wear if they fancied themselves) the comprador got me a pony and I started out to the manufactory. There were soldier sentries at the entrance, but no difficulty was made about admitting me. I was shown into the presence of some high official, offered white sweet cake and wine, then a cigar, and was taken over the factory. Whether the same plan of manufacture is carried on to-day I know not, but the pounding of the tobacco leaves with flat stones, by women or girls, on thin wooden tables made a deafening noise, comparable to very noisy machinery. Of the courtesy shown me I can only speak in the highest terms.

I was also very successful in regard to my mid-day meal, to which I was directed by a monk from the window of some religious house, who heard me inquiring after the manner of Englishmen. When Admiral Dewey sailed into Manilla Bay, I know that I remembered the stately courtesy I had there experienced and felt sorry that the modern world had broken in upon it. We all know that it is no trouble for a Spaniard to die as a brave man should, but to have modernity thrust down his throat, at the sacrifice of his life's teachings, entitles him to the sympathy of every Briton who cherishes his own hereditary rights and privileges.

At the time of year that we were at Manilla the wind blew pretty constantly down the harbour; it was consequently a fair wind out, and the custom obtained there to some extent of helping another ship to get under way. There was one point of seamanship over which much argument took place, and this was whether, getting under way with a fair wind, it was the correct thing to leave the afteryards square, or to fill them as soon as possible. I could argue it either way myself, but it was a source of never-failing criticism whichever way was adopted. In our case the afteryards were left square.

Our run down the China Sea was a pleasant one, through Gaspar Straits and so down to Sunda, where we were becalmed for ten days, to the intense exasperation of every one. Even the supply of the mangosteen procured at Anger Point did not compensate for this. Lest it should seem that I overrate the charms of fresh fruit, let me say that no one who has not eaten mangosteen is qualified to form a fair opinion. Unfortunately, the fruit is so delicate it hardly stands carriage, for I have never seen one away from its place of growth. It is, however, probably the daintiest and most delicious fruit that grows.

Once clear of the Straits, our good fortune returned to us and we made a fine run across to the Cape. The ship was rapidly fouling, but the old man hung on to the canvas with all his wonted pertinacity, and very little wind got past us that could be put to any use. As an instance, once in a morning watch I was keeping, I saw a foretopgallant-studdingsail depart in its entirety; tack, sheet and halliards parted at the same moment, and where the sail went I never saw. It was the only time such an occurrence took place in my experience, but it gives an idea of how canvas was carried.

In due course we got to Queenstown, and, getting orders for London, arrived at St. Katherine's dock without further incident. I was not anxious to make another trip in that ship as I wanted to see other fashions, so took my discharge and went down home once more. I parted from Captain Craigie with regret, for I had profound respect for him, and he had helped me on the passage home to coach myself for my first mate's examination.

That was the next thing to encounter, so once again to John Newton and the Wells Street associations! This time I stayed at the Sailors' Home while passing, and spent my spare time looking for a ship. The details of this examination do not seem to have left any lasting impression upon me. I got through all right, and passed in seamanship before Captain Domett, but I remember there were one or two critical moments when my certificate seemed to waver in the balance.

Then began once more in earnest the search for a ship that was to my liking. There was in those days a place frequented by shipowners called the "Jerusalem." I was never clear as to what went on there exactly, but one of the officials was a Mr. Paddle, and to him I took a letter from a friend. By this interposition I secured a berth as second mate in a tea clipper called the *Omba*, belonging to the firm of Killick & Martin.

The *Omba* was a fine composite built ship of about eight hundred tons, well found in all respects, and altogether I was not displeased with my bargain. But she turned out to be by no means the ship of my aspirations, for I often found myself wondering why it was not possible for officers of a ship to carry out their duties in a gentlemanly manner. I had seen that the officers in the *Essex* were gentlemen and could do their work, and I hoped it might be my good fortune to again sail in a ship where the decencies of life might receive some little attention. There was some show of refinement in the ship, but not much, although nothing was wanting to secure it but the will.

The skipper was an Englishman hailing from close to Deal; the mate was a Scotchman, herculean in size and apparently simple in manner on first acquaintance. This simplicity, however, disappeared as the ship left the dock, and he stood revealed as big a hustler as it had been my fortune to come across—a voice like a bull, dauntless courage, and in the technique of his calling with little if anything to learn. I have seen him swing the deep sea lead (thirty-two pounds) over his head with two fathoms of line for drift, and it will be realised that this was no common accomplishment. At all events I could not do it; in fact I did not try, nor did any other man in the ship, but when he started to go aloft, *via* the main tack and up the weather leaches to the main royal yard, it became necessary for me also to acquire that accomplishment, at all events if my end of the stick was to be properly supported. And in the end I think that at that particular game I beat him. We were never on cordial terms, for I was not his sort, and curiously enough both he and the skipper resented my holding a certificate superior to my rating. In fact, the old man once observed, "Look here, Mr. Crutchley, you seem to think that mate's certificate of yours makes you a gentleman: there's only one gentleman in this ship, that's me; if there's to be another then it's the mate, not you!" That statement appeared to me to be quite adequate, and not to be controverted.

There was, however, a third mate with whom I did associate. Tom Boulton was a nice boy, and we had much in common. Further, he liked the same books that I did. It is many years since I saw him, but I know he rose to the command of fine sailing-ships, afterwards setting up in some business on shore. Of all those I knew in the sailing-ship days he is the only survivor that I have recently been in touch with. As for the rest of the crew, there were some boys living in the half-deck with the warrant officers. I think they were special lads, more or less friends of the owners and well born, but long years afterwards, when I commanded a steamer, I saw a certain foolish expression on the face of my boatswain, and my mind went back, prompting the question, "Were you ever in the *Omba*?" I knew I recognised that expression. He was one of the boys; his father was a doctor, but he himself only a waster who could never do any good for himself or any one.

About this period the theory of compass compensation for local attraction was understood by the few, and composite ships were supposed to be more difficult to adjust than iron or steel ones. So we made fast to the buoys off Greenhithe while the operation was being gone through, afterwards making the best of our way down-Channel in charge of a pilot whom we landed off the Isle of Wight. The wind soon after this came out from the westward, and we had the pleasure of working her down-Channel in company with many other biggish ships. I remember one we were often in company with—she was called the *Liberator*, and she sailed well. We had the misfortune to knock the mast out of a trawler somewhere off the Start; I do not think it was our fault, though I doubt not the ship paid.

It fell to me to write the letter to the owner describing the circumstances, and how it occurred, for the old man was not fluent with his pen. I shall later on give an instance of how letter-writing was regarded by many masters.

During the first part of the passage out there was no particular incident, save that we boarded a little schooner in order to send home letters. She was a Spaniard, and the skipper was as polite as his countrymen usually are, begging me to accept the present of a box of cigars, which, needless to say, I was glad to do. It was my first experience of boating on a line swell, and it came as a surprise.

We made a fair passage through the Trades and commenced to run the Easting down. The skipper decided to run through the Straits of Sunda and up the China Sea in preference to the eastern passage, but that did not hinder him from getting well down into the "roaring forties." As a general thing no one minded much being up to the waist in water, but higher than that was unpleasant, for it induced a suggestion of swimming that had its drawbacks.

The ship had fine bulwarks, nearer six feet high than five, and she was fairly deep in the pickle too, but the way she took the water over in heaps when she was running was uncomfortable. There was no fuss about it, but just one steady cataract, that at times gave the relieving ports all they could do to get clear of it before another lot came along. I am not going to say that at any time she was filled up to the top of the bulwarks, but it seemed very much like it, and I do not believe we took the maintopgallantsail in while we were down south, for the old man carried canvas like a hero. Our best day's run was 335 miles—a very respectable performance, but it was fortunate there was no ice about.

Up through the Straits of Sunda and the smooth tract of sea immediately north of them, which always struck me as being so eminently quiet and peaceful. The passage through Gaspar Straits was not looked forward to by many masters with much pleasure, but I suppose that with steam all its difficulties have disappeared. We had only to anchor once, but when we got higher up the sea into the Bashee Channel we caught something that was worth having from the point of view of experience.

I cannot state the exact position of the ship when this happened, seeing that I did no navigation save an occasional star latitude when the skipper wanted one, but it was somewhere in the Bashee Channel and the wind blew from one direction only—I think it was N.N.E. We took in bit by bit every scrap of canvas down to a lower maintopsail and a mizzen-staysail; in due course both these sails disappeared in rags, and it was a brand-new maintopsail too. It was blowing far too hard for a big sea to get up, but at times a vicious one would come along and smash something; for instance, one hit her on the starboard bow and started the knight-heads—a very curious accident. There she lay for the better part of twenty-four hours without a rag of canvas, and heeling over about a steady forty-seven degrees—(I may say that a clinometer I had rigged early on the trip was regarded as one of my fads). I suppose the rain also helped to keep the sea down, but on one occasion I saw the watch at the pumps fairly overwhelmed, and I scarcely expected to find any of them left.

At last it ended. The ship came upright, we got canvas on her, and found that we were not very far from land. It is really comical the manner in which sailors take things for granted. I should not have dared to ask the skipper to see the chart, and had we all known of the danger it would have done no good, so perhaps it was for the best.

The following story I believe to be true, it was told me by Captain Ballard, C.M.G., in these words: "Once in a cyclone the — — was off Mauritius; we could not help ourselves, and I saw we must be swept upon — — Island, when it would all have been over. I went aft to tell the people in the saloon, but stopped half-way; I thought it could do no good, and would only worry them before it was necessary; but she was either swept over the island by the tidal wave or else we missed it."

But what an awful mess that ship was in; as a rule she was spic and span, the acme of neatness, but now a survey of our state was pitiable. The laniards of the lower rigging on the lee side were so chafed that it was doubtful if they would last to port, and altogether the rigging had suffered greatly. But Providence was good to us, and we got in without much more trouble, although it was a beat up the China Sea.

When I speak of the customary neatness of our rigging I in no way exaggerate. As an instance of my meaning, most people know that to save chafe on the backstays in the way of the lower yards, wooden battens are usually seized to the backstays. That was far too rough a method for us. We had the backstays served with unlaid strands of wire rigging, and if any one wishes to try his hand at putting that on, he is welcome to the job so far as I am concerned, for it came to my lot frequently to have to show men that the operation of serving with stiff wire was a possible one.

It was early winter when we arrived at Shanghai and fairly cold. There were a lot of ships in the harbour, and among them was the *Lauderdale*, of which George Davies was now mate. We renewed our friendship, and had lots to talk over. I think he obtained command of that ship on her next voyage, and was never again heard of. There was also a ship called the *Loudoun Castle*, whose skipper had the dire misfortune to incur the enmity of our mate, which led to disagreeables for the following absurd reason. A party of skippers were with our old man talking in the cabin, and the topic of discussion was the writing of letters home to the owner, an operation sometimes considered a difficulty. One of the guests happened to say that when he wrote home he turned the mate out of the cabin, imagined he had the owner opposite him, and then wrote as if he were speaking to him. There was no great harm in that, one would say, but our mate heard it, and attributing it rightly or wrongly to the captain of the *Loudoun Castle*, made it a personal matter that a mate should be asked to leave the cabin. There was considerable trouble over the matter, and I very stupidly went to a lot of trouble to make peace in a business in which I had no concern whatever.

We discharged our cargo in due course, and in spite of the bucketing we found there had been no leaking or damage to speak of. Then we commenced preparing for the homeward cargo of tea. Now, as all people know, tea is a very light commodity, and the ship had to be ballasted to stiffen her. The second mate is supposed to supervise the stowage, but in this case the mate did. To save space he did not leave a sufficient thickness of ballast on the turn of the bilge, and so some tea was spoiled. I heard afterwards it was put down to the fault of "that second mate," although I had nothing whatever to do with it. It is one of the prettiest operations conceivable to see Chinamen stowing a cargo of tea—great heavy mallets are used, and the tiers are built up with almost mathematical accuracy.

We carried several boats bottom upwards on skids, and these were filled with every article we could bring up from any place below where tea could be stowed, and with the cargo work went on the repairing of the rigging. Here I can illustrate how splendid a sailor the mate was. We rove new laniards to the lower rigging fore and aft. It was bitterly cold weather, yet such care was taken over the business that they did not require to be set up again when we got into warm weather, or touched for the remainder of the voyage, and let no man say he stretched the rope to ruin, for it was not so, but the strain was put on properly.

We had rather a good day's leave on shore there. Pony-riding seemed the correct thing to do, and most of us were duly shot off by the sudden swerve of the beast into some haunt of seamen with which we were unacquainted. We also foregathered with some of the officers of the old P. & O. paddler *Ganges*. Nothing of note occurred, however, and in due course the ship was fully loaded, all the officers were given the usual bounty of tea as a present, and we prepared to make the start homewards.

We had taken on board three passengers, a clergyman and his wife and child. A lady at table was a novelty for us, but they were nice people, and I in my spare time got the loan of many books, and for the first time made acquaintance with a series of back numbers of the *Saturday Review*. I can remember a lot of the smart and caustic writing they contained even now.

We had to beat out to sea, and in doing so discovered that the ship was rather tender with a beam wind, the royals made an appreciable difference, but thus it was and we had to make the best of it. To beat out was fairly hard work, for we had to tack so frequently that there was no time to coil the braces down; as they came in, so they went out. But the pilot was a smart fellow and handled the ship beautifully.

Once outside there was a fair wind down the China Sea and we started to make the best of it. We carried royal stunsails and let very little wind get past us. The canvas was good, the gear was good, not a moment was lost in trimming or making sail, and we did well.

One morning, it was my watch, I had rather a scare, for I suddenly made out breakers on the port bow and I had not the least idea that there was land in the vicinity. I yelled down the skylight for the skipper, and at once began to brace up and haul off. The old man came on deck in a hurry, and was graciously pleased to consider that I had done well to avoid running on top of the Pescadore Islands, which with a slack look-out might easily have happened.

There was a certain amount of confusion in getting clear, and to make matters more complex we heard a great riot going on in the cabin, and clouds of steam were arising therefrom. It seems that as we came to the wind, the cabin stove fetched way to leeward and capsized, scattering the lighted coals. The crash brought the parson out of his cabin and he promptly made use of all the liquids he could lay hands upon, thus creating a condition combining safety with a filthy smell.

The skipper was good enough to say that we kept a very good look-out in my watch, even if the proverbial second mate's slackness was apparent in other matters, but looking back at this little episode after the lapse of years, it seems to me there was no excuse for not warning the officer of the watch that there was a possibility of the ship making a bad course. I trust that a different order of things now exists, but in that ship it would have been little short of sacrilege to ask to see a chart, or to inquire as to the ship's position. I should have been informed with biting sarcasm, "When I want you to navigate the ship, Mr. So-and-So, I will let you know, meantime, I am quite capable."

We had great luck down the China Sea, through the straits and as far as St. Helena, which we made in sixty days from Shanghai. But when we reached the line our troubles began. There we ran into a stark calm that lasted for three weeks, and tried the patience of all. More especially did it affect the captain, as was but natural, and his extravagances were at times very comical. On the first part of the trip, when all had gone well, no one concerned themselves about the proverbial ill-luck which attends the carriage of parsons by sea, but it now seemed to have improved by keeping. It had been the custom of the skipper to make up a dummy whist party with the parson and his wife, but this was now discontinued, and the old man's text as he tramped the poop was loudly spoken and often. "Oh, if the Lord will only forgive me this once for carrying a parson I'll never do it any more." One night he solemnly brought up a pack of cards and consigned them with many varied and choice imprecations to the deep. I cannot, however, consider that he was an artist in the use of language—there was too much sameness and repetition about it.

Whether it was owing to the foregoing incantation I do not know, but we did eventually get away from the line. Our passage, however, was completely spoiled, and at the end of it we were shamefully outsailed by that celebrated clipper the *Jerusalem*. We were going up-Channel with a fine southerly wind that was about a-beam, but, as I have said before, we were a bit tender and could not usefully under those conditions carry all the sail we should have wished. The *Jerusalem* passed us to windward under all plain sail, and we felt the beating badly, for we could not carry our royals without burying the lee side to the detriment of our speed. Off Beechy Head, however, we took on board a hoveller as a Channel pilot, and I can hear even now the sigh of relief the old man gave as he welcomed him on board.

There is nothing more to chronicle of that ship; I had made up my mind she did not suit me—nor I her—so we parted with scant regret on either side.

There was in the East India Docks a vessel called the *Albuera*. She belonged to the firm of John Willis & Co., and rejoiced in a double row of painted ports. To her I transferred my services. Her captain, Gissing by name, was a nice fellow, and we should have got on together, but my fortune was now in the ascendant, and I left her to take up the berth in steam that was then becoming the ambition of all young seamen. The Suez Canal was open, and it required no great prescience to foresee the end of sails. The modern sailing-ship that was then being built, however, was very beautiful. Let me instance one as an example, the *Lothair*; she was afterwards commanded by Tom Boulton, but she was built on the lines of a yacht and was as beautiful, although the modern ship never had the stately grace of the old frigate-built Indiaman.

CHAPTER V

"The liner she's a lady by the paint upon her face,
An' if she meets an accident they count it sore disgrace."

Kipling

Good-bye to sail! The chance had come to make the plunge that was rendered inevitable by the opening of the Suez Canal and the march of modern invention. It was sad to realise that the sailing-ship was becoming a back number and that the future for the sea lay with steam—a means of propulsion that would for ever put in the background the manly management of masts, yards and sails. To-day, the period in which this country won its greatest triumphs on the sea is commonly referred to (even in the Royal Navy) as the "stick and string time," but I am old-fashioned enough to believe that the seamen of the past were in their way as clever engineers as the men that fit and drive the modern turbine engines.

In the museum of the Royal United Service Institution is to be seen a fully rigged model of the old *Cornwallis*. Stand by the side of it and try to realise the exquisite skill that was necessary to rig that vessel, and then keep the masts in her through all the varied experiences that would befall. How, pitching in a head sea, every stay must bear its due proportion of strain or something would go! Consider the friction and chafe that would be constantly taking place with rope rigging, and the unceasing vigilance that was necessary to preserve it intact, and then, if you know enough to realise what it meant, sneer if you will at the days of stick and string, but forgive those who look back with regret at what was the inevitable eclipse of a notable phase in a very noble calling.

The sailing-ship man had a little doubt in his mind as to how he should properly rank the steamship man. I had on the previous voyage heard engineer officers in a mail steamer speak disparagingly of the seamanlike qualities of the ship's officers—such, for instance, as an order to the engine-room, "Half a turn sideways if you can; if you can't never mind." Not to be believed for a moment, but still we sailors doubted as to how they ought to rank in the hierarchy of the sea. It was also said by the same engineers that they had a chief officer who was worth anything in bad weather, for he could go round the decks with such a beautiful command of language that nothing ever went wrong with them, and so the conclave with whom I discussed the matter concluded that there might possibly be an opening for one that had graduated even in a hard school of seamanship. Need I say that, in spite of chaff and theoretical leanings, I was unfeignedly thankful to be offered the berth of third mate in the mail steamer *Roman* belonging to the Union Steamship Company, of Southampton. I said good-bye to Captain Gissing of the *Albuera* with regret, and proceeded with all due haste to take up my appointment.

It was in July 1870 that I first set eyes upon the *Roman*. It was evening and she was deserted save by an old shipkeeper, who having been an officer in the very early days of the company was willing enough to gossip, and satisfy such curiosity as I was not backward to confess on the subject of my new surroundings.

U.S.S. "ROMAN"

U.S.S. "NYANZA"

U.S.S. "AFRICAN"

Naturally the first things that caught my eyes were the ship's spars, and there I was gratified; she being rigged with yards beautifully squared, sail covers on, and royal and topgallant-yards up and down the lower rigging in approved man-of-war fashion. Next, the decks were clean, and there was a look of the old Blackwall liner about the paintwork that spoke well for her. Altogether she bore an air of prosperity that made me think my lines had fallen in pleasant places. My first impression in this case was the right one, for I doubt if I ever had an unhappy day on board that ship. She had originally been built with a flush deck by Lungley of Deptford, on a so-called unsinkable principle, but the exigencies of increasing trade had caused the company to build a poop on her to a great sacrifice of good looks. She carried it well, however, and years afterwards they even lengthened and put a forecastle upon her, from which you descended by a ladder to the bowsprit to get at the jib.

On the day after my arrival I reported myself at the office to the Marine Superintendent, Captain R. W. Ker, R.N.R., and learned from him that I was on a trial voyage, and that my tenure of office depended upon my suitability for the company's service. With this information I was perfectly satisfied, and went down to the ship to present my appointment to Captain Warleigh. Things were then done with a good deal of form, and I trust I may be forgiven a certain amount of regret that a system which gave excellent results has been departed from. The policy of "hustle" is not the only one productive of good results.

My new captain was somewhat of a revelation. He received me as one gentleman would another, and when he chose he could be particularly agreeable. His appearance was decidedly prepossessing, and he had a pair of steely blue eyes that could on occasions show a very lurid light. Let me say at once that I always found him a kind friend, though years afterwards we had differences of opinion. Warleigh was a very fine character and would have been an ornament to any service; he was not, however, physically strong, having suffered greatly from fever contracted on the Mauritius service. When he had asked me some few questions as to where I had been and what I did there, he called to the chief officer, whose name was Coathupe, and introduced me to him in the following manner: "Curly, this is our new third, show him round and help him feel his feet, will you?" The freedom of speech, I afterwards learnt, was owing to the fact that Warleigh had only been promoted the previous voyage, and as he and Coathupe had been great friends when officers together, the skipper was on more free and easy terms with his chief than would otherwise have been the case. Fred Coathupe was one of those gifted mortals liked by every one; indeed, I cannot call to mind any occasion on which I knew him to lose his temper. There was little if anything of the sailor in his manner, but for all that he was a smart officer and kept his ship in excellent order. We proceeded in search of the second officer, whom we found in the shed tallying cargo—or going through the form of doing so—for let me say here, that to put a steamer's officer on to do clerk's work is both unfair and a farce. I know that in some cases it is done to-day, but I feel sure that the loss entailed by an imperfect record of cargo carried is far more than would pay for the time of a clerk who has been properly trained to the work. In sailing-ship days, when there was no hurry, the mate could sit on the rail and do his tallying easily enough, but not so now.

Reginald Leigh, the "second," was a man with a very keen sense of humour, never at a loss for a reply to any curious remark that might be addressed to him, and altogether gifted with a flow of language that on occasion compelled even the admiration of the victim to whom it might be addressed. I could tell amusing stories on this subject, but think I will refrain from details. Indications of them may appear, however, in future pages. Leigh made my acquaintance with a humorous grin, observed that "It was a good dog that barked when it was told," that was his motto, and would I just relieve him for a little time with the tally book? He and I had to share the same cabin, and we were on very good terms, the one difference of opinion being that he abhorred tobacco, while I and my pipe were good friends. When the ship was not full of passengers the captain gave permission for the third to use one of the saloon cabins, and indeed the fashion in the service was for every one to be made as comfortable as possible. The captain, throughout the company's service, was a very important personage. Under him the chief officer was practically supreme in all matters. If, for instance, one of the crew had a grievance and wished to represent it to the chief, he had first to secure the attention and support of a warrant or petty officer who would certify to his statement and accompany him aft to lay it before the chief officer.

It may not be out of place here to say a few words about Southampton as it then was—not the great home of mammoth liners it is to-day—but a nice, quiet little place with just enough of the best sort of shipping to make it of considerable importance. The people who lived there did not seem very keen about encouraging shipping, they rather preferred it to be considered the county town, and to rely upon the support of the county families; at all events that is what the townsfolk used to say if one pointed out the vast potentialities of the port. I confess that to visit the place to-day makes me look back to the old times with keen regret, for a Southampton sailor in the early 'seventies could with truth take unto himself the thanksgiving of the Pharisee when he contemplated the despised Publican.

Firstly, to mention the shipping companies in their order of precedence, there was the Royal Mail Steam Packet Company. This was, and is, I believe, the only steamship company incorporated by Royal charter, and it had various quaint privileges denied to others. It is difficult even now to arrive at them, but the tie between the Royal Navy and the Royal Mail has been close, and undoubtedly the line was at one time more or less under the active patronage of the government of the day. Its ships were well officered, and there was fairly rapid promotion, for the climate of the West Indies taken all round was not very conducive to longevity, owing to the fevers that were at that time very common.

The Union Company drew many of its officers from the Royal Mail, and there was consequently a good deal of intercourse between the two services. Antagonism existed, however, to a considerable extent between the officers of the Royal Mail and the P. & O. service; they would not foregather on any condition, the reason being that each was jealous of the other. Either, however, would associate with us, for they could and did say in a patronising tone: "Oh, yes, that's a very nice little company of yours, quite nice," little thinking what it would grow to in the very near future. At that time the Royal Mail was modernising its fleet. It still had running such paddle steamers as the *La Plata* and *Shannon,* and the contrast between these and the new *Elbe* was very marked. I happened to know an officer named Teddy Griffiths who was appointed to the latter ship, and he, in describing his first visit to her, declared she was so spacious and intricate that he lost his way, and sat down crying on a hatch until a boy came along and showed him the way out. Be that as it may, we spent many a cheery evening on board that ship, for we were young, we could sing a good song, and we had the gift of good fellowship—which I regret is not always appreciated at its proper value when one is its owner. It may lead you into undue exuberance, but it's a valuable possession to be able to see the best that's in your immediate surroundings.

Whether the Royal Mail or the P. & O. was entitled to the first place might be a matter of debate, but there is no doubt that in the matter of looks the P. & O. was an easy first. Their ships lay in the outer basin and always presented a beautiful appearance. Vessels like the *Mooltan*, *Poonah* and many more of the same class were even then being superseded by newer ships like the *Australia*, *Bangalore* and *Kaiser-I-Hind*, newer and more up-to-date, but not to be compared for appearance with the older vessels. With rigging and sails in perfect order they were all that the eye of a sailor could desire.

Mentioning that these vessels lay in the outer basin reminds me that the rise and fall of tide at Southampton was considerable, and that at times the bowsprits of these old-fashioned ships, extending as they frequently did over the lines of rails on the quay at low water, were level with the lines of railway trucks. One day an artist in mischief quietly hooked a truck coupling to a neighbouring bowsprit bobstay. As the tide rose so did the truck, and great was the interest taken in the incident. I never heard that the culprit was discovered, and he deserved immunity for his genius.

Beyond the Channel Mail steamers, a few grain ships, and the North German Lloyd ships, there was little traffic to the docks. The German ships were fine vessels, well managed, and the local pilots who had the handling of them always spoke in the highest terms of the qualifications of their officers. It struck me at the time in a vague sort of way that it was curious the Germans should have such fine craft. It is easy to see now that they were in the early stages of the thirst for sea power. Apropos of this matter, I might mention that the Union Company had just sent out their steamer *Dane* (Captain Ballard) with sealed orders, but as we afterwards learned on an expedition to the Western Islands to warn a German training-ship for officers that war had been declared between France and Germany.

No notice of Southampton in the early 'seventies would be complete without the mention of Queen's Terrace and the Canute Hotel. The Terrace was, generally speaking, the abode of the officers of the vessels in harbour. As a rule the landladies were a good sort, looked after us well and did not unduly rob us. They were also fairly patient and long-suffering where our misdeeds were concerned. For the days were not long enough for all we tried to crowd into them, and the nights were very short and bed was to most of us a last resort. The experiences were many and varied, but there was mostly the charm of novelty about them. Some officers rather favoured a ladder that would afford an exit through the backyard from their bedroom windows when it was undesirable for various reasons to make use of the front door. The Canute Hotel was the general rendezvous of all officers in port for lunch. It was kept by Mrs. Hyles, who in her way would have mothered the lot of us. She supplied most excellent chops, the remembrance of which and the appetites that devoured them lingers to the present day. I have only one ground of complaint against that good lady and I may as well state it now.

There was a music hall in Southampton called the Royal York which was well attended by officers generally. When I had been in command about two years, Mrs. Hyles was managing it. One night Charlie Hight, a most respectable official of the National Provincial Bank, and myself thought we would like to see the York once more if we could do so in safety and with no loss of dignity. We consulted Mrs. Hyles, who said, "You shall have my own private box," and we went there. That was all right, but she afterwards extended a similar favour to three young doctors from Netley who had been dining very well if not too wisely. At one period of the performance there was a lady on the stage known as Jenny Hill, or the "Vital Spot," and these young doctors commenced to chaff her. She stood on the stage and dressed them down properly, for which she was applauded by the audience, but as we were also occupants of the box addressed, we tried to make ourselves as inconspicuous as possible, I especially so, for I could see my third officer in the stalls taking a great interest in the proceedings. Our box was at the end of a long gallery, filled with people, which had to be traversed to obtain exit, and when the doctors departed, the whole house rose and howled at them. Charlie and I sat fast, thinking that we should slip away later unobserved, but no such luck. After an hour we tried to go, but got rather a worse doing than the actual culprits. It only shows how accidents may happen to respectable well-meaning men if they stray from the paths of strict propriety.

It was amusing at times to observe the feeling between the P. & O. and the West Indian Mail men. For instance, one of the former would say, "Now, Mrs. Hyles, when you have quite finished with those brass-bound gentlemen will you spare me a little attention?" That was called for because the uniform of the P. & O. men was conspicuously plain and neat in contrast with the rather liberal use of gold lace by the West Indian Co. I think it may be found that a history of the Royal Mail Company would prove a valuable book if any one acquainted with the legends of the Company would write it, for it seems a pity that such interesting matter should be lost. Such stories, for instance, as permission being given to wear epaulets, "any number above two," and an authentic statement as to when the white hat for full dress was finally dispensed with. These may be trivial matters, but the traditions of the sea service are precious to those who still love the Briton's heritage, and the records of the merchant service are as much part of the country's history as are those of the Royal Navy.

To leave the shore details and come back once more to the *Roman*, it was then the custom of the Company the day before the ship sailed to muster the crew, and go through fire and boat drill, and a very good custom too. It was a respectable show to see the men fallen in, dressed in uniform and saluting in proper fashion as their names were called over, the officers dressed in frock coats trimmed to the company's fashion. The captain's uniform had evidently been copied from that of the Trinity Masters, an excellent example, and it always appeared to me that it was a mistake to too closely follow the uniform of the Royal Navy. It is, I am aware, commonly done, but it would show better taste if it were discontinued.

Naturally this condition of things appealed to me vastly, and I may say gave a liking for the service which never departed. Years afterwards when I had sought "fields afresh," it was said of me that "as well expect the planets to have left their orbits as me to sever my connection with the company," and I am more than ever sure now that it was the biggest mistake in the many that I have to record. I firmly believe that that service was the last stronghold of the conservatism of the sea.

At the time of which I am now writing it was customary to leave Southampton two days before the date of sailing from Plymouth. The Company's vessels were not powerful enough to make sure of their passage against a strong adverse wind, and cases were frequent when it was found necessary to put the vessel under fore and aft canvas, and reproduce in a mild form the tactics of sailing-ships with a head wind.

We also took a Channel pilot who was ordinarily employed as the Company's pilot. His name was William Waters. He was a man of strong character, and stronger language. There was little of the *suaviter in modo* about him, but he was a sailor, and could handle a ship for all she was worth. Many are the stories that might be told of incidents that occurred during those trips down-Channel, but they would lose much of their point if their text were departed from, and as much of it is unprintable, there is nothing to do save leave it alone. But never shall I forget William's language to the man in charge of a small schooner without any lights that we found in close proximity to us one dark night. In reply to a forcible question concerning lights, the reply came up, "Sure, sir, they've gone out." This reminds me of another Irishman, Pat Malony, afterwards one of the Company's captains, who being in the hold when he was fourth officer, was asked, "How many lights have you down there, Malony?" He replied, "Six, sir, but they're all gone out."

The fore and aft canvas carried by the Union ships was peculiar to those vessels. I never saw anything quite like it, though I believe the P. & O. Company at one time had something very similar. The trysails were set on very large booms, and the gaffs were hoisted by the steam winches. They were quite easily handled if once people knew the way to do it, but at first it required a good deal of faith to see a steam winch tearing away with throat and peak halliards. I can't say I ever saw an accident, but years afterwards in the same ship with the same spars and sails, it was sad to see how the old skill had departed from the hands that worked them. They seemed to have lost the knowledge that to work big fore-and-afters, the throat should always be higher than the peak in hoisting, but that principle takes a lot of driving into the heads of people. There was also another peculiarity in the rig of these ships, the lower yards were fitted to lower across the rails when steaming against a head wind. The Jeer falls were always kept rove, and I have on occasion, when dealing with baffling winds about the line, seen royal, topgallant and lower yards up and down three times in a day. It took about twenty minutes to complete the job.

Nothing of special importance occurred on the way down-Channel on this voyage, but it was a novel experience to be left in charge of a steamer's bridge for the first time. It was frequently the custom to double the watches in narrow waters, but on this particular occasion the captain did not do so. He left me entirely to myself, although I had the impression that he kept a very careful eye on all that transpired in that first watch. It was an excellent way to let a new man feel his feet, but on no occasion did the captain interfere with me when carrying on the duty of officer of the watch.

We did a thing leaving Plymouth that is not often done, we ran well into Cawsand Bay to pick up a gentleman and his wife as passengers from a shore boat. He had formerly been one of the Company's captains, and report, rightly or not, said that he being an old friend, Warleigh had taken him away in this fashion to save him from his creditors. I dare say it was likely enough, for there was no breach of the law in doing as we did. The ex-captain afterwards made a fortune on the diamond fields. Needless to say we were fairly filled with passengers, but it is one of the difficulties in writing this story to know just how much or how little one should say on that particular subject. There was every inducement for passengers and officers to be on friendly terms. We messed with them, and they were always treated as though they were guests. There was a lot of spare time to get through, and it was expected that the officers would take the lead in devising amusement to pass the time. The contract speed for the mails was seven and a half knots and the passage was seldom made under thirty-five days, and gave one ample opportunity to acquire a very fair knowledge of whether one's fellows were amiable or otherwise.

The Cape Colony in those days was a small place, and I soon began to discover that almost every one of our own nationality took an interest in the officering of the mail steamers, and to do bare justice to the hospitality universally extended to us on shore, we were generally welcome guests wherever we went. Therefore, there was a great amount of good feeling on all sides, and disagreeables were rare.

Particularly fortunate in this respect were we on the occasion of my first voyage in steam. We had a most agreeable set of passengers, and at our first port of call, Madeira, we were put into quarantine. We found the Company's ship *Northam* there, and as she was in a similar plight, homeward bound, we foregathered with her officers and passengers. I was greatly struck by the good tone that seemed to pervade the Company's ships, and was immensely pleased at my good fortune in being able to take a share in it.

When Cape Town was reached, it was customary to fire two guns as an announcement that the English mail had arrived. These were answered by two fired from the castle, for in those days this was an event. Upon this particular occasion we carried out the news of the outbreak of the Franco-German War. This, however, did not seem to greatly interest our visiting officials, who were then full of the discovery of the diamond fields, and it may be said that we on our side did not realise the vast importance of this new discovery. There was no cable in those days, and the near interior of South Africa was an unexplored country. We landed our Natal passengers, who were sent up the coast in a smaller vessel called the *Natal*, and said good-bye with regret to one of the best of fellows, a sugar-planter called Tom Milner, whose memory is still green to old Natalians.

Cape Town docks were at that time open for sailing-ships and small vessels, but we discharged our cargo in Table Bay to sailing lighters. Little more than the commencement of the present magnificent breakwater had been made, and it was not an infrequent occurrence for vessels to drive on shore when it blew hard from the north-west. The Table Bay boatmen were very splendid seamen. In the worst weather a well-fitted anchor boat would keep the sea, and if a vessel was driving, or had parted her cable, they were very clever at passing on board the end of a big coir cable, the other end of which was fast to an anchor they had let go to windward.

Before we left Table Bay, the homeward-bound mail steamer came in—the *Briton*, afterwards H.M.S. *Dromedary*. She looked a small but beautiful little ship, as she came in with yards squared to a nicety, sail covers on, nicely painted, and generally speaking spick and span. She looked thoroughly workmanlike and typical of her captain, by name George Rawlinson Vyvyan, of whom more anon. On a preceding voyage the *Briton* had lost her propeller and had run into Vigo at the rate of three hundred miles in a day under canvas only, which was plain proof that sail was not carried in those ships for ornament only.

In due course we completed our trip to Algoa Bay, discharged our cargo and loaded wool for home, calling at Table Bay on the way back to fill up with cargo and passengers. We had amongst our passengers one very accomplished man named Woollaston, who took great pains both to teach me écarté and indicate the sort of reading that would be useful to me; I retain grateful memories of him. On the passage home the S.E. trades blew strongly. The *Roman* on that voyage had a two-bladed propeller; this we fixed up and down when the engines were stopped, and for two days we ran over ten knots with no steam at all. As that was well over contract speed it was thought desirable to save coal, but the pursuance of that policy brought about the opposition which in time absorbed the original line of mail steamers.

Captain Warleigh was naturally anxious to make the most of the sailing powers of the ship, and as I was last out of a sailing-ship, I was pleased to find that one and all permitted me to trim canvas to my heart's content, and I was encouraged to do so by every one except the boatswain, who did not like the officer of the watch to interfere with details. He was told, however, by the chief, that if other officers left the work to him, that was no reason why every one should, and after that there was no trouble, for he was a decent sailor man. This business of canvas helped me materially with the captain, who told me one evening he would do all he could to retain me in the Company's service, for which I was grateful. My advice to any young fellow joining a new service would be to try how much they will let you do even to the usurpation of what may be the work of other people—do the work, and do it well—it pays.

When we got home the ship was immediately taken in hand to fit up for an extra crowd of passengers. I was confirmed in my appointment, and we got a new chief officer named Alex J. Garrett, a man as strong as Hercules and as obstinate as a mule, a good sailor, and a good friend where he took a fancy. He was very good to me, and gave me the run of his father's house in Southampton. I may say that the father was a clergyman, but Garrett's proclivities did not run that way much; he had been trained in one of the old Blackwall liners of Smith's, and represented the type of officer capable of filling any position with credit. He had a short and effective way of managing the crew, and rejoiced in the nickname of "three-fingered Jack." In the matter of our crews the men often stuck by the same chief officer, voyage after voyage. They were mostly a very decent lot and, in sharp contrast to the present day, the firemen were probably the best men on board. They as a rule had been seamen taken into the stokehold because of their steady conduct. In those days the glands of the engines were made tight by hempen or cotton packing, and this was made in the form of square sennit by firemen, and they had to make lots of it. The pressure of steam in the main engines was about fourteen pounds. There were no spring safety valves, and at each moderate roll of the ship there would be the escape of a large puff of steam brought about by decrease of pressure on the weighted bar that controlled the safety valve. This loss of steam was a very considerable item, but the time for reform had not then arrived, and we were all content to pursue the old and pleasant road of "as you were."

In addition to the main and second saloons we now had first-class accommodation fitted up in the midship and after between-decks. The ship had been built with a view to this being done if necessary; there were consequently ports fitted that only required to be brought into use to provide light and ventilation. These cabins were of the rough-and-ready description, but they were eagerly snapped up by the first crowd of adventurers making for the diamond fields. There were names among those people that were well known in South Africa in after years. Many of them did well, some came to grief, and one of the brightest of them all, Albert Ward, had his career ended fighting for his adopted country in the Cowie Bush. We also had on board the Roman Catholic Bishop of Cape Town with several priests, who were mostly good fellows. Their presence gave us, according to sea superstition, promise of a good passage which was not falsified. It is a curious fact that Anglican clergy are generally credited with bringing *bad* weather.

We left Plymouth, leaving behind us various would-be passengers who had come off in the vain hope of getting a passage. On the passage to Madeira I was very friendly with a young man named Brett, who was going to spend the winter there. He was, I believe, a great man afterwards in the Isle of Wight. At all events I know he must have been known to the police, for one evening some months later we had been dining together, and then finding a stray horse wandering about the High Street, Southampton, we took it to the police station and wished to give it in charge for disorderly conduct. The sergeant in charge seemed disposed to think it was we who were disorderly, but my companion took charge and saved the situation in a masterly manner. I never looked him up afterwards, but it was a pleasant friendship of young men while it lasted, and the faculty for friendship does not improve with age.

The passage to Madeira was rather a rough one. Crossing the Bay the wind was just abaft the beam, and Warleigh was disposed to make the most of it. One first watch I had been hanging on to the canvas in the good old-fashioned style, but it had taken a bit of doing to get her to stand up decently when the squalls came down, and Leigh, when he came on deck, would not take charge until the canvas was reduced. He did not care to take the extra care necessary to carry it, and I dare say he was right, but with a good ship and a good crew I loved the job. We got to Madeira in good time, and there are few changes more striking than the beauty of a fine morning at Madeira after you have had a dusting across the Bay.

To my surprise when we anchored the skipper sent for me, and asked whether I could ride? A reply in the affirmative brought me an invitation to go on shore and ride with him, as he could provide a mount. It did not take me long to get into riding clothes, and we had a most delightful scramble over the hills. I am afraid we rather exceeded the speed limit in the town, but the officials in Funchal were fairly tolerant when once you were on shore, although inexorable over matters of quarantine, and, moreover, the influence of the Blandy family, which was very considerable, was always devoted to making things go as smoothly as possible; in fact there was always a touch of old world courtesy in all the business relations with our agents at Madeira. Needless to say, that on our return to the ship it was every button on duty once more.

With the number of people we had on board it was necessary to duplicate each meal. I presided at first breakfast at 8 a.m., and first dinner at 3.30 p.m. These meals were mostly attended by the younger and more rowdy element, who naturally seemed to gravitate in my direction, but the skipper was pleased on one occasion to express his approval of the way in which I represented him at the head of the table, and that gave me great pleasure. There is little need in these days to describe what life on board ship was like; athletics, cards and sweepstakes absorbed much time. Add to this a little music, and perhaps amateur theatricals, and you obtain a fair list of the methods, mostly employed successfully, to pass the time.

They were a lively crowd on that journey, and the officers of the watch had to keep the quartermaster pretty much on the *qui vive* to prevent sheer mischief, for with a number of young fellows in a confined space with nothing to do save to try how they can create diversion for themselves, what one does not think of the other does. The passage ended in a great spree at Cape Town, and the party separated to their varying fortunes.

On this voyage we went into Cape Town Docks for the first time. It was a very awkward entrance, and it is not given to every man to handle a ship under steam in the vicinity of a pier. Warleigh, however, acquitted himself well, and I can only say that his first performance was a marked success in comparison with mine.

When lying in Algoa Bay loading for home, the ship was rather well thought of. The skipper was very particular as to the stowing of the sails, and the chief was quite as keen. We lay there with royal yards across and fancied ourselves no end. I should mention that along the rails forward, all our ships in those days carried an immense coir spring for putting on the cables if riding out a south-easter. It was probably ten inches in diameter, and in use would stretch and take up like a bit of elastic, but I do not now feel sure by any means that the plan of riding out a gale in shallow waters, as we then did, was the best course. Far better weather is made in fifteen to seventeen fathoms of water.

As showing the vagaries of sea-sickness, the skipper, Leigh, Trotman, the chief engineer, myself and four men pulled out one day to fish on the Roman rock. We duly anchored upon it, and at the expiration of an hour, when we had caught many fish, every soul in the boat was sea-sick with the exception of the chief engineer. The motion of a boat at anchor under some circumstances is disgusting, very, but Trotman fairly had the laugh of us all.

On the return trip from Algoa Bay we went into dock to complete loading, and there occurred an incident I shall always remember with amusement. Leigh had taken under his protection a curious specimen of a pariah dog that used to prowl round the docks, and the poor beast was rather at a loss to understand the vast amount of consideration shown him. He was permitted to sleep in his master's cabin and generally was made a pet of. One night after dinner, when we had a young fellow named Hanbury dining with us, Leigh had retired to his cabin, got into his pyjamas and prepared to go to sleep, attended by the faithful hound. Now, as it happened, Hanbury had a dog also, a bull terrier, and as Garrett, Hanbury and I went to say good-night to Leigh, the dog came also. No sooner did he catch sight of the stray dog than he went for him, and the next moment the two were on the top of Leigh in his bunk, indulging in a wonderful scuffle. It was a trifle difficult to differentiate between barks and yells, for Leigh under the dogs was yelling to Garrett to take the dogs away, and that was eventually done—when we were able to stop laughing. That was the finish of the good time of the pariah dog.

We had a fine passage home, a lovely run across the Bay with a strong fair wind. I find in a note-book certain caustic comments on the wisdom or otherwise of running under whole topsails, and taking in the foresail, but age brings a certain amount of charity with it, and the skipper might possibly have had reasons for his actions which he did not impart to us. I remember the matter rather well, for some of the gear of the foresail had parted, and I lost some of the skin off my fingers in helping to furl the sail. They had, I suppose, become soft for want of work. There was no need to have gone aloft, but it was a stiffish job, and I fancied myself if there was anything out of the way to be done. "Zeal, Mr. Simple, zeal!"

When we got to Southampton the skipper had to change over to the *Briton*, a very quick turn round, and I never again had the pleasure of sailing with him.

Our next captain, I am glad to say, is still alive and well, honoured and respected by all who know him. He is now Sir George R. Vyvyan, K.C.M.G., the late Deputy Master of the Trinity House, and it was my great good fortune to sail with him more than once.

If I were to attempt to record events of separate voyages this reminiscence would run to an intolerable length, therefore I think that I will mention only certain occurrences that impressed themselves on me during the time I served as third officer, and so bring this chapter to an end. Let me place on record my thankfulness that I was never deprived of my watch-keeping privilege. It was the custom in some ships in narrow waters to give the watches to the chief and second officers only. Both my captains held, however, that if a man was not fit to keep a watch in one place, he was not fit in another, and really this reasoning is the true one, for once in charge of the bridge of a steamer you have to deal, as a rule without notice, with whatever may happen, and it is a little lowering to the self-respect of even a young officer to infer that he is not at all times capable of taking charge of the ship.

Now it is not pleasant to find fault with anything in that service, but the days of steam were comparatively young, and there were numbers of things that were not rated at their real importance. I will mention two only. There was no engine-room telegraph and orders were shouted down the engine-room skylight; and secondly, and of still more importance, there was no recognised standard compass. The ship was steered right aft on the poop, and there was a binnacle on either side; the starboard one was that by which the ship was navigated, and that speaks so eloquently that no further comment is necessary. If any captain had proposed expenditure to provide a suitable navigating instrument such as a well-placed standard compass, I doubt if his wishes would have been listened to. He would have been told that surely he could do as others had done. It was reserved for Sir W. Thompson, afterwards Lord Kelvin, to first convert the shipbuilders on the Clyde to the belief that it was necessary to provide a suitable location for a standard compass, and then to confer that greatest boon that was ever given to seamen, a really sound and effective compass.

This voyage was the last one on which the mail steamer called at Plymouth on the outward trip. For some years after this there was a good deal of see-saw about calling at that port to take or land mails. Now that steamers have such power that they can be certain of landing mails at Southampton by a stated time, there is no reason why the western port should be visited, but at the time of which I write a trip down-Channel to Plymouth in a low-powered steamer was a hard experience in the winter time.

We had now lots of passengers both ways, and the ship was a very comfortable one to be in. There was no great change in the routine, and the ship was always kept in apple-pie order. The Saturday inspection was as thorough as it was possible to be. The Southampton ships were, I think, unique in the matter of the inspection of the crews' quarters. Whether the fashion was set by the Royal Mail or the P. & O. I hesitate to say, but it was the custom, and a good one.

There was one little matter that made a great impression on my mind on that voyage, and I have never forgotten it. On the visit to Table Bay homeward bound we did not go into dock, but finished loading in the bay. One morning at lunch time the skipper came into the saloon in his riding togs. I suppose I looked at him hungrily, for he asked me if I would like to go with him, saying he would mount me. When I had quite got my breath, of course I said yes, and hurried off to change into suitable clothes. Well, we went on shore and had a glorious ride, visiting his friends at Bishopscourt and Newlands. Such kindness was not a common occurrence. It set me an example as to the way junior officers might be treated where the opportunity arose, and in after years I tried to do likewise.

On that passage home we had as passengers Mr. Molteno (afterwards Sir John Molteno, the first premier of Cape Colony under responsible government) and two of his charming daughters. When they returned to the Colony I was always welcomed at Claremont by the family, and some time later, when I was in command of the *Mexican*, I had the great pleasure and pride of entertaining some of the family in the finest ship of the line.

Do any of my readers know what "coal fever" is? It is a nasty disorder prevalent in small-power steamers, when a doubt arises as to the sufficiency or otherwise of the coal on board to take the ship into port. It was rather common in some of our ships, but I never saw it arrive at the crisis when the ship's woodwork had to be sacrificed, an occurrence which has been known to take place. In some cases preparation has been made to cut up derricks and every available thing that would burn. I should say that the worst evil that can befall a ship-master is to be cursed with a chief engineer who cannot keep a correct account of coal expended.

I propose to relate one incident more that occurred during my service as third, for it has its amusing side.

When in Cape Town dock on one occasion it was blowing hard outside, and there was a nasty run in the dock causing the ship to strain at her moorings and bump heavily against a shoulder in the dock wall that took us about the main rigging. Unknown to any of us we started some rivets in the side. On the way round to Algoa Bay we had bad weather, and arriving at the anchorage, went in rather further than was usually done, causing the lighthouse-keeper to say we were on shore. The ship did not touch, however, and had ample water under her.

When the captain was asked if he had been on shore, he said no, and his word was, of course, taken; but a day or so afterwards it transpired that we had made water in the afterhold, and people knowing nothing about the dock episode revived the story of our grounding. The port captain, Skead, a really good fellow, again approached our captain, saying that as an accident had occurred would he formally deny that the lighthouse-keeper's story was true? That was enough to set the skipper going. He stated in incisive language that he had already done so, but that if the port captain chose to accept the word of a "reptile" against his, he was at liberty to do so and take what steps he pleased.

The result was a court of inquiry, at which about half the ship's company attended and swore we had not touched the bottom. The ship was acquitted, but the port captain afterwards observed to me, "To my dying day I shall believe you were all perjurers."

On the homeward trip on one occasion we met the outward-bound steamer *Celt*, one of ours, and passed within hailing distance. Before the captains could get a word in there was a chorus from our passengers: "What won the Grand National?" Answered from an equal chorus: "The Lamb." We had one or two breakdowns, between that and the Channel, and on one occasion I remember hoisting the mainyard by the passengers only, the inducement to help being that if we did not hurry up they would not see the Derby. That was Favonius' year.

When the time came to leave the *Roman*, I was pleased to get my promotion, but sorry to lose my shipmates. I was rather lucky, two of my seniors had just resigned in order to try their luck at the diamond fields. One was named Johnson, and I don't know what eventually became of him; but the other was Doveton, who, as Major of the Imperial Horse, was killed at Wagon Hill. At one time serving in the *Cambrian* when she put into Saldana Bay short of coal, he rode to Cape Town for help in record time, for he was one of our best riders, and a first-class all-round man.

The Company had bought from the Royal Mail their paddle steamer, *Danube*, had converted her into a screw, and generally made a very nice little ship of her. She was commanded by Captain Baynton, who was commodore. She was, therefore, the best ship in the Company, and I was very proud when I mustered on her as second officer. It was true that I was told I should have to change with a senior then serving on the coast ship, but that in no way detracted from my satisfaction.

CHAPTER VI

"Fair is our lot—O, goodly is our heritage!"—Kipling.

The *Danube*, as I have already stated, was a converted paddler, and in our eyes loomed as a big ship. As we went to muster, Captain Baynton casually drew attention to the fact that a few years ago they were serving in vessels that were not as long, as from the taffrail to the mainmast, and used his favourite expression: "It's marvellous!" Now the *Danube* was about three hundred feet long, so that may give some idea of the size of the vessels that the Union Company made a commencement with. Baynton was one of the men who upheld the best traditions of the merchant service. In person he was short and unduly stout, but the possessor of great natural dignity, brave as a lion, and with an eye that brooked no contradiction. He had me under arrest one morning for a short time, and my fault so far as I could gather was that I had looked at him in a manner he disapproved of. But we were afterwards great friends and I had a most sincere regard for him. I think that the earlier portion of his life had been spent in the service of the Royal Mail, and he commanded the *Medway* when she towed H.M.S. *Britannia* in for the bombardment of the forts at Sebastopol. As he once told me, his wife and a faithful attendant named Anne were with him on that occasion, and he further explained that when he had finished with the flagship and went to see about them, they were sitting on camp-stools on one of the sponsons amused at watching the shots fall. It may be mentioned here that when the question of towing the flagship under fire was raised, the crew of the *Medway* gladly acquiesced, with the understanding that if fatalities occurred their families were to receive the same consideration financially as if they had been serving in corresponding rank in the Royal Navy.

Our chief, Sammy Valler, was quite a character in his way, but does not call for comment specially; the third was a nice enough youngster but as weak as water, and his own enemy. He took a great fancy to me, and if we had remained shipmates I fancy his career might have been better than it was. Altogether it was a good ship's company, and I was very glad to get to sea. As it was a first voyage we were naturally trying what we could get out of the ship, and, going down-Channel the first night out, I nearly ran over a sailing-ship which was going the same way as ourselves without even showing a binnacle light over the stern. I did call the captain, who came on the bridge and made a few cursory remarks concerning the iniquities of sailing-ships generally, after which he retired. If Baynton could not trust the officer of the watch, he got some one he could trust. A master who is too much on the bridge is not an unmixed blessing, for he lessens the sense of responsibility in the officer of the watch, and, strange though it may seem to a landsman, the bridge under ordinary conditions is not his place. Baynton realised this and acted accordingly. The weather we experienced for the first day or two was such as to cause the ship to roll heavily, and the rigging, being new, stretched to an abnormal amount, so much so that it had to be "swiftered in" until we could get into quiet water. I watched this operation with some interest as it was carried on under the supervision of the chief and the boatswain, and inclined as I was to criticise steamboat sailors, I confessed to myself that it was done in a seamanlike manner. I think it was the same night in the middle watch that the wind came out fresh and free from the northward and I was able to get the square canvas on her. It was a treat to do so, for although lots of the gear was foul, sail never having been set before, the way she showed her sense of the attention was beautiful to see. In these days of twin screws and massive ships canvas would mean little, but in well-sparred, fine-lined steamers, canvas was then like water to a thirsty plant, and imparted a motion and buoyancy that were delightful to experience. To the speed of the *Danube* canvas would add at least two knots.

The remainder of the voyage passed without any event of interest, and in due course we got to Algoa Bay and commenced to load for home. We had started a new plan of stowing our own cargoes of wool, and naturally the second officer had charge of the business. This was rather a novelty and I was taking a great interest in the entire job. One day the chief and I wanted to go on shore to a ball to which we had been invited, and the captain had given us free permission to do so, saying with a certain amount of sarcasm, that if all the officers went, and the boatswain as well, he thought we might find the ship afloat when we returned. However, we made allowance for the fact that the atmosphere was a little sultry. I was on that day just finishing the stowing of the after orlop deck, when a voice from above gave notice that the captain was coming down. He duly made his appearance, being lowered in a big basket known as a cheese basket, variously used for discharging small boxes of cheese and also for landing timid passengers into boats in bad weather. There was a space into which I was determined to get a bale of wool, but there was considerable trouble in doing so, and Baynton, having comfortably seated himself in a chair I had procured for him, expressed a decided opinion that the job was impossible. His remarks continued to be of a very caustic nature, until the bale being in its place, he observed: "Now I suppose you think you are a dam clever fellow," and as he did not patronise hold ladders, shouted out for his return conveyance. There must be many still alive who can picture this scene to themselves.

We went to our dance and had a splendid time, and I know that in this season of the Coronation I shall meet stately ladies who though unfortunately no longer young, helped on that occasion to make the sun rise far too quickly. On our return to Table Bay, Nemesis overtook me. I was far too comfortable and contented and consequently had to turn over to the coasting steamer *Natal*, a little craft of under 500 tons. The man I relieved was named Borlase, commonly known as "handsome Henry"; he was my senior and had managed to work the oracle with the Company's agents, and my skipper had not objected. My shipmates in the *Danube* gave me a very cheery farewell dinner and send off, and I entered upon my new experience with a lot of curiosity, for the tales of the coast were many and various.

It is not an easy matter after many years to put events in quite their right perspective, especially when many things were happening at the same time, but the history of that little ship was a fairly crowded one. In the first place she had recently been sent home with the mails, when the proper mail steamer had broken down. They had then greatly increased her passenger accommodation by building a saloon on deck, which was an advantage, and as at that time the Franco-German war was on, there was a clause in the ship's articles when they were opened at Southampton that was unusual and, if I may say so, more's the pity! It ran as follows: "The said crew agree to fight and defend the ship to the best of their ability, at the discretion of the said master." Advantage had not been taken of the chance to reboiler the ship, and this was an endless source of trouble, for it always made sailing-day a period of uncertainty. It was the old story of putting a new patch on an old garment, and a patch on one place often caused a break-out in another.

But, as in all the Company's ships, the personnel of the officers was of the best. Ballard was skipper; I have referred to him in connection with a previous experience. He was a sailor, curiously quiet until roused, when he could make the sparks fly with a vengeance; very self-contained, but always ready and willing to do a good turn if he could to any one. I am happy to say I won his confidence. The chief was the ill-fated Edward Manning, afterwards lost in the *Teuton*. His end was in keeping with his life, for probably no man ever kept himself under more complete control than did Manning. Knowing his work thoroughly, he seldom if ever raised his voice; nothing ruffled—outwardly at least—the calm serenity of his temper. I only saw him move hastily twice; once to get the helm over when I was shaving a point rather closely, and again to fling me a rope's end when, in lifting the end of a buoyed cable, the boat was capsized and we were all in the ditch.

He was a very fine character, and a good shipmate. Our third, Harrison, was a good man too, but after a short time he was relieved by Jones, of whom more anon.

The duties of the *Natal* were to make a trip monthly between Cape Town and Durban, taking up the mail and passengers brought out by the mail steamer coming to Cape Town, and feeding her in a similar manner from Natal. It usually took about two days to accomplish the transhipment. There was a certain amount of novelty in this work, for it was rather out of the beaten track, and the eastern ports were in a very primitive state of development. Take in the first place East London, then a very difficult port to enter even with the smallest craft. The mouth of the Buffalo river, which made the port, was closed by a sand bar that at times was impassable even by a lifeboat. The method of working was for lighters to haul out by surf lines laid over the bar and extending a fair distance into the anchorage; the ship that had cargo or passengers to discharge anchored as closely in as was prudent and then ran a warp to the buoyed end of the surf line for the lighter to reach the ship by; the work was rough, very, and the boatmen were in perfect keeping with their surroundings. I should not like to do the men an injustice, but they seemed to be the scourings of the roughness and rascality of the world. Their lives were mostly in their hands, and they did not attach much value either to them or the language with which they adorned them. It was no uncommon thing when there was a sea on the bar—and there mostly was—to see a breaker sweep a surf boat from end to end. The men generally managed to hold on, but fatal accidents were not infrequent. These boats would frequently land passengers, who were carefully battened down and in almost complete darkness while the passage was being accomplished. Both at this port and Durban, passengers were put into the lighters in large baskets lowered by the cargo whips, and if the ship were rolling it would be no uncommon occurrence to see a basket containing perhaps three or four men and women hoisted half way out and held fast by derrick and stay until the roll had subsided. People got used to it, however, and no improvement was made until the visit of the Empress Eugènie to South Africa, when it occurred to some genius that a wicker cage might be made with a door in the side which would obviate the necessity for lifting the ladies into the basket. If, however, the ladies were young and good-looking there was never much difficulty noticeable in finding volunteers to take on this arduous duty.

Leaving East London the navigation of the ship was conducted on different lines to that adopted to the westward. There one could steer a course and be moderately confident of making it within reasonable limits, but between East London and Natal you had to face the full force of the

Mozambique current, which mostly ran anything between three and five knots to the south-west, unless you were close in shore, when you were sometimes, but not always, favoured with a drain of eddy current.

With a vessel steaming perhaps nine knots it was therefore necessary to keep as much inshore as could be done with safety. To set a course was not possible; during the daylight hours the ship was steered by the coastline, and when darkness closed in a course was set which ran parallel to the land by the chart, yet caught the current on the port bow, with the result that when daylight came the ship would be thirty miles out, or more, fighting the full strength of an adverse current. The nett result was that passages between East London and Natal were a very uncertain quantity.

I took to this sort of watch-keeping in the daylight very kindly. The coast was mostly like English parkland, and I set myself to learn it as thoroughly as possible; in this I was assisted in every possible manner by the captain, who spared no pains to point out the various places by name. It was interesting work, for it gave one a chance to exercise one's initiative which was in no way checked by my seniors.

Durban harbour in those days was not the ample port it is now. Under the best conditions there might be perhaps sixteen feet of water on the bar at high tide. It was more often twelve or even less. Outside the bar there were the remains of three attempts to improve the harbour, but each one had been a failure. There was an impression that any of them might have been a success if it had been persevered with, but money had been too scarce to push the experiment to a successful ending. There was, however, one man who even then had made up his mind that Durban should be a port, and he lived long enough to realise his ambition. His name was Harry Escombe, afterwards "Right Honourable." If Harry Escombe and Cecil Rhodes were alive to-day there would be some backbone in the councils of the Empire. But this is a digression.

There was a good deal of formality about getting the little *Natal* into the Bluff Channel, a dignified port captain, an oracular pilot, lots of signalling and a final pointing for the bar. Whether we touched or not I cannot remember; most likely we did, for it was a very common occurrence—but anyhow we got in, moored in the Bluff Channel, and looked around us with satisfaction. There was every reason to do so. A beautiful harbour, a hearty welcome from all, and an utter absence of anything approximating to bustle. Further it was the land of the Zulu, who was relied upon to do all the hard work. I suppose that it would be difficult to find finer specimens of muscular humanity than were the Zulus who did the shipwork; their scanty raiment appeared perhaps inadequate to the white ladies who were then making their first acquaintance with the manners and customs of the country, but if modernity has now insisted upon trousers in the towns of Natal, it has destroyed a picturesque side of the national life.

Natal was absolutely different from any other part of South Africa, inasmuch as it was mainly British! In Cape Town you heard as much Dutch spoken as English, if not more. Towns like Stellenbosch or Wellington might be called all Dutch, and I remember when I first visited those places I wondered in a vague sort of way how it happened that the British flag flew over them, by which it is evident that I had not learned my history properly. But in Durban there was a different atmosphere. It was essentially British and the inhabitants prided themselves upon being up to date and live specimens of colonists. They were, moreover, intensely loyal, and fully realised what their country was going to be in the future.

I was sitting in the Durban Club one Sunday afternoon and certain men were arguing as to the possibility of a railway between Durban and Pietermaritzburg, the journey in those days being made by mail cart. Escombe brought the matter to a head with the following words addressed to a sugar planter named Tom Milner, a splendid fellow who had come out with me on the first voyage of the *Roman*: "Look here, Milner, I will give you a shilling a day until I go by train from Durban to Maritzburg; after that you shall pay my butcher's bill for life!—is it a bet?" Milner said yes, and this being in 1872 he received his cheque yearly until about eight years later when the railway was built and the bet was compromised. I fancy he paid back two shillings for each one received.

No one walked in Natal. If a man wished to go one hundred yards down the street, the Kaffir boy invariably brought his horse. There was never any difficulty in borrowing a mount. The people were most generous and hospitable; but underlying it all there was the sure knowledge that the great Zulu power in the north would some day have to be reckoned with. There was one little incident that happened about this time that should find a place here, for it shows that even then the minds of Germans were fixed upon the great expansion of their nation. There was a small German trading steamer on the coast called the *Bismarck*. She was commanded by a very fine fellow named Staats, who wore a magnificent beard. On one occasion he had a difference of opinion with the Point boatmen, who were not quite as bad as the East London men, although very nearly, and they declared they would cut off his beard. Staats, however, set them at defiance, and declared that the German flag was sufficient to prevent such an outrage even then, and would be for all time. The men admired his pluck and cheered him, for it took a bit of doing.

When I left the *Roman*, Leigh presented me with a suit of canvas clothes which he had found useful. In the daytime I lived in them, for the forehold of the Natal was not a place adapted for the wear of fine raiment. The principal articles we took away were raw hides, sugar and wool, and the smell of those hides was a thing to remember. There was no trouble in getting cargo either stowed or discharged, but an officer had to be there all the time, and in a canvas rig it was possible to sit down. The Zulus would work well if you did not lose your temper, and as they happened to approve of me I never had any trouble with them.

One voyage was much like another, but sailing day at Natal offered considerable variety, for it depended upon the vagaries of the bar. I have known passengers and their friends come down four days in succession and be detained for want of water. Those days, however, usually resulted in a sort of picnic on the bluff—and were most enjoyable. It was a treat to see the way the girls could negotiate the steep slope under the lighthouse, and if the idea was to go up town, there would be a rush for the point, with not too much care exercised as to whose pony you mounted to get there. Upon one occasion we stuck on the bar for over half-an-hour, bumping fairly heavily, but she was a well-built little ship and it did not seem to do much harm; it used to jar the spars a good deal though. On the passage down the coast we would call at the ports, weather permitting and pick up such passengers and cargo as we could, transhipping to the mail steamer in Cape Town Docks.

After a few trips I got some knowledge of the upper part of the coast, and experienced a dislike to being set off miles in the middle watch by the current. I therefore sounded the skipper as to whether he would let me exercise my judgment in keeping her in when I could see well. I found he was agreeable that I should do so, and I used to report to him every hour, and hand the ship over to the chief at 4 a.m. well in shore. This led to a considerable shortening of the passage up the coast; but it told against me in one way, for when I wanted to get home the old man said, "No, the ship has made much better passages up since you've been here and I shan't let you go." That was a bit hard, for there was a lot of promotion going on at home, new men being taken in as chief, and I out of it all, as was said, for lack of experience.

On one passage down we were anchored at East London, and a breeze of wind came on from the sea. Seven sailing-ships went on shore that night, one, a brig called the *Nant-y-Glo*, driving close past us. At that we decided to slip and go to sea without loss of time; we did so, but, picking up the cable next day when we were fast to the slip rope in the cutter, the ship drifted down on us, fouled the rope with her propeller and capsized us all into the water. That was one of the occasions when I saw Manning run. Curiously enough, we let go another anchor, and when we picked it up brought up the other cable that we had slipped foul of it, so all was joy once more.

But the boilers were in that sad condition that it was necessary to go in for thorough repairs. We had had to delay our sailing from Cape Town for four days through bad leaks, on one occasion; and as the Company had just got the contract for the Zanzibar mail we went in for a thorough overhaul. This was towards the end of 1872, and a good two months were spent over the operation. When it was finished, we found the *Natal* painted yellow, the better to withstand the anticipated heat of Zanzibar.

Before we started the first voyage on the new route, we made a trial trip to Saldanah Bay, and took up with us as visitors many of the principal people in the Cape, including Mr. Molteno, the premier, and his two sons. I wonder if one of those sons, now an M.P. and director of a steamship company, remembers firing one of our twelve-pounder signal-guns under my tuition? It was a very jolly trip, and we all enjoyed ourselves immensely. We changed our chief officer about this time, and got in his place an officer named Barker, a man of no striking personality but a good fellow, who always went about the deck humming, and had a most curious voice.

When we left Natal behind us on the first upward trip I think we all felt like Columbus when he started on his voyage of discovery. The East Coast of Africa was very imperfectly known, and the charts were by no means reliable guides. It was a mercy that in those early days the craft we were navigating were small, and drawing little water, or I fear that there would have been a good few landmarks left by the pioneers. Delagoa Bay, for instance, splendid harbour though it is, was absolutely without a solitary buoy to give a friendly lead, and the land in the immediate vicinity at the entrance is not conspicuous enough to give any definite leading marks. No actual mishap occurred either going in or coming out, but we had enough experience of the various tides to show us that it was no place to take liberties with. Quillemane, which is the port at the mouth of the Zambesi, was also touched at; here again was a river entrance apparently big enough to take in any ship, but there was the same failing—imperfect survey and lack of competent pilotage. Presumably in the future this will be one of the big ports of the world, but at that time it was considered as a place to be avoided at all hazards.

It was a change to get to Mozambique, where there was a harbour with plenty of water, and sufficiently well surveyed to make negotiation easy; it was also a striking-looking place from the sea, with a magnificent old fort built (so report had it) of stone brought from Portugal early in the sixteenth century. The work accomplished by those early navigators and settlers was simply marvellous; it made one wonder why it was that people who had been so enterprising and splendid as explorers should have so terribly deteriorated. May the Gods avert a similar fate for Britain! So far as we could gather the country in the immediate vicinity of the settlement was rich and fertile, but no strong or satisfactory rule had then been established, and the entire place seemed to be marking time.

A strong current sets down the coast past Cape Delgado, but we had fine and favourable weather for the run into Zanzibar. The entrance to the anchorage is narrow in one or two places, but in the absence of buoys the ship could in the daylight be easily conned from aloft between the coral reefs, though that indeed was hardly necessary. But it was not advisable to attempt the narrow passes in the hours of darkness, and consequently the mail steamer bound south usually left before noon. Our first arrival at Zanzibar was on a Sunday, with a temperature of ninety-seven degrees in the shade—not a breath of wind, and the water so clear that the bottom could be seen in ten fathoms. We found H.M.S. *Daphne* at anchor, and also the B.I. steamer *Punjaub*, which was concerned in the mail contract from Zanzibar northward.

About this time there was some excitement at home concerning slavery at Zanzibar, and Sir Bartle Frere paid a visit to the place in the *Enchantress*. He arrived the day we left. There was also fitting out a Livingstone expedition under the leadership of Colonel Pelly. There is no need here to go into any description of the place itself, except to say that it was quaint, the people well disposed towards the British, and that slavery as then practised, was on the whole a respectable institution, although more than one black man swam off to the ship and begged to be taken down the coast. Indeed, in after years we were frequently asked by friends at the Cape and Natal to bring them down a black boy for service, and there was never any difficulty in procuring them. There were at times very strong winds of hurricane force, and the previous year the island had been visited by one that did great damage.

We had a slight specimen of this sort of thing. One morning we had just commenced working cargo in the usual manner, taking it in from lighters, when a dense cloud gathered to the N.W., and occasional flashes of lightning were seen. About 7.30 a.m. down came the squall with great fury. We got up steam, but had no occasion to use it although a small dhow full of cargo that was made fast to us went down, and the beach was strewn with dhows driven from their moorings. I saw a roof—part of the Sultan's palace—lift at one side, roll up like a piece of paper and blow over into the courtyard with a mighty crash, but I did not hear it if killed many people. By noon the weather had changed, the wind was gone, and people commenced to pick up the pieces and resume the ordinary routine of life.

Shortly afterwards we left for Natal, passing H.M.S. *Briton* on the road. One trip on this route was much like another, but we spent a very fair portion of every month in Natal harbour. The last voyage I made was under somewhat altered circumstances, for Captain Ballard had been appointed to the *Basuto*, and Barker was in acting command of the *Natal*. I, of course, got an acting appointment as chief which tended to stir up in my mind a taste or longing to participate in that stream of promotion that was flowing at Southampton, but which did not flow my way. I tried vainly for some time to get home, but as long as Ballard commanded the *Natal* I could not manage it, for he would not let me go. He was very good-humoured, however, in granting leave.

On one occasion I greatly wanted to go to a dance at Maritzburg to be held on a Monday night. A great friend of mine, and one well-known and liked by all, named Manisty, offered to find me the necessary mounts and to ride with me. We started off on Sunday afternoon, arriving at Maritzburg at 9 a.m. on Monday, sleeping some hours on the road. After a bath and breakfast we rode to a place fifteen miles out, and in again to a dinner and the dance, which was kept up till 5 a.m. Then I changed my clothes, got on my horse, and started for Durban, arriving on board by 6 p.m. in time for dinner. My companion on the road down was a cheery soul named Innes. It rained heavily all the time, but it was the most enjoyable ride I ever had. It was fifty-seven miles between the towns, and the journey totalled 144 miles in just over two days, but I had relays of horses to do it, although there were some of all sorts amongst them.

Soon after Ballard left the *Natal* to join the *Basuto* we met her in Natal harbour, and I arranged to change into that ship for the run to Cape Town, and the transfer to a home ship. Here for the first time I met a notable character in the person of Harry Owen, who was chief of that ship, and one of those who had been put over the heads of many. He was in those days one of the cheeriest of companions one could well find, and also a reckless dare devil. We first foregathered over the matter of firing a royal salute on the Queen's birthday. We had two big guns in the *Natal*, the *Basuto* had three little ones, but as the ships were alongside each other the combined salute was done in a fairly respectable manner. I can't say more than that, but no one was killed or hurt, and after all that counts for a little. Here also I first met Bishop Colenso, who would come on board our ships in the Bluff Channel and simply delight us with his charming companionship; he was shipmate with me afterwards and was fond of sailors, but it always seemed strange to me to be on even conversational terms with the man whose book on algebra had given me as a boy so much trouble to master. I transferred to the *Basuto* as second officer and thus came under Owen's orders. He was the worst man at relieving a watch I ever knew. We dined at 6 p.m., and if I had the dinner look-out, he never showed up on the bridge before 7.30 p.m., for the chief was always relieved for dinner. This was rather a tax on the second, who had to turn out at midnight, but it came to an end in a few days, and I turned over to the *European* for the passage home, acting as third officer. About this period the *Roman* had had an accident and returned to Cape Town for repairs. She had had a difference of opinion with some rocks off Dassen Island, and the *European* was instructed to make the best passage home with the news, for there was no cable in those days. She was for her time a fast ship, steaming a good twelve, which was exceptional for us, and every one was delighted; she was comfortable and there was a nice crowd of passengers on board. Our skipper was named Jeffries, a curious compound, who did not make friends easily, but where he did, stuck to them. I should like to tell many stories about him, but refrain. His great hobby was whist, and he played a fair game, but his main fault was that he had little tact in dealing with awkward people, and this on one occasion, coupled with his having also a tactless chief officer, led to a lot of reckless young passengers throwing overboard a great portion of his cabin furniture, including various embroidered covers by which he set great store. I personally got on well with him, and I adopted when my time came many hints that he gave me as to various duties that the officer of the watch should perform.

We made a good passage home. I was favourably received, and after a spell of sick leave, which I had asked for to enable me to leave the coast, I was sent down to Dundee to join the *American*, the newest ship then fitting out. My application for sick leave was not humbug, however; I had had a touch of the sun one afternoon riding from the point to Durban, and the particular way the ailment should be treated caused a marked difference of opinion between two celebrated London physicians.

There was a very delightful old Scotchman who kept an hotel where we stayed in Dundee. His family were as hospitable as himself; I think the house was called the Globe, but anyhow it was close to the dock where the *American* was fitting out. One remark of his impressed itself upon my memory: "Ye ken we have a' things in season in the good toon o' Dundee," and it seemed as if a good time was specially in season at that period. The builders of the ship, Stevens & Co. and some of their connections named Crowdace, were particularly attentive and civil to us all, but I entirely fail to remember who was chief officer of that ship. Baynton was in command and Mrs. Baynton was also with him. She came round to Southampton in the ship, and it was a fortunate day for me when she did so, for it enabled me to make a friendship that, apart from the pleasure it gave me, was of infinite value as far as my future prospects were concerned. To any young man I would say that if you come in touch with the ladies connected with your seniors or superiors, use your best efforts to interest and be agreeable to them, for apart from the advantage you derive from association with women possessing presumably "the knowledge of life," you never know where it may not possibly be in their power to put in a word in the home circle that may be of benefit to you in your professional career. Some men may sneer at this advice, but my experience is that it is good. At all events Mrs. Baynton was a good friend to me.

When we got to Southampton there were many changes going on in the officering of the ships, and in the midst of it stood out the fact that there was a captain and a chief officer short who would have to come from somewhere. The manager of the Company in Southampton at that time was Mr. G. Y. Mercer; he had been with it from its creation, and possessed great power. He was a far greater man even than the marine superintendent. Now Mrs. Mercer and Mrs. Baynton were great friends, and it may be mentioned that the latter lived in a very charming house at Shirley, called Trafalgar Lodge; it was an ideal place for the people living in it. I was invited to dine there one evening, and doing so met Mr. and Mrs. Mercer. It was fairly evident to me afterwards why I had been invited, for after the ladies had left the table and the men were discussing things generally Mr. Mercer made the casual remark that "Nothing was certain in this world, not even that Crutchley would go out as second of the *American*." Very shortly after this I was appointed to the *Syria* as chief, and my skipper was Garrett, late of the *Roman*, his first voyage in command. This opened up to me a new vista of boundless possibilities, for the ship was one of our best. Both the skipper and myself were new brooms and most anxious to sweep clean. Our second was named Merritt, a nice fellow who came from Cape Town. Garrett liked him very much, and when a year or so afterwards Merritt died as the result of an accident, was inconsolable for months.

U.S.S "SYRIA"

(From a painting by Willie Fleming of Cape Town)

The passage out was uneventful, but when we got to Algoa Bay we had some time to spend there. The ship was in beautiful order, even to the satisfaction of the skipper, who took a delight in trying to find out something amiss out of sheer mischief and for the love of tormenting me. Not that I minded in the least—it was good training—but for some reason or other it came to the front that there were one or two anchors and chains on the bottom in the vicinity of where we were anchored, and Garrett told me to find them and pick them up. I started to sweep and soon got fast to something heavy, and the work of recovery began. I picked up an anchor and chain, claimed as belonging to one of the Castle line, another anchor and chain, and also heavy moorings laid down for the company's ships some years before. On the last day I was engaged in this operation, Garrett took Merritt on shore to the races, leaving me with a pious adjuration to be sure not to kill any one. It's rather a mercy we had no accident, for we were dealing with heavy weights with makeshift gear. However, it was done, though when we got home the skipper was asked his reason for picking up the company's moorings. There is no doubt, however, that it was a good piece of work, for it cleared a large space of the best anchoring ground; they were moorings that would have held a liner of today, but the place was not suitable for them.

On the passage home we called at St. Helena, and as there was some spare room in the afterhold, we took in a great number of casks of whale oil for Southampton. They were old and leaky and made an awful mess of my beautifully clean teak deck before we could stow them in the after lower hold. I had grave misgivings about them from the first, but had to do as I was told. When we got off Ushant there was a heavy beam sea and the ship rolled badly, with the result that they all collapsed and not a single cask was landed. It took days to clean the hold, and there had to be an extension of protest and all sorts of trouble to get clear of the liability for loss, and to put it on the shoulders of the insurance people.

When we arrived at Southampton, Garrett was relieved of his command and so far as I remember was appointed to a new coasting steamer. With him he took Merritt, who was succeeded by Dacre Bremer, an old Wigram's man and a very nice fellow. The new captain was H. E. Draper, and even now after a lapse of years I find a difficulty in rightly defining his character. I was with him a long time in various ships, and found him kind and considerate; he had, however, a caustic wit that was very telling, and which was perhaps nourished at the expense of other more important qualities. I fail to remember anything of particular note that occurred either on the outward passage or on the coast, but homeward bound in the S.E. trades one beautiful Sunday afternoon I, with many others, was having a delightful sleep. I woke up feeling an awful vibration with the impression that the end of the world was upon us. As I tumbled out on deck the masts seemed to be bending together, and the first thing I remember was seeing the chief engineer making for the engine-room and driving before him some firemen who were trying to escape. The vibration soon ceased, and then we were informed that the main shaft had broken well aft in the tunnel, that it had very nearly gone through the side of the ship, that what remained was bent in the stern tube, and that we must stop the ship's way until it was so secured that the propeller would not revolve. Now we were too far north to fetch St. Helena under canvas, for although the ship was brig-rigged and sailed fairly well, it was no use trying conclusions on a wind with the S.E. trade, so when the shaft was secured we set course for Ascension, and in due course made the island dead to leeward. The trouble was to get the ship before the wind, but it was done by a little scheming, and we rounded the east side of the island and luffed up for the anchorage in quite the approved sailing-ship fashion. The skipper, however, would not risk going into the proper anchorage, so we put the anchor down some distance out, and warped further in next day, in charge, much to my disgust, of a Naval lieutenant whose interference was to my mind quite unnecessary. Beggars, however, could not afford to be choosers. After a considerable amount of consultation it was decided that we should endeavour to trim the ship by the head so that we could unship the propeller, and that we should try and do this before the arrival of the *American*, which was expected in about a month, in the hope that she would give us a tow home. We had a fair number of passengers on board, but fortunately they could spend lots of their time on shore, where they were very welcome. Many of them, in fact nearly all, were ultimately transhipped to the *Northam*, which came in before the *American*, but it was no use looking to her for a tow; it took her all her time to get about herself. She did, however, bring Captain East, R.N., the new captain of the island, who, had he come earlier, would, I fancy, have advised other steps than those we had taken. It was then too late, however, for we had failed to trim the ship sufficiently by the head to get at the propeller, and had had to content ourselves with securing it with a length of stream chain, replacing all the cargo we had shifted and leaving the ship on an even keel. Thinking it all over, it seems rather a mercy that she did not capsize with us, for we took a good many liberties with her.

One evening Captain East was detained on board as the "rollers" were in, and a vessel in the offing was seen making signals. As they could not get off from the shore, I went in our gig to see what they wanted. She was the barque *Dione* short of provisions, and the skipper was very glad to avail himself of my assistance and that of the boat's crew to get into the anchorage. I stood well over to the eastern point, tacked ship close in shore and then steered for the stern of the *Syria*, luffed up as I rounded it, and then, laying everything flat aback, put the anchor down in a beautiful inshore berth, where she got what she wanted the next day and went on her way rejoicing. That was the last sailing-ship I handled.

While waiting for the *American* we proceeded to get ready our towing gear, and for this purpose we got from the naval stores two big hawsers. One was a thirteen inch and a beautiful bit of rope, the other one as it turned out was afflicted with dry rot and gave a lot of trouble at odd times. We had none of us had any experience in the towing of ships, and I am greatly afraid the preparations we made were of an unsatisfactory nature, for we provided for four tow-lines, and that was three too many. By the light of experience it is easy to see that one large hawser shackled on to a bower cable which could be veered to any extent required by the ship being towed, would have given all the elasticity required to prevent breakage, and the towing ship could have slipped her end at any time she thought it necessary. In due time the *American* arrived, with Captain Baynton in command. She had a fair number of passengers too, who were not overjoyed when they learned that their passage would be delayed by towing us. But Baynton decided he would do it, and the hawsers were passed. We sent some firemen on board her, but before we got under way Baynton hailed us to send for them back, which we did, as he observed, "They want a nursemaid to look after them."

What the poor devils had done to offend him I know not, but he was of a very peppery nature, and had little patience with any obstruction. The scene getting those ships out of the roadstead must have been a source of high entertainment to the onlookers, and it was in no way creditable even as a first rehearsal. There are two things necessary to those carrying out such an operation—patience and moderation of language. Unfortunately we were none of us burdened with either, but we managed to get away after indulging in comments on all and sundry, to which the Commination Service would have seemed mild. We parted hawsers and generally made as big a mess of things as was possible. That scene, however, had its use, for when we could think it over it was a fine object lesson for the future. It all arose from the fact that there were two masters, and that was the weakness which was evident on many future occasions.

There is little need for me to go into daily detail. We carried the S.E. trade well north, and one morning we were informed by means of a black board exhibited over the stern of the *American* that we were to go into Goree for coal, and this we did. When we got there it was found that there was very little to be obtained, in fact only enough to take us to St. Vincent in the Cape Verde Islands. It would have been well if the *American* had gone there alone, filled up with coal and come back for us to tow in the comparatively smooth water near the land, but that was no part of Baynton's idea. He had towed us so far, and did not intend to lose sight of us until he saw us safe so far as salvage was concerned, so over we went to St. Vincent, where the N.E. trade nearly always blows half a gale. There we found lots of ships and transports, for the Ashanti War was just over and the troops were being sent home. I seem to remember also that there were certain complications concerning anchorages, differences of opinion in fact, but before we had been there long in came the *Roman* homeward bound with Garrett in command, and to her the *American* transhipped such of her passengers as could be accommodated. We also, as did the *American*, took on board some of the returning troops, mostly the married men. Incidentally I may mention that the trooper *Tamar* was at anchor to windward of us, and I saw one afternoon a young lieutenant do the best bit of boat-sailing it was ever my good fortune to witness. I wish I could remember his name. When matters had been arranged we started again on our homeward way. It was blowing hard from the N.E., and as we left the harbour the tow-ropes at times stood out stiff as the ships pitched to it, but, as we found in time, it is easier to tow with a head wind than with a fair one. There were incidents in that trip that would have made the fortunes of a comic writer and artist, but they would run to too great length here. We called at Madeira for coal and set out on the last stage of the journey. There was a S.W. gale in the Bay of Biscay in which the ships parted company, and we were lost sight of for some time, but picked up again the next day, and again taken in tow for the run up-Channel. It was a Sunday, and remarks had been passed that we only wanted a really good collision to make our experiences complete, and as it happened we got it.

It was a fine cold night in March, and the Portland lights were in sight. I was in my cabin asleep, for all was going well, when in rushed the chief engineer asking for my tomahawk to cut the tow-ropes. I grabbed it myself and jumped on deck habited in a scarlet flannel sleeping suit, such as some of us rather affected at the time. There I found that a large sailing-ship had struck the *American* on the port side, making a big hole in her, and knocking down the engine-room skylight on top of the engines, so that they could not be moved. The *Syria's* helm for some reason had been starboarded and we passed the stern of the sailing-ship dragging our tow-ropes with us; when these tightened the two steamers drew alongside one another and the *Aracan*, as the sailing-ship was called, lay across our two sterns. No one that was playing an acting part can describe a scene such as that. I can only record certain, impressions—I looked over the side and saw the interior of the ladies' saloon of the *American* through a great hole in the side, a stewardess standing with a candle in her hand in blank amazement. On the quarter-deck of the *American* was Baynton as cool as a fish, with his chief beside him, saying that there were plenty to do the running about, all *he* wanted was his engines cleared. At the after end of the *Syria* was a crowd trying to board the *American*, thinking we were sinking. At the fore end of the *American* another crowd were coming on board us under similar delusion, and to add to it all some Irish women were yelling blue murder either from fright or devilment, I know not which. I got some of our boats in the water by the skipper's orders and then went on board the *Aracan*, whose crew had left her, to get her clear of our stern. This I succeeded in doing. She drifted a short distance away and went down by the head, her masts crashing as the sails felt the water on her downward plunge. She had been loaded with ammunition for Hong Kong, and it was rather a mercy that nothing caused an explosion, for her bow was flattened in like a wall where she had sailed into the *American's* side. When I got back to the *Syria* I got orders to hoist the boats, and, hailing one to come alongside, I asked who was in charge, "Sergeant Dighton, sir," came back the reply. She was manned mostly by volunteers from marine artillery, passengers, and that incident always struck me as being comical. By this time they had cleared the *American's* engines, and Baynton, seeing that the tow-ropes hung clear of his propeller, went full speed ahead like the fiend he was. Any other man would have got a spring out to separate the ships, but he meant to be out of it at the first minute at all costs—it was rather a mercy that we did not have some of the sticks down. Beyond a few breakages, however, little harm was done to us, and one of the tow-ropes held, so that we proceeded on our way to Southampton I cannot say how, but we got there the next day and I for one was not sorry.

There is a good deal of incident, even when you get on shore, over a collision case. The solicitor's clerks are very busy collecting or procuring evidence of sorts. I believe there is more honest perjury in collision cases than in any other. It appears to me that no two men view the same thing in exactly the same light. Thus—

(*a*) There is the thing as it happened.

(*b*) The thing as each individual thought it happened.

(*c*) The thing that you state in court, after your solicitor has persuaded you the particular manner in which it ought to have happened.

After we got a new crank-shaft and repaired damages we had a change of captains. Draper had to stay behind for the law business, and I was once more shipmate with Vyvyan. The voyage passed pleasantly and without incident. I had been warned before leaving Southampton to hold myself in readiness to transfer to a coasting steamer, but as no one gave me positive orders to go I made the complete trip, one of the most pleasurable of all, the passage home being very jolly, with nice passengers.

I was ordered out as a passenger in the *African* to serve on the coast, and was told it was a compliment to be selected for the post, but that will need another chapter.

CHAPTER VII

"One meets now and then with polished men, who know everything." — Emerson.

I regretted to leave the *Syria* chiefly because I had grown to thoroughly appreciate the character of my captain, and to enjoy the many talks we had on subjects connected with the sea and matters relating to seamen. He was an exceptional man, as his after career has proved, but he was not liked by every one, and for the matter of that, what man worth his salt ever is? When I had arrived home, Captain Ker, the superintendent, asked me why I had not stayed on the coast, to which I replied that no man bade me do so.

"Then you will go out in the *African* as a passenger," he retorted, "and relieve Mr. Owen."

That passage to the Cape was memorable to me for many things that I need not here detail. Baynton was in command and Leigh was chief officer. The third I remember was one of those charming ne'er-do-wells that one occasionally meets. His name is suppressed. He soon disappeared, but he was talented, a good sailor, a good musician and a man who was the enemy of no one but himself. I found it very nice to have plenty of leisure with an exceptionally nice crowd of passengers. Some of them are my friends now, but time has played sad havoc amongst them. One of the best was Sutton Vane, the talented dramatic writer; he and I played principal parts in a farce enacted on the passage, and as Myles na Coppylene observed, "God be with thim good old days." I make my best bow to you even now, my fair shipmates, even if I do not mention your names. Captain Baynton was kind enough to accept my help as a navigator, and as he was laid up for a great portion of the trip it was a pleasure to me to be of service to him. The officers in some cases might have resented the interference of an officer on passage, but somehow few people thought of opposing "old Ted," as he was styled behind his back. In a similar way Vyvyan was usually called "Lord George," while in after years I have been given to understand that I was commonly spoken of as "Buffalo Bill."

We arrived at Cape Town in due course and went our respective ways; mine as it turned out was to be one of the most difficult I ever traversed, for it led me to the *Basuto*, and of all the heartbreaking ships that were, she was the worst. A north-country slop-built craft, of low power, with a long poop and a short well and forecastle, she could not be kept clean with the expenditure of labour that it was practicable to devote to that purpose, for be it remembered that the diamond fields had disorganised the usual steady routine of coast work, and there was considerable difficulty in keeping a crew at all. Thus discipline could not be maintained in the same manner that was possible on the home route. I know that had it not been for the unflinching support given us by the resident magistrate at Cape Town, Mr. John Campbell, we should have had a difficulty in keeping the ships going. I gladly bear my best testimony to his just and common-sense reading of the Merchant Shipping Act, and also to the manner in which he administered it. On sailing day it was no uncommon thing to be obliged to go up town in a hansom cab, find your men half drunk, and then sit upon them in the cab until you could get them safely on board and in irons until they were sober. The *Basuto*, with Captain Draper in command and Harry Owen as chief, had been rather a warm corner, so when I relieved Owen I knew pretty well what was in store for me, and truly I was in no way disappointed. There was always trouble with some portion of the crew, and it was no uncommon matter being obliged to use more than moral persuasion to carry on the work of the ship. Owen had been in the habit of carrying a shooting-iron, and had found it useful to encourage the belief that he had been schooled as a Yankee mate, but a pistol never seemed to me to be a necessary precaution.

In connection with the employment of physical force on board ship I and others were quite recently greatly amused by the experiences of a captain of one of the Irrawaddy flotilla steamers, recounted as follows: "The best peacemaker you can have is a sandbag about a foot long and an inch thick; I and my mate and engineer have one, and we never find it beyond us to clear the deck of a crowd." I should think it would be better than a belaying-pin, which is at times an awkward thing to carry in your sea boot.

Be that as it may I found that practically everything was left in my hands on board the *Basuto*, and that suited me excellently. We spent our time between Cape Town and Zanzibar; there was no use hurrying, for the ship could only go a certain pace, and if we missed one mail we were in time for the next one, but nothing possible was spared to do our work well. We were fortunate in having as second officer a man I had the greatest respect for as a seaman, E. T. Jones, and further I found by practical experience that he was a good man in an emergency, and was to be absolutely relied upon. When in Natal we had the use of a large ship's boat belonging to the Company, rigged as a cutter. It was a sight to see Jones sail her single-handed, but then he had served his time with the Trinity House.

For some reason it had been decided that Captain Ker should leave Southampton as marine superintendent, and reside at Cape Town as manager of the Company in South Africa. When he arrived in Cape Town he found the *Basuto* after a refit, looking very spick-and-span, and I suppose conceived the idea that that was her usual condition, which was bad luck for me. There had never been any great cordiality between us and there was to be less in future, for try as I might there was always something wrong about my ship in his view, and he resented, I think, meeting officers at houses where he visited, especially as ladies do not always pay that deference to superior position to which its owner may think himself entitled. But be that as it may the fact remains that there was no love lost between us.

From time to time we carried as passengers many distinguished men, or those who were in the way of becoming so. Especially do I remember two clerical dignitaries; Bishop Colenso was one. He once confessed to me a feeling of irritation because the new Bishop of Cape Town was to be enthroned by one who was his junior in the Church of England, he himself being precluded from officiating by reason of opinions he had put forward. In due time the new bishop also travelled with us, and when we got the usual dose of bad weather in consequence he declined to turn in, saying with a merry twinkle in his eye that it would be undignified if anything happened, for a bishop to be seen without his gaiters. He is an archbishop now, but at the time I write of his hair was black, and he was not above a bout at singlestick.

Just about this time there was a good deal of national unrest, extending from Zululand to East London. It was shortly after the Langalibalele trouble, and on our way down the coast we were ordered to call at the Kowie and tow to Algoa Bay an American ship called *Tecumseh*, which had lost her rudder. Captain Ker came up to supervise the operation, and we also took on board as a passenger Mr. J. A. Froude, the historian, who was then on his way to England. He had been touring the country in order to form his own opinion on the political situation for the benefit of his friend Lord Carnarvon, and one may be permitted the remark that it was a great pity he did not take a more careful survey of the situation, for South African politics were not then to be learned in a three months' sojourn in the country, or for that matter in six either. At all events he failed to recognise the fact that the situation was summed up in lines from Alice through the Looking-Glass.

"The eldest oyster winked his eye, and shook his hoary head,
Meaning to say he did not choose to leave the oyster bed."

In my own mind I have always held Mr. Froude responsible for the Boer rising which culminated at Majuba.

Of course when it comes to doing an unusual job things cannot be expected to work quite smoothly, and they did not on this occasion. I had been on board the *Tecumseh* and rigged up a makeshift rudder with stream chain, and returned to my own ship to get the towing-gear ready for a start at daylight. In the morning, of course, I was up betimes, and had as I thought the situation to myself. There was one A.B. who was constantly giving me trouble when there was anything to do, and usually required correcting by some method before the day was out. On this particular occasion I thought I would make the correction before the day began, so as to have no further trouble, when looking round I found Mr. Froude paying me quite as much attention as I thought was necessary. He inquired whether that was my usual method of maintaining discipline, to which I replied in the affirmative, and the incident closed. We towed that ship to Algoa Bay all right, but two captains in one ship are quite unnecessary. Captain Ker, however, would interfere, and at the end of the towage drew down on himself the wrath and language of the Yankee skipper, expressed in a masterly manner, to which I listened with an unholy satisfaction.

On another occasion when he was taking a passage I remember him giving me an order to alter course without consulting Draper, that was an absolutely unwarrantable action, manager for South Africa though he was. His last exploit at sea was, however, splendid. Another manager was appointed, and he took command of one of the Company's ships that went on the rocks at Ushant one winter's night. He saved crew, passengers, mails and specie in twenty minutes, and it took a man to do that.

When we got to Cape Town there was an amusing incident. One Sunday Jones and I, with some cheery souls, went out to lunch at Coghills at Wynberg. Mr. Froude was at the table talking in loud tones about his great lady friends at home. There was also present Mr. Savage, one of our directors, whom Jones did not happen to know. In the midst of lunch Jones started to tell his friends how he had acquired some beautiful ostrich feathers from a bird he had travelled with. I could not stop him for my legs were not long enough, but I watched Savage's face until he said, interrupting dryly, "I hope those feathers were not on freight, Mr. Jones." Many at the table could see the joke and there was a peal of laughter.

I was not sorry when after about twelve months I managed to get a transfer home. I may mention here, however, the end of the *Basuto*. She had various peculiarities, one of which was a playful habit of half filling her after hold with water. Of course that never had anything to do with the tunnel or the engine-room, so said the engineers at least; I had my own opinion on the matter. Then, again, she was infested with rats, and we got into a habit of shooting at them with small revolvers in the evenings when we were in harbour. I say little of minor depravities such as the anchor always fouling the stem when we got it. Anyhow, she stayed on the coast about two years after I left her, and then came home and was sold to some Frenchmen. The rest of the tale about her is as it was told to me. The new owners did not understand all her little failings as we had done; one fellow pulled a broomstick out of a hole one morning, and that started an inrush of water which they could not cope with. I heard that when the crew left her they did not even stop the engines—but I do not vouch for the truth of this particular yarn.

I got my passage home in the *Nyanza* as supernumerary second. Warleigh was skipper, William Somerset Ward was chief and Henry Barnes was second. I forget the others. Now Ward was one of the men who had been brought in over my head when the yarn was that they wanted "more experienced men" (contrast that with the cry of to-day of too old at forty). He was one of Green's men and a very fine officer. He had brought with him many of the old Blackwall fashions, one of which was that the men of both watches should answer to their names when the watch was relieved. That was a plan that I took with me from that ship for the rest of my sea career, but it was an unpopular proceeding though most useful from a disciplinary point of view. Barnes on the other hand I had known since my first voyage to sea, when he was in the *Elphinstone*. His appearance was fiery and his character did not belie it, but he was a really good fellow at heart and I liked him. Trouble soon arose. Warleigh wrote in the night order-book that the dinner look-outs were to be kept alternately by the second, supernumerary second, and fourth officers. As a rule they were kept by the third and fourth only, so Barnes got the idea that Warleigh was unduly favouring me, although I was actually Barnes' senior in the Company. He accordingly walked into the captain's cabin the next morning and shut the door. No one ever knew exactly what transpired. Barnes was a big noisy man, and Warleigh slight and quiet. There was doubtless plain speaking, for when Barnes reappeared he went to his cabin and remained under arrest until we arrived home, when he left the service. He told me afterwards that he had told Warleigh "he could make his bally chum second mate, and perhaps that would please him"; but it always struck me that he sacrificed his prospects for absolutely no reason.

We reached Southampton with no incident calling for special note, and in due course I was sent for by the managing director, Mr. Mercer, who informed me that I had been sent home by Captain Ker as my ship was always behindhand with work, and I was constantly putting my men in prison. "But," said he in his most kindly manner, "as this is so different a report from that which you have always had I am going to send you out as chief of the *Roman*." I thanked him to the best of my ability, and was delighted with the change. My new skipper was A. W. Brooke-Smith, with whom I never had any unpleasantness, and whose friendship I value to-day. He told me confidentially that he was delighted to have me for chief; but that we should have a warm time on the coast as Ker hated me and would be sure to find fault. Before we sailed Warleigh came to see me one morning to offer a bit of advice. It was "Don't do so much yourself; make the other officers do more." Ever after I acted upon this; it did not increase my popularity with my fellows, but the counsel was good. Popularity may be paid for too dearly, and after all it is our superiors that we should try to please. Brooke-Smith was a great stickler for orders being obeyed to the letter without any consideration as to discretionary power. He also was given to making unreasonable demands upon one's power of performance. For instance, on Saturday at 9 a.m. he would give an order to send down topsail-yards, and then expect the ship to be as fit for inspection at 11 a.m. as if nothing extra had been done. Lower and upper yards were all in the day's work, but topsail-yards were an innovation, and hardly fair play for Saturday morning. However, it was done, and all went off well. When in that ship I had the good fortune to make many friends, one of whom was Herbert Rhodes (brother of the Colossus). What a splendid character that man had—a head to plan, a hand to execute and the heart of a child. I think I was the last of all his friends to see him before his untimely end.

Then again, one passage home there was Lord Rossmore and his brother the Hon. Peter Westenra. Very lively companions they were—I never met their equals in that respect. They never seemed to want to sleep, and if there was any mischief to be done there was no need to call for volunteers. They were cheery shipmates and left a pleasant remembrance behind them. Also do I well remember Captain Byng, R.N., the commander of the *Active*, Admiral Hewitt's flagship. He also was a cheery soul, and we habitually spent our evenings together. I learned from him many tricks in the trade of managing men.

I now had rather more time to attend to my personal affairs, and one important matter was to get my master's certificate. I could now ask for leave to go to town to pass, and was furnished with excellent references both from the Company and my captains. We had as marine superintendent at this time Captain Walter Dixon, who had commanded the Company's ships for years. He was a very excellent man for the post, kind, courteous and considerate. But in spite of agreeable qualities there was never any doubt as to his ability to enforce his will, and his word went a long way with the Board of Direction. In addition he was the keenest of sportsmen. He simply loved horses and sport, and rather affected a horsey style of dress. He did me many a good turn, as it will give me pleasure to relate.

Passing for master at the time I write of was no great ordeal, but it was a somewhat tricky one for this reason—the examiners in seamanship were necessarily old sailing-ship men. It may be presumed that they considered a steamship man as a sort of inferior being, or shall we say a hybrid being—at best a makeshift seaman. The fact was that many officers who had grown up in steamers had not had my experience in sail, or the opportunity of picking up the old art of sailoring, and it will be realised that there were times when they might find themselves a little uncomfortable in the examination-room. I was to see an instance of this. Naturally, I went again to John Newton for a final rub up, although I had been coaching myself for some time past, for there were always new fads to be prepared for on the part of the examiners. But I greatly fear that I was again the bad boy of the class, for Newton would at times look at me with grave eyes, and did not commit himself to any optimistic view of my chances of success.

The eventful day at length came round when our fates were to be decided. I remember that I made a mistake in my figures which I was given an opportunity to correct, for every possible bit of fair play was given. The examiner in this particular matter sat next me at a recent Trinity House luncheon, a younger brother like myself, and I reminded him of ancient times with pleasure.

But after the navigation came the seamanship and that was "quite another story." Captain Steel was my examiner and he proceeded to put me through the mill in a most thorough manner. At last he got on the topic of handling a sailing-ship under short canvas in heavy weather. He proceeded on a system which supposed various changes of wind, and finally asked me what I would do under certain conditions. I was nonplussed. Then he brought in Captain Dommett who was engaged in the next room examining a chief officer from the Royal Mail and told him where I was puzzled. Finally he left me with a diagram to study while they both went into the next room to put the same question to the West India Mail man. Suddenly the right answer came to me. It was only catchy in a room, it would have been palpable at sea in practice, and when Captain Steel returned I merely told him that the answer was "Wear ship." That was the conclusion of the examination, and I was complimented upon having done well, but the man in the next room was not so fortunate. To pluck a chief officer of tried ability in a first-class line is a serious matter, and rightly before doing so the examiner took a second opinion. The unfortunate officer in this case had got through his figures without a mistake, and far better than I had, but for want of sailing-ship experience he was sent back to sea in a steamer "to gain experience" to answer such a question as had nearly done for me. That was one of the bright days of my life, for I thought the ball was at my feet as I sped to the telegraph office to send a wire to Captain Dixon, who took considerable interest in the careers of his officers. He used to consider that he could put his hand on men suitable to perform any service, and was proud of it. After that I went to John Newton, where there was a gathering of plucked ones. Newton was surprised at my success and asked me if I was a Freemason, to which I replied in the negative, for the absurd belief was entertained that my passing was due to the correctness of that surmise. I wished him a cordial good-bye with many thanks for the trouble he had taken over me.

About this time I received my commission as a sub-lieutenant in the Royal Naval Reserve, and to this day I am uncertain whether it was a good day's work or a bad one when I did so. I also got married.

The command of the *Roman* was now changed to Captain S. R. P. Caines, a man of considerable character, but of no great discretion. He was probably his own greatest enemy, for as a shipmate I found him all that could be desired. He did not care much to associate with passengers, except at meal times, and usually spent his evening in my cabin, or rather I should say came and smoked for two hours when I came off watch. Needless to say that when skipper and chief were on these terms the work of the ship went on well, and we rather fancied ourselves in the old *Roman* and thought we could show other ships how to do things properly.

We were nearly always lucky in our crews, for the men got to know what was expected of them, and I know that I egged the skipper on to many an innovation. For instance, one day in Algoa Bay I was curious to see how long it would take to get all boats out to abandon ship. This we did suddenly one day, with the result that including fire drill and rehoisting all boats, forty minutes was the time taken. I also learned there to pay attention to boats. One time, leaving Southampton, a fireman (drunk) got on the rail, and saying that he was going back to his wife, jumped overboard in the Needles passage. The second officer (Pybus), the third, two quarter-masters and myself, jumped into the boat fitted with Clifford's gear, dropped her into the water, picked up our man, and were hoisted up and proceeding in eight minutes; that was pretty smart work, but I had personally seen that boat was in order half-an-hour previously. I fear that Clifford's patent is no longer as popular as it was. True that it is a little expensive to keep up, and requires care if used with a heavy boat, but with it a boat may be dropped in the water with perfect safety, no matter what the speed of the vessel may be, and I know that I stuck to it for the time I was at sea. Then again, it was our custom habitually to strip the ship as much as possible when steaming against the S.E. trade. I was anxious to find out what difference it would make if in addition to sending down yards, we housed our topmasts. When this came to be done, however, I found out what I had let myself in for. It was a heavy job to carry out at sea, but as it made the difference of a quarter of a knot in speed, I had to do it each voyage. On the last occasion we did the job between 7 and 9 a.m. and had a day's work afterwards, but getting the topmasts up again was at times a ticklish operation. However, we never killed any one.

There is an incident that I may mention when on one occasion most of the crew got drunk and out of hand at sea. It was one Saturday night and a beautiful moonlight one at that. Where the men got the drink from we never knew, but there was violence and a free fight more or less before getting some of them in irons and tied up to the mainboom for security until they were sober. We had a young parson on board, the Rev. R. H. Fair, a Cape boy, who had been a Cambridge athlete, and is now rector of West Meon. His distress was great at having no legitimate excuse for taking part in the scrum, but he had a share in it after all. While it was at its height I was forced backward over a door-sill, and had it not been for Fair's action in pulling off my assailant I should have had the worst of it. It all ended without serious consequences and the men were heartily ashamed of themselves next morning. We punished some of them when we got to Southampton. About this time, August 1877, I took long leave, and left the old ship with regret. I wanted to put in some Naval Reserve drill and to the best of my recollection there was then no drill ship at Southampton. Anyhow, I had to stay in London in order to drill on board H.M.S. *President*, and of it I will only say here that while the instructors were possibly the best that could be found in the navy and the teaching of the first order, there seemed always to be an under-current of indifference so far as the officers were concerned. I was anxious to learn, and did not get nearly enough to satisfy me. I got on my certificate "has been energetic and very attentive," but had acquired a taste for the Queen's service, which very often caused me to pay less attention than I might have done to things more intimately connected with money-getting.

Suddenly I received instruction to join the *Danube*, and went to Southampton once more, where I found my old skipper Draper in command and the ship taken up for troops. To the best of my belief it was the headquarters of the 32nd and they were going to Queenstown, South Africa. Trooping is an experience that improves on acquaintance, but one was apt in those days to think that the embarkation officials were unduly fussy. In reality they were nothing of the sort, for to keep troops healthy too great care cannot be exercised. The naval captain who was inspecting told me that as he knew boats were a hobby of mine, he intended to leave that matter to me.

I think the officer in command of the troops, Major Rogers, V.C., was an unmarried man, for he was grimly satirical on embarkation day on the subject of officers looking after their wives' band-boxes instead of seeing to their men. He and I became on very good terms. In point of fact they were all a most agreeable lot, if I except two junior officers whom I could not get on with at all. The ladies were charming, but it was a little amusing at times to hear them expressing their candid opinions of some of their colleagues. There was also as a passenger going to Natal, Major Mitchell, afterwards Sir Charles Mitchell, K.C.M.G., a very striking personality. I think he had been in the Marines. He made my acquaintance by approving of the manner in which the decks were cleaned in the morning. He used the expression that "they were like a hound's tooth," and as that smacked greatly of salt water, we took to one another and formed a friendship that lasted longer than differences of opinions. He had a most wonderful memory. I remember his sitting on the quarterdeck with a crowd of people (mostly ladies) round him, and reciting without a note the "Lay of the last Minstrel," and doing it in such a manner as to hold his audience spellbound. I often met him, after the voyage was over, in various parts of the world. He showed ever the same courteous cheery personality so valuable to a public man.

There was nothing of exciting interest on the passage; things went smoothly, but the following incident deserves to be told. The officer commanding the troops visited the troops' quarters every morning at eleven with his officers and me in attendance. There were sentries posted in different parts of the ship, and one was stationed by the principal hatchway. Some point was raised as we were going below, and the O.C. turned to the sentry and said, "Go and find Sergeant So-and-So." The man, a youngster, flushed very red and said, "I must not leave my post, sir." The O.C. turned red too and said, "But I tell you to go," and again received the same reply. By this time the O.C. had got his breath, some one else was sent, and the sentry was told that he had done quite right. I observed to the O.C. when the inspection was over that I fancied that chap would soon get promotion and I found that the O.C. shared my view. It was an interesting case to me, for I wondered in the circumstances whether a sailor sentry would have hesitated to obey an immediate order from his C.O.

One other story of an entirely different nature. Fatigue parties were at times told off to clean paintwork about the decks, and they were usually in the care of an able seaman who put them in the way of doing it properly. One afternoon I was out of sight but within earshot of a party working with a seaman named McRae, a man I could trust to do anything, but an awfully wild scoundrel if he got out of hand. Said one of the young Tommies, "What would you do if you hadn't got us to clean the ship for you?" Said McRae,

"If it was not for the likes of you carrion there'd be no dirt to clean." I retired to my cabin for a big laugh over that. I think we landed the regiment at East London, using cheese baskets to put the men into the lighters, and in due course we started homewards, but there was an incident in Algoa Bay that I should like to tell the truth about at last. At this time there was a good deal of rivalry between some of the ships, as to which had made the fastest passage, and some brilliant genius conceived the idea of making the image of a brass cock with his wings extended in the act of crowing. This was mounted on the jackstaff of the commodore's ship the *German*, but many of us thought that she did not deserve the trophy, for even the old *Roman*, which was then in port, had made a wonderful run after a smart chief engineer had altered the lead of his slide valves. Be that as it may, it would be good business to score a point off the chief of the *German*, if we could manage to do so. There was one officer in the *Danube* who was born for mischief, his name was Samuel Pechell. Afterwards he came into a baronetcy and soon died. But at the time I write of he was third or fourth officer. There were many ships in the Bay, some belonging to the Currie fleet, so that suspicion would be divided as to the perpetrators of the robbery, especially as it was said that some people from the *Conway Castle* had made a previous attempt at Cape Town. It was a bright moonlight night, shortly after 3 a.m., when Sammy Pechell and McRae having covered our dingy with white sheets, started to paddle ahead of the *American*, and drop down to her bows hanging on by the cable. Like a monkey McRae was up the cable, and in less time than it takes me to write these lines was down again with the coveted bird. I had grave suspicions that the *Melrose*, one of the Currie coasters just coming in, had seen the job, but I suppose that a boat under the bow of an opposition ship did not interest them. There was a watch too in the *German*, for "seven bells" were struck just after the cock disappeared. We had intended to put it up on the *Roman*, but I vetoed anything further that night. The bird was afterwards packed in a game hamper and set to Wait, the chief officer, in Southampton. Next morning there was a fine hubbub all round the fleet; there may have been suspicions but no certainty, for many thought it had been done by some of the Currie men. In due course I told my skipper, who dwelt on the enormity of stealing the commodore's bird and told me I ought to be sacked for encouraging such a thing. Dear old Captain Coxwell was the commodore, and his remarks to me the next time we met were picturesque, but never shall I forget distinctly seeing McRae cross himself before he shinned up that cable. All the people in the *German* were quite mad over the episode, and I am afraid that Pechell had a bad time of it afterwards when he had to sail with McLean Wait, who I fancy had got to the truth of the business.

There is just one remark I would make in passing, and that is on the liability to be caught at misdoing at any time. On the passage home entering the Channel, we were put into double watches of six hours each—and six hours is a long watch in cold weather, as it then was; Pechell was my junior, and was supposed to supervise the forecastle look-out, but really was a good deal on the bridge with me. I had the first watch, which ended at 2 a.m., and about one o'clock I said to Pechell, "Go down to my cabin, have a tot yourself, and bring me up a glass of hot grog, as soon as you can." He went, and shortly afterwards the skipper came on the bridge and took possession of the weather corner under the screen. I heard my door open and up came Sam. Not seeing the skipper in the dark, he observed audibly, "There you are, sir, I made it stiff!" The reek of whisky on the night air was palpable as I drank it, and Draper made sarcastic comments. I must, however, do him the justice to say that he seldom troubled me, and I am certain would sooner have brought me refreshment himself rather than that I should put foot off the bridge.

When we got to Southampton that time it was on a Sunday, and my only regret was that Captain Dixon was not down to see the ship. She was in such order that she satisfied even me, and Draper, a very particular and natty man, could not offer even a suggestion, for her appearance represented the culmination of all the years I had served as chief in learning how to put and keep a ship in proper order. But I was growing dissatisfied, there were men being placed in command who were new comers compared with me, and as there was an old saying, "that modesty was a sweet thing in a woman but not worth a rap in a man," I put such remnants as I had in my pocket and laid siege to Captain Dixon. My friend, Mrs. Baynton, had also been having a few simple words on my account with more than one of the directors, one of whom (Mr. Savage) had said to me some little time previously, "that I was all right, but that they thought I hardly carried ballast enough." To this I retorted that I had a wife and surely that was enough to give one stability. Captain Dixon was most kind. I pointed out that I was fit for command and that I hoped he would help me, to which he replied that he would be pleased to make me Captain Crutchley, but that unfortunately he could not make ships. He would, however, keep me at home, so that I might be on the spot if a vacancy occurred. I do not remember who relieved me, but I left the *Danube* to make myself generally useful in various companies' ships in port. At that time there were few men who considered it necessary to pass the Board of Trade examination in steam, but as I could make the time fit in I did so, and if such a certificate is useful to a master on even one occasion it is well worth the trouble of obtaining. It helped me materially on one occasion. There were two engineer examiners, and the experience was a new one for them, but they took no unfair advantage of their superior knowledge, and I had the satisfaction of seeing my certificate endorsed with the words "Passed in Steam." My practical examination took place in the engine-room of the *Asiatic*, and curiously enough, two days afterwards I was ordered to act for her captain in taking the ship down the river. At this time there was another chief officer also on shore, A. McLean Wait, who had been chief of the *German*. I did not dream that other people might be pulling strings that might hamper me, but there was more going on than I was aware of. I should state that although Wait was actually my junior in the Company he had held a good command previous to joining it, and it was generally considered that he was marked for early promotion. He and I were good friends, and I had assisted him at a function in the *German* when she was a new ship. He was a man of considerable attainments, but somehow there was a something in his manner which did not attract people; he had lots of good friends, however, and nature had been kind to him so far as personal appearance was concerned.

One morning I had taken some specie that had been landed from one of our ships to the Bank of England, and having done so went to report the fact to the Company's office in Leadenhall Street. When leaving I met Wait going in; I had a chat with him afterwards, going to spend an hour at the Aquarium before returning to Southampton. There were two things with which I was not acquainted. One was that there was a Board Meeting that day, the other that the command of the *American* was vacant and that Wait had been sent for with a view to giving it to him. He was called before the Board, and there some comment was made as to his having lost a ship; this appeared to go against him, for the word came out to ask for me. I was not to be found, and Wait was appointed, for the ship was shortly to sail. This shows on what trifles things hang, for the few weeks seniority he got by this gave him a series of chances which might well have formed part of my life's story. It kept him in command when the Company's fleet was reduced, and afterwards permitted him to become marine superintendent, and subsequently the Company's agent in New York. We always maintained a cordial if casual correspondence.

There were a number of new ships being built for the Company's service, and it was now the turn of the *Pretoria* to make her appearance. Great things were expected of her, and when the *African* came home George Larmer was taken from her and given command of the new vessel. This made another vacancy, and it was then my turn to be summoned to the directors. Sir Benjamin Phillips was chairman, and the chair on his right hand was always reserved for the master under *dissection*. On this occasion the experience was a pleasing one, for in his most courtly manner he observed, "Captain Crutchley, if you will always consider that the Company's honour, so far as the *African* is concerned, is entrusted to your keeping, you will please and satisfy us: now, will you give us the pleasure of your company to lunch?"

It is strange, but though the remembrance of that day is very dim, I always recollect those words and the grave courtesy with which they were spoken. The directors were naturally men of varying temperaments. There had formerly been a director I never met, whom I will designate as H, whose business it was to rebuke a master whenever such a proceeding in the opinion of the Board became necessary. It was stated that he had a great talent for language, on which point I ought to tell a story. He was a merchant, and had in his business a nephew who was known as Mr. John (afterwards a cordial friend of mine) who, on some provocation, had told one of the clerks that he was a damn fool. The clerk complained to H, who looking him full in the face said, in his broad Scotch accent: "Whether Mr. John was right or wrong to *call* you a fool, I'll no tak' upon mysel' to determine, but ye *are* a damn fool—ye are—ye are—ye are." And the man fled.

When I come to think it over, that Board of Directors was good for a straightforward conservative policy, but as events proved was not well fitted to deal with the more exacting conditions entailed by the competition of modern shipowning. In fact it was not up to date, and it never took to itself the leaven that would enable it to cope with the situation created by the opposition of the Castle Company. It was the greatest of all pities when the flag of the Union Company was merged into that of the Castle Line. It was doubtless a proud day for Sir Donald Currie, but I shall always maintain it as discreditable to those who permitted the transfer, and particularly so to the chief actor in the surrender. The transfer did not take place during my term of service in the Company, but it was galling even to an old employé to see the armour of Achilles appropriated by a hated Trojan.

I had previously made a passage in the *African*, so that my first command was in no way a stranger to me. She was a pretty little ship of rather more than 2000 tons gross, with a fine long poop and comfortable accommodation for passengers. Her speed under steam alone was something over ten knots, but with the help of canvas and a strong fair wind she could touch 300 miles a day. That was not often, however. My cabin was in the poop right forward on the starboard side, and it had the disadvantage that, except in very fine weather, one could not sit there with the saloon door open. But to overcome this there were times when I had a canvas screen nailed up to overcome the trouble, for it was not necessary to stay on the bridge always. The worst thing about the ship was the compass. The standard was a large spirit compass that was always giving trouble, and the steering compass on the bridge was close to a mass of iron tanks, stanchions and disturbing matter generally, so that it was almost impossible to compensate for local disturbance. In every other way the ship was perfectly found, but this little matter of a proper compass, on which so much depended, was one that was driven to the background and slighted by every one. It was no part of my business either as a junior to find fault. I had to take that which had satisfied my predecessors, and as it happened she had been commanded by Captain Dixon before he was made superintendent, as well as Captain Baynton, the commodore. My policy was to lie low and get what I could as time went on. There was a story told of a certain captain, a very tall man, who mentioned to the deputy superintendent that his berth was not long enough for him to sleep in. This, it is said, was reported to Mr. Mercer, who replied in his usually dry manner, "If the man cannot fit into the berth, we must find one that can; fortunately the world is wide and the field is large." The last half of the answer was often hinted at if inconvenient requests were made.

There were a very nice set of officers in the ship; but the chief was a senior man, and it is a little awkward to come the skipper over one of your colleagues. He was a Cape man named Chiappini, and was afterwards killed by an accidental fall when serving in the *Arab*. The third was a youngster named East, the son of Quartermain East of Tichborne claimant fame. First and last he sailed with me for many years, and there was a great friendship between us. The second, Walter Foster, was also a nice fellow, but very delicate, though plucky to the backbone. The engineers also were a good set. The chief, Ernest Gearing, is now I believe one of the leading lights in the engineering world, and it was easy to discover even then that his acquirements were of no common order. Lastly let me mention Henry Black, the second engineer. There was no great amount of sympathy between us at any time, but he sailed with me as chief engineer during the greater part of my sea career.

I have gone into this detail with a view to showing the sort of men the Company's ships were manned with. Sailing day came at last; there were not many passengers, but one of our directors came down to see the ship off, bringing with him one of his very charming daughters, who was kind enough to wish me luck and a successful command. I took it as a good omen, and if I do not mention her name, it is in no sense that I have forgotten it, or the graceful kindness shown me on more than one occasion. We arrived at Plymouth in due course, and there I learned to my great satisfaction that my friend Harry Escombe had decided at the last minute to take a passage with me. He arrived on board in due course, and I started on a new experience—that of being my own master. This particular voyage we were on was a novelty also, for the people at Algoa Bay had been complaining they did not get their goods as quickly in proportion as the Cape Town people. We were therefore to call at St. Vincent to pick up the latest cable news and then to go to Algoa Bay direct, passing by Cape Town. We were also to go to Natal.

I rather think that some small smattering of commercial education should be imparted to holders of certificates, and one thing that should certainly be driven into their heads is that to send a letter on business without keeping a copy is little short of crime. I did not learn that lesson for a long time, but I wish now I had copies of the letters in which I gave the various incidents of the voyages to my chiefs at home. Captain Dixon had asked me to write to him fully, which I always did, even going so far as to relate gossip, but the letters to the secretary were necessarily of a more reserved order. For rightly or wrongly a secretary is usually considered by the staff afloat as the enemy of all mankind. It is natural enough, for as a rule the wiggings come through him, and he on his part gradually acquires the idea that he is quite competent to instruct a master upon any subject—that he is in short a vicarious person inheriting the combined wisdom of the board. This pretension is not in every case acknowledged. I regret to state that I rather carried with me the impression that masters had natural enemies, but when I consider the number of years I lived without keeping any journal, or record of events, I am not prepared to argue that they do not indirectly invite trouble. I know that the search necessary to make dates fit in for this narrative has been by no means inconsiderable, and the good offices of Admiral Inglefield of Lloyd's has helped me to overcome past omissions. He caused a record of my commands to be made, thus helping me materially to put facts in the order in which they occurred.

It would not have been possible to get a finer start than we had on that voyage, with a beautiful fine N.E. wind that took us well down to St. Vincent. I find that we were running close upon 300 miles for several days, and then came the job of taking the ship into port on a fair moonlight night, not by any means a difficult matter when you are used to it, but if you permit it to get upon your imagination, curious results are at times obtained. I had made up my mind from past experiences that show irresolution on the bridge I would not! I had seen so many skippers wandering into an anchorage, and driving every one mad in the course of getting a berth, that I was determined not to lay myself open to such a reproach. I once sailed with a man who if he had the whole anchorage to choose from would go and give a solitary vessel a foul berth, simply because he did not know where he wanted to go. I saw him do it once in Natal Roads. Again, constantly stopping or easing the engines by guesswork ought to be avoided when coming to an anchorage, but I am talking of long ago, and I dare say the men of today know exactly when to ease their engines so as not to lose time.

On this particular occasion I thought I knew where I wanted to go, and was going there in a hurry. I anchored rather sooner than I had meant to do, but it was all right, and Escombe came to congratulate me on the way I had brought the ship in. I had, however, already discovered that there was a much better berth than the one I was in, and had given orders to get the anchor and shift at once, which I did, carefully keeping my reasons to myself for so doing. I may remark that in most places steamers anchor closer inshore than sailing ships. In St. Vincent they reverse this order of things.

We coaled up and left in due course. There were not many saloon passengers, but we were a very cheery party. It was distinctly the commencement of a liberal education to have the intimate acquaintance of a man like Escombe, who in addition to great natural gifts had acquired an omniverous appetite for knowledge. Especially keen was he upon astronomy, and his store of information was always open to draw upon. Even in the intricacies of a seaman's calling he was well versed, for his practice at the bar had put many strange cases before him to unravel.

There was not much else that called for comment before we reached Algoa Bay. Here Escombe transhipped to a coasting steamer in order to reach Natal sooner than we should, for we had to discharge a portion of our cargo. He did so against my advice, and as he did not save the time he anticipated, forfeited a bet to me of the best pair of binocular glasses to be got at Baker's of Holborn. They lasted me for my time at sea, and I never saw a better pair. In Algoa Bay the *Dunrobin Castle* was at anchor. She was commanded by Alec Winchester, who was a splendid seaman and a marvel at handling his ship. My old friend, Barnes, was also chief officer there, for Mr. Currie, as he then was, was always pleased to snap up any good officer who was leaving our service. By this time there was a little better feeling between the two services, and I know that Alec Winchester put me up to many things concerning a ship which few learn save by actual experience, and I am glad to acknowledge the obligation. We went on to Natal, finished our discharge and loading, and in due course arrived at Table Bay on the homeward trip one Sunday afternoon.

As it was getting dusk and there was more than a bit of a south-easter blowing, I should like to pass over this incident, but cannot in fairness to the truth of this story.

The entrance to Cape Town dock in those days bore a resemblance to a donkey's hind leg, inasmuch, as there was a crook in it. The inside of this crook was formed by the end of a stone wall and a small jetty, and it was arranged that we were to stay in the lock or entrance until we sailed. I started to get in, but as the two insides of the crook were to leeward of me, I found myself hitting the end of the stone pier rather hard while the stern of the ship rested gracefully on the jetty. The *African*, I thank Providence for it, had a clipper bow. "Go forward," said I to the third officer, "and see how much of her is smashed up." He returned with the information that the ship was intact and uninjured. She had only run up the stone wall a little, and displaced a big stone or two. By this time we had got out hawsers and warped her to windward (where we remained until sailing day), and an hour afterwards were sitting at dinner. I thought many kind things concerning Providence, but even then I fear I did not realise to the full what my obligations were.

Sailing day came, still blowing hard from S.E., and I had to back the ship out stern first. I did not look forward with any degree of confidence to the job, but kept a face of brass to all and sundry. Warleigh, who was there in dock, came and chatted just before I started, and pointed out with perfect accuracy just exactly how the ship would behave under stern way. It was very good of him and I told him so. We got out with no accident; in fact, I was satisfied, and I have frequently noticed that if I have that feeling, most people concerned share it with me.

An hour after the time fixed for our departure the *Warwick Castle*, Mr. Currie's newest and fastest ship, was to leave. She was commanded by Captain Webster, who I was told had promised to make an exhibition of my ship. As soon as I was clear of the breakwater I got the canvas on and I rather fancy my chief engineer had got the needle too, for although we saw the *Warwick* come out of the Bay, gain on us she could not, and we saw her astern for a day or more, when we lost sight of her. The reason, of course, was that we had a spanking trade wind, and our canvas helped us. We carried a fair wind to Cape Verde and then I knew that our advantage was over. When we arrived at Madeira, the other ship had left some hours, but we were told that Captain Webster had spent some time in the stokehole of the *Warwick*, and was furious at his inability to pass us.

As showing the relative merits of Southampton and London as ports for southern-going steamers, let me mention that my ship was docked and discharging, and I had been to London and seen my directors before the *Warwick Castle* had passed Gravesend. There was nothing of special note that happened between Madeira and Plymouth, but I left the latter port at five on a December afternoon with a fog coming on. I kept her going, and was justified in doing so by the fact that I hit nothing. At last, getting into I think it was nine fathoms of water, I turned her round due west and saw the Needles light red on my starboard beam. I need say no more than that Providence perhaps showed partiality even to the end on my first voyage.

I should say that when I met my directors Mr. Mercer was kind enough to say that I had made a remarkable passage to Madeira.

CHAPTER VIII

"'Tis a pity ... that truth, Brother Toby, should shut herself
up in such impregnable fastnesses." —Sterne.

It was a very comfortable feeling, to find myself one of the circle that I
had looked up to and envied so long, but it did not appear to me that I was
in any way a different person to that which I had ever been. I mean that I
experienced none of that feeling of proud omnipotence which I had always
imagined to be part and parcel of a master. Perhaps this was partly due to
the fact that my old crony Harry Owen was in port, preparatory to sailing
for Natal in command of a tug built for the Company's service. Certainly no
one could be serious for long in his company.

The *Union*, as she was called, was a peculiar craft, for she had a propeller
at each end, with a shaft extending from one end to the other, the object
being to prevent racing on the short seas of Natal bar by always having one
propeller in the water. Bernard Copp, now Captain Copp of Southampton,
and one of the last of the old crowd, was chief officer, and I think that
the events of that passage might have been chronicled with advantage as
they were related to me, in language of extreme raciness. I passed her off
Agullas on the next voyage, and she arrived at Natal in safety after many
vicissitudes.

It was no part of my business to grumble, but I felt inclined to when I
learned that we were to have ten days at home and sail on Christmas Day of
all days. It was an outrage, for there was no necessity for it; it was just one
of those sardonic jokes that directors collectively at times take a delight in.
We were to carry no passengers, but were to make a somewhat longer trip
than usual, for after going up to and down from Natal, we were to make a
trip to Zanzibar before returning home, in fact it was to be a five months'
voyage. Never shall I forget that Christmas morning. We were to leave at
noon, and every one seemed anxious to kick us out and go back to their own
firesides, also I had more than an idea that several of the crew had not got
quite over Christmas Eve. I had a boatswain named Barrett, a good man,
but one who wanted some handling. We got outside the Needles and found
a stiff breeze blowing, with too much wind to carry whole trysails, so the
job was to put in a reef and set them. By this time most of the crew were

asleep, and my chief officer was hardly the man physically to get a move on them, so I proceeded in the first place to the boatswain's cabin. It was touch-and-go how it went, but Barrett was sober enough to retain a pride in his manhood, and after that there was no more trouble. He was a man of powerful physique, so the crew appeared in a twinkling, like bees from a disturbed hive, and the work was soon done. The doctor, who was named Ernest Walters and now practises in Essex, proved himself a good useful man when occasion arose, even outside his own work.

I had been trying to see what I could do to improve the compasses in dock, with so unsatisfactory a result that I did not feel sure whether I should make the Start or Ushant going down Channel, for we were not to call at Plymouth that trip. I had to replace a much-loathed compensation at the first opportunity, but we did fairly well on the whole, coming in for a fair dusting, however, as we got off Finisterre. About this time there were two schools of thought as to the best way to handle a steamer in bad weather. One party maintained that head on to the sea was the correct plan, the other people varied in detail but agreed in denouncing the end-on principle. On this occasion I tried the end-on plan, but came to the conclusion, which I have since retained, that almost any position is better in really bad weather; of course the size of the vessel has a great deal to do with it.

To the best of my belief we got to Cape Town and docked on the morning of January 22, 1879, the day on which the battle of Insandlwana was fought. We had a good bit of cargo to land, and there was no great hurry. That evening I was in town, gossiping at the club or something of the sort about 11 p.m., when a rumour was whispered of a great British defeat. All the Company's shore officials were in the country or in bed, and it occurred to me that there were troops in Cape Town who would have to be moved up to Natal, also that I was the man to do it in a hurry. I made at once for the office of the *Cape Argus* and, by dint of an exercise of modesty, got hold of the Editor. I wish I could remember his name. He was not popular, but on this occasion showed me every courtesy. Without giving particulars, he told me a disaster had happened, and that reinforcements were urgently wanted at the Front. That was enough for my purpose. I made straight for Government House, from there to the Castle, and then went down to the ship, knowing that I had secured the job to take what troops there were to Natal. This was all the more satisfactory because there were three or four Currie ships in the dock that could have sailed at short notice, but I doubt if they could have gone as fast as we did. When daylight came in I set every one to work to get the cargo out of the 'tween decks to make room for the troops, and must say my fellows worked like good ones. That afternoon I went up to see Sir Gordon Sprigg, who was then Premier, and promised that

I would not anchor between the Cape and Natal. By the courtesy of Captain A. D. W. Browne, Captain and Adjutant of 2nd Battalion, The King's Own Regiment, I am able to quote from the regimental records.

"The detachment at Capetown (*i. e.* C, G, and half E companies, with Major Elliott, Captains Knox and Leggett, and Lieutenants Bonomi and Ridley) was brought at a few hours' notice to Maritzburg, sailing in the s.s. *African* on January 23, and landing at Durban on 26th." I take leave, however, to doubt the absolute accuracy of this record for the following reason. The disaster happened on the 22nd. Certainly one day elapsed, for it was in the afternoon of the 23rd that I saw Sir Gordon Sprigg, and I have a distinct recollection of going out of dock in a thick fog before breakfast, and the caution of the port captain that there was a big sailing ship at anchor very near the dock entrance. This discrepancy, however, is of no great importance. There was one little incident in the embarkation of the troops that took my fancy very much. Said young Bonomi, "Did you notice, major, when we left that the barracks were on fire?" as if the matter were one of the smallest importance only. If they were burning, at all events they were soon extinguished.

We left Cape Town docks in a thick fog, which, however, cleared when we got to the entrance of the Bay, and we made the best of our way round the coast. We had to call in at Algoa Bay, but I did not anchor, as I had to do (though for a few minutes only) at East London, and on the evening of the 26th we were all very thankful to make the Bluff light at Natal where we anchored about 8 p.m. I should explain that by common report it was one of the threats of Cetewayo that one night he would come in and put out the big candle on the Bluff, meaning the lighthouse, so that when we saw the light it gave us relief, for we knew at all events that the worst had not happened. It is an easy matter to think it over quietly now, but at the time there was a great deal of uncertainty as to what the Zulu power was really capable of, and on the previous voyage I had heard Judge Lushington Phillips, who knew the country thoroughly, make the remark that if we tackled the Zulus we should have many empty saddles before the affair was finished, which unfortunately was a true forecast.

Captain Baynton was acting now as the Company's manager in Natal. He came off at the earliest moment and disembarked the troops; he also gave me instruction to land one of the *African*'s twelve pounder guns, with all its necessary equipment, for the defence of the Pynetown laager. This was done, and the gun was duly mounted, though never used.

There is no doubt that at that time Durban was very uncertain as to what would happen. A decision had been come to that if the worst came to the worst they would all have to take to the ships, and consequently great wooden barricades had been hastily run up across the Point to assist in resisting any victorious Impi that might be out on that particular piece of business. Very many of the stoutly built houses in Durban were loop-holed with sandbags, and the entire male population was being organised for the best resistance possible. On the first evening I landed I went into some big hall, I forget which it was, and saw the inspector of police, Alexander, putting the townsmen through their drill with old Snider rifles. There never was a more attentive class. So far as my remembrance serves me, there was not at this time any naval officer to superintend at the Point; all that sort of thing came in the course of the next month or so.

But although Rorke's Drift had been fought and the Zulu rush stayed, the ordinary trade had to be carried on, and I was soon dispatched down the coast again. It is wonderful in these cases of emergency what can be effected by the display of pluck and experience. In all the excitement which prevailed, Baynton was unmoved, save with some little scorn, perhaps, for those who took too seriously the normal reverses of war. The 24th regiment, which was cut up at Isandlwana, was a great favourite with every one, and I had known many of the officers intimately, and enjoyed the hospitality of their mess. To this day Pat Daley's picture hangs in my bedroom as a memento of one of the cherished friendships of early days, for he was of the best of them, but old Ted was sternly practical, and retailed for the benefit of the uninitiated the lessons he had learned in the Crimean War. As it happened, on the previous voyage home I had with me, as passengers, wives and children of officers who were killed, and the disaster came to me with a great sense of personal loss.

It was found by experience that the Zanzibar mail work could be better done by larger vessels than those we had on the coast, and the *African* was to be the first of our intermediates to make the trip. One of our captains, H. De La Cour Travers, had been on shore on the East Coast for some little time on Company's business, and he came up the coast with me. Nothing of importance occurred, but our stay at Zanzibar was a very pleasant one. Leaving that port there were two passengers of interest. One was Archibald Forbes, the other Lord William Beresford. Of the great war correspondent there is little that is fresh to be said, but the following anecdote may be permissible: I did not like card-playing in the saloon on Sundays, and said so, but when I was in my cabin dozing after dinner with one eye open, some of the others came to Forbes, asking him to play and to disregard me. "No," said Forbes, "the skipper isn't a bad chap, and he doesn't like it, so there will be no play," and there was not. This was the more noticeable, for I had had to address a few unpleasant remarks to him on a certain subject. With regard to Lord William it was another matter. We most of us have an idea of the energies of the Beresford family, but here was the quintessence of it. I first met him jumping down the steps of De Sousa's shop, just as a child would do, both feet together. We were soon on very good terms, and I owe to him my introduction to Gordon's poems and some other things of a like nature. He was full of romance, and in order to get a look in at the Zulu War was taking letters from Lord Lytton, the Governor-General of India, whose A.D.C. he had been. I never saw him again after I said goodbye in Durban Club, with the words "Luck and a V.C." He got both.

Natal Roads was a different place in April to what it had been in January or even March. There was a great collection of steamships there, and the entire harbour was very busy. We skippers found it a little awkward to get on shore and come off again, for the Company's tug was almost the only reliable conveyance, and she could not spare individual attention to our ship only. Eventually the Curries got a tug of their own, and that made matters better. The *African* was now bound home, and things were working very smoothly. Sailing from Cape Town, however, we stayed in the Bay for some hours to pick up some celebrities who wished to sail with us. Amongst these was the Rev. Charles Clarke, the celebrated elocutionist. We became great friends, and I enjoyed his society very much. The saloon was full of passengers, and I well remember the events of that sailing day. I had to deal with peppery men standing up for their rights on the one hand, and the supplications of beauty in distress on the other, whilst looking on with calm serenity were the wonderful eyes that years afterwards were to be my guiding stars. I had to exercise considerable diplomacy to arrange matters, but eventually it was done, and peace reigned for the rest of the trip. Upon that occasion we had a really live ship's mother, and any one who has travelled much knows what that means; but she was a charming, good-natured soul, and her husband was the best tempered man I think I ever met. In case they are still alive and chance upon these lines, I should like to say that the kindest remembrances of them remain, for we were shipmates afterwards on more than one occasion. There was a very fair spell at home that time, and I had my first experience of playing expert witness in a law case. It related to the loss of a vessel on Point Padrone in Algoa Bay, and the fees we received were grateful and comforting, but the masterly summing up of the case by the then Master of the Rolls, Sir George Jessel, was a thing to remember.

We were still on the direct Algoa Bay, Natal and Zanzibar route, which was out to Natal—then to the Cape—then Zanzibar and home *via* Cape Town. Calling at Delagoa Bay on the outward trip we took on board H. E. Governor Castilho, who was proceeding to Mozambique. He was a naval officer by profession (Portuguese) and had been well known for some years as Consul in Cape Town. He was a man of very marked ability, and spoke English perfectly. I once asked him how it was he spoke our tongue with such purity. His reply was "You learned to speak from your nurse. I learned my English from the *Spectator*." I quite recently had a pleasant reminder of our old friendship, for he sent me his photograph. He is now an admiral, and I have to mention him more than once in these pages. There is always a certain rivalry between seamen, and it was not wanting in this case. Mozambique is a port that in those days was not entered during the hours of darkness, as there were no leading lights to ensure safe navigation. It was dark before we made the light on St. George's Island, and Castilho observed to me that I should have to anchor outside. The spirit of opposition made me reply that I should go inside. To make a long story short I turned in just a little too soon, and the port lead gave "half four" just north of the Island light. It was coral formation and that meant very close to the bottom. Castilho, who was on the bridge said, "You are on the north side," but I knew better, ported the helm, went full speed and was into safety once more. But it was touch-and-go. However, by this time I had got confidence on the bridge, and, thank Heaven, it never left me. I left my friend the Governor at Mozambique, for he told me he was going to the Cape *en route* for home with me on the downward trip.

Need I say that there are times when masters of ships are charged with delicate commissions? The trip under notice was a case in point. The agent of a company, if properly accredited, is supposed to exercise the powers of the owners if need arises, but the master is also the owners' representative so far as his ship is concerned. The point is a nice one, as to how far it lies in the power of an agent to supersede the master's authority, but the problem is not perhaps now so difficult when there are so many facilities for cabling information. In my time, however, our masters were not taking more orders from the smaller agencies than they could comfortably manage. Our Zanzibar agent was a man rather awkward to deal with, but he always consulted me before deciding any point concerning any ship. When I left Cape Town I was charged by our chief agent, afterwards Sir T. E. Fuller, K.C.M.G. (as to whose authority there was no doubt), to confer with the Zanzibar agent as to the Company's accounts, which were apparently in a somewhat backward condition. This was rather a delicate matter, but I did my best and the affair passed off very well as I thought, and I received the assurance that the accounts should be forthcoming without more delay. H.M.S. *London* was the station ship at Zanzibar for the suppression of the slave traffic, and naturally we were on good terms with the various officers, and on the morning we were to leave I went to the Sultan's levee with them. The preceding evening we had illuminated the ship with blue lights, as it was Ramadan time, and H.H. Seyyed Burghesh was kind enough to compliment me on the appearance of the *African*, for from his watch-tower he could see all that went on. The levee was over by 10 a.m. and I went on board in order to sail at noon.

About 12.30 the agent arrived with the ship's papers, and I casually observed that I was very fond of punctuality, little dreaming of the mine I was setting fire to. Amongst other things he said something about wishing to send some particular sort of ox and a goat to Algoa Bay. I judged that he had intended to do so, and thought no more about it. We left the port and proceeded through the pass all right. But unknown to me, and while I was at the levee, the Sultan had sent on board (as it turned out eventually as a present to me in recognition of our fireworks) an ox and a goat, which I imagined when I saw them were the ox and the goat referred to by the agent to be landed in Algoa Bay. There that matter can rest for the present, but there is more to follow. At Mozambique we picked up both the old and the new Governors of Delagoa Bay and a Major Da Andrade who was to be landed at Quillimane. I think he has since played an important part in Portuguese East Africa. When we got to Quillimane there was no sign of craft coming out, so, after long waiting, we put the passengers, mails and specie on board an Arab schooner anchored outside, and left for Delagoa Bay. It may appear in these days a loose way of doing business, but there was then no help for it.

About this time Delagoa Bay was in a very poor state politically. There was government by an autocracy, not always a wise one at that, and the management of the natives was a source of considerable profit to the so-called emigration agents. In fact, affairs were in bad confusion and I scarcely think Castilho was sorry to turn his back on the scene of his late governorship, for events had been a little too hard to manage.

We got down to the shoals as it was getting dusk and a heavy sea was breaking on many of the shoal patches. There were no marks or lights, so I put her at one of the dark patches of water and she came through all right, in fact it was about as safe a plan as could have been adopted. But I will admit it was rough-and-ready navigation, adapted to the needs of the time and also the circumstances of the case. We got to Cape Town in due course on the way home. There, to my satisfaction, I met my friend, Herbert Rhodes, and got up a little luncheon party on board to celebrate the occasion. I thought I had picked my party well, for I had Castilho and Rhodes, who sat opposite one another and next to me. There was F. St. Leger, "the Saint," as the dear old editor of the *Cape Times* was commonly called, Peter van Breda, and others whose names do not now occur to me. I was greatly surprised to find that Castilho did not talk willingly to Rhodes, and that the latter had some reason for mirth which he did not impart to me at the time. When we left the table Castilho observed to me, "If I could have have laid hold of your friend in Delagoa Bay, he would have gone to jail for a long time." I was a bit astonished, but the party then broke up. Here was the reason of it all. For some years past there had been a lot of young Englishmen coming to South Africa in search of adventure, and there was very little that was too hot or too heavy for some of them to tackle in one way or the other. Some were soldiers, I remember Major Goodall and Captain Elton in the early 'seventies; then there were young men such as Dawnay, Reggie Fairlie, Campbell, and others like Rhodes. They might be hunting, or transport riding, or exploring, but one was fairly confident that no piece of mischief was passed that could by any means be negotiated. Now, some little way up the river that runs into Delagoa Bay there lived a dusky potentate whose soul thirsted for the possession of some piece of artillery, be it ever so small, and as proof of his earnestness offered in return a tumbler full of diamonds. I never heard that they were to be of any fixed value, but they ought to have been, for the Portuguese strictly forbade the importation of artillery of any sort or kind, and it would go hard with any one engaged in smuggling. I am not certain who Rhodes's companions were, but some of those I have mentioned were surely in the job. They chartered a little schooner at Natal, named the *Pelham*, then got a six-pounder old brass gun, which they smuggled on shore at Delagoa Bay one night and buried in the mangrove bushes above the town. They got their diamonds and, then, instead of getting on board their craft as sensible, or older, men would have done, they proceeded to paint Lourenço Marques red, in the brightest coloured paint procurable. There was a certain lady there with very sharp ears who, forming a conclusion, gave the game away to the authorities, and the young adventurers owed their freedom to the fact that there did not happen to be a Portuguese gunboat in Delagoa Bay, as there usually was. Doubtless, however, that absence had been taken into consideration. This was the last occasion but one on which I saw my friend Rhodes. The last was when he came off to my ship at Quillimane, a short time after this, to bring some ivory tusks for home, to get some Eno's fruit salt, and if possible a toothbrush, and chiefly to see me. It seems that he had got some great shooting concession from a chief up country and was going the next day to take possession of it. We had a long yarn about mutual friends, and that was the last of him, for some accident happened at the camp fire the next day, and he was so burned that death in agony was the end of a man who in my mind always stands as an embodiment of Charles Ravenshoe.

About this time I had as passenger the late Arthur Sketchly, of "Mrs. Brown" fame, going out to write that lady's adventures in South Africa. He was a man of great bulk and moved slowly. One night at dinner, some boys were very happy and jolly. He turned to me, saying, "Young men! Young men! they can run, jump, laugh, eat, make love, do anything. Ugh, I hate 'em!"

On my next passage from home we got a very severe dusting just south of the Bay of Biscay. I find by my notes that we lost a lifeboat, got the bridge rails smashed, man washed from the wheel, and various other damages; but these things will happen at times. We got to Algoa Bay on December 25, 1879, and there the fun began concerning the ox and goat being landed in an unauthorised manner, and I was liable for all sorts of fines. Further, I was told that the Zanzibar agent had written about a "buffalo and a calf," and these were not as described. Given these circumstances there can be lots of correspondence and, as in this case, serious results. About this time I was in severe domestic trouble, such as shakes a man to his foundations, but fortunately, perhaps, if you happen to be a cogwheel of a machine you are kept grinding and so have less time to brood over the workings of fate. I was thankful for the companionship of two of my passengers, one Herbert De La Rue, and the other Fred Struben, both of whom are now well-known men. We got to Zanzibar, and there it was reported to me that the agent had been spreading reports concerning my sobriety when I left the port on the previous voyage. I did not concern myself about this until the agent made the statement to my chief officer. It was all over the "ox and goat," for the statement was that I was told in good plain English by the agent that they were a present to me from the Sultan, but I was not in a fit state to comprehend what was said. Now on the morning in question I had been, as I have said, to the Sultan's levee and had not touched intoxicants at the time of leaving port. The inference that coffee and sherbet had influenced me was of course unbearable. However, as the statement was persisted in there was no alternative but to take the matter before the Consul. There were numbers of independent witnesses from the shore to testify on my behalf, and the agent was fined and mulcted in costs. They had a fine expeditious way of doing business in that court, for a defendant is ordered to appear "forthwith." To close the incident, there was some talk in the harbour about the "cheek" of a master putting an agent in the court, but I knew that unless I took immediate steps the lie might have lasted my lifetime. The next time I faced my board and the business came up, the chairman, Sir Benjamin Phillips, said to me, "We think that you acted quite rightly, sir," and that was all that I required. I should like also to put on record my sense of appreciation of the kindness of Sir John and Lady Kirk, Sir

John being at that time Political Agent at Zanzibar. The remainder of this voyage, so far as I was concerned, was uneventful, save that I found it quite necessary to really practise star navigation. I had then with me, as chief officer, Franz K. Thimm, an old Worcester boy, and he seconded my efforts by all the means in his power. Between us we came to the conclusion that we could be, if necessary, independent of daylight observations, and that state of things was useful on a coast where currents often run both strongly and in uncertain directions. But, apart from its usefulness during the whole of my sea career, I never lost a sense of wonderment that man could compile such a book as the Nautical Almanac. To step on deck, take three or four all-round shots at stars, and then go in and place the ship to a nicety, gives one cause for reflection and thankfulness for the work of the great discoverers who have so benefited those who came after them.

When we arrived home there were some changes made. Wait, who I have explained was my senior in command by a few days, was in port in the *American*, and there was then building on the Clyde the *Trojan*, to which it was necessary to appoint a master, to finally supervise her fitting out, and bring her round to Southampton.

One day Wait was ordered to go north—and I to the *American*, then Wait was ordered back to his old ship and I to the *Trojan*. This was rather a fortunate thing for me, as on the passage out, when on the line, the *American* broke her screw shaft and sank. Fortunately all hands were saved, to the infinite credit of her captain and officers. Captain Hepworth, R.N.R., C.B., of the meteorological office, was then chief officer, and my old friend Jones of the *Basuto* was the second. I came to hear of the accident in the following manner. I was in my lodgings one afternoon when the office messenger, Fancourt, came in with a face of great importance, "Captain Dixon's compliments, and he would like to see you at once." Those who have known Fancourt will realise the manner in which the message was delivered, for I really believe he thought he ran the Company, in the same manner that the limelight man dominates the stage. I went to the office of my chief, who paid me a great compliment or else was pulling my leg. The table was covered with charts, and he said, "The *American* has sunk in lat. — — long. — —. All hands saved in the boats. I want you to tell me where we should look to find these boats, for I conclude you know more about it than any of us." As it happened I was wrong in my estimate, for the boats were picked up by ships, but the currents, both the Guinea and Equatorial, might have played a part in their destination. Some of the passengers had a second shipwreck in the vessel that picked them up and there were fatalities. I cannot quite remember how the news first reached home, but several details stood out rather prominently. One was that the theatre on the poop, where theatricals had taken place the preceding evening, was conspicuous as she sank, and also that the second officer had been seen getting the butcher's water-tank into his lifeboat. That was typical of Jones, essentially a practical seaman. I asked him afterwards to tell me about it, and whether he had any trouble at all. "When I got down in the boat," he said, "to get things in order I chucked out several bundles of things that were no use and took up room, one of which belonged to the cook, who resented my action. I just told him that if he said more I would see that he followed his bundle, and there was no more trouble." It has always been a matter of congratulation to me that I escaped being in that business. Captain Wait was very justly highly complimented for his action, and his officers, too, received their meed of recognition.

I duly went north to take over the *Trojan*. She was a ship of something under four thousand tons, but that was big for us in these days. Taken all round she was one of the nicest little ships I ever had to do with, and curiously enough she was the *second* ship that carried an electric light. I fancy the *City of Berlin* was the first, but the *Trojan* was the second. It was merely an arc lamp in the saloon, and Captain Dixon referred to it as "one of the chairman's fads." A special cabin also was being fitted up to bring home the Empress Eugenie from the Cape. She had travelled out in the *German*. I found the two brothers Thompson, who built the ship, very agreeable, and they did their best to make my stay pleasant. Leaving Clydebank on the top of high water we actually bridged the Clyde, by accident it was true, but we might easily have been in a very awkward fix. We went into the Gareloch to adjust our compasses, and there I first had the pleasure of meeting Sir William Thompson, afterwards Lord Kelvin. Seamen should be eternally grateful to him, for in addition to a perfect compass, he gave us also a sounding machine which, if fairly used, is simply invaluable. I once asked him, some years after this, for I am pleased to say that I retained his friendship, why he could not give us a reliable log that would register the ship's speed accurately. He replied that there would be no difficulty in doing that, but as it would engender a false confidence he thought it better left alone, for surface currents that could not be accounted for would falsify the correctness of any log. We did not run our official trials in the north, but at Stokes Bay. On the way round Captain Dixon was with us, and I learned that I was to take the ship out. This, I thought at the time, was a little too good to be true, for I knew some senior would come along and hustle me out of her, and after we had our speed trial in Stokes Bay, sure enough Travers had managed to so work it that he came home in the *Asiatic* and the exchange was duly effected. My connection with the *Trojan* was not a long one, but for many reasons it was eminently pleasant. For instance, it had given me an opportunity to meet, unofficially as it were, most of my directors, and it convinced me that there were times when they could behave as human beings. I should specially like to mention the unvarying courtesy of Mr. Giles, who had succeeded to the chair. He was then member for Southampton, and his dinner-parties at Radleys, to which all our captains in port were invited, were functions much appreciated by those asked to attend.

There have been many ugly ships afloat—the *Basuto*, for instance—but for sheer naked ugliness and brutality unashamed, the *Asiatic* must be given the palm. She was built at some north-country port, and had a bow like a circular haystack. When she was light and a breeze was blowing, very nice handling was required to prevent her taking charge herself. But she had her good points: for one thing there was a decent compass, and she handled well in fine weather; for the rest she was comfortable enough at sea, but had not been well attended to as regards her upkeep, and wore a slovenly aspect altogether. This I at once set myself to remedy, and she presented a vastly different appearance the next time she came into Southampton. We of course were on the intermediate service, but when we arrived at Zanzibar for some reason there was great jollification going on, in which we participated. I gave a dinner and ball attended by every lady in the place, except two—the French consul's wife and sister. They were absent, as the captain of a French man-of-war told me in strict confidence, because the unmarried sister's dress was prettier than that of madam. The fact remains that we mustered, I think, eight ladies, and they were very well pleased. What was of more importance, however, to my mind, was a shooting match got up between the officers of the cable-laying ship, H.M.S. *London*, and ourselves. The *London* found the rifles and the ammunition, and P. G. VanderByl, one of the lieutenants, was in charge of the *London* team. I had known his people at the Cape for years past, and was afterwards shipmates with him in the old *Devastation*. We sailed up the harbour in one of the *London's* sailing cutters; they had several, and very fancifully named they were—after the names then in vogue on the front pages of waltz music. This one was called *Olga*, and she was navigated and conned by VanderByl as if she had been a battleship. It is, perhaps, needless to say that we were fairly well provided also for a picnic. I had in my team a great big hulking quartermaster whom I had seen do very well on the range at home, and I was relying upon him and some of my officers to make a good show. To make a long story short, the *Londons* shot abominably, and we did rather worse, the cable ship being a bad third. My quartermaster was a distinct failure. The *Londons* were delighted to find they were not beaten, for it turned out afterwards that their captain would have been vexed had they been. It was at this time that I made the acquaintance of Captain Ouless,

R.N., who was navigator to the *London*. I always found navigating officers most willing to help a shipmaster with the time, or any information that may be at their disposal. I fancy it was on this voyage also that I first met H. M. Stanley. I was taken by one of the officers from the consulate, a nice fellow named Holmwood, into a large, low, fairly light room. A small white man was leaning against the wall, and squatted all round the room were the men Stanley was engaging for his trip to the interior. It was a rather remarkable gathering, but if the truth be told, neither then nor afterwards did he give me the impression of being the remarkable man he in reality was. There was also in the port that beautiful yacht the *Lancashire Witch*, afterwards bought by the Admiralty for a surveying craft. She was owned by Sir Thomas Hesketh, but I do not remember making his acquaintance. The Sultan's forces were then under the command of a British naval officer named Matthews, and it was very remarkable the success that attended his efforts. His men regarded him with immense respect and veneration, and would have gone through fire and water for him. It was quite a sight to see them drilling in the square in front of the palace. I ought also to say that the Sultan was most generous in providing horses for visitors who wished to ride. He had a sort of a henchman called Mahomet, who spoke very good English, but was not, if my memory serves me, an unswerving Mohamedan, for at times he admired the wines of France. Although afflicted badly with elephantiasis, a very common complaint there, he would always manage any little matter that might be required on shore, but naturally he liked his perquisites and saw that he got them. If report spoke correctly, he could have told the tale as to how the death of gallant Captain Brownrigg, R.N., was brought about, but as I cannot state facts it is little use talking over that sad story.

There were quite a nice lot of passengers for the homeward trip from Natal and the Cape, amongst them a newly married couple, the bride being a very beautiful Dutch girl. Before we left the Cape there was quite a gay time. One day we started out in a drag for a picnic at Newlands, but it came on to rain badly. There was a man I knew lived near to where we were, named Raphael Bensusan, and he was a good fellow, so we drove up to the house. He was not in, but his brother, or a male relative was, and he joined us in our picnic on the floor of the dining-room, for as it happened the house was half shut up. That was a very jolly afternoon, and the day ended with one of those balls in the Exchange Building that went far to make Cape Town one of the pleasantest places to know.

The following story is absolutely true, and shows how circumstances at times seem to try and assist the hangman to put the rope round the victim's neck. It was my custom when in command to sleep in the afternoon, and then remain about well into the middle watch. In the *Asiatic* my cabin was at the fore end of the saloon on the starboard side. One night, about half-past twelve, I was sitting up with a Captain Le Breton, smoking and yarning. The door was open, windows and ports also, for the night was very warm. This was before the time of electric lamps, and my cabin was lit by a moderator lamp, and another one hung in the saloon, for ordinary cabin lights were extinguished at 11 p.m. save when by the doctor's orders they were kept burning. Suddenly in rushed a girl, yelling that some one was looking into her cabin through the porthole, and asking to be saved, flung herself down in a chair, and went off into a faint. Just at that moment a puff of wind blew my lamp out, a thing that had not happened before to my knowledge. Then I went for the lamp in the saloon, which also went out, after which I got the quartermaster's bull's-eye, and went and called the stewardess, who took the frightened girl back to her cabin and put things straight once more. When I and my companion were alone again I asked him, if he was on a jury, would he believe in such a combination of circumstances, and he gave an unhesitating No, and I can certainly say, Neither would I.

The *Asiatic* got back to Southampton looking so smart that she hardly knew herself. It's really wrong to make fun of my ship, but on her first voyage, when she was commanded by Captain Coxwell, the commodore, on her arrival in Algoa Bay he was chaffed by his acquaintances upon his skill in bringing in his ship stern first, for they pretended to believe that no vessel in existence could have a bow like the *Asiatic*. They might almost have been forgiven for the belief.

Back now once more to the *African*, for as far as seniority went I was in my proper place there. The directors had come to the conclusion that they would run a monthly line to Hamburg, in connection with the intermediate service to Zanzibar, and the *African* was the first one to undertake this business. Our chairman, Mr. Giles, who had carried out engineering work at Cuxhaven, thought it fair to masters to send them over first as passengers to let them see what the Elbe was like before taking their ships there. This was a considerate act, for a frozen river was a novel experience to me, if not to others. I therefore took passage in one of the General Steam Navigation ships. The Elbe was frozen over, and it was curious to see the steamer charging a great floe of ice and splitting and rending her way through it all. The main difficulty, however, appeared to be that the injection water occasionally froze, and there they had to use a special contrivance for blowing steam through the injection plate. I duly wired that information home, but no notice was taken of it, and I had just the same bother in the *African*. One could not help being impressed by the iron order imposed upon all and sundry in Hamburg. The people lived by rule, and they lived well;

the docks were in excellent order and far better fitted than were ours, either in London or Southampton. I was taken by the Company's agent to a ball where the admission was sixpence. It was 2 a.m. and there were about three thousand people of the working class present, but not a sign of rowdiness or any one the worse for drink. It was something of a revelation, but there was a great deal more to be learned than that. I suppose I, as most young Britons of the period, had the idea firmly fixed in my mind that we were the one people in the world, and that no one else counted. Our agent was a very nice fellow, and we never had the smallest friction, but somehow or other he managed to convey to my mind that there was a nation of Germans that intended to become, as they thought themselves then, top dogs of the world. I have mentioned an earlier instance of this already.

I saw all I could and went back to bring my ship over, and if any one is under the impression that the North Sea is a nice place to navigate they are welcome to their belief. It is not mine. I suppose that in time those trading there become accustomed to it, but it must make seamen of them, and this factor should be taken into consideration when appraising the worth of our Teutonic cousins as possible rivals at sea.

It is undoubtedly a good thing to have a change of route. Constantly trading between the same places is pleasant in many ways, but you see little that is fresh, and the mind has a tendency to run in a groove, which is not healthy. And again, fresh faces and places sharpen your wits, and remove the impression that you have learned all that there is to know.

A first trip up the Elbe in the winter time was a fine corrective for any feeling of stagnation. The Company was kind enough to supply us with a North Sea pilot, a shipmaster acquainted with those waters, but I had no idea of letting him do aught else than consult me. In this case he was not anxious to assume any responsibility, but arriving one night after dark at the mouth of the Elbe, we got on board as a pilot a little old man, who gave one the idea of Rip Van Winkle. There was a lot of ice coming down, and I was considerably surprised when the pilot asked me to put the anchor down with the ship making at least six knots through the water. It was quite all right, however, and next day we got to Hamburg.

My instructions were to give a dinner and entertainment to some of the shipping magnates, and that I proceeded to do, sending out invitations on the advice of our agent. The eventful evening came round, and I had had some doubt for a day or so as to the strict sobriety of my chief steward. As dinner was proceeding I looked backwards where I could see the pantry, and then observed the steward in a helpless state of inebriety. He caught a look from me that would have sufficed to wither an anchor, but he was too far gone to be affected. My own personal servant and the head waiter pulled us through, however, all right. The dessert was hardly on the table when one of the guests was on his feet proposing the health of the Kaiser, and the rest got up and yelled "Hoch" enough to lift the deck beams. I sat fast and said nothing, for the situation was an awkward one. I was host, but it was a British ship, and our Queen had to come first, so when the national ebullition had died down, I got on my feet as I said to propose the first toast of the evening, "The Queen and the Kaiser." That was perhaps too great a concession, but it was better than discord under the circumstances. It was duly honoured and the rest was harmony, for I had provided music. My servant at that time was a perfect attendant; I scarcely needed to tell him anything, for he had the faculty of anticipating my wishes. There was one of the guests who was needlessly pro-German throughout the evening, but at the end of it he had to be put into a cab and sent home. I fancy that for his final brandy and soda he must have had brandy and gin. I gave no instruction or hint on the matter, but I had the impression that honours were about easy at the finish. A day or so afterwards he came to wish me *bon voyage*, but he did not seem very well, and I doubt if he meant it. It was so cold in Hamburg that the steam winches on deck had to be kept moving all night when not in use, to prevent them freezing, and as the ice-breaker was not then properly at work we had to cut our own way through the ice going down the river. When we got back to Southampton the ship's sides at the water line were bare of paint, and the steel side was as bare as a knife and the same colour.

When we reached Natal in the course of that voyage, we heard of the outbreak of the first Boer war, which commenced by the shooting down of one of our regiments without any declaration of hostilities. I will only say this, that the feeling between the Dutch and the British was then, and for many years afterwards, so acute that the last Boer war was the inevitable outcome of it, and for this state of things I, in my own mind, have always considered Mr. Froude and his friends responsible. Left to themselves, the Boers would have accepted the ruling of Sir Bartle Frere, had his administration in the Transvaal been carried out as he intended it should be.

My chief officer in the *African* was a man I have mentioned before, E. T. Jones, who wore an abnormally large black beard, from which he had acquired the soubriquet of "Black Jones." I had the very highest regard for him in every way. When we arrived home in February 1881, as a matter of course I went to London to see the directors. At that time the *Roman* had been chartered to take out troops to Natal. There was then no master appointed to her, and I was questioned as to the ability of my chief officer, to which I replied that he was as good a man as I was. But, said one director, "is that the man with a black beard that looks like a pirate?" and the conversation closed with a laugh, and the intimation that they would come to Southampton to see about it. When I returned that evening I got hold of Jones, and much against his will took him to a barber's and had his beard off. It was a time for heroic measures, for that use of the shears probably decided the matter in his favour. As, however, it would not do to send out troops with a man whose first voyage it was in command, he took the *African* and I the *Roman*, with orders to change again on the coast. As I write this I have before me a letter signed by the officers who travelled in the *Roman*, thanking me for a pleasant passage. The first signature is Finch White, major 85th Light Infantry, commanding troops. It is followed by F. Grenfell, lieutenant-colonel 60th rifles (now Field-Marshal Lord Grenfell). Amongst many others comes R. B. Lane, major rifle brigade (now General Sir R. B. Lane), D. N. Stewart, 2nd lieutenant 92nd Highlanders, who afterwards achieved honours in many parts of the empire, and Charles E. Knox, captain 85th regiment, one of our best generals in the late war. They were a pleasant crowd to travel with, and the passage passed without a hitch, but so far as I was personally concerned I had a little trouble, for on the line I discovered that my carpenter had been neglectful of his duties, and we had only one day's water on board. I said nothing about it but put on the condenser night and day until we had refilled our tanks. I then put an officer in charge of them, but my chief engineer rose manfully to that occasion, for it was not pleasant to have many hundreds of men depending entirely upon condensed supplies. Major Lane and I became very intimate. He had a wonderful personality which attracted every one, and I doubt not he still retains it. One evening he and I caught a booby, and the question was the best use to put it to. Colonel Grenfell was then asleep, and we thought it might be a good idea to put the bird in his bunk. We put that squawking beast on top of him as he lay, but he never turned a hair, only said, "Ugh! take the beastly thing away," and we did. It was no small test of a man's nerve, however, since tried and verified in many a tight corner. One thing struck me, however, on that trip, and it was the great interest taken by the officers in theological works of all sorts. There was a fine collection on board, and I remember reading one called *The Approaching End of the Age*, by Gratton Guinness, which proved beyond the shadow of a doubt that the world must end by 1894.

Going into Cape Town dock it was blowing a strong south-easter and the ship was listing heavily to starboard. We got the troops over to the port side and that put her upright in a trice. It was very smartly done, but they only wanted a word to do what was wanted. Then we learned that the war was over. I fancy that Lord Roberts had already arrived and returned, and there were loud murmurs of discontent all round. We went on to Natal, however, and landed our troops. The late Admiral Andoe and Sir Edward Chichester were there disembarking officers, and they gave me a very nice certificate for the manner in which the entire job had been performed. By the way, I had a bet with Colonel Grenfell that the Government that made the peace would not last six months, but I was wrong in the sequel.

On the way back to the Cape I had with me as passenger Sir J. H. De Villiers, the Lord Chief Justice, who told me that had peace not been made the whole of South Africa would have risen in revolt, so perhaps things were as well as they were. I got back into my own ship at Mossel Bay, and resumed regular work once more.

CHAPTER IX

"And the world went very well then."—Mel. B. Spurr.

I was glad to make the transfer with Jones at Mossel Bay. For one reason it gave him a fair chance of retaining his command, for the *Roman* was to remain on the coast, and I also gave a certain sigh of satisfaction as I saw the blue ensign once again at the stern of the *African*, for she was a nice little ship and I was very fond of her. When I got on board I found that Ballard and his wife were taking the passage home with me. It is a curious sensation after you have been under the orders of a man to meet him upon terms of equality, and to this day some of my old officers, now in command, cannot get over the inclination to say "Sir" to me. I remember remonstrating with one of them some little time ago. He replied, "Well, I always said sir to you, and I always shall." He was an Irishman, and the episode took place in the House of Commons, whither he had dragged me to meet some of the leaders of the Irish party. It was on that occasion that I first met John Burns, now the Right Honourable, who, speaking of the then recently concluded Boer War, observed that we had beaten "better men than ourselves," from which statement, guided by my past experience, I mildly dissented. On that passage home I lost overboard my boatswain, and to the best of my recollection he was the only man that parted company with me in that manner during my career at sea. I have known one or two instances of people disappearing on board ship, when the inference was they had gone overboard, but he was the only case of a man falling overboard, and not being picked up It happened this way. We were half way across the Bay and the ship was rolling, with the promise of bad weather coming, when I gave the orders to get the anchors inboard, for they had been left at the bows on leaving Madeira. It was neither a dangerous nor a difficult operation, but I had spoken to the man that morning and, curiously enough, remarked to my chief the far-away look in his eyes. I think now that he was what the Scotch call "fey," and that the hand of Fate was upon him then. At all events he was unshipping a piece of iron rail when he slipped overboard, hanging on to the rail, and sank like a stone. I was on the poop myself and had a boat in the water immediately, but he never came to the surface again. We cruised round for at least an hour, and then I asked the men if anything more could be done. All agreed the case was hopeless, so we kept along on our course again. When next in Southampton I sent a circular letter to the captains of all our ships asking them to make a collection for the widow. They very kindly did so, and a sufficient sum was obtained to set her up in a small shop in comfortable circumstances, but she never forgave me, I was told, because when she came to my lodgings with a sister prepared to make a scene, I declined the interview. I dare say I was wrong, but I had had trouble enough of my own, and my old landlady, a very privileged person hailing from the West Country, when announcing the callers volunteered the advice, "Doan't 'e see her, sir," and I thought the advice good.

The ways of conscience are curious and it manifests itself at times in absurd fashion—here is an instance. Lodging in the same house was a chief officer, with whom I had been very friendly in years past, and was on good terms with then. One morning my landlady came to me with a request that I would go up-stairs and see Mr. — — who had something important to say. I went, and there was my friend in bed, crying. It seems he had been out on the spree the day before, had inherited a bad headache, and had sent for me to say that he was going round to see his captain and confess his delinquency. Words were no use for a case of this sort. A threat of a hammering, duly translated into fact, ultimately brought home the light of reason to a good fellow who would have made a most excellent curate, but was too gentle to be a success at sea.

On the next voyage we were loading for home when instruction arrived that the *African* was to remain on the coast, and do the mail service between the Cape and Natal. Trade on the coast was good, and it was no longer policy to depend upon the services of such vessels as the little *Natal*. The *African* was very well suited for the work, which was comparatively easy— at sea for at the outside ten days a month, and the remainder of the time in harbour at the Cape or Natal. Unfortunately we could not cross the bar at the latter port. Looking back at this period of my life it occurs to me that it was good, and that I was not sufficiently appreciative at the time. There was an excellent ship's company; my chief, named Smythe, was afterwards long years in command and was a first-rate man; the other officers left nothing to be desired; there was a cook who satisfied all the passengers, and the ship was very nicely kept and popular on the coast. I had a sort of rough shelter built on the bridge for me, and when at sea always spent my nights there, for there was ample time to sleep when in port, but when the master of a mail steamer runs her on the principles of a yacht it is apt to prove a little expensive. At that time, however, there seemed to be lots of money about, for people were always wanting some commission carried out that could be done without any infringement of the Company's regulations. I find by reference to old letter books that in my letters to the home authorities I mention the fact that we seemed exceptionally fortunate so far as weather was concerned, and indeed the luck in this respect seems to run in cycles. I cannot remember that there was anything approaching bad weather during our spell on the coast. But I had one little accident which cost me a wigging. One night coming down the coast I had discharged a considerable quantity of sugar into a large lighter at East London, finishing about 9 p.m. The lighter could not then be taken inside, and the boatmen asked me if I would give them a tow up alongside a steamer that was ahead of us. I thought it well to do so and accordingly steamed up at a fair distance from the vessel ahead, going very slowly, and eventually stopping the engines while the lighter sheered off. The current by this time was setting us towards the *Balmuir*, the vessel I was taking the lighter to, and some one on board her sung out, "Hard a port, captain, full speed ahead." A second later and that would have been my order. As it was, wrath at the interference or impertinence surged uppermost, and I ordered: "Steady the helm, full speed." That also would have put things straight, but the engines had stuck a little on the centre and the two ships rolled towards one another, my starboard quarter-boats catching her on the bow, and suffering severely in the contact.

This was just after the loss of the *Teuton*, and many people had acquired nerves in consequence when travelling, so in addition to the crashing of the boats, the yells of the women passengers were not nice to listen to. As soon as the engine moved there was no more trouble, and Captain Gibbs, who had been chief of the *Essex* when I was in her, and now commanded a steamer called the *Clifton*, very kindly lowered a boat and came alongside to ask if he could do anything for me. There was nothing to be done but proceed, which I did. Of course retribution was bound to follow; it came in the shape of a letter from Captain Dixon, to whom, of course, I had reported the occurrence. In conveying an intimation from the directors as to the future avoidance of what "might be termed somewhat lubberly conduct," he regretted that my helping other people had obliged him personally to address such a letter to me, but the "lubberly conduct" was underlined viciously by him, and I could picture the expression on his face as he did it, knowing perfectly well that it would create on me its calculated effect, though quite realising that it was all just bad luck. It was not the only time in my experience, however, that ill-timed advice was productive of disaster, for to quote the words of A. L. Gordon: "Take it kindly." "No—I never could."

It was about this period (the close of 1881) that the value of the Transvaal goldfields began to be discovered. That meant much, and at the end of the year General Sir Evelyn Wood was leaving Natal with some of his staff.

If my recollection is correct he had been acting as Lieutenant Governor of Natal. There are one or two incidents in connection with this matter that I may as well put on record.

The bar at Natal was a very uncertain quantity. The channel at times was fairly good, for harbour works in a small way were going on practically always, but there were occasions when it was very bad and very shallow. When I knew that Sir Evelyn was to go with me as far as Delagoa Bay I determined to make him as welcome as possible, and show all the attention I could, although I had not had the honour of meeting him. There was to be a farewell dance given in Durban at which he would take his leave, he having already taken up his quarters at the Alexandra Hotel at the Point. I reasoned that if, instead of going from the dance to the hotel, he could come straight on board the *African*, it would be a great saving of time and trouble, for we were to leave at daylight in the morning.

Accordingly I got the skipper of our tug, the *Union*, who had been boatswain with me previously, to agree to take the passage of the bar in the dark as soon as the party arrived at the Point, and I also gave my chief orders that when the tug was nearing the ship, he was to illuminate mastheads and yardarms with coloured lights. I was reckoning, however, without my host. In the afternoon I went on shore, and as I landed at the Point I met the General with some officer—I think it was Major Lane—who introduced me to him, and he immediately invited me to dine. I replied that I had no evening clothes on shore, to which he replied that I had better find some. At that time there was at the Point an ex-Naval Lieutenant named Woodruffe. I remember that he had been Flag Lieutenant to Sir Harry Keppel in China. We were great friends, and had consumed much midnight oil—and other things—together, for he was one of the nicest fellows I ever met, and was liked by every one. He was commonly called "Chummy," and as it happened he was about my size. To him I went in my dilemma and borrowed his clothes, he waiving in my favour his intention of going to the dance, so that I duly appeared at dinner time, and in answer to the General's query I told him how the clothes were procured, which seemed to tickle his fancy. We had a very jolly dinner, and I gathered why they were going home *via* the East Coast, for they wanted to have a look at Egypt, as they were greatly interested in a certain Major Kitchener whom they all seemed to think a great deal of. The General said he would be very pleased to embark on his return from the ball, from attending which I begged to be excused and went to return borrowed plumes and get on board the *Union*.

Here Nemesis overtook me. About the last man I should have expected to find there was Captain Baynton. According to all canons of civilisation he ought to have been comfortably spending his evening in his house at the head of the Bay, engaged in that gracious hospitality for which he was famous, but it seems he had by some means got wind of my intention to cross the bar in the dark and had come down determined to stop it. He opened the conversation by saying that as the General was to sail at daylight, he thought he himself would sleep on board the *Union*, so as to make his farewell easier than coming to the Point so early. Vainly did I explain that the bar was easy and safe; there was the old grim look and stony glare.

"Yes, you go and stick the General on the bar, and a fine d— — fool I shall look. You don't start before daylight." And neither did we.

On that particular passage I had with me amongst others as passenger the Rev. E. L. Berthon, the inventor of the boats bearing his name. He was a remarkable man in many ways. For one thing, though he was sixty-nine years of age, he was as active as a cat, and was greatly distressed because on an occasion of boat drill at sea, just to show him the time it would take to pick up a lifebuoy, I would not let him be lowered in the Clifford boat, the ship running a good thirteen before a fresh breeze. I mention this incident, for the evolution was performed on the spur of the moment during a conversation with him, and on referring to a letter to Captain Dixon as to the efficiency on the ship, I find that the boat with the lifebuoy was being hooked on in five and a half minutes.

In his book entitled *A Retrospect of Eight Decades*, Mr. Berthon mentions the days spent by him on board the *African*, but was not complimentary concerning the crew. I wrote to him on the subject and received a letter in reply in which he stated that I had myself addressed them collectively as a pack of cab-drivers, but I submit that a man may take liberties with his own which other people have no right to do.

The general and Major Fraser came on board with me at daybreak in the morning, and the next day they were duly landed at Delagoa Bay, where they were to transfer to another mail steamer, and we on Christmas Day, 1881, left again for Natal. That evening we had a very remarkable exhibition of electric phenomena, which I never saw equalled. We had been running down the coast with a nice fair wind and all sail set, but as dusk came on, heavy clouds gathered ahead and as a shift of wind looked imminent, I took in all canvas and hustled the men a bit to get it stowed quickly. (This was the matter to which Berthon had referred.) No sooner was it done than the wind headed us with a rush and the rain came down in torrents, accompanied with a fine display of real South African lightning. At the same time there was a shower of corposants, and mastheads, yards and stays were thickly covered with them. The effect was weird in the extreme, and although the phenomenon is often mentioned as common I cannot recall seeing it to any marked degree more than twice. This squall lasted about an hour, after which the weather cleared.

After about eight months of this coasting work we were ordered home, for we had a defective crank-shaft, concerning which I might point a moral were it desirable to do so, but as we reached Southampton without mishap it is as well to let by-gones be by-gones. My connection with the *African* was not severed until March 1883, but the preceding twelve months were of considerable interest to me. I was married for the second time at the Cape, and all the ships in port displayed as much bunting as they possessed, Mr. Currie's ship dressing with the Union flag in the place of honour. My directors also gave me permission to take my wife home in the *African*; for which favour I hope I was sufficiently grateful, and as we now regularly ran to Hamburg to pick up cargo for the Cape I had to thank Mr. Mercer for more than one similar favour on this continental trip. But the time arrived when I came across a junior in a better ship than I had, and I changed to the *Nubian*.

She was a much bigger ship than my last one, but there was no great difference in their respective speeds. She had two funnels, however, and the captain's cabin was situated between them, which did not make for comfort in hot weather. Generally speaking she was a fine, comfortable craft. We were taking out guns and stores to Simon's Bay in addition to our other cargo, and amongst our passengers was Captain Warton (of cricket fame), and a very charming lady of the theatrical profession about whose flaxen locks I should dearly like to tell a story. But woman-like it may be said, she emerged victorious from a considerable ordeal, so let it pass at that.

I was instructed to make coal consumption trials, and that I did to the best of my ability. The passage out was uneventful, and in due course we left Cape Town at noon for the trip round to Simons Town. A number of people had been given a passage for the trip, which was of about four hours' duration, and I remember that I took the ship inside the Bellows Rock. There was, of course, no risk in doing so, but it was not usual for big ships. We picked up a nice anchorage in close proximity to H.M.S. *Boadicea*, the flagship of Admiral Sir Nowell Salmon, V.C., etc., the Commander-in-Chief on the Cape station, from whom, as from his officers, I received the greatest kindness and courtesy. Sir Nowell, however, would not permit any Sunday work, and that delayed us a little, but the stay was quite a pleasant one.

In due time we got to Algoa Bay, where the *Mexican*, our newest ship (then on her first voyage), lay at anchor. She was commanded by the Commodore of the Fleet, Captain Coxwell, who at that time was laid up unwell on board her. I should say that my fair-haired passenger was still on board, bound for Natal. One evening after dinner it was commencing to freshen from the S.E. and a nasty toss of a sea was on. Coxwell sent me a message asking that I would go over and see him as he had something particular to say. I proceeded to do so, and in response to the wish of the before-mentioned lady, but against my wish, I took her with me. We got to the *Mexican* all right, the wind freshening all the time, but when it was time to return there was some sea on, and prudence would have dictated remaining for the night. To this, however, my passenger would not listen, and taking me on one side observed, "If I am drowned in the attempt, you must take me back tonight, for I've no chalk to do my eyebrows with tomorrow." Yielding to this *force majeure* we shoved off, and after a considerable dusting got safely on board my own ship again. I was glad to have seen the *Mexican*. She was then the last word in fine ships on the Cape route, and it filled me with longing to be master of such a splendid craft.

We made a decent trip home, and on arrival at Southampton found that Captain Coxwell had been invalided and that the command of the *Mexican* was vacant. Better still, there was no one at home senior to myself, and it was not long before I got a hint that my chances were rosy. Sure enough I got the command, hardly believing in my own good luck. That ship was a beauty. It is true she was only square-rigged on the foremast, but her lower yard was ninety-seven feet long, and that sufficed to give a spread of square canvas of no inconsiderable proportion—in fact, there were four reefs in her topsail. Contrasted with the ships of to-day she might not show to advantage, but she was beautifully fitted, and when it came to handling under steam she was a dream of delight. Although only a single-screw ship, her turning powers were marvellous, and I made use of them to the fullest extent. John Tyson was chief officer. He is now one of the senior captains of the Union-Castle line, and it goes seriously against the grain to write those words, for it seems to me that the Union Company is absorbed by the newcomer and its old identity lost. I never could see the necessity for the amalgamation, and think it was a sad day when the old Company's flag was merged into that of the Castle line. My lament being absolutely sentimental does not of course carry the least weight in an age when commercialism is of the first importance, but I think that in the long run it will be found that the punishment will fit the crime, for there is no instance of *one* great company being successful in retaining a mail service which on public grounds should be shared by two. For a chief engineer there was Charles Du Santoy, than whom there were few better men afloat. We had been shipmates in the old *Roman*, and consequently I was well satisfied with everything. On the day we left Southampton there was quite a gathering of my friends to see the ship off and to wish us luck. Being the crack ship of the line we were of course full of passengers, and a very pleasant crowd they were, but on the way to Madeira the ship rolled to such an extent as to in some measure disgrace herself. There was a cross swell, it was true, but she had been badly stowed, and given too great a metacentric height. It was a quantity of cement which had been put quite low down in ship which caused her to misbehave on that occasion. As showing how ships are affected by their treatment I may mention that on that passage home an old gentleman came up to me, (it was William Acutt of Natal, Uncle William he was commonly called). "This is a funny ship, captain," he said; "when I let go my cabin door it does not slam," for she scarcely had any motion.

It was a glorious passage from Madeira outward. The weather was fine, the passengers were contented and happy, and altogether we were sorry when we got to the Cape and each went their separate ways. There had been some discussion on the previous voyage as to whether the ship could lay in the Company's berth, or whether she was not too big to do so. There was only one way to settle this, and that was to put her in it and try. This I did, and I remember there were some complimentary notices in the Cape papers on the transaction. We went up the coast that time as far as East London, and had the best of luck in getting rid of our cargo. I profited greatly by the study of a little work on South African coast weather by my friend Captain Hepworth, who had obtained a wonderful insight into it. To know what the weather on that coast is likely to be is no small advantage in taking up an anchorage. Further, I began to discover that Harry Escombe was more than right in his remarks, and that to keep pace with the time there could be no resting on your oars, but a constant search for, and acquisition of knowledge. On the road back to Algoa Bay my old coasting knowledge saved me some miles, for time was short to save daylight. She was doing fourteen knots, and I slipped along inside Bird Island with happy results.

H.M.S. *Boadicea* was there, and we resumed former acquaintance, but when sailing day came Admiral Salmon expressed a wish that we should not leave before midnight, as a ball was to take place and a young lady friend of his wished to see a little of it. He promised to put her on board by midnight, observing that mail steamer captains were only like "so many tame cats," and as the agent was agreeable we stayed until that hour, when we left for the Cape. In the early hours of the morning, however, we had an accident. The strap of the high-pressure eccentric got hot and seized to the sheave, the result being a breakdown which might have been very considerably worse. This, however, was just one of those cases when my chief engineer was at his best. He hung up the end of the link with a piece of chain, and a screw to adjust its proper length, and in a short time was ready to proceed, but was not prepared under any conditions to turn the engines astern. We got into Table Bay the next evening, but had to creep in very cautiously to get the anchor down. We were visited from the shore, and arrangements were made to repair damages, we remaining in the bay until they were completed. This was dreadful; it meant delay in final loading and coaling, and also meant things being in a mess on sailing day. I went to bed considering the matter. Daybreak brought one of those beautiful fine mornings when it is a pleasure to be alive. I had had all night to think over the problem and had made up my mind as to what was the proper thing to do. I ordered steam to move, and sent for John Tyson, my chief. To him I said, "Get the stern anchor ready for letting go (we had a stern davit) and bend on to it the biggest hawser we have; see that the hawser is taken to the bitts so that it can be veered, and let me know when it is ready." In due course this was done, and shortening in the bower cable I steamed the ship round on her anchor until she was pointed for the dock entrance, but as she had swung a little too far before I got the anchor, I had to let it go again and repeat the operation, this time with success. As soon as the ship's nose was inside the entrance I let go the stern anchor, and veering on the hawser and holding on as required we got to our berth without the least trouble or damage. I ought, however, to have buoyed the stern anchor, for it gave some trouble to trip to the boat that picked it up. All went on now swimmingly, and we were spick and span when sailing day came. I think the evolution I had performed was considered to have been a little risky by the powers that were, but as it came off all right nothing was said to me. The *Cape Times*, however, in commenting upon it said that as far as they knew this was the third time in history that such a thing had been done, the other two instances being St. Paul on the occasion of his shipwreck, and Admiral Lord Nelson at the Battle of the Nile! We made a very fine passage home, something just over eighteen days; it was not a record but something very close to it. There are upon my bookshelves now some very pleasant mementoes of kindly souls who helped to make a delightful and memorable trip for me.

I come to the conclusion that it is possible to say too much to your directors, unless you make it exceedingly clear what the point is you wish to bring out. I was being questioned as to the cause of the excessive rolling on the outward passage, which some of the passengers had written home about, and tried to explain that when a ship with a great beam started to roll, she naturally swung through a big arc of space, and that consequently people felt it more. This was construed into a criticism on my part of the build of the ship, than which nothing was further from my thoughts, and I was told afterwards it did not do me any good when the question arose as to my giving up the ship to a senior man. It is on such accidents, if there are such things, that human destinies hang. We had a very nice time in Southampton. I was able to pass my mornings at drill on the old *Trincomalee*, and one afternoon I was successful in taking the all-comers prize at the Hampshire rifle meeting. This gave me great pleasure, for the volunteers were very wroth at being beaten by a sailor.

On the next passage out we called at St. Helena, and I had my first opportunity of visiting Longwood. It was a morning I shall never forget. As we got up to the high land the weather was misty, with a drizzle of rain, and it was not possible, to me at all events, to avoid the thought of the torture it must have been to that great master mind who ended his days there on that weather-swept spot. The house in which he had lived gave me the impression of having only recently been vacated, and the bust of the Great Emperor by Thorswalden seemed to dominate the place with his personality. No work of art that I have seen has impressed me in the manner that did, for the grandeur of the face is most imposing, and surely not one ever to be rivalled in marble. Resist the feeling as one might, the very place seemed permeated with the being of the mighty spirit that sped from within those humble walls.

There was nothing more to call for comment on the outward trip. There were many nice people and several sportsmen who arranged all sorts of sports and pastimes. I remember one remarkable boxing-match. In the final bout there came together a big bluejacket and a little featherweight of a man, which recalled the meeting of David and Goliath. When the word was given to begin, the little fellow rushed in to close quarters and set up no end of a mill, doing this with extraordinary impunity, for the big fellow could have knocked him silly if he had got home. When the bout was over, the referee, a military officer of proved knowledge of boxing, awarded the prize to the big man as being the best boxer, the little man getting a prize as a good fighter.

In the *Nubian* I had had a compass that had been tried and proved during a great many voyages. In the *Mexican* we had one of the best, but we were only now finding out how to adjust Sir Wm. Thompson's compass for changes of latitude. On this particular voyage I pulled mine to pieces in Algoa Bay and re-adjusted it by stellar azimuths. It was a long operation, but it was well worth doing, and no one can appreciate the value of a really good compass until they have been well broken in by attempting to navigate with an indifferent one. There was one other little matter that may well be mentioned. The *Mexican* always seemed to us all to be a brilliantly lit ship, and oil lamps appeared to meet every requirement, but as soon as the electric light came in, we all wondered how we had managed to exist in what was by comparison a state of semi-darkness.

Once more in Cape Town, homeward bound, and coming events did not cast their shadows before, for little did I think as I took her out of dock in the most approved "show off" fashion that it would be the last time I should do so. Sailing days at the Cape for the mail steamers were red-letter days, when all men interested came down to criticise the way in which the various ships were handled. On this particular occasion I managed to retain my reputation, but the pitcher sometimes goes to the well once too often, and I fear I was what the boys call "coxy" over what I could do with that ship. Altogether that was one of the days of my life on which I felt pleased with myself, and it may be observed that there have not been many of them. Sailing day at the Cape was once well described by Leigh, who, speaking of visitors generally, said, "They come on board in ballast trim, and leave drawing twenty-seven feet by the stern."

Few things would give me greater pleasure now than to revisit the old scenes and see how the modern school of men deal with the great ships they command, but the early negotiators of Cape Town dock had a fair amount of pioneer work to do. We learned as we went along.

My chief recollection of that last trip home was that I first made the acquaintance of Clark Russell's novels, and on my arrival at Southampton I wrote him a letter expressing my admiration of them, which resulted in a friendship still unbroken. There are few men who have so faithfully painted life at sea as it really was. His *Wreck of the Grosvenor* is simply a marvel of realism, having only one equal so far as my knowledge serves me,—Dana's *Two Years before the Mast.*

Southampton dock came at last, and it was with little pleasure that I learned the Commodore was at home without a ship and that I should have to make way for him. It was no use kicking against the pricks; seniority was the law of the service and it had to be abided by, so I turned the *Mexican* over with regret to Ballard, and once more joined the army of the "stand-bys."

But it was in reality much worse than merely standing down. At the end of the year 1883 the trade to the Cape was in a very depressed condition, and it was not found possible to keep all the ships employed. Consequently "rotten row" began to fill up, and there were many masters and officers on shore on half pay. "Economy and retrenchment" became the watchword of the board of direction, and the Union Company was by no means singular in commencing its retrenchment policy by seeing how much it could possibly save from the pay of the sea-going staff. There was one favourite question commonly asked of masters by directors. "Did not we consider the difference of pay to be too great between the chief officer and the master?"

and we always rightly and religiously answered "No," for the chiefs were content to wait their turn and the masters knew perfectly well that if any levelling was to be done, it would not be in the upward but the opposite direction. The blow descended at last, however, for, taking advantage of an indiscretion by a prominent master, to whom pay was no great object, the Company gave him the choice of signing a new agreement for less pay, or being unemployed for an indefinite period. The master in question was taken completely by surprise and signed without consultation with any of us, and the path of the directors was then easy, for the rest of us had no choice but to follow suit. I remember, though, that when he came from the office and told me what he had just done, I made use of remarks that might have strained a great friendship of many years' standing.

At this time many of our intermediate ships had been put into the North American trade, amongst them the *Nubian* with my old friend Jones in command. They were in no way fit for the trade. As showing the difficulty of finding two seamen who will take the same view of any situation I may mention that during a conversation at dinner one night I said to Jones that he was the only man of my acquaintance to whose opinion I would defer on a point of seamanship. Shortly after this he was telling me how he had run for Holyhead in bad weather and let go both anchors at once to bring the ship up. I at once proceeded to argue stoutly that he was entirely wrong in doing so, and if he were alive today, which unfortunately he is not, that point would serve for an unending difference of opinion.

There was now a chance to put in a good spell of drill on board the *Trincomalee*, and this I took full advantage of, but the system of training officers which obtained in those days was not one calculated to give the best results. In that particular ship the commanding officer was always most anxious to do everything possible to further the interests of officers on drill, but the guns were hopelessly obsolete, and indeed the ship was shortly after replaced by an up-to-date vessel. I think it was about this time that I succeeded in obtaining for officers the loan of a confidential book from which they could obtain useful information.

I had found it necessary to take steps to obtain my promotion in the Royal Naval Reserve, for at this time very little attention was paid to the officering of this force. Admiral Sir Augustus Phillimore was the admiral superintendent, and with him I obtained an interview which I did not consider to be by any means satisfactory. He informed me that he considered the rank of sub-lieutenant was ample for the master of a mail steamer, and with that I had to content myself, but when H.R.H. the late Duke of Edinburgh became admiral superintendent I renewed my application in writing and was promptly granted the rank of lieutenant.

Between one thing and another the time in no way hung heavily with me. I was on half-pay, it was true, but that was the worst of it, and there is no doubt I should soon have had another command, but it cannot be denied that losing the *Mexican* had made me discontented, and that frame of mind is not a healthy one.

One morning I received a circular letter from Captain Dixon, enclosing one from the manager of the New Zealand Shipping Co., asking if any of the Union Company staff would wish to apply for the command of their new ship the *Ruapehu*. I had no wish to do so, and after talking to Captain Dixon, gave no further thought to the matter. Incidentally, I heard the names of Captains Leigh and Griffin mentioned in connection with the command. One morning, I think it was Christmas Eve, I saw the two of them standing outside Kelways Hotel engaged in animated conversation, so I walked to them and joined in. Naturally I asked, "What about the New Zealand ship?"

I was answered that both of them had accepted the command and both had given it up. I asked why, and learned that they disapproved of going into regions where ice might be encountered, and also that neither of them cared to contemplate the passage of Magellan Straits upon the homeward passage. Well, it was very absurd of me, but I said as the ship was to sail on January 12 they had not played the game with the New Zealand Company, also that the honour of the Company was at stake, and immediately walked over to the telegraph office and sent a wire offering to take the ship for them. I received an immediate reply asking me to go to town and see them as soon as possible.

When I got home that day my action was not altogether approved of, in fact it was strongly deprecated, but the die was cast and there was the end of it. I went to town next day, it must have been Christmas Day, for the London streets were deserted and the office of the Company was only open to meet me. The London Manager took me to the West End to meet the General Manager, Mr. Coster, and before I had time to turn round I had promised to go to Glasgow and bring the ship round to London. I must say that my new employers were very nice people, and evinced a strong desire to meet my wishes in every way possible, but it was a sad time for me when I turned out into the street and realised that it was no longer the Union Company's flag I should sail under, and that my most cherished connections were to be severed. I regarded it, and rightly, as the opening of a new page in the book of life which I had not yet had the chance to glance at, but the only thing was to go through with the undertaking and make the best of it; so I got back to Southampton, spent the rest of my Christmas Day in the conventional manner, and next evening saw me in the limited mail for Glasgow.

I found the ship at the tail of the bank off Greenock, and she was quite good-looking enough to please me; but as soon as I put foot on board her it was evident that for so long a run she was too small to pay. I was not quite correct, however, in this, for I was not then acquainted with the frozen meat trade and its possibilities. I found as chief officer a man from the Union Company, and there also others from the same source, so that I was not in the midst of strangers. The ship was well fitted in every respect, and she had, what was then rare even in first-class ships, an electric light installation. There were two dynamos, but from the first they gave considerable trouble. Still, Fairfield had had a very free hand in turning out the ship, and that notable yard was not in the habit of making many mistakes.

On the 28th the manager and others came down from London and we ran a short trial. It was on this occasion that I first met Mr. Pearce, afterwards Sir William, who had built the ship. We were, I think, mutually satisfied with one another. The ship steamed well, and the next day we started for London and reached Gravesend on the last day of the year, remaining there for the night. In the early hours of the morning a small steamer caught one of her backstays on our bowsprit and pulled her mainmast down, but as she did not stop to leave a card, and no damage was done to us, I am ignorant to this day as to what vessel it was. I do know, however, that the Scotch pilot who brought us round, and others of his countrymen on board, paid a midnight visit to me to be sure that I properly welcomed the New Year. We duly moored in the Royal Albert Dock the next day.

I found from the commencement, as was only natural, that there was a vast difference between my old Company and the present one. There, things had gone on well-defined lines, here there were no lines at all, and the machinery was hardly in evidence that was to trace them. My general instructions were that my ship was to be brought to the standard of the best mail steamer afloat, and I must say that any recommendation I made received the greatest attention; but when one has lived under a fairly consistent discipline its loss is felt very much. Our marine superintendent was Captain Underwood, who had been selected from the staff of the Union Company of New Zealand, and I always found him a very nice fellow to work with. As superintending engineer we had Archibald Thompson, who had filled the same position in my late Company, of which it will be seen there was a very strong leaven. The New Zealand Company had for many years run a line of sailing-ships between London and New Zealand. They consequently had many well-tried officers in their employ who were perfectly competent to command in sailing-ships, yet lacked any knowledge of steam. Certain of them, however, were placed in the new steamers as second officers, and naturally were rather inclined to regard the newcomers as interlopers. Further, when Mr. Coster and the New Zealand directors decided to commence with steam, they chartered vessels to commence the service until their own ships could be built, among them being the *Ionic* and others belonging to the White Star Line. These ships were fitted with refrigerating chambers and plant, and when released by the Company were chartered by the Shaw Savill Co., so that the New Zealand Company people had done their best to popularise these ships, and the opposition reaped a certain reward from their efforts. Also it let in the White Star Line, which was no inconsiderable item. Some time previously the Union Company had had the chance to tender for this particular traffic, but I do not think the directors fully grasped the future of the frozen meat trade. I know that Captain Dixon had not regarded it with any favour, but it was a great chance missed. In point of fact we were here face to face with a situation not unlike that between the Union Company and Donald Currie, and it might have been forecasted that the best business men would win in the struggle.

I found a warm welcome waiting for me at the office, and a pressing invitation for my wife and self to go and stay at the house of the manager, Mr. Strickland. At dinner that night we had the pleasure of meeting my old friend, the Rev. R. Fair, who I found had told my new chief more to my credit than was perhaps my due. A new ship and a new voyage, however, deserve a new chapter.

CHAPTER X

"As she lifts and scuds on the Long Trail—the trail that is always new!"—Kipling.

N.Z.S. CO'S. "RUAPEHU"

The *Ruapehu* was a handsome ship; there were no straight lines about her, for the Clyde shipbuilders realised to the full that it was possible to combine beauty with utility. There was perhaps a suggestion of the Denny ships in the early New Zealand fleet, but, be that as it may, there was no mistaking the clipper bow which was the certain mark that indicated a ship turned out from Fairfield. I cannot say that she was in any way ideal, but she was decidedly good for her time, necessarily suffering somewhat from having been built in a hurry. With the *Mexican* still fresh in my memory I was naturally inclined to make comparisons, but all things being taken into consideration I found no great reason to be dissatisfied with new conditions. Indeed, so far as outward appearance went there was every reason to feel proud of my new command. She was a novelty in many ways, one being that she was lit by electricity, an advantage then quite exceptional. Another important feature was the freezing plant, which in reality represented the real *raison d'être* of the whole line. It was then thought, and I am not certain that the idea does not largely obtain to-day, that competition for first-class passenger traffic could not be successfully carried on with the P. & O. ships. The fact remained, however, that we could land our mails in Melbourne *via* Hobart sooner than could be done by the P. & O. Company, and that fact must have had an important influence in speeding up the Australian mail contract *via* the Canal.

Amongst the crew I found a strong leaven from the Union Company, including an excellent boatswain and quartermasters, for which I was very thankful; and I took an early opportunity in dock of mustering all hands so that I could see exactly what I had got. This step met with the strong approval of Captain Underwood, who warmly supported me in all measures that I suggested for ensuring a consistent discipline in the new company. Two ships had preceded mine, so that it might be considered a fair trial as to who would obtain the best result, but I had made up my mind that I was to work for the old fashions which had obtained in Southampton, and it is not altogether an easy matter to import into London any custom that may have obtained elsewhere.

There was one distinct novelty in the *Ruapehu*. We carried six midshipmen, or rather "company's apprentices," but this practice was discontinued after being tried for several voyages. It was a praiseworthy attempt to meet the inevitable demand for facilities to train officers, but it was a little too early. Indeed the New Zealand Shipping Company had from its commencement been remarkable for its forward and enlightened policy, and its constant endeavour to make use of the latest improvement found useful after scientific inquiry.

Our passenger list in the saloon was not a large one. There were about forty people, but let it be said at once that a more agreeable set were never got together in any ship. We called at Plymouth to embark mails and passengers, and I also received a wire from the manager telling me not to be beaten to the Cape by the *Athenian*; but as we were not calling there, it must have been sent under a misapprehension, which I could easily understand when I came to consider the track we had to follow to make the shortest mileage to Hobart. To decide upon a composite track is not an easy matter when the application of the great circle is possible. In this particular case, taking Cape Verde as the westernmost longitude, the great circle track to Hobart would pass somewhere close to St. Helena, but to follow it would have been to steam against the very heart of the S.E. trades, and that I knew would be a heartbreaking performance if they were blowing hard. I therefore decided to pass about 600 miles to the westward of the Cape, which would entirely do away with any chance of being reported from Cape Point, but which would, I hoped, bring me sooner into the region of the "brave west winds" and also to the latitude where the degrees of longitude were greatly shorter in actual distance, for according to the best advice I could then obtain latitude 45° S. was about the best parallel on which to run down the Easting. In later voyages when I had more experience I formed a somewhat different opinion.

Calling at Santa Cruz on the outward passage we were somewhat unfortunate, for Teneriffe had recently been visited by a serious gale from the S.E. which had greatly interfered with the coaling plant. I had not coaled there before, and greatly fear that I made myself very objectionable to Brothers Hamilton, our agents, for I was driving for all I was worth, and instituted comparison between their procedure in the way of coaling and what was done in Madeira, to the great disparagement of Santa Cruz. As it turned out, it was as well that I did give them a good shake-up, although I know it must have been a sore trial to both the brothers to stand anything in the way of faultfinding. They soon saw, however, that if their port was to get its share of the newly growing trade they would have to bring their plant up-to-date, and they did so as speedily as possible. Our little difference of opinion left no ill-effects, and was the commencement of a pleasant acquaintance only terminated by the inevitable. But as showing that I had reason for complaint, it cost me fifteen hours of a passage that I knew was being carefully watched at both ends of the world. This first passage was absolutely uneventful. I cannot recall any unpleasantness even, save and except the fact that we did not experience the westerly winds we anticipated, and had no opportunity of finding out what the ship could really do with a strong fair wind with canvas set. I can find mention of heavy swells, but only an occasional breeze at force 7, the highest day's run being 328 miles. It must be remembered, however, that the day only contained about twenty-three and a half hours, so that the average speed for the passage was 12·8 knots. This put us into Hobart on February 21, and was not as good a passage as we had hoped for. Although the ship was only built to do 12½ knots, it was expected she would do considerably better than that in actual practice, and in point of fact she did.

Darkness in these days cannot be allowed to hinder one. If there are no lighthouses people have to do without them, as all those did who made Hobart from the westward. It was nasty navigation to go for that land in the dark, for there were several outlying dangers that might very easily bring a ship to grief. On this occasion I made the land at one a.m. and a dark night at that, but when I subsequently saw what the coast was like by daylight, I liked it even less. On the other hand when once the land is made the coast leading to and up the Derwent river is singularly beautiful, and many parts of it rejoice in good old Kentish names, showing very clearly the origin of some of its first settlers. My instructions were to make the ship a "show" ship, and to offer the townsmen hospitality. Accordingly after we had coaled we made preparation for a big luncheon party to which were invited members of the government and the leading people of the place. It was a most successful function, and in responding to a toast I took the opportunity of pointing out that if anyone on a future voyage lost wives or families on their way to Hobart by being wrecked on the west coast for want of a light, they would not be able to say that they had not been warned. The language might have been brutal, but I was feeling the matter keenly and I am glad to say the words went home. We had a most successful and enjoyable function, which every one appreciated, and the good people of Hobart had every opportunity of seeing what was described in the manager's letter of instruction as "my noble ship." It may be as well to state that we had anticipated the Brindisi mail. A lot of time had been wasted as far as a quick passage to New Zealand was concerned, first at Santa Cruz and then at Hobart, but no time was lost when the last of our guests was over the side, and we made the best of our way for Auckland. The remembrance of going into that port is very vivid even now, for although I had been there once as a boy, that gave me no help in taking a ship into what were practically unknown waters. On the passage out I had of course studied my charts carefully, and had formed my expectations of what the various places would look like, and as it turned out my surmises were not very wide of the mark. Indeed I am inclined to think that navigating a ship into port is better done if it is learned from a chart than by acquiring local knowledge by actual inspection. I found latterly even on the Cape route that it was better to steer known courses entering or leaving port than merely to con the ship by sight. And here I had a very curious experience tending to strengthen my argument. I steered perfectly safe but close courses round various corners, passed inside an island towards the entrance of the harbour, after which I picked up a pilot who told me that ships seldom used that passage because of the dangerous patches in it. That was quite true, but the dangers were charted and no hindrance to safe navigation, and a mile in distance often helps towards saving a tide or securing daylight into an anchorage. Further, if a ship is being watched carefully, as she must be in narrow waters, she is in my opinion far safer than if she is taking the broadest part of the channel anyhow. I do not, however, wish to dogmatise, only to point out that for many reasons it is desirable to be accurate even when traversing waters that are well known.

There is little need to say anything concerning the beauties of Auckland Harbour. Kipling has said it all in "The Seven Seas." And certainly as I saw it that afternoon it well deserved the praises bestowed upon it. But my mind went back to that other afternoon, twenty years before, when I was there under vastly different conditions. In my mind I could see again that beautiful ship *Tyburnia* anchored under the shadow of that wonderful crater Rangitoto, and the harbour crowded with transports of all description, dominated by the imposing presence of H.M.S. *Miranda*. And in the very berth at the Queen's Wharf where one lay in the little *Alwynton* we now lay in the finest ship that had yet been in the harbour. I confess to having experienced a feeling of pride, though unfortunately its duration was short.

It would have been difficult to find fault with the welcome that was extended both to the ship and myself personally. Perhaps the first feeling of annoyance was caused by the pertinacity of the newspaper reporters, for we had not had anything of the sort at the Cape, and I did not then realise, as I have since done to the full, how very useful it is to get all the advertisement possible. But it was gently hinted to me that interviews were the custom of the country and that it was desirable to fall in with it. This once being understood there was no more trouble.

Again we were to be a show ship, and do a lot of entertaining, and the Company's directors were coming up from Christchurch to do the thing properly. I looked forward to their advent with no great degree of pleasure, for at best directors are kittle cattle to handle. But in this particular case I found myself confronted with as nice a group of men as one could wish to meet. Indeed, the general impression made upon me by the New Zealand men I had met was that they were as a whole vastly superior to the average colonial man one had been in the habit of meeting. In fact it was easy to recognise a considerable leaven of public school boys from the old country. The Northern Club at Auckland had opened its hospitable doors to me the day before the arrival of my directors from the south, and I was playing a game of billiards with an exceedingly nice fellow I had met there. His name was John Studholm, and at the conclusion of our game he observed casually that he was one of the directors of the New Zealand Steamship Company. I am glad to say that it was the commencement of a friendship that lasted.

When I met my group of directors on board the ship they were all highly pleased with what they saw, for I fancy that in one or two of the earlier ships they had not been altogether happy in the selection of a crew. New Zealand was not a very suitable place for the maintenance of good discipline if a crew were disposed to get a little out of hand, for the democratic element was very strong, and Jack got to assume that he was quite as good as his master. I had, however, been fortunate in the main in getting a decent lot together, and though the ship's discipline was as strict as was consonant with its due maintenance, we had succeeded in persuading the crowd that they should fancy themselves as belonging to a smart ship and behave accordingly. An average good crew seldom go wrong if you handle them precisely as you would a lot of school-boys; in fact they are much easier to manage. I had an opportunity of hearing a curious instance of this *esprit de corps*. One night the San Francisco mailboat lay alongside us, the *Alameda*, and in the darkness I came out of my cabin to get cool before turning in. Below me I could overhear one of my Jacks talking to one of the men from the other ship, who asked what was the speed of the *Ruapehu*. Quoth my man, "Oh, she will steam seventeen easily, but we are not going to let her out this voyage." After that piece of embroidery it would have been difficult to persuade me that Jack took no pride in his ship.

There was one thing that I hated about the ship, and that was the hideous yellow colour with which the masts and yards were painted. In London there were other things to do than point out its ugliness, but now was a fine chance. Mr. Murray Aynsley was the chairman. He had a brother, a celebrated admiral in the service, and had himself seen the work of our ships in the Black Sea at the time of the Crimean War. To him, as an authority, I pointed out how much nicer it would be to adopt a different style of colouring, and how much smarter the ship would look. My reasoning took effect, and I was given permission to use my own judgment on the matter. I promptly set my chief to work to transform her into the most approved Union Company fashion, and in a very short time she was looking like a yacht, with sail covers on, upper yards down and in the lower rigging, and not a rope slack or awry. She was a picture, and one worth looking at. All the Company's ships were afterwards painted in a similar manner.

Bashfulness or undue modesty cannot be claimed as an attribute for our colonial fellow countrymen; they simply swarmed over the ship whenever they got the chance, and no place was sacred to them. I never found any one turned into my bunk, but it would not have surprised me had I done so, and I am afraid that many people did not like the strictness with which the gangways were kept. The first Sunday the ship was open to all, and at times the crowd was so great that we had to deny admission until there was room created by people leaving. The preceding day there had been an "At Home" which had been well attended by the youth, wealth and beauty of Auckland, and on one evening we gave a dinner to which all the notables in the Colony were invited and which was very well attended. Some doubt had been expressed as to the ability of the ship's cook to carry it through, but this scepticism was unfounded, for it was a first-class performance and the function went off well. I had to speak, which was a little awkward, but I scarcely think I trod very heavily on any one's toes. As the ship was to remain some time on the coast there was no great hurry to get away, and I made several very nice acquaintances. One evening I went to what was called a clairvoyant entertainment by a certain professor whose name I will not mention for obvious reasons. It was a clever, striking and withal an uncanny performance, for the lights appeared to burn blue to me, and if the evil one had appeared with a due smell of sulphur it would have seemed to be in perfect keeping with the surroundings. When it was over I made it my business to meet the professor, and ask him to lunch with me next day, which he did. He was a very nice fellow, and when I asked him to tell me how his performance was done he observed that it was a curious request to make, but if I promised secrecy he would do so. He did, with the result that since then I have never quite trusted my own senses, but he maintained that his mesmeric power over his wife, which was part of the show, was real and effective.

When sailing day came there was a great crowd on the wharf to see us off, and from photographs taken we must have looked very fine, but we had then to discover that coal counted as well as looks. The directors were going down the coast with me, and naturally desired to make a smart passage to Wellington. We had filled up with New Zealand coal; they said it was Westport and first-class steam coal. Be that as it may, our people proved unable to get steam properly, and there was considerable disappointment. I could not question the logic of proven facts, however, and had to make the best I could of a severe disappointment. It occurred to me about that time that the engine-room should occupy a greater share of my thoughts than it had hitherto done—the ship's company generally were at their very best and my chiefs were delighted. It seems that they were curious to see how a complete stranger would take his ship into Wellington, and Murray Aynsley told me afterwards that it pleased them. Wellington is a perfectly easy place to enter, but its looks are against it in daylight, for the reefs and rocks at the entrance look nasty until the channel is open. As a precautionary measure I eased to half speed just at the entrance, but I had so learned the place from the chart that it did not give me the least uneasiness. When the head of the harbour was reached a pilot came off to take the ship alongside the wharf, and it must be confessed that for handling large ships under their own steam these men in all the New Zealand ports showed a wonderful aptitude. This Wellington pilot in particular was an extraordinarily good man.

As preceding ships had been show ships here, we had a comparatively quiet time. The question of good or bad coal cropped up when we were filling our bunkers, and I am afraid that any one with a less perfect temper than Captain Rose, our manager there, would have been seriously put out with me. I was acting for the best, as I thought, but my knowledge was limited. About this time the Orient Company had their ship the *Austral* sunk at her moorings in Sydney harbour. She was coaling at the time, and as it was night time only a warrant officer was in charge. I had long thought that an officer should always be on duty night or day in a valuable ship, and from that time forth, with the concurrence of my superiors, the third officer was relieved from all work in harbour save looking after the ship between the hours of 9 p.m. and 5 a.m. This was a distinctly good move in many ways; it certainly had the effect of causing men on leave to return quietly and not draw attention to themselves. From Wellington we went to Dunedin, or rather Port Chalmers as the port was then called. Here again was a sample of the pluck and energy of the colonists who would have ports everywhere. They were even then dredging a channel by which large ships would be able to reach Dunedin, and here a misfortune overtook me. The whole of the forepart of the ship was fitted as a cooling chamber for the carriage of frozen sheep. We had commenced taking in some, when suddenly it was reported that the freezing engine had broken down. An expert was telegraphed for to Christchurch and he duly came, shook his head and said nothing could be done, for the bedplate of the engine was broken and no insurance company would take the risk of a frozen cargo with a patched-up engine. It is useless now to say all I thought on the matter, but I believed the damage could have been made good. It was settled that we were to go home with a general cargo and no frozen meat. As the freight was then twopence per pound it will be seen this was a serious loss, incurred as I still believe by wilful damage.

Our final port of call was Lyttleton, the seaport of Christchurch, the cathedral city and the most English of all New Zealand towns. Here was the Company's head office, and it was considered to be the home port of the Company. At the time I cannot remember whether we had the word Lyttleton or London on the stern as our port of registry, but I know that shortly afterwards there was some correspondence with the builders on that subject.

As we were continuing our rôle of show ship, and as the ship was being delayed so as to ensure a full passenger list homeward, it was thought desirable to put her in drydock, and it certainly was a great advantage to start clean for the homeward passage. I found it necessary about this time to draw the reins of discipline a little tighter, and as an outward and visible sign ordered a Sunday morning muster. This was duly carried out as it would have been at sea, and it caused the growlers (mostly in the engine-room) to think I had behind me greater powers than I really possessed. But the plan answered.

We gave one beautiful dance on board, to which the directors issued invitations. It was a great success and brought together a great number of charming people. When we were ready to start for home I do not think that anything had been left undone that could have increased the popularity of the ship.

The question of the route to be followed homeward was one that gave me considerable difficulty to decide. I was not in the least degree shy of accepting advice, in fact I sought it, but having had little experience in navigating southern latitudes, and bearing in mind all the tales I had heard about ice and kindred subjects, I was naturally anxious to do the right thing. I knew, moreover, that our two new ships had made excellent passages to Rio. By chance I met my old friend, Captain Gibbs, and from him I got the advice, "Hear what they all say, and when you get out, act as you think fit," which left me exactly where I was. But the general impression left upon me was, get down to Lat. 50° S. by the great circle track and then run the Easting down on that parallel. I duly carried out the plan as far as human endurance permitted me to do so (for I had not then the practical knowledge of great circle sailing I afterwards acquired) when I attempted it. Let me explain. Lat. 50° S. was reached three days out from Lyttleton, and from there to Cape Horn by a Mercator line was a stated distance. But there are two sides to this line—one the polar side, or the great circle, which shortens the distance immensely, the other the equatorial side which very considerably lengthens it. Now to run the Easting down in Lat. 50 was to do so on the equatorial side of the Mercator line, and flesh and blood was not strong enough to do that. I tried for three days with something like the following result—A run of say 320 miles, and nearing my port only say 280. That would not do, so ice or no ice I took to the Mercator track, and having succeeded in spoiling my run to Rio saw not a scrap of ice, nor did I have the least trouble in any way. It must, however, be admitted that for a stranger to look at the ice chart he would think that bergs were as plentiful as potatoes in their patch, and might be inclined to disregard his knowledge that hundreds and thousands of voyages had been safely made by sailing-ships in high latitudes, and that what one man had done could be accomplished by another. However, both I and the Company paid for my lack of experience, though we both profited by it in the long run. It should also be said that upon this trip there was little help from canvas. The passage home was made by dint of sheer hard steaming, greatly assisted by the fact that we had not to provide steam to keep the freezing engine going. We left Lyttleton for the homeward passage full of passengers, and it would not be difficult to give the full details of the life on board if it were desirable to quote from the pages of the *Ruapehu Satirist*, a weekly journal that was read with considerable interest. Its editor was decidedly a free-lance, and spared no one. It may be stated, however, that it would be hard to exaggerate the mischief that can be made by a few sheets of paper, a little ink, and lively imagination. I think I can say that summary suppression was the fate of most on-board-ship newspapers with which I came in contact.

I was rather anxious about making the land near the Horn, for as the days went by it was evident that only by fine weather should we be enabled to see anything before dark. This may seem absurd to-day, but to run on a close course, as I was doing in darkness, for a land I had never seen, was not a very pleasant job. It had to be done, however, and this specially emphasises my former remarks as to the desirability of never losing a mile or a minute when making a passage. As luck would have it on this occasion we made Ildefonso, looking like a streak of smoke from a steamer funnel, just as darkness was setting in. After that there was no more trouble and we passed one mile south of Cape Horn about midnight. There was no difficulty in recognising its shape from the rough sketches on charts and in sailing directions. We ran through the straits of Le Maire, and arrived at Rio without incident.

Sydney may be beautiful, Auckland is acknowledged to be, but to my imagination Rio is unsurpassed in loveliness by any place I have seen. There is no intention of attempting to describe it here, that is beyond the power of any ordinary mortal, but until one has seen the sun rise in Rio Harbour the most beautiful sight in the world had yet to be experienced.

Naturally all our passengers went on shore, for the coaling was to take twenty-four hours, and I have a very keen remembrance of bringing a very lively crowd off with me in the small hours of the morning. I had picked them up in a cafe at the top of the Rua D'Orviedor, where every one appeared to be in a good temper and Englishmen exceedingly popular. Repentance, I doubt not, was the predominant feeling next day, for mixed drinks with strange and strong tobacco are apt to make the ordinary hat feel a little heavy in the morning.

The remainder of the passage was not such as to call for special comment. My attempt to dodge the N.E. trade was not the success I hoped it would have been; we ran through the anchorage at Santa Cruz at midnight, making noise enough to wake the dead, and leaving particulars behind us in a sort of pyrotechnic washing-tub, so that we might be reported home by cablegram, and finally arrived at Plymouth after a passage the steaming time of which was 38 days 8 hours and 37 minutes. I find that both Plymouth papers call this the fastest passage on record, and for some reason it made a stir in London, for when we got to town I met my old friend Mr. Trapp, and his words were, "Is that your ship that we are all talking about?" I said "Yes." "I suppose," he remarked, "you ran all night and did not shorten sail in the hours of darkness." The old gentleman was back in his thoughts to the usages and customs that had obtained in the days of the Napoleonic wars when he had been privateering.

However that may be, the passage was a success; my chief had brought her into London looking spic and span in the most approved Southampton fashion. Both the chairman and the manager were waiting to meet the ship at the docks, and they were so pleased with her appearance that they altered the paint of all the other ships to the fashion we had set. In the *Daily Telegraph* of June 17, Clark Russell had an article on the passage. It was to all intents and purposes a good performance, but to the day of my death I shall always look back to it with regret, for had I taken a better course to Cape Horn than I did, it might have been a passage that would have held the record for years yet to come. I think, however, that at the finish I had the record for passages both ways.

On the next voyage I had with me the chairman of the company, Mr. J. L. Coster, who was in his way a type of the coming New Zealander. He was a keen, clever man, determined that whatever he had to do with should be the best procurable, daring and ambitious to the last degree. He stuck to his friends, and loathed his enemies with a deadly enmity. He had formerly been, I believe, manager of the Bank of New Zealand, but was now certainly the leading spirit of the shipping company and determined that no one should wrest from them their supremacy. I had seen a good deal of my chairman and others connected with the Company in London, and looked forward to a very pleasant passage, for Coster and I got on very well indeed.

About the time that we were to sail the Shaw Savill Company were sending out the White Star steamer *Coptic*, having on board her as passenger Sir Henry Loch, the governor of Victoria, who was to be landed at Hobart. It was the first run of the *Coptic* on this route, and to us she was an unknown quantity, but this I knew, that although she sailed three days before us it was my business to get to Hobart first, and I intended to spare no effort to do so. The fates seemed adverse to us, however, and gave the worst weather I ever saw. The run out to Madeira was a good one, but we lost nine hours there coaling. We spent the time very pleasantly on a ride inland, and enjoyed the proverbial hospitality of the Blandy family at their beautiful villa. We left filled up with coal and in the cheeriest spirits.

I should mention that I now had as chief engineer my old chief from the *African*, and knew that though stubborn as a mule he was a first-class man, and not likely to indulge me with unpleasant surprises. In fact he was rather safe than brilliant, and under the particular circumstances I could not have done better, for on this occasion I had not taken special pains in the selection of my crew, having left it to be done in the ordinary manner. When we were one day to the south of Cape Verde, it was a beautiful Sunday afternoon, we sighted a steamer coming towards us, and by her rig and the position she was in, I knew that it was the *Athenian* homeward bound, Warleigh being her captain. Coster, who was with me at the time, asked me to speak her and ask if she had seen the *Coptic*. And if so where; for if we had that information we should be able to judge fairly well what our relative speeds were. Accordingly we hoisted a signal, asking the *Athenian* to close as she was on our port side, but instead of doing so she sheered further off. Not to disappoint my chairman I steered across her stern and came up on her starboard side, when I found, much to my surprise, that Warleigh had stopped his engines, and his manœuvre brought us a good deal closer that I intended. No harm was done, however, and we got the information that the *Coptic* had been spoken 150 miles to the southward of the Western Breaker. This gave us the information we wanted, and thanking Warleigh I put on full speed and resumed my course. But there was something about the business I did not like, we had been too near an accident to please me, and meeting Warleigh some voyages after in Cape Town I asked him why he had stopped his engines. There had been, I may say, a little coolness between us for some time over some misunderstanding that ought never to have occurred. He replied, "I thought that you intended to steam round me, to show your superior speed, and determined that I would stop to let you do it." I was rather hurt to think he could have thought me capable of such a piece of rudeness, and told him so, upon which we buried the hatchet for good and all.

We were not to call at the Cape, so there was no need to debate as to the track to be pursued, as it was the winter months down south. I determined to go well south, and save all the miles I could, but reckoned without my host on this occasion. I had intended to go south of Prince Edward's Islands, but had to turn tail to a S.W. gale and very heavy sea. Had I held my course I should not have made good progress, damage would probably have been done to the ship, and the passengers' lives would have been unbearable. The chart I used on that voyage lies before me as I write. Again I tried to pass south of the Crozets, and again I had to turn and run. As the weather moderated I again tried to get south, but my chairman, learning my intention, observed that I was an obstinate man and if I got into trouble I was not to expect help from him. In other words, he had had enough of high southern latitudes. Of this I am certain—the weather down south runs in cycles; for the first four years I was on that route the weather was frequently more than average bad, and my tracks on the chart at times gave one the idea of a dog's hind leg. For when there is plenty of sea room in a passenger ship, it is in my opinion worth while to run a point or so off a course, if by so doing the ship makes better weather and goes along comfortably. It was held by some experienced masters of steamers in that trade that a course once set should not be departed from. I still, however, hold to my view that it pays to let the ship take the seas as easily as possible, and it also requires no skill to knock a ship to pieces.

I was rather amused by an observation made by my chief engineer. The weather was fairly bad and I asked him how he liked it. He replied, "This is all right I dare say for sailing-ships, but it's no place for steamboats." Of course the engines required the greatest care, for at times they raced very badly. It was our luck, however, on this occasion to get a really fine specimen of a gale of wind, and although all things are comparative I think that it would not have been possible for it to blow harder than it did or for a bigger sea to get up.

It was my custom when running the Easting down to habitually carry a reef in the topsails, setting topgallantsails over them; it was the survival of an old Blackwall fashion brought about by long experience of whole topsails, which showed that they were unwieldy to handle in really bad weather. One seldom cared to reef so long as the wind was fair, and if by force of wind it became necessary to do so, more time was lost over the operation than if a single reef had been in all the time, for in most gales a reefed topsail could be carried so long as the wind was fair. Added to this, however, steamboat passengers were not fond of a disturbance overhead such as would be caused by a stiff job of handling canvas in the night time, and all things taken into consideration, I am certain that in stormy latitudes it was a good plan to adopt, for it did not pay to blow away canvas in a steamer. On this particular occasion we had struck a streak of abnormally bad weather. For some days the barometer had been showing a steady fall, and on the morning of July 1, 1884, at 8 a.m., it stood at 27·94, with a furious gale from the W.N.W. Shortly after 10 a.m. it was 27·73, after which the weather improved. The weather appeared so threatening the day before, and it was blowing so hard, that I had had the close reefs put in, with a reef in the foresail, so that when the worst came there was nothing more to be done than stand on the bridge and speculate as to what was coming next, sometimes dodging a mass of snow that was frequently blown out of the belly of the maintopsail. All the time there was the knowledge that ice might be encountered, for we had passed bergs a day or two previously. In the chart-room, which I occasionally visited, I could stand before the aneroid and see the hand going backward; in fact I have now the rough pencil notes I made from time to time of what was to me a novel experience.

Fortunately the ship steered beautifully, and also she was not by any means deep, for the coal burnt had lightened her considerably, but at times when going down the front of a wave she would throw her stern up and the engines would race furiously, giving them anxious times in the engine-room. When this took place, at the other end of the ship the bowsprit and a portion of the forecastle would be dipping into the rear of the wave ahead. I think it was the only time I ever saw such an occurrence, for be it remembered the ship was 420 feet over all, and by comparison to the size of the waves, she was behaving like a whale-boat on a big surf. As I do not wish my veracity to be impeached I forbear from speculation on the height of the waves from trough to crest, but I have often thought since that one might have been treated to an unpleasant surprise.

As it was we came through the breeze without parting a rope yarn, Mr. Coster expressing his regret that the builder of the ship was not with us to see how beautifully she behaved. We were running down our Easting in Lat. 47° S., and I eventually came to the conclusion that that was a bad parallel and that further south was much better. About this time too the chief engineer made the discovery that he was short of coal, and consequently we had to reduce expenditure, to the detriment of our speed. We again made the land at Tasmania in bad dark weather, and off the south point of the island I made out the outline of a big ship outside me. We knew it must be one of two things, either H.M.S. *Nelson*, the Australian flagship, or the *Coptic*. As daylight came in we found to our intense delight it was the latter ship, and the firemen of the watch below turned out of their own accord to help in the stokehold. We passed her easily and anchored at Hobart, reporting having passed the *Coptic* off Cape Connella. That was all very well so far as we were concerned, but the port authorities were anxious to keep the best berth for the Governor's ship, and we were of the opinion that it should have been first come first served. She arrived an hour after we did and I am sorry to say got the best attention. When on shore that day I met the captain of the *Coptic*, and found that they had been in our vicinity when we had encountered bad weather, but further south. He told me he had never seen weather like it, even in the Atlantic at its worst. Three whole main topsails had been blown away, and in reply to my inquiry why he had not reefed down, said with a patronising smile that "it was not White Star fashion to reef; if a whole sail would not stand, then let it go." I failed to see the beauty of the argument. We found that we had a serious shortage of coal in our bunkers, and there was considerable difficulty in getting a fresh supply. Eventually we did get a collier barque alongside, but there was a good deal of unpleasantness. Mr. Coster in his autocratic manner was furious at losing time, and I am afraid that I was very rude to that collier captain (who was a very good fellow) when he refused to let us have any more, because his ship was as light as was safe, while all the time I believed he was keeping it for the *Coptic*. We left the next day with a bare supply, trusting to good luck. Fortunately we got it, but if the truth must be told, we arrived at Wellington with less than forty tons of coal on board. However, we had made the passage to Wellington in forty-three and a half days, including two days stoppages, at an average speed of 12·99 knots, with which my chairman was well satisfied, for he had seen the difficulties. It was winter time in New Zealand when we arrived, but it was very pleasant. There was a general election taking place, and Mr. Coster stood and was elected for one of the Christchurch divisions. It is, perhaps, needless to observe that it was a period of great jubilation to us all, but it did not last long as our stay in the country was only to be a fortnight. We were to leave full of cargo, frozen meat, and passengers, but before we got away my chairman came to lunch on board. He told me to express his satisfaction to the ship's company generally, but said he could not say enough to me. As a sign of his appreciation, however, he had cabled home that I was to have the big new ship and could always count upon him as a friend.

It must have been a bad spell of weather about that period, for it took fifteen days to get to the Horn. There was a great deal of head wind and sea, for I find in my abstract "pitching bow and stern under," and a record of bad weather generally, while before we rounded the Horn we found that we had lost one of our propeller blades. This was a bad job, for it gave the engines a very jumpy action, and was equivalent to entirely spoiling the passage, for we could never now pick up the time we had lost. I have since thought that the foundry where these particular blades were cast must have hit upon a streak of bad metal, for I certainly seemed to have the luck of losing blades which was not shared by any other of our ships.

Our ill fortune lasted us to Rio; but before we got there I had one little excitement that may as well be chronicled. It was the custom of the ship, weather permitting, for the crew to bring out and air bedding, and clean out their quarters for inspection by me on Saturday mornings. This had been done hitherto without a murmur reaching my ears. The weather prior to rounding Cape Horn was too bad to permit the weekly routine, but when we were drawing near to fine weather I gave the usual order, and was astonished to hear that the firemen refused to comply. I really cannot remember now, but I think the seamen did; at all events, I gave the order to muster on the poop, and the malcontents obeyed the order. Now if they had graduated in a rowdy sailing-ship in the 'sixties and had meant business, they would have remained in the forecastle and placed the onus of getting them out upon me. But they were modern recreants and did not understand the particular methods by which a skipper may effectively be set at defiance.

As soon as they had quitted the forecastle and come on the poop, I had the doors of their quarters shut and guarded, effectively cutting off retreat. Then calling over the names as they stood on the ship's articles, I asked the first man if he intended to clean his quarters. His reply was that his mates in London had told them that they were not to obey that particular order. My reply was that they could reckon with their mates in London when they got there, but that in the meantime they had to reckon with me, here and now. A renewed refusal and my order was "irons," duly carried out. Five men went through the same formula, and the rest gave in; they were all kept aft and sent forward in batches to do their share of the work.

This outbreak of insubordination could not have been put down so easily if I had not had a good lot of officers to back me, although, as the men knew, I should have taken extreme measures had there been any show of violence. Where they could have embarrassed me would have been for the entire lot to have continued their refusal, for then I might have been put to inconvenience to find lock-up accommodation for them all, but I knew the passage was hopelessly spoiled, so thought it just as well to fight out a question of principle when circumstances were in my favour. I recollected afterwards that when we left the London docks some men on the quay made loud and angry remarks concerning the importation of Southampton fashions to London and I have no doubt that a certain resolution of defiance had been duly arranged, although it was very ill thought out.

After that little breeze things went on quietly and in due course we got to Rio. I remember taking some young ladies to see a circus, which was in some ways novel, and I doubt not that if these lines meet their eyes they will remember the incident well and laugh at the recollection. There was no other incident of note and I duly started for home, not thinking it worth while to make a fuss about the loss of one propeller blade, but some days before we got to Madeira we lost another, and then it became a serious matter, so I wired home for instruction, feeling that it was just as well that some one else should take a little responsibility. For although a ship *can* paddle along with only one blade or even a portion of one, it was due to every one concerned in the ship's welfare that the risk should be known, in order that if trouble did come it might be met. I got a reply to proceed "with caution," and it occurred to me that the last two words were rather superfluous if quite natural. We completed the voyage in safety, for the weather was favourable and our progress good, although there was a most objectionable vibration. What was very satisfactory was that the passengers left the ship well pleased with everything in spite of our mishaps.

That was the end of my connection with the *Ruapehu*. I had gained a considerable amount of experience in her, it had got me out of the old groove, and I had become reconciled to my lot. The worst of the business was the longer voyages, and the knowledge that in the near future our stay in London would be materially curtailed, as New Zealand was to be considered the home port. But with it all there was a fine sense of exhilaration. There was enough use to be made of canvas in order to get the best out of the ships—that reminded one of some of the best traditions of the sea—and we perpetuated so far as we could those of the old customs that would or could exist side by side with steam. The ships were well found and there was no stint of anything required to put them on a really first-class level. As, however, might have been anticipated in a new steam company, after some time it became necessary to take a more careful survey of what was really being done. Bidding adieu to my ship I now transferred my interest to the new ship *Kaikoura*.

CHAPTER XI

"She walked the waters like a thing of life."

N.Z.S.S. "KAIKOURA"

(From a painting by Willie Fleming of Cape Town)

I suppose that all seamen have cherished a particular liking for some particular ship they have sailed in; a long association seems to establish a sympathy between the mind that controls and the dull steel that gives effect to the task required of it. Kipling had some such idea in his mind when he wrote "The Ship that found Herself," and almost insensibly the idea is imbibed that the ship is a sentient thing whose behaviour can be accurately forecasted under any given conditions. I never had that feeling quite for the *Mexican*—my acquaintance was not long enough to permit it to grow into absolute confidence which it assuredly would have done had time been granted, but for my new ship it was altogether different. I took her twenty-three voyages round the world, and she never disappointed me, or failed to come up to expectation at any time. She could do anything that was reasonably asked of her, and I am vain enough to think she sulked when she lost the hand upon her that she had grown accustomed to, for she never did much afterwards. As it was put to me by a prominent official, "She never seemed to have a day's luck after you left her."

On my way to Glasgow I was delighted with the idea that there was to be a really big ship for me. I knew that she was to be forty feet longer than my last one, and at that time a five thousand ton ship was thought to be a pretty fair size. At all events many of us had the idea that with over four hundred feet in length the evil of pitching would be reduced to a minimum. Both *Mexican* and *Ruapehu* were 390 feet, and at times they could under provocation really distinguish themselves, but this extra forty feet, it was thought, would put an entirely different aspect on a ship's behaviour in a heavy head sea. It was a vain hope, for I have known the *Kaikoura*, when light, pitch and scend through a vertical arc of thirteen degrees, which was both trying to the stomach and the temper, for although I was never actually sea-sick after my second voyage to sea, a heavy bout or spell of pitching always made me feel uncomfortable.

From the train, when nearing Fairfield, I saw two ships in the yard alongside one another; one appeared to be big, the other small, and I said to myself that the big one was mine. It was a vain surmise—the big one was the Cunard *Etruria* and the small one the *Kaikoura*, but she was a fine ship for all that. She was too far advanced in building for me to suggest any but minor alterations, but I was glad to see that many defects I had pointed out in the earlier ships had been remedied. She was not, however, nearly so far advanced as the advertised date of her sailing led me to suppose she would be, and after being with her some little time I wrote to London saying it was an utter impossibility for us to leave the Clyde on the date mentioned. A reply came back saying that Sir William Pearce (the head of the Fairfield firm) assured them she would be ready by the time specified. Then began a wonderful piece of work—a small army of workmen invaded the ship, each bringing some part of the ship's internal fittings with him. For instance, you could see the panelling of the saloons grow as you watched, the pieces having all been fitted in the workshops, and only requiring to be fixed in place; further, the work was well done, for up to the time of my leaving the ship she showed no sign of hurried workmanship. The engines had all been erected and tried in the engine-shed before being placed in the ship. She arrived at completion without a hitch, and on the appointed day we went for our steam trials on the measured mile and made, as nearly as my recollection serves, nearly fifteen knots. Mr. Bryce Douglas, the engineer to the firm, represented the builders, and Mr. Strickland the Company. Mr. Bryce Douglas and I got on very well together, and I for one regretted greatly his death shortly afterwards.

It must not be supposed that the saloon or passengers' quarters were in any way completed. We had, in fact, some scores of workmen going round to London in order to finish the work by the time she arrived there.

There were also some dozen gentlemen with us, mostly scientific men who had been given a complimentary run round. In one respect there was a marked advance on former ships, for the electric light installation was a great improvement and scarcely ever gave any trouble; in fact it may be considered that by this time the problem of lighting ships by electricity had been satisfactorily solved. We left the Clyde on the morning of October 20, having on board a channel pilot in whom the builders had the greatest faith, for I scarcely think that the Company were to take the delivery before she arrived in London Docks in a completed state. On that point I am not certain. There was no doubt I was master, but the pilot was not in any way anxious to get orders from me. I had no great reason, however, to be dissatisfied. All went well until the evening of the 21st, when we were off Portland, a dark, clear night with a light westerly wind. We were passing many sailing ships standing off shore on the starboard tack, and, in attempting to clear a Danish barque, there unfortunately developed a difference of opinion on our bridge as to what was to be done, and we hit her very hard. Fortunately she was timber loaded and did not sink, although her crew left her and came on board my ship, seeing red, after the manner of excited Scandinavians. I was a little puzzled what to do, for I had no time to waste, so for the first and last time called a council of my officers, asking for suggestions. It was decided that we should send a lifeboat with a crew to stand by her, to keep a light burning to warn off other ships, and to see if she could be got into port. When we proceeded to carry out the plan the master and crew of the barque begged to be given the lifeboat and to go themselves, and I, very weakly as I now think, did as they wished. At all events it let us get on, and that was the all-important point just then, for we were in no way damaged and our paint on the bow was hardly scratched. The barque duly got through the Needles and I think put into Cowes, from which place our lifeboat was returned. We arrived in London without further adventure, and once again I had an experience of law. The short stay we had was fully taken up with depositions and consultations, but as I have already expressed my views on that subject I need not recapitulate further than to say it was "the same old game" to get clear of this matter. When the case was tried it was given against us, the truth, as I believe, being that they got scared at our close proximity and tacked the ship under our bows, thinking we were not giving way to them. I think the court was of this opinion also, but I can imagine that our ship, (a blaze of light being kept going for the workmen) and approaching a sailing ship at great speed, was perhaps a trial to weak nerves. At all events they were all in a howling funk when I saw them. That was No. 1 collision. We had all our work cut out to get the ship ready for sailing day. She was booked up full of passengers, and there was an apparently endless stream of stores and equipment coming down to the last minute. To the credit of the Company be it said that the work was done, and done properly. I cannot remember that anything was omitted.

The worst part of the business was that I had in the main a new set of officers, although my chief engineer from the last ship was with me. It is of the greatest advantage in a case like this to have people with you that you know you can depend upon, and with the best intentions in the world you cannot have this feeling with strangers. It must be remembered that a new ship is always something in the nature of a surprise-packet. On the afternoon of October 25 we left the dock, and by the time we got to Gravesend it was quite dark with a strong ebb tide running, and the reach full of ships, mostly at anchor. As we were to stay there the night it was necessary to turn the ship round, and when we got across the river there was not a great deal of room for anything to get past us. This was discovered by one of the Aberdeen steamers called the *Ban Righ*, for in sweeping past and under our stern she cleared the whole of her starboard side of bridge, deckhouses, bulwarks, etc., and she also dented our stern and carried away rudder chains and some of our ornamental gilt work. There were circumstances connected with this that would have made a cat laugh, but a very stiff upper lip had to be kept, and I greatly admired the admirably cool way in which the incident was treated by Mr. Strickland, the London manager, who had come down the river with us and alluded to the collision as "a river bump." I went down the river in a tug to see the extent of the damage to the other ship, and the next day we left for Plymouth. This collision No. 2 was, I believe, settled by both parties bearing their own damages, for not even a bench of judges could have rightly apportioned the blame in this case. I find by abstract that we left Plymouth at 7.30 a.m. on the morning of the 28th, after a fairly strenuous week's work.

The ship, as I have said, was full of passengers. In the saloon we had a number of representative Christchurch people, and they were very nice to get on with. In every community there is nearly always some prominent spirit that will give the rest a lead, and this is especially the case on board ship on a long voyage. From extended observation I would venture the remark that nineteen days is about the maximum period for which people will dwell together in unity. After that time a great deal of forbearance and tact is required to make things go smoothly and well. As may be imagined there were in this case little shortcomings that might with some degree of justice have been found fault with, but there was one man who was determined that all should go well. His name was Tom Acland, and we became great friends. He has now, alas, gone to join the majority, but his memory remains a pleasant one with many. He ensured peace in the saloon, but in the second cabin it was another business. There were a lot of old Australians bound for Hobart, and nothing was right so far as they were concerned. On more than one occasion it was necessary to talk very straightly to some of the ringleaders, and eventually they sent a letter to the directors complaining of my conduct to them, the result of which was a unanimous vote of confidence in me by the Board. We got to the Cape without any incident calling for special mention, this being the first time I had called there since joining the new Company. It was pleasant to see the old faces once more and, further, to find they were glad to see me. As we had to take in a lot of coal the people travelling had a fine chance for a run on shore, added to which the ship was steaming well and giving every satisfaction. This, unfortunately, was not to last, but still, when we got away once more, she began to show me what she really could do when she got the canvas on her. I find there was one day's run of 369 miles for a day thirty-six minutes short of the twenty-four hours, and that was faster travelling than I had ever done before. One day it became necessary for some reason to open up the high-pressure cylinder. I had been down in the engine-room having a look at what was going on and saw nothing very out of the ordinary for a new ship, but I had noticed that something was being done to the escape valve at the lower end of the cylinder. When the engines were again started there was a great crash and they immediately stopped. This was a twenty-fours hours' job, for a piece was broken off the rim of the high-pressure piston, and the explanation I accepted for the accident was that a small spanner had been left in the steam port by the builders and that it had just rolled out. There are some explanations that it is well to accept even when they may not be altogether satisfactory. I thought in this case the main thing was to get the damage repaired, and let those immediately concerned fight it out when they got home. The engineers made a good job of the repairs and in due course we proceeded gaily. There had been a fine fair wind during the stoppage of the engines and we had sailed 155 miles.

There were various incidents between this and Hobart more or less unpleasant, one in particular. A young married couple had the misfortune to see a child of theirs die of some infantile ailment and it had to be buried that evening. There was in the saloon a very charming elderly lady who was great on evangelism and preaching, appealing to the emotions after the style of the Salvation Army. While I was reading the Burial Service this lady had got an audience of women in the saloon and was rapidly making a scene. The burial had been kept as quiet as possible, but after it was over the doctor came up to me and said, "I wish you would come down to the saloon, sir, and say a few words, or else Mrs. — — will have every woman in the ship in hysterics." I did so, and many speedily recovered sufficiently to suggest that I was a brute for stopping the proceedings—very funny the ideas that strike people under certain conditions.

It was always my endeavour to have the men prepared for emergencies, and many have thought at times that I was unduly particular in this matter. The crew, for instance, never knew when they would be called to fire quarters. Saturday was of course the most convenient day, but the objection to a fixed day was that every one had a fair surmise that the bell rang for drill only, and that was not the same thing as calling upon people unexpectedly. When it came to the actual test my scheme worked well. Again, when boats were manned, they were always provisioned, for stores were kept in a portable state in order to facilitate this matter. I found that boats could be provisioned and swung out ready for lowering in four minutes, and that as a general thing without taking any undue risks; I have only seen one man go overboard at boat drill. That was in the *African* during a fresh breeze, but we soon had him again. There is more harm done by undue haste than by the trifling delay in first seeing that things are properly prepared for the work to be done. Another very good spirit to introduce is to make the crew fancy themselves and take a pride in their ship. It seemed to me that this plan also worked excellently.

There was no further incident on that passage, but on arriving at Port Chalmers we discovered that our misfortunes were not quite over. There was a Government tug assisting to get us alongside the jetty, and by some bad management on its part it ran into our propeller, which cut through its side as though it had been a piece of paper. The tug consequently made the best of her way to the beach, getting lower in the water as she proceeded, but she eventually reached the shore. This was the third smash I had had in just over seven weeks. I was about tired of being made a cockshy of, and the occurrence generally had not improved my equanimity.

When we had made fast I went on the jetty, and having had the turning gear put in, was watching the blades of the propeller to ascertain what, if any, damage had been done to them, when an elderly man whom I did not know came fussing up to me asking, "What's the matter?" I replied, I am afraid rather shortly, that I did not see what business it was of his, on which he informed me that he would soon let me know all about that, and took himself off. I then discovered that he was a Government engineer surveyor, but one of the very old school. There was no great damage done to anything, and we soon made arrangements to repair the damage done on the passage, but I did not consider it a casualty, nor did I think it necessary to report it as such to the customs. But gossip spreads, and the next day I received a little note from the collector of customs asking me to go to Dunedin and see him. I did so, and found in the room my friend of the previous morning. The collector, who was a very nice man, liked and respected by every one, told me he had heard I had had a casualty on the outward passage, and had not reported it. I replied that I did not consider there had been a casualty and therefore no need to report anything, as the damage was slight and to be easily repaired. Upon this the engineer broke out that he considered there had been a casualty and "What did I know about it anyway?" This elicited the reply from me, as I considered under extreme provocation, that "I had a steam certificate and he had not." This closed the conversation and I was not further molested. How it was finally settled I really forget, but my engineer opponent and I were afterwards very good friends. I write of this incident because I have frequently been put to considerable trouble by Custom House officials who have pressed for unnecessary details, and in fact have told me that if even so small a thing as a piston-spring breaks it should be entered in the official log as a casualty, but this I always stoutly refused to do, claiming in this a reasonable amount of discretion. And again, in colonial ports a ship's name is nearly as delicate as that of a woman, and as easily damaged. A report of a casualty at the Custom House is good copy for every newspaper reporter that can get hold of it, embellishing what may have happened with every fanciful idea that it can possibly bear. There is yet a graver aspect in which this subject may be viewed—it reduces the discretionary power of the master of the ship, and that appeared to me to be a thing quite worth fighting for.

During the remainder of our stay in New Zealand we went the round of the big ports and left Wellington finally for home. I find that I had not adopted then a high southern route to the Horn, for although we made an average speed of 13½ knots we did not make a good passage to Rio. We passed the Horn, however, in broad daylight and I came to the conclusion that there were several matters connected with hydrographical details that would be better for being looked into. The old stagers had gone on their way accepting everything on the chart for granted. I was navigating so far as I could to learn. Here is a case in point. I was passing Cape Horn at what I believed to be a mile's distance. I took the danger angle at its recorded height and immediately hauled out, for the angle put us apparently too close in, and I could trust my eyes. That was jotted down for future investigation, as were my compass deviations nearing the Horn, which, if the variation lines on the chart were correct, I could not account for. We made the passage home under forty days total or thirty-eight days actual steaming time, but I hoped we should some day do a great deal better than that. We were given a fair spell at home this time, for there was a lot to put in order, and as it happened our collision case had to be tried. I did not like the ordeal, nor do I think I came well out of it. We lost the case, but not one word of fault-finding was said to me. About this time Sir W. Pearce commenced to take more interest in the Company and various changes began to manifest themselves, but they did not at that time detract in any way from the efficiency of the ship or cause any inconvenience.

On our next voyage we started with the best of luck and made a fine passage out to Santa Cruz. We had on board a great number of single women emigrants, who were berthed right aft in the ship, and were really in charge of the matron and the doctor. I was not supposed to have anything to do with them, save inspect their quarters once a day, and to settle differences if the matron and doctor could not do so. On more voyages than this one it happened that the said matron and doctor would goad the women into rebellion over some trifle, and when they had become unmanageable would send for me to put matters straight. I had learned by experience that you could lead a crowd like that by dint of a little judicious humbug, but drive them you could not. By the time I had sat and talked for ten minutes, the row was always over, but it was necessarily at the sacrifice of some apparent or fancied dignity on the part of the officials in direct charge of them. Scarcely to be wondered at, for matrons are given rather to domineer, and young doctors mostly are green as cabbages outside their own particular job.

There was one other event on this voyage. I had been permitted to select my own chief officer, and I induced a man to come with me who had been third in the *African*—Tom East—the son of Quartermain East of Claimant fame. He was of the bulldog breed, a good sailor, a good officer, and loyal to the heart's core. We had disagreements at times, but we liked and respected one another, and when the separation came it was with mutual regret. Further, I grieve to say he has now joined the majority. Half the trouble is lifted from the shoulders of the master if he has a chief he can rely upon to carry out his orders. For if the master's voice is heard at all, it should be a clear intimation that the attention of every one is called for, and that the ordinary routine is departed from.

Two days out from Santa Cruz we lost a propeller blade, and we consequently waggled down to the Cape at reduced speed, thankful that we encountered no really bad weather, for we were only making about eleven knots to the hour. On arriving at Cape Town we went alongside the outer jetty and made arrangements with a diver to take off the broken blade and put on a spare one. I was assured that the operation was practicable, and that it had been successfully done in other similar cases. It did not strike me, however, as looking very promising. In just under a day and a half the job was done for what it was worth. I knew it was a risk, but desired to save the expense of dry docking the ship. On the other hand, I should not have been justified in taking the ship from a place of safety with a damaged propeller, so the course adopted I hoped would prove the happy compromise. In this I was mistaken, for ten days afterwards the new blade dropped off altogether. By that time we were half way to Wellington with a nice fair wind and, by easing the engines considerably, could make very fair running. In point of fact, in spite of our mishaps our average speed for the entire distance was 12·94 knots, and the steaming time was forty-one and a half days. We went south to Lyttleton in due course and were again put into working order, but there was not much time given us in the country, for in less than a fortnight we were on the track again for home, the round trip taking three months and six days. By this time I was getting acclimatised to the surroundings down south, and was making shorter cuts to Cape Horn each passage. On this particular occasion, although it was the depth of the Antarctic winter and a little ice was seen, we had fine fair winds. Every one concerned was delighted with the ship, and the passage home was made in a total time of thirty-seven days nine hours, or steaming time of thirty-six days four hours—an average speed of 13·3 with the freezing engines all working. To deal with this matter once for all it may be said that her best passage out was thirty-nine days eight hours total time.

"KAIKOURA" IN HARBOUR

No pains were spared on my part to make the ship as fine a specimen of a first-class steamer as possible, and it was always a matter of certainty that when we arrived in port we should be the best-looking ship there. By a little contriving I had succeeded in getting dummy yards made for the mizzen mast. They were only used in port, and they came down with the Blue Peter when we started on homeward passages, for although they were used once or twice in London, it was never possible to do the ship's appearance justice with no proper crew on board her. On the other hand, in colonial ports that matter had my special attention, and I so impressed my views upon the officers that in time they had as keen an eye as myself for a slack rope or a yard not quite square. I have reason to know that this peculiarity of the ship was noticed on all sides, and only quite recently I got a letter on business from a complete stranger who reminded me incidentally that he had seen the ship years ago and recalled her appearance and her smartness.

Things at times go very wrong even with the best intention, as the following case will illustrate. The Governor of New Zealand was then Sir William Jervois, an officer who had served his country in many ways with great distinction. One day in Lyttleton he accepted an invitation to come and see the ship and to lunch on board. I was very keen upon doing the thing in first-rate style, so, having two Naval Reserve officers and a crew of Reserve men, it seemed to me that we might turn out a decent Guard of Honour. My second officer was given charge of that business, for I knew that he was well up in his drill. We borrowed the arms and the men were very decently turned out. When his Excellency came on board there was a decent "present," the Governor's flag was broken at the main, and all went very gaily, the lunch was excellent and every one was pleased, but here was disaster. Many ladies and townspeople had come on board as visitors and were chattering gaily with the officer of the guard, who had let his men disperse for dinner or stand easy. The Governor rather suddenly rose from the table to depart, and before my officer again got his men together, the necessity for them had departed. I do not think that I ever felt quite so angry, but a sense of the ridiculous reduced the feeling to some sarcastic remarks that I should not have liked to be the recipient of. His Excellency, however, in no way remarked upon the incident, but I doubt not he enjoyed a quiet laugh at the *contretemps*. He was uniformly kind to me, and I entertain a grateful remembrance of hospitality and courtesy displayed to me and mine by Lady Jervois and himself.

About this time the late Admiral Sir George Tryon, K.C.B., was Commander-in-Chief on the Australian station, and his was a personality to be remembered. He was good enough to treat me with a great amount of consideration, and indeed went out of his way to encourage a growth of good feeling between the Royal Navy and the Merchant Service. I saw a good deal of him, and so far as I could discern he made no distinction between me and one of his own captains. I think I may truly say that it was mainly the intercourse with him which turned my mind to a study of naval matters, and caused me to write the various papers I have on the possibilities of war service by merchant steamers.

This was just after the Pendjeh war scare, when a Russian cruiser had turned up most unexpectedly at Wellington. My ship had been taken by Government, but for some reason was returned, and the *Coptic* was taken in her place. There was some little trouble in getting the crew of that ship to take war risks, but having mustered my men and put the question to them, they agreed to a man to do as I did. With that assurance I went to call on the Governor to ask him to requisition my ship, but for some reason unknown to me it was not done, much to my disappointment.

They were a splendid lot of officers on board the flagship H.M.S. *Nelson*, but a matter of thirty years makes a great clearance. It is not so very long, however, since I met a man who reminded me of an incident concerning a lot of them who, having been to a ball, had come on board my ship to put up for the night, and wanted to know what I could do to amuse them. I had then on board as guests two parsons, one of whom was the Rev. Eliot Chambers, an old navy man himself, so I replied that there were two parsons on board and they were at liberty to draw them if they pleased. Chambers heard this, slipped out of bed and bolted his door, but the other fellow was fetched out in scant attire to join the general revelry, and a very pleasant time it was.

The flag captain was Atwell Lake, now an admiral, and he was a tireless talker. One evening General Sir George Whitmore, who was commanding in New Zealand, invited two members of the Government, Lake and myself, to dine with him, and a very fine dinner he gave us too. But Sir George was also a tireless talker, and I fancy that Lake went there prepared to vanquish him at the game, for he started to talk at the commencement of dinner, kept us all interested, and Sir George never got a word in edgeways the whole of the time.

It must not be supposed that during the Russian war scare New Zealand was altogether unprepared. There were both forts and mine fields, and the latter were very well equipped. As for the forts, they had been constructed, I believe, under the directions of Sir W. Jervois himself, who was a skilled engineer, though, as I happened to know, he and the naval commander-in-chief held different estimates as to their specific value. At various times I think I went over nearly all of those forts with Sir George Whitmore, and formed the impression that the material was excellent, for they seemed to have ordered the best of everything. On one occasion, some years afterwards, I was visiting the forts at Otago Heads in company with the then Minister of Defence, afterwards the Right Hon. Richard Seddon, and this seems a fit place to give an anecdote quite characteristic of the man. The officer commanding expressed a wish to have another gun mounted in a particular place that he pointed out. After some demur Seddon agreed to give this, but said the Government could not afford luxuries. Some one chipped in with "That's what the *Daily* — — says about you having a special train to go from — — to — —." "Oh," replied Seddon; "they say that, do they? Well, in future I will have a special train a great deal oftener than I have done." He quite understood the way to deal with his fellow-countrymen, and most of them admired him immensely for his sheer dominating personality.

The social clubs in the principal towns were great institutions and of most hospitable tendencies the whole time that I was in the mail service. I was free of them all as an honorary member, and it seems to me rather a pity that we do not reciprocate this hospitality to any great extent when colonial visitors come to London. There is, of course, reciprocity between certain clubs all the world over, but generally speaking it is a difficult matter to obtain for a colonial friend in this country. The Fernhill, Northern, Wellington, Canterbury and Christchurch clubs were most kind, and I have pleasant memories of them all. Perhaps the last named appealed to me more than any, but then Christchurch itself was the most English place I ever set foot in. It had evolved its own atmosphere, habits and customs. There was also another famous institution known as "Coker's Hotel." Here the personality of the proprietor was decidedly an asset, and Jack Coker was liked and respected by every one with whom he came in contact. He had been a sailor, I think an old man-of-war's man, but had the instinct of good breeding which made him welcome in any company. I remember on one occasion there had been a great ball in Christchurch given to the officers of the Australian squadron. Many of them were staying at Coker's, and when we returned in the early hours he was chaired in recognition of something he had done by two post captains, a first lieutenant and myself, and as he expressed it afterwards, "It was the proudest moment of my life, but a little bit risky," and it was. But there was a homelike atmosphere in that hotel which I have never found elsewhere, and which disappeared with the man who had created it.

There was an incident connected with a dinner to celebrate the inception of the Midland Railway which is noteworthy in the light of recent events and would no longer be possible. The function was held on October 21, and I was called upon to respond to the toast of the Navy, having had due notice of what was expected of me. I did so in some sort of fashion, but when I went to lunch on board my ship the next day, my chief observed in his plain-spoken way that I had made a nice mess of it the preceding evening. "How?" I asked. "It was the anniversary of Trafalgar," he said, "and you didn't mention it." It is well to remember that a similar lapse would no longer be possible, for through the genius of Arnold White in suggesting that a wreath should be laid on the Nelson Columns on Trafalgar day, and the efforts of the Navy League in giving effect to the idea, the event is now celebrated from one end of the empire to the other. Certainly there is no child in New Zealand to-day ignorant of the fact that October 21 is Trafalgar day, and attaches due importance to it accordingly.

THE MASTER OF THE "KAIKOURA"

It was rather the fashion both in Australia and New Zealand about this period to take great interest in anything that resembled a race between two well-known steamers. In fact it reminded me of Mark Twain's stories of racing on the Mississippi. There were two vessels on the coast about the speeds of which all sorts of tales were told. One was the *Takapuna*, an express vessel carrying the mail from Wellington to Auckland *via* the west coast; the other was the *Rotomahana*, a beautiful vessel built by Denny's and credited with a speed of seventeen knots. At all events she was supposed to be the fastest thing on the coast and I dare say was. But we in the *Kaikoura* had rather an idea that we could do a bit of steaming on a pinch, and so it came to pass that these two ships were lying in Wellington harbour one fine afternoon both bound to Lyttelton and to sail about the same time. The idea of racing had not entered my head at the time of my leaving the wharf, and as lookers-on said afterwards, "I went down the middle of the harbour as usual with a leadsman in both chains." That was chaff, of course, but I never cut corners unduly fine. On this particular occasion the *Rotomahana* left a short time after me, and to my astonishment came and squeezed in between me and the first turning point. She was crowded with passengers going down to Christchurch races, and they howled at us in derision, holding up rope ends and offering us a tow if we wanted one. We had started under easy steam, as was usual in coasting, and we had in fact been overhauled very quickly, but the indignity of the proceeding rather vexed me, so I sent for my chief engineer, and pointed out that it was not desirable we should be made a laughing-stock of. He replied that he "supposed it was to be Elder (meaning Fairfield) against Denny," to which I assented, and he went below, but I shall always hold the opinion that there had been some talk on shore between the rival engineers. Be that as it may, the lead the *Rotomahana* had got by this time did not increase, but she still ostentatiously trailed her coat. There was no doubt under ordinary steaming conditions our then rival was the faster ship, for she had far greater horse-power proportionately than we, but on this occasion she had a full load of cargo and we were flying light. Our displacement, in fact, was inconsiderable, and as the water was smooth as a mill pond, it was equal to having our horse-power in a vessel half our size. To make a long story short, we let my ship go and we simply raced past our friend *Rotomahana*, got to Lyttelton an hour and a half to the good, and were safely moored and piped down before she got into dock. The race caused a good deal of comment, for the result was surprising. Every one did not see that we owed the win to being light, and having the luck of smooth water, but the fact remained that we had the fastest run between those ports to our credit for many years, until H.M.S. *Orlando* took it away from us. The captain of the *Rotomahana* was a very splendid skipper named Cary. He had done numbers of fine things on the coast, and was commonly spoken of by a somewhat fiery sobriquet. I was informed that he did not like his beating, but he was not the first challenger to fail.

I had two outbreaks of fire which deserve to be chronicled. One happened at sea and the other in harbour. On the first occasion it was midway between New Zealand and Cape Horn when it was reported to me that one of the coal bunkers was on fire. It gave me a nasty sensation for a moment, but it was night time, no fuss was made, and a few hours put an end to the trouble. It tires me to hear men talk about the bad behaviour of British merchant seamen in emergencies of this sort. It is my experience that, except during periods of strike or general labour unrest, you can do anything with them.

The next fire was a more serious matter, for there were complications which made the matter more difficult. It is a most excellent maxim to keep on good terms with the port authorities wherever you may be, but occasionally you come across personalities with whom smooth working is impossible. The port captain at Lyttelton had on one occasion fallen foul of my second officer, who was carrying out some order I had given him, and my man had retorted in language perhaps more forcible than polite. That was, strictly speaking, quite wrong, although natural, for all my people knew quite well that though I exercised the right of free speech to them, I did not permit any one else to do so, and was always ready to take their part if it were necessary. In this case the port captain complained to the head office in Christchurch, and I received a letter written by the order of the directors instructing me to severely reprimand the officer in question for his unguarded language to the port official. I regret that I have destroyed that correspondence, for I remember replying to the directors that I had carried out their instructions, but that the "cavalry forms of speech" indulged in on both sides had not originated with my ship, and so the incident closed with a rankling remembrance on the part of the port captain, and a sort of *civis Romanus sum* feeling on the part of my ship's company.

Well, one Sunday evening in Lyttelton harbour we had just finished dinner when East came to me and reported that there was a big fire in the forward coal bunker, and that the refrigerating-room bulkhead was very hot. We were to sail for home in three days, we were coaled up, and had on board a large quantity of frozen meat stowed in the immediate vicinity of the seat of the fire. I shall never be sufficiently thankful that it was my habit to spend Sundays on board, for had I not been there it would have been very awkward. Without any fuss we got the pumps to work. The men, being fortunately most on board, fell quickly into their places, and having put an officer in the gangway to prevent any one coming on board, I thought things were in a fairly satisfactory condition. But about this time two things happened. One was the advent on the scene of the port captain, who demanded admittance, which upon consideration I could not well refuse, for, as he argued, you don't start pumps on a Sunday evening unless there is something the matter. The other occurrence was the intimation that the deck of the second saloon was getting hot and smoking. The port captain wished to summon the local fire brigade and take charge; to this proposal I would not listen, but said I would accept the services of his tug-boat's pump if she could come alongside, which in course of time she did. By this time it was known in Christchurch that something was wrong, but as there were no trains running so late on Sunday, the Company's manager, Mr. Bennett, made, I believe, record time over the hills down to Lyttelton, arriving in time to see the end of it all.

Underneath the wooden deck of the second saloon was a steel one which was now red hot, and flames were showing. My endeavour was to pierce the steel deck so as to get water directly upon the fire, but this was rather difficult, and for one awful moment the idea flashed across me, "You have refused help. Is the job going to beat you?"

Now H.M.S. *Rapid* was in port, and Lieut. Sparks, R.N., her first lieutenant, a friend of mine, was, I knew, in command at that time. To him I dispatched my second officer to ask that he would send me means to blow a hole through the deck. Like the good fellow he was he did exactly what I asked, no more and no less, for it would have been easy for him to have gained a lot of kudos had he done more than I asked. He sent his gunner and a cake or two of gun cotton, and with that in reserve I knew it would be all right. As it turned out we did not need it, for the carpenters had managed to get through the steel, and we were then able to put a heavy flow of water right in the heart of the fire, and our troubles were soon over.

My fellows had worked splendidly—Clifford, the third officer, going into such an atmosphere of smoke and heat in the endeavour to get a hose to bear on the flames, that I had to order him to desist, and he was dragged up by a rope that was fast round his waist. No set of officers and men could have given a better performance, for by midnight the fire was entirely subdued, and the damage done was confined to some twisted steel decks and woodwork that could be repaired before it was time to sail for home. The directors caused a letter to be written thanking me and the officers for our exertions, and sending a sum of money to be divided between those men of the ship's company who were actually employed in putting the fire out.

On the succeeding voyage to Lyttelton my friend the port captain tried to induce the Company to make me appear before a Harbour Board tribunal, at which matters concerning the line of action I had taken were to be inquired into, but the Company said they were not intending to play that game, and as the powers that were were equally anxious to avoid any unpleasantness, no more was heard of the affair. I suppose that technically I was wrong, for a ship in port is to some extent under the orders of the local authorities. But I was always very jealous of any attempt to encroach upon my prerogative as "master." It is a very fine designation and title, but to my mind it carries with it the obligation to maintain its meaning. I was never particularly anxious to take the courtesy title of captain which is commonly assumed on shore by those in charge of merchantmen. Mr. — —, master s.s. — —, looks quite well enough on a visiting card.

In this same year 1889 I was asked to attend a meeting of the Hobart Chamber of Commerce in order that I might receive the thanks of the Chamber for taking my ship alongside the Dunn Street pier. It reminded me somewhat of an old *Mexican* episode. A most flattering resolution was passed and I was congratulated upon the fact that the light on the western land I had advocated seven years previously was now actually in course of construction. That sort of thing was gratifying, although no special merit attached to my action, for the pier was large enough to accommodate a far larger ship than mine was.

Among the intimates that I had in New Zealand was Captain Edwin, R.N., the meteorologist, who resided in Wellington. We had many tastes in common, for he was one of the old school and had learned his business thoroughly, commencing with the bombardment of Sebastopol, at which time he was serving as a midshipman in the *Albion*, and his stories of the bluejackets of the period, of fights between the men on the lower deck, of men, when dying of cholera, asking an officer to hold their hands, these and other matters were graphic in the extreme. As a specimen of his powers as a *raconteur* the following is an extract from one of his letters to me —

"By the bye, I had a curious dream lately; I had departed this life and found myself covered with feathers and fitted with a pair of three folding wings like an albatross, and was outward bound; being not used to flying, and off my first letter, I did not get on very well; and found I was putting my tail too hard over, which frequently brought me broadside on. After a while I settled down, but made rather heavy weather of it; and a lot of clipper chaps passed me on the way. When I had been out about a month, I heard a fellow coming up astern, and before long he hailed me and it turned out to be you: 'Hullo, Crutchley,' said I; 'where are you bound?' 'Gabriel for orders,' said you. 'Same here,' said I; and we flapped along together. After a good while we saw a faint sort of pale light ahead and you remarked that you thought we were running into ice; after some time we made out that it looked like a fog bank, with a bright place in it, and on coming nearer we saw that in this bright part there was a high gate, so we eased down and worked our tails a little so as to be sure we had everything in readiness; for not being accustomed to being up under feathers we were a little anxious; all, however, went well and we both perched on the gate in a masterly style and folded our wings very neatly. We had no sooner landed, so to speak, when a bell rang twice, and immediately a voice hailed us and asked who we were; when we had replied, the voice said: 'Tell the Recorder that two fellows have come for orders!' Presently we heard someone say, 'What name was it? Ah! yes: I see; Crutchley, Master Mariner, Lieutenant Naval Reserve, rather bad style both. Dear me! Dreadful record! I am afraid he must go on. Who did you say the other fellow was? Edwin: I have him! Why, dear me! This is very sad! Naval officer, and bad at that; send him on at *once!*' So then we heard the first one hail us. 'Outside there! You Crutchley! Edwin! Go round by the left immediately.' But we didn't see it, being sailormen and willing to contest the point; so we called out that we wanted a rest, being very tired and thirsty—could they not let us come inside and sit down for a while? (you see, that gate was not good holding ground), but a loud voice said, 'Go away! be off immediately! We shall have others here to deal with directly.' But we held on; presently a long pole came out of the fog and proceeded to shove us off and in so doing gave us some pretty hard knocks. Still we held on; but at last we each got a most awful punch with the pole end which made us let go, and we so far forgot ourselves as to say cuss words; whereupon there came a clap of thunder and we found ourselves tumbling about anyhow. When we got way upon us again and could see, we found that my starboard wing was singed and that the feathers on your head were badly burned. We consulted what to do, and as we could only just see the light we knew that we must have been blown a long way off shore; we therefore decided to work up to it again, and though we flapped our level best and tried all we knew, we could not rise the light at all and had to give it up. We then noticed that we seemed to be in a strong set, for the light was broad away on the starboard bow, while on the port bow there was a reddish glow which made us feel rather creepy, and we both remarked that we had got into a kind of haze which had a sort of burnt powdery smell. We saw the white light dip, but it comforted us a bit to see that the other did not get any redder—we kept ourselves under easy speed with a bright look-out all round, and to make all sure, one of us wore ship every hour, just dropping a little to leeward and coming up again. Time went by slowly, but we didn't care about making much headway 'to the left,' and at last we sighted something moving, and carefully edged down on it in open order. As we got nearer we saw it had wings and we made it out to be a hoary old chap of a decidedly Egyptian head, but there was no mistaking him, for he was a real true blue old sailorman by the way he worked his wings, which showed he had been a long time afloat, and we could not but admire his style. As we came up he sheered off, but we were one on each side of him and had evidently plenty of wing power in reserve, so he stopped and took a long pull at a bottle that he hauled out from under his port wing and then hove a deep sigh. Now the sight of that bottle did us good and we hailed

My Life at Sea | 191

him, saying that if he didn't want it all we should be glad of a drop, for we had *come a long way*; he looked at us compassionately and shook his head: 'No such luck,' says he; 'why, I've been sucking this bottle for nigh on to four thousand years and can't get a drop out of it! Though it seems to be good stuff, too! But there,' says he, *'that's your job.'* He was a pleasant old fellow and was telling us that he commanded a squadron of war boats on the African Lakes under King Rameses the First, and was just deploring the degeneracy of the seamen of the present day, when he suddenly said, 'Here comes the Old Man,' and the way he spread his wings was a sight to see."

There was one incident that may be set down here as worthy of notice. It relates to the period of unrest that was manifest in the maritime world both at home and oversea in the year 1889. Some portion of that time we were in New Zealand, and so far as we were concerned the affair culminated in the port of Lyttelton. On August 31 I had arranged for a dinner-party in the evening, but an urgent message came down from Christchurch that I was to attend a consultation at the head office that evening at eight o'clock. The strike at that time was in full swing, and the previous day we had seen officers leaving one of the Union Company's ships owing to the pressure brought to bear on them by the men. They did, however, leave the masters of all vessels unmolested. By great good fortune my wife happened to be making that voyage by the courtesy of the directors, so that I could leave my chief to do the honours to my guests, and the lady to represent me. When I got to the office the matter for discussion was whether we could get the ship away to her date in spite of the labour troubles, and to that I gave an unhesitating affirmative, provided that I was allowed to manage the matter in my own way. This was on the Sunday evening, and with that understanding we separated. Monday passed by, so did Tuesday, with varying incidents, and as I did not leave the ship I formed the view that the next day might see trouble, so I was up very early. I knew we were ready for a move in the engine-room, and that my only chance lay in a surprise. The Company's manager and myself were walking the quarter deck, off which was the only gangway, when a fireman came along and was going on shore, when I stopped him, and forbade him leaving the ship. He wanted to know why he could not go, and was told no one could leave the ship. That, of course, let the cat out of the bag, but I was prepared and they were not, so with the help of the officers we kept the crew on board until we got into the stream, where they soon found themselves, much to their disgust. To this they gave somewhat free expression, the firemen being the most aggrieved. There was one gratifying thing about it all. One of the quartermasters, a man that had been with me many years, and that I had rescued once from a painful ending with the help of another man, came to me surreptitiously and said he was asked by our men to say that if there was trouble with the firemen I had only to say the word and they would take them on and give them a hiding. This made me laugh, but there was no more trouble and we sailed to time next day. That time when we arrived in London we had to get the ship loaded as best we could, the officers driving winches and hydraulic cranes. It was then that the rumour was spread that John Burns was coming down with a crowd of dockers to stop the work, but fortunately the rumours were never crystallised, and I know that the ship's reputation at this time facilitated greatly the task of getting a crew for the next voyage.

CHAPTER XII

"And I have loved thee, Ocean! and my joy
Of youthful sports was on thy breast to be
Borne, like thy bubbles, onward." —Byron.

SHAKING A REEF OUT

The late Clark Russell and I were at one time great cronies, and consumed a good deal of midnight oil, and other things, discussing the sea and its varied incidents. He was a seaman more by instinct than by experience. He had, of course, served at sea, but for some few years only, and yet he seemed to be the embodiment of sea lore for all time. Trifles that would be passed without notice by the ordinary observer, were absorbed by him and fitted into their proper place in his conception of the grandeur of the sea and all that appertained to it. No one man in his experience ever saw one half of the incidents Clark Russell has related, but his instinct was unerring, and as to his power of description there can be no question. Let me instance one example. "A slip of a moon westering fast" may not appeal to the uninitiate, but to a nautical mind it is most eloquent and expresses exactly the meaning it was intended to convey in the fewest possible words. To my mind this phrase is only equalled by Kipling in "as foot by foot we creep o'er the viewless, hueless deep, to the sob of the questing lead." Both these quotations stand out as unique in compression of vast matter.

There was one point on which Clark Russell and I did not agree. He maintained that it was possible to have at the same time a dense fog and a gale of wind. I maintained the contrary, for at that time I had never seen the combination, and believed, like most people, that wind was the enemy of fog and soon dispersed it. As it happened I was wrong, for on my very next voyage I had a most convincing proof of my error, which I duly acknowledged. We were running our easting down on the parallel of 46° S., and from Lon. 62° E. to 140° E. we got no observation of sun, moon or stars. I find the distance between observations is logged as 3,216 miles for ten days; during a great part of which period it was blowing a hard gale and a thick fog. To make matters better we also shed a propeller blade, but that was only an incident which slightly lengthened the passage. The really interesting point about this experience was the demonstration of the invaluable qualities of Lord Kelvin's compass.

In a paper I had read at the Royal United Service Institution I made mention of its value to navigation, and some little time after this I was asked by the inventor, then Sir William Thomson, if I would testify to this in a case that he was bringing before the law courts to stop the infringement of his patent right. I was able to state the following—

Between the longitudes I have mentioned the variation of the compass or magnetic variation changes from about 30° W. to 10° E., for the locality is in the vicinity of the centre from which the variation lines radiate. It was consequently necessary to alter the compass course at stated times to maintain the due east tract we wished to take, and at certain times the alteration of a degree was made every two, three, or four hours. My last observation showed Lat. 45° 58', the next one 45° 53', so that in the ten days, run without sights, we were only five miles out in our latitude.

To be called as an expert witness in such an interesting case as this one was, is not a disagreeable experience. It was then that I first met Sir John Fisher, now Lord Fisher, who with Admiral Hotham and two staff-captains were subpœnaed to represent the Navy. I fancy that Sir Charles Hotham was then one of the Sea Lords, and Lord Fisher was then a Captain. Captain Squire Lecky, the author of *Wrinkles in Navigation*, and myself stood for the merchant service. It was the time of the Parnell trial, and the present Lord Chief Justice, who represented the Crown in that inquiry, was secured by

Sir William Thomson to take charge of his case. I must confess that all we sailors were looking forward with a kind of amused interest to see what the lawyers would do when dealing with the magnetism of iron ships, and as it happened I had one of the treats of my life. Sir Richard Webster, as he then was, coming in fresh from the Parnell case, proceeded to explain, in words that were to be understood by all, the theory of the deviation of the compass in iron or steel ships, the defects of compasses prior to Sir Wm. Thomson's, and the advantages to which his invention had given birth—all this in the clearest possible language and with the most convincing mastery. He spoke one whole day and part of the next, and, so far as I personally was concerned, taught me more about what I considered was a special subject of my own than I ever knew before. Sitting near Lord Alverstone at dinner some little time since, I reminded him of the case, and he said it was an agreeable change, at the time, to the other case he was engaged on. Sir William Thomson won his case and wrote me a letter of cordial thanks for the help I had given him in the matter. The most humorous thing in that trial was the spectacle of Captain John Fisher in the witness-box in the dusk of an autumn afternoon, looking like a school-boy, and suggesting by his demeanour that so far as he knew anything, green grass was his colour. But he recalled a youthful episode of a piece of string tied to a compass to keep it lively by jerking it. He also recalled how at the bombardment of Alexandria, he had been standing looking at one of the Thomson compasses to see how it was affected by the *Inflexible's* gunfire, when a big gun being fired lifted his cap off but did not seriously affect the compass. Those days spent in Court were of extreme interest, for it was a ding-dong fight between scientific men of the first rank.

While on the subject of accurate navigation I should like to say that an invaluable adjunct to a successful navigator is a reliable "instinct." In some men this is developed very strongly. I first saw it in Craigie of the *Lord of the Isles*. He was also a splendid navigator, and on more than one occasion I heard him say when leaning over the chart: "Our reckoning puts us here" (pointing with his finger), "but I ken she's here," pointing to quite another place. He was always right too. I had the sense to a certain extent, and it kept me out of trouble more than once.

When navigating in high, or comparatively high southern latitudes, there is always a possibility of encountering ice in large or small quantities. There are, of course, certain localities where there is a greater likelihood of meeting with it than others; for instance, as a very unusual occurrence, icebergs have been seen from the Cape of Good Hope itself; but no one would ever expect to see them there again, or take precaution against them in foggy weather. In the austral summer and autumn months there is a greater possibility of seeing ice anywhere than at any other time, and again in the winter months you occasionally come across stray bergs that have got out of their properly recognised course and are wandering about aimlessly, a nuisance to every one. Such an example of ice out of place may be found in Dana's *Two Years before the Mast*, where he relates his experience in the month of July off the Horn. I should think that occurrence was quite abnormal, but it is mentioned to show that there is never any certainty as to where ice may or may not be, and in thick weather a master has to decide whether the risk of ice is such as to justify him in taking precautions which will lengthen the time of his passage. Now in the matter of navigating in a fog there are certain rules laid down by which you will be judged by a court of law if you come to grief, but those rules apply principally to those waters where vessels do mostly congregate, although as far as I know they are applicable everywhere. Generally speaking the rule is that in fog, mist, or falling snow, all vessels are to proceed at a "moderate" speed, which brings about some absurdities. "Moderate speed" in a Mauretania might be nine knots or so, which in a low-power steamer would be full speed. On the other hand if, in a dense fog, all ships stopped, they could not harm one another, although they might drift out of position.

Down south of course the danger of collision with ships was infinitesimal; with ice it was another matter, and I consequently resolved in my own mind that if I could not see I should either go full speed or stop. On one occasion, half-way across the Indian Ocean, a dense fog came on. I had seen no ice, nor had I any particular reason to suppose I should do so, but the fog was dense, so much so that I could not see either end of the ship from the bridge. I did not like to stop, but eventually about 8 p.m. I stopped the engines and lay all night without moving. Though it is needless to say I had run before in a fog scores of times, on this occasion I did not do so, nor could I give any definite reason for my action. But when daylight came and the fog blew away we saw around us at various distances a dozen or fifteen big icebergs. Of course, we might have passed them safely, but, on the other hand, had a difference of opinion as to right of way taken place between us we should probably have added one more to the mysteries of the sea.

I ran down to one of those bergs to see if I could get an echo from the steam-whistle. It was then clear weather and the echo was quite perfect, but whether it would be so in fog I am unable to say. Clark Russell wrote an article on this incident in the *Daily Telegraph*.

I think the only other occasion on which I was delayed by ice, and it was again stray ice too, was on a homeward passage, and it was winter time. It was coming on dirty weather when, at the close of the afternoon, such as it was, ice was reported—and a good deal of it. Another case of the homeless dog, but it had to be attended to. The wind was strong from the north-west with the usual mist and drizzle, the night coming down as dark as pitch. Again I decided I could not run with any degree of safety, so brought the ship to the wind under her trysails, heading about N.N.E. with the engines moving as slowly as possible. About ten o'clock the glass was falling rapidly, and a terrific squall came down. The quartermaster observed to me, or rather shouted, "She is coming to against her helm, sir." This was rather interesting, so I said to the officer of the watch, "If she knows what to do better than I, let her do it; stop the engines." He did so. By this time the main trysail was blown clean out of the bolt ropes, but in the roar of the weather I did not hear it go. The wind had now shifted to the west, but the ship lay broadside to the sea without shipping any water. This was because I had put my oil bag equipment to work, and my experience of it was most satisfactory. After some hours the weather cleared sufficiently for us to put the helm up and proceed. We saw no more ice after that night.

Before leaving this subject of Antarctic ice it may be of interest to note some of its characteristics. Firstly its size. On one occasion we passed a flat-topped mass which at a distance of fifteen miles subtended a horizontal arc of twenty-four degrees, and another berg was passed having in it an arch big enough for a ship to go through. As nearly as we could compute, the arch was about 270 feet high.

Once, far south by the Nimrod Islands, crossing the great ice-bearing current, we saw some bergs which were very remarkable inasmuch as they appeared to be stratified, and when in one position reminded one of enormous tulips. I embodied the experiences of that trip in a paper read before the Australian Science Congress, and still hope that the source of that particular ice-bearing current will be investigated by one of the Antarctic expeditions.

At the time I first took a ship round Cape Horn the charts left a good deal to be desired. As an instance of what I mean, Cape Horn itself was noted as about 500 feet high. From my own observations I was certain this was not correct, and calling on the Hydrographer, Sir W. Wharton, K.C.B., one day, I assured him that it was at least 1,200 feet high. He replied that this was impossible, "for Fitzroy had a station on top of Cape Horn," meaning Admiral Fitzroy, who had made the original survey from which our chart was drawn. This was in 1885, and within a very few days of this interview I received a letter written by direction of the Hydrographer thanking me for observations that had enabled him to correct the lines of variation near Cape Horn, and stating that the French survey of 1882–3 had fixed the height of that promontory as 1,394 feet. My observations were afterwards verified by Captain Clayton, R.N., of H.M.S. *Diamond*, for magnetic observations made in an iron ship are always regarded with a certain suspicion. I must say, however, that I always found Sir William Wharton quite willing and even anxious to receive any information that might be useful, and the Superintendent of Compasses, Captain Creak, R.N., F.R.S., was most helpful and encouraging, even to coming on board the *Kaikoura* and assisting me to compensate the compass for heeling error. Previous to this there had always been some mystery as to the so-called vagaries of ships' compasses off Cape Horn, the truth being that the variation lines as shown on the charts were in places as much as five degrees wrong. It came to my lot to make the correction through my taking nothing for granted which I could not verify.

I had the great good fortune once to get a fair wind between Cape Horn and Rio that satisfied even me, and about that time also I became convinced that the quickest way home was outside the Falkland Islands. I had consistently taken a track through the Straits of Le Maire, but, save under exceptional circumstances, I am confident that is the wrong course for a vessel bound to Rio. It is true that you experience fine weather off Cape Horn sometimes, but it is rare, and the sailing directions commenting on the subject say "that each fine day should be received thankfully as it comes." For when bad weather sets in it comes suddenly, often accompanied with heavy and dense snow. On one occasion I was entering the Straits about midnight when snow came down heavily. From the best bearings I could get while the weather was still fairly clear I believed I was pointing fair for the middle of the passage, but I did not feel by any means happy in the matter, for the tides or currents thereabouts run strongly and uncertainly, swayed largely by the prevailing wind. I had to decide pretty quickly too. If I slowed down or stopped I could not tell where I might be set, so I came to the conclusion it was better to shoulder the risk and let her go. I did so and it came out all right, but I made a mental resolve that I would not be caught that way again.

A HANDY MAINSAIL WHICH DOES NOT
DRIVE SMOKE DOWN ON THE BRIDGE

The phenomenal fair wind which I have referred to was in the month of April. We had made a fairly decent passage to Cape Horn and passed outside the Falkland Islands as far at Lat. 44° S. when the wind began to blow strong from the north-east, with a falling glass, and at the same time showed an inclination to shift further to the eastward. Here, I thought, is a possibility of deriving some benefit if, as I concluded, a cyclonic system was passing to the eastward and we were on the south-east corner of it. There was a good bit of sea running, but I let her go off and set fore-and-afters. I was rewarded by the wind freeing still more, so that before dark I got the single reefed topsails and foresail on her, which was about as much as she would stand, for the sea was just abaft the beam, increasing all the time, and the ship was lurching very badly. That night stands out as one of my pleasantest recollections of sailoring, for there was a clear sea in front of us, as much wind as we wanted, and the need for good handling if the most was to be made of it. About midnight we were getting another pull on the weather braces, and the men of the watch were finding that it taxed all their energies to do it, for she was lurching horribly. The chief engineer came staggering along the poop to me to ask whether I could do anything to keep her steadier, as she had more than once rolled her vacuum away. This meant that her injection plate had been out of water, and I could readily believe it. I told him it was getting better all the time, so he must make the best of it, and with that he had to be content. By morning the ship was on her course again, the wind aft, and we with topgallant sails set running about 16 knots. In three days we ran 1,064 miles, an average of close upon 15 knots, and that with all the freezing engines going, but the *Kaikoura* was as grateful for canvas as a thirsty man for drink, and revelled in the real sea dance. I felt rather pleased with myself over that business, but it was all vanity, for we got to Rio before they expected us, and there was no coal ready. The actual steaming time between Wellington and Plymouth was thirty-seven days three hours, or an average speed of just over 13 knots.

While on this question of route some word must necessarily be given to the Straits of Magellan, the passage through which figured largely in the advertisement for passengers. Very wisely, however, no strict instruction was ever given to the masters to adopt that route; it was left entirely to their discretion. At that time there was great rivalry to make the fastest passage, both between our own ships and those of the opposition line, and to this day I do not really know who did the fastest passage home, although I believe I did. Naturally, under those circumstances, when a ship was in a good position for rounding Cape Horn, it required some powerful argument to make a master go out of his way to increase his distance, and undertake what is at best the risky navigation of that magnificent waterway. For absolute grandeur the western portion of the Strait is unsurpassed, but when a ship is in a hurry there is little inclination or inducement to stop to admire scenery. As it happened, however, in my case the "powerful argument" was supplied. Leaving England in November 1885, we had on board a full complement of passengers, and among them were General Sir Patrick and Lady McDougall and the Earl and Countess of Dalhousie. They were intending to make the "round trip" in the ship, and the passage of the Straits was, I fancy, an event they all looked forward to. I never had more pleasant passengers. As it happened Sir Patrick's reading and mine had been on very similar lines, and conversation at meal times was by no means dull. Lord Dalhousie had been in the Navy and was still a sailor at heart; he was also a great student of Shakespeare. Lady Dalhousie also had had some experience of the sea when her husband was Commander of the *Britannia*, apart from any other. It is superfluous but natural to remark that she was charming as she was handsome, and whenever she could further the harmony of the ship she spared no pains to do so. We made a very fine passage to within four days of Cape Town, when we dropped a propeller blade. We were at dinner at the time it went. I felt it, and looking across the saloon caught the eye of my chief engineer, which had sought mine. I said nothing and hoped it had passed unnoticed, but one of my lady friends at table had caught the look and artlessly inquired why the chief engineer had left the table in the middle of dinner. It is little use trying to hide anything, for we had to ease the engines, but even then we made a good run to the Cape.

When we got to Table Bay, I was not trusting to any divers' work. We put her in dock, discharged an atom of cargo, and then dry-docked her, cargo and all, replaced the blade, reshipped the little cargo we had discharged, coaled and left again in about thirty-two hours, which was not bad work all things being considered, for, much as I liked Cape Town and its people, there were certain interests there that were very pleased to welcome a "daily stranger" in distress. We had to make what is known as a "particular average" of this matter in New Zealand, and few things cause more irritation to consignees, but there would have been no excuse for me if I had incurred needless risk which could be avoided by reasonable expenditure. The remainder of the passage to Port Chalmers was made without incident; but on the last night some young men amongst the first-class passengers had too much to drink, and succeeded in making themselves asses, and a nuisance to their fellow passengers. The Port Chalmers pilot took us in on the ebb tide and succeeded in putting us on a sandbank, where we stayed until the next high water. There was no harm done, but a lot of inquiries were afterwards made about it at the London Custom House. Our steaming time out that passage was 39 days, 9 hours.

The new order of progress was now inaugurated, and we were having our long spell in port at the New Zealand end. In all we had six weeks there, but we left for home in the middle of February, and then I had to face the music. I knew the *Doric* was to sail the day after us, therefore I was loth to lose the time involved by the passage of the Straits, for the *Doric* and *Kaikoura* always ran very jealously of one another, and I was confident our rival would stick to the great circle. I also knew that if she once caught sight of us we should never hear the last of it, for Captain Jennings, who was my very great friend, never lost an opportunity of impressing upon me the immense superiority of the *Doric* and White Star fashions generally. With this I naturally disagreed, although Jennings himself was one of the finest specimens of an old seaman it was possible to come across. As we drew down towards the Horn the questions with which I was plied concerning the Straits and my intentions grew more and more pointed. We had a fine fair wind, and I was loth to lose its benefit, but as it became eventually a personal matter I shifted my helm for the Straits and was fortunate enough to make them at daybreak, so that I had a really long day's run in front of me. Needless to say, my passengers were delighted, for the scenery, if wild, was very magnificent, and to tell the truth I enjoyed the trip myself, now that I had had a reasonable excuse for losing time. There was no difficulty in navigating so long as one could see, but in that locality the weather changes with great suddenness and one watches it carefully from hour to hour. We passed the remains of more than one big steamer, stranded and deserted.

Some speculation took place as to what the fate of their crews had been, for at that time the natives of Tierra del Fuego were cannibals. We were fortunate, and anchored at Sandy Point about nine in the evening, just after dark. We started at daybreak again, and carried a fair tide through the narrows, and that being so we raced past the land at the speed of a railway train, the current running perhaps nine knots, and the water one mass of boiling impetuosity. When we were past Cape Virgins that afternoon I sat down to play a rubber of whist with very great equanimity. We reached Rio in due course one morning, but coaling was very slow and detained us until late in the afternoon of the next day, by which time, as I anticipated, our friend the *Doric* had made her appearance, and I knew that for all eternity Jennings and his crowd would relate how they caught up the *Kaikoura*.

On this occasion in Rio (it was before the revolution) the Emperor favoured me with an intimation that he would be pleased to visit the ship. He did so, and inspected her very minutely, afterwards lunching, to the great relief of his staff, who had been attending some religious ceremony for the whole of the morning, and had confided to me that they were desperately hungry. His Majesty was extremely gracious, and the function was a very pleasant one. There was no further incident on the passage, and when we got to Plymouth early one morning, we were boarded by several friends of Lord Dalhousie who came to announce that he had been appointed Secretary of State for Scotland, and how both he and the Countess must be on shore with the least possible loss of time. They had been exceedingly popular in the ship, and the following voyage every officer received from them a souvenir of a pleasant voyage. I personally cherish a little hand-painted Christmas card, for Lady Dalhousie was fond of painting and had made some wonderful studies of sunlight effects at Rio.

There are few more puzzling things than a dense fog on shore, even in a well-known locality, but at sea it at times causes the most fantastic incidents, one of which I propose to now relate. We were bound down-Channel for Plymouth with a Channel pilot (Posgate) in charge, and when off the Start it came on a thick fog. I will confess that I was rather given to navigation under these conditions, so I kept on until I knew that we were not very far from Plymouth Breakwater, when the anchor was put down. Nevertheless, it is not pleasant to be anchored in the fairway of the Channel, for there is considerable risk of some one blundering into you, and a sharp look-out was being kept whenever the fog thinned a little, to pick up the breakwater light. About nine in the evening it was made out very dimly, but yet sufficiently well for me to get under way, and in a short time we picked up the Plymouth pilot, who then took charge. The fog was then heavy, but we kept the loom of the light and passed it, the pilot being very anxious to use port helm more than seemed to me to be warranted. At last I said, "How do you want to go, Pilot?" "About N.E. ½ E. sir," was the reply, to which the London man said, "But you are E.N.E. now." Said the Plymouth man, "Never mind, sir, port please." At which I stopped the engines, although we were moving very slowly. Shortly after this the chief sung out from the forecastle, "A man-o'-war close ahead of us," and immediately afterwards, "No, no, it's the breakwater fort!" I turned astern full speed, despite remonstrances from both pilots that I should foul moorings and buoys, and as she backed out she just shaved the fort with her bowsprit, which thereby got a cant that it carried for the rest of its days. I asked the chief, East it was, if she had touched, but he like a good man said, "No," and indeed it was the lightest possible graze. Eventually we anchored, nothing the worse for our novel experience. I forget now what I said to the Plymouth pilot—no doubt it was something very polite—but it was hardly ever possible to take Cousin Jacker really seriously, for they knew themselves that they were frequently as useful as a fifth wheel to a coach. The moral of this story is, if there is a moral, that if one had tried to do as we did on a fine day the chances are that we could not have done it, and indeed, there are times now when I can hardly understand how it took place. It did, however, and exactly in the manner I have described.

I must admit that during my entire sea experiences I was singularly immune from any serious accidents. That was my good fortune. But there were disagreeables at times. On one occasion we were hampered by a bad epidemic of scarlet fever, and some very cantankerous people in the saloon could not see that I had to act for the welfare of all, and that it was consequently necessary to sacrifice some room to secure isolation and hospital accommodation. To mend matters we had an accident that gave a deal of trouble. In one of the orlop decks was stowed a great quantity of casks of oil, illuminants for the New Zealand lighthouses. By some mischance one of them worked loose, and before it was realised the whole lot were adrift—for the ship was rolling badly—dashing from side to side, eventually smashing and deluging the orlop deck and lower hold with oil. It was a matter of difficulty and some danger to secure the casks that were left, for there was a curious cross swell on, and try as I might I could not persuade her to keep quiet. The men worked well, however, although the fumes affected their eyes badly. Great quantities were baled up in buckets and thrown overboard, but enough was unavoidably left to damage an enormous quantity of cargo in the lower hold. That was one of the few disagreeable trips I had.

On the other hand there were passages where people made everything a pleasure, and one very cheery time we had three young Englishmen not very long from college. One was Lord Burford, another was named Conolly, and the third was Seely, now (1912) Under-Secretary for War, who was even then exercising considerable influence by perfect manners and a knowledge of the world rare in one so young. Lord Burford has since that time succeeded to the dukedom of St. Albans. He has the most graceful seat on horseback I ever saw. Conolly, who afterwards joined the Scots Greys, sleeps with his fellows, the bravest and best, under the turf in the Transvaal. The reason I specially mention these three young men is that they had the happy knack of getting everything they wanted, and at the same time making it a pleasure for other people to give it them. It is true that three tandems at one time bulked rather largely in the streets of Wellington and caused a little comment, but the New Zealanders with whom the friends came in contact liked them, even to the extent of delaying the start of an express train while they laid in a stock of provisions for a journey. Conolly alone made the complete voyage with me, and on the run down to the Horn developed a taste for going aloft to handle canvas in bad weather. I did not like the risk he incurred, but could not well oppose it, and fortunately no accident happened.

Although I had by this time lost touch with a great deal concerning the Cape I had the good fortune at odd times when calling there to see old friends when they were gathered together for any special function. On one occasion there were some warships in the bay and a ball was taking place that night at Government House, to which I was invited. Coaling would be finished, I knew, by nine in the evening, and my anxiety was to get all my passengers safely on board, for it was coming on a south-easter. That, however, was safely managed, and then, having seen the gangway pulled up, I started for the shore and had a couple of hours amongst old friends and enjoyed it to my heart's content. I returned to the ship by midnight and got under way at once. I suppose I really had no right to take those three hours, but it was the only time I ever lost a minute on a passage, and the exception does not make me feel repentant even now.

I think it was that passage that I had the satisfaction of carrying out a very great scientist, Sir Julius Von Haast. We were friends, and I had the greatest respect for his views and attainments. He gave me a great deal of his time, and for one thing thoroughly convinced me that our national system of free imports involved ultimate disaster. Geology, however, was his forte, and his reputation in this science was world-wide. I regret to say he died shortly after landing in New Zealand.

Towards the close of my voyaging I became involved in the after-effects of the various seamen's strikes, and the dangerous spirit of unrest and insubordination generated by them. The power of the master of a merchant ship, be she a collier or be she an *Olympic*, is a very uncertain quantity, inasmuch as it is limited only by the necessity of the case that is being dealt with. In other words, you can act as you consider the occasion rightly demands you should do, but you stand to be called upon to defend your action when you get on shore.

It will thus be seen that the discipline clauses of the Merchant Shipping Act leave a great deal to the discretion of the judicial authority that may be dealing with any particular case, and it can well be realised that some magistrates would view offences against discipline with a more lenient spirit than others. Again, and I am well aware of the gravity of the words I am using, it is not the Board of Trade that has whittled down the master's authority voluntarily, but it is the deliberate action of shipowners, who, curiously enough, have done more than any other agency to destroy authority on board ship. So long as a master was certain of support from the owner, so long would he act unflinchingly if necessity arose. But in many cases a master will hesitate to involve himself in law when he knows that in doing so he will get no support from his owners. Quite recently the master of a great mail steamer told me that it would not do to have any trouble with his crew, "for the Company would not like it," a policy, I submit, which is simply asking for trouble, for the men of to-day fully realise that a clever lawyer can make a plausible case from very slight grounds. Hence arises the crying need of *one uniform administration* of the Merchant Shipping Act, for as it is dealt with at present there is *no* uniformity of practice.

I had occasion to take part in a police court case in Wellington where a fireman was being prosecuted for assaulting my second officer and knocking some of his teeth out. It was a particularly bad case, and deserved the extreme penalty that could be awarded for that offence, but the magistrate took an entirely different view and only inflicted half the maximum penalty.

I was rather put out at this and am afraid that I showed it, for I told the stipendiary that I should advise my officers in future to carry something for their own defence, as they got little protection from the police. This was rather unfortunate, for some little time afterwards, I think it was the next voyage, there was a shooting case which caused a good deal of comment and which nearly got me into serious trouble. The facts were as follows. Two mates of sailing vessels had got themselves disliked by certain seamen belonging to their own and other vessels. They had been threatened, and consequently kept together for mutual protection, one of them, as they went on shore one Sunday morning, putting a revolver in his pocket. They were met by men in search of them with hostile intent, and the mate in possession of the revolver was knocked down. Fearing worse treatment he fired at his assailant from his pocket, and the aggressor fell shot through the heart. It is to be noticed that although this feud had been in existence some little time there was no sign of any police supervision or watching until the mischief was complete. The two men were put on trial for wilful murder together, but the judge ruled that they were to be tried separately. Consequently the man who fired the shot was first tried, and sentenced to a long term of penal servitude. This was on a Saturday. The next day I sat down and wrote a long letter to the *New Zealand Times*, which was published on the Monday; in it I pointed out former complaints of my own as to police inefficiency, and concluded with an appeal for mitigation of sentence. I did not mention the other man, who had to stand his trial on the Monday. This man was acquitted, but the public prosecutor was furious at my interference in the case. He and I were on very friendly terms as far as whist players went, but meeting me in the Club on Monday afternoon he told me that I had been guilty of contempt of court, and would have to take the consequences. I think, however, that it was just one of those touch-and-go cases where it would have been difficult to convict, for I heard no more of the matter. The man who was acquitted came down to my ship on the Tuesday morning, and meeting East in the gangway told him that he had come to thank me for getting him off, to which my chief replied, "Clear out at once! The old man don't want to see you, I know!" and really he was quite right. So ended that episode; but I did not make many friends over what was really a fight for principle, and to this day I cherish animosity against a Christchurch newspaper that, taking this case as a handle, attacked me falsely and bitterly in my absence, when I had no opportunity of replying.

By this time I had become tired to some extent of spending so much time at sea; I wanted for one thing to do some training in the *Excellent*, and for another my wife had been so pulled down by repeated attacks of influenza that it was necessary I should look more closely after my family affairs. I accordingly thought I would stay at home for a voyage, and one fine summer's afternoon I took my leave of the old ship that had served me so well, and as I stood by Manor Way Station seeing the blue ensign replaced by a red one I felt as though I was taking farewell of a much-loved friend. I never saw the *Kaikoura* again, but grieved to hear that she had met her fate at the shipbreaker's hands. She deserved a better ending.

It is one thing to be a Naval Reserve officer in command of a fine ship in peace time, but it is quite another matter to give up separate command, inferior to the Navy as it is, and take your place as one of the eighteen hundred or so units that carry on the principal duties of H.M. Navy. This fact had long been dimly recognised by me, although in all my periods of drill service I had always been shown a great deal of consideration.

As soon as one had reported at Whale Island one's identity was lost in the particular class in which one was merged, and I thanked goodness that drill had always been rather a hobby of mine, and that I could hold my own respectably with other lieutenants of the senior class to which I was attached. Indeed, I discovered that so far as actual drill was concerned the teaching of the drill ships had been very thorough. It was only that here one was faced with the handling of the latest and newest weapons. In other respects the lieutenants of the regular service had not been better instructed than we were.

The senior staff officer was a lieutenant named Waymouth, now captain of a battleship, and he it was who put us through our gunnery tests, and lectured on those matters requiring explanation and blackboard diagrams, such as hydraulics and kindred matters. He was a wonderfully gifted man, and had the rather rare faculty of being able to impart his knowledge to others. He had, I think, made gunnery his particular study, for there was no possible question concerning any gun in the service the answer to which was not immediately forthcoming. Indeed, so far as I could judge, the whole staff of the *Excellent* had reached a standard of efficiency and excellence it would have been difficult to find fault with. The first lieutenant, Adair— now admiral—was a man of great personal character.

The torpedo school, H.M.S. *Vernon*, was another thing altogether, and here I suffered considerably from my inability to chase "X." Highly interesting though the lectures were, they required a knowledge of algebra, which, though learned in my school-days, I had entirely forgotten. As it happened I had to leave the course before the examination, so my shortcomings were not discovered. I had been through all the practical work connected with mining, etc., but as the Whitehead came last of all I did not then make its acquaintance. The following year I was appointed to H.M.S. *Devastation* for the naval manœuvres, at which I was highly pleased, and duly proceeded to join her when she was lying in historic Mutton Cove. She was commanded by Captain Oxley, who gave me a very cordial welcome, and her first lieutenant was none other than my old acquaintance of Zanzibar, P. G. Vanderbyl. The other lieutenants were all men who have since done well in the service, and one with whom I was on specially good terms, named Hall, I found acting as inspecting captain of submarines when I was down at a review at the invitation of the Admiralty just a year or two ago. With that peculiarity men in the service have, Captain Hall hardly looked a day older.

Service in the *Devastation* was a novelty. She was one of the earlier types of ironclads, and at the time she was built was of considerable utility, but as a sea-going craft she was not a thing of joy. Even in that capacity, though, she had her good points, one of which was her extreme steadiness in a sea-way, but on the other hand, the ventilation below left much to be desired, and in anything like bad weather, when the ship was closed down, a considerable amount of potted air was consumed by every one.

We left Plymouth the morning after I joined her to join the fleet at Portland. We were making our best possible speed, but she was a ship that resented being driven beyond a certain pace, for when doing anything over ten or eleven knots her steering was erratic to the last degree. A yaw of three points on either side was of constant occurrence, and my sympathies went out to the chief engineer, who stood looking at her wake in grim calculation of an enormous amount of wasted energy. In due course we joined up at Portland with the Red Fleet under the command of Admiral Fitzroy. Compared with our fleets of to-day it was a motley gathering. The best vessels in the manœuvres were four ships of the *Royal Sovereign* class, all allotted to the Red Fleet, while first-class cruisers were put into the line of battle to make up sufficient numbers to carry out the scheme of operations. But if the Red Fleet was one of all sorts, the Blue Fleet was still worse, for with the exception of some armoured and other cruisers, there were not in it any two homogeneous ships. This, be it remembered, was in 1894. It would be interesting to hear the comments of an admiral to-day if he were given the command of a fleet of battleships consisting of six different types, such as *Alexandra, Barfleur, Benbow, Inflexible, Colossus,* and *Edinburgh.* It speaks well for the capacity of the officers in charge that they were able to obtain satisfactory results from so strange a mixture, but that really was the transition time of the Navy, for since that date ships have been built with a view to homogeneity.

No object would be served by relating the details of those manœuvres. I shall content myself with one or two remarks upon occurrences that impressed themselves upon me. We left Portland in due course for a week's manœuvres in the Channel, and Admiral Fitzroy expressed his satisfaction at the manner in which they were performed. We then put into Falmouth to coal and get ready for the battle that would probably take place between the opposing Fleets. By this time the crew and officers had got used to the ship and to one another. We had on board about thirty Naval Reserve men and they fell to my division; the great mistake made was in putting them on board with an insufficient kit. This led to all sorts of excuses being made for them, and it was easy to see that instructions had been given that they were to be treated with a very light hand. This they were not slow to discover. They were not a bad lot, but it was unsatisfactory to me to have to handle them under those conditions, and when the captain expressed his satisfaction at their general appearance, I had to take it seriously, but knew that Falstaff's regiment must have been in his thoughts. The matter of inferior appearance by some members of a ship's company is no trifling matter.

We left Falmouth one evening to cruise off Ushant, waiting for a declaration of war. We knew the plan of manœuvres but not the exact hour of commencement. It was blowing freshly from the S.W. and the *Devastation* with her low ends was like a half-tide rock. In fact only the superstructure was negotiable, and the greatest care had to be exercised to prevent water from getting below; even then there was a fair quantity on the maindeck. But she had this advantage—when every vessel in company was rolling we were almost motionless; certainly we never had the fiddles on the ward-room table. The *Resolution* rolled badly, and had to haul out of the line to try and secure a boat which came to grief. Life in the small craft must have been wearisome in the extreme, for they had a motion that approximated in speed to the pendulum of a clock.

When the appointed time arrived our Fleet started off up the Irish Channel, and one day at noon all the cruisers were sent on ahead at full speed to try both to elude the enemy and to join hands with our friends separated from us by an opposing Fleet. They parted company from us like a flock of swallows, and then came the turn of our battleships to put on full speed, for the admiral had determined to push on, leaving us as slowest ship to make the best of our way after him. I shall never forget that run. The night was dark, we were showing no lights, and the foredeck was one mass of white creaming water. We saw lots of ships, but there was no trouble in keeping clear of them, and I am not sure that the sight in the engine-room was not as interesting as any, for there was no difficulty in keeping steam, and the engines were being driven for all they were worth, all being done without the least trouble or fuss. About nine o'clock the next morning we sighted our Fleet, which was hanging back for us, as they had sighted their enemy. In a short time we were all at it as hard as we could go, engaged in the sham battle of South Rock. Two things were noticeable. In the middle of it all a Norwegian sailing collier drove down through the contending lines, which had to keep clear of her; and, secondly, the splendid appearance of Admiral Dale's Fleet as they came to our assistance headed by the *Empress of India* and the *Repulse*. As is usual in such matters both sides claimed the victory. After this the hostile Fleets separated, we putting into Belfast and our adversaries into Queenstown, but as there was no certainty that hostilities were over we got out torpedo-nets for the night. They were not wanted, however. On our way to Portsmouth on the return trip we had some time at our disposal. It was a fine August afternoon in mid-Channel; all the ships stopped their engines and turned eight points to starboard; those ships which had a band used it; the men were piped to bathe, and some boats were used for visiting purposes. The impression left on my mind was that our "home was on the deep," and that the custom of centuries would keep it inviolate.

In due course we got to Spithead, where I left the ship, and so practically ended my sea career. I landed with a very decided opinion that there was a deal of truth in the old adage that "standing rigging makes bad running gear." I had been in command so long that a subordinate position irked me, although I trust that fact was never apparent. Still I feel confident that for a man to become a satisfactory Reserve officer it is necessary he should get his experience as early as possible, and it is matter for satisfaction that this has now been recognised.

I quitted the sea with deep regret, and were my time coming over again, I should, even with my present knowledge, unhesitatingly adopt it as a calling. But if Britons value their heritage "the sea" they will see that British ships are manned by British men, and take some pains to bring this about by encouraging the youth of the country to adopt the sea as a calling. It is a *man's* life in a properly found and officered ship; it is also necessary that, as I have pointed out on many occasions, our long-sea-route steamships should be given the means to protect themselves against the guns of a hostile merchant vessel that has been armed for the special purpose of preying upon our commerce.